IN THE SERPENT'S WAKE

IN THE SERPENT'S WAKE

RACHEL HARTMAN

RANDOM HOUSE New York

Text copyright © 2022 by Rachel Hartman
Jacket art copyright © 2022 by Simon Prades

All rights reserved. Published in the United States by Random House Children's Books, a division of Penguin Random House LLC, New York.

Random House and the colophon are registered trademarks of Penguin Random House LLC.

Visit us on the Web! GetUnderlined.com

Educators and librarians, for a variety of teaching tools, visit us at RHTeachersLibrarians.com

Library of Congress Cataloging-in-Publication Data
Names: Hartman, Rachel, author.
Title: In the serpent's wake / Rachel Hartman.
Description: First edition. | New York: Random House Children's Books, [2022] |
Summary: "Tess Dombegh sails south as a spy, hunting for evidence of politically motivated crimes while also hunting for the last World Serpent that could save her friend Pathka"—Provided by publisher.
Identifiers: LCCN 2021016138 (print) | LCCN 2021016139 (ebook) |
ISBN 978-1-101-93132-5 (trade) | ISBN 978-1-101-93133-2 (lib. bdg.) |
ISBN 978-0-593-48720-4 (int'l) | ISBN 978-1-101-93134-9 (ebook) |
Subjects: CYAC: Fantasy. | Spies—Fiction.
Classification: LCC PZ7.H26736 In 2022 (print) | LCC PZ7.H26736 (ebook) |
DDC [Fic]—dc23

The text of this book is set in 11.5-point Adobe Caslon.
Interior design by Ken Crossland

Printed in the United States of America
10 9 8 7 6 5 4 3 2 1
First Edition

For Karen New:

It was the least I could do.

Prologue

Once there was a girl named Tess,
Who'd got herself in a wretched mess.
She'd sneaked out late and been quite wild.
She'd finally borne a bastard child.
In consequence of all her sin,
She became a servant to her twin.

She kept her hopes and dreams tamped down
Until the wedding day rolled around.
Sweet Jeanne, so innocent, wed a duke,
While Tess got drunk and fought and puked
And brought the evening to a close
By breaking the duke's brother's nose.

The road, the road, the beckoning road
(Seraphina her boots bestowed).
Tess ran off, ashamed and bowed,
Along the endless road.

In Trowebridge she found a workshop
Where quigutl toiled on thniks nonstop.
Her old friend Pathka was there in chains
And forced to work for worldly gains.
Tess helped him escape that nest,
So he told her of his mystical quest:

Deep underground in a cavern vast
A huge World Serpent was said to exist.
Pathka hoped to join dreams with it,
For that would constitute quigutl bliss.
Tess didn't quite believe, but knew
That Pathka's purpose could be hers, too.

The road, the road, the endless road,
Tess took clothes from a hapless clod.
Pathka taught her to steal her food,
Along the wondrous road.

From dawn to dusk, they walked all day,
And met strange folk along their way:
Two louts and an old man on the run,
Some shepherdesses and a singing nun.
They went spelunking for the serpent's trail,
Pathka's child, Kikiu, on their tail.

And as she walked, Tess understood
That walking on was a definite good.
She let herself look back and feel,

Process her grief and begin to heal.
Her child, long dead, she learned to mourn,
And now looked forward to each new dawn.

The road, the road, the wondrous road!
These are the gifts that it bestowed:
Perspective, forgiveness, a lightened load,
Along the healing road.

Tess joined a road crew and got to work,
Tamping roadbed and moving dirt.
Pathka searched in the caverns deep,
But of the serpent there was no peep.
Tess doubted that the monster was real,
And that's when she fell down a hole.

The tunnel led to a cavern huge
Beneath the monastery of St. Prue's.
The monks above knew about the snake
That lived underground and made the earth shake.
Tess made a friend, one Frai Moldi,
Took him underground, the serpent to see.

The road, the road, the healing road.
They saw the serpent; the serpent glowed.
Comfort and joy is what it showed:
The end of an endless road.

Pathka stayed and dreamed with it,
But Tess couldn't quite bring herself to quit
The road that long had been her home.
She carried on south, continued to roam.
She helped a maid escape a priest,
Arrived in Segosh, and decided to rest.

She spent the winter with Josquin dear,
Who helped her grapple with one last fear.
Her former lover, Will by name,
Had forced himself on her without shame.
She'd blamed herself for not being strong,
Rather than the man who'd done her wrong.

The road, the road, the endless road,
The past never ended; on it flowed.
Will that villain get what he's owed,
Upon the winding road?

Tess had abandoned one last dream:
To make a splash on the scholarly scene.
At the Academy she gave a talk
On what she'd found on her long walk.
The masters lauded her telling and showing,
Then sought the serpent without her knowing.

They killed the creature for science's sake;
Pathka, bound to it, felt his mind break.
Kikiu rushed in to save her kin,

Blaming Tess for all, to Tess's chagrin.
To save Pathka's life, Tess offered her arm,
Which Pathka bit, transferring the harm.

The road, the road, the winding road,
We try our best, but our best is flawed.
Pathka's mind wasn't quite restored,
There on the striving road.

Seraphina then came to town,
And gave Tess a mission from the Crown.
Tess didn't like to leave Josquin,
But the time had come for her to move on.
She went to the port town of Mardou
To find a countess and join her crew.

Young Jacomo, he found her there.
He told her her twin was pregnant and scared.
But Tess wasn't ready to go along;
As far as she'd come, she didn't feel strong.
She asked Jacomo to come away;
They'd travel the road for one more day.

The road, the road, the striving road,
The past and future ebbed and flowed.
On the horizon adventure glowed,
The never-ending road.

One

*R*emember, Worthy One:
   The world knew nothing at first. Then it gave birth to plants, who noticed what sunlight tasted like, and worms, who reveled in the luxuriant touch of soil. Soon the world's bright birds were perceiving the color of sound, its playful quigutl discerned the shapes of smells, and myriad eyes of every kind discovered sight and saw differently.

   Behind these senses were minds—so many! The world was too vast to fit into just one mind; it needed millions of them to consider itself from every possible angle.

   The difficulty with minds is that each perceives itself as a separate thing, alone. And so the minds spin stories to bridge the gaps between them, like a spider's web. There are a million stories, and yet they are all one.

   But come, Mind of the World. Open your eyes.
   We have teased apart one filament, which might be a beginning.

Once upon a time (*the world always starts with time*), a dragon scholar climbed the stairs of an inn in the bustling port city of Mardou.

   There were fifty-six stairs. It only felt like twice as many as yesterday.

The dragon was in human form, a saarantras; they wouldn't have fit in the stairwell otherwise. They paused on each landing, leaning on a hooked cane. Dragons shouldn't feel irritated or bitter, but Scholar Spira was usually in enough pain to feel a bit of both.

Today their irritation was directed at Professor the dragon Ondir, who seemed determined to meddle endlessly with Spira's expedition. Their bitterness was for their knees, which gritted and stabbed with every step as if they were full of broken glass.

At the top of the stairs, muffled voices were audible behind the professor's door. Spira couldn't discern the words, but a sniff at the doorknob answered their most pertinent question. The person they'd come to complain about—the person Ondir had foisted onto Spira at the last minute, whose hundred barrels of pyria were even now being loaded onto the *Sweet Jessia*—had arrived before them. This was going to be awkward.

Spira feared no awkwardness, however. Spira was born awkward.

They flung wide the door without knocking.

"Enter," said Professor the dragon Ondir, rather too late.

The room was large and well appointed, with a view of the sea. A four-poster bed loomed at the end, curtains drawn (like a market stall, Spira thought). The right wall was dominated by windows, the left by a broad, roaring hearth.

Ondir, whose chair faced the door, was tall and gaunt like a proper saarantras (and utterly unlike Spira). His guest, facing him, looked to be much shorter. Spira could see only tightly curled hair, so fair as to be almost white.

"Lord Hamish, have you met Scholar Spira, leader of our expedition?" said Ondir.

"We weren't properly introduced," said the pale man, leaping up to perform the elaborate genuflections Southlanders called courtesy.

Dragons generally ignored such performative nonsense and never bothered learning to distinguish one degree of courtesy from another. Spira had bothered. Spira had Tathlann's syndrome; their egg had been ripped from the maternal oviduct before the last, crucial hormonal infusions. Spira had no maternal memories, none of the basic knowledge other dragons hatched with: language; flight; who was likely to eat you. Ondir had once calculated that a dragon with Tathlann's syndrome must study four times harder just to make up for that congenital deficit.

Spira had taken it upon themself to study 6.3 times harder. It paid off in surprising ways.

Lord Hamish gave five-sixteenths courtesy—the tiniest increment more than they deserved. Either the man was insulting them, or he had an idiosyncratic sense of humor. Spira didn't care which; the fact got filed away for later.

His lordship, pale and petite, was dressed head to toe in cream-colored wool. His doublet and breeches were expensively cut but almost aggressively unadorned. His soft boots were the color of parchment, and his earrings (four per ear, very unusual) looked like little woolly cocoons. The only contrasting darkness on his person was a pair of smoked-glass spectacles.

He finished his manner-dance, saying, "Thank you for agreeing to take me along."

Spira had agreed to no such thing. Given a choice, Spira wouldn't be on this expedition themself. The risks outweighed the benefits by more than sixty-eight to one. The scholars in the high towers of the Mootseye had calculated the precise ratio out to twenty decimal places and concluded thereby that the expedition should be led by their most expendable researcher, the one who made everyone uncomfortable.

Spira considered disconcerting others a cultivated skill, in fact. They aimed their most off-putting stare at Lord Hamish and said, "Are those your hundred barrels of pyria cluttering up my hold and endangering my expedition?"

Lord Hamish's face fell in confusion. "One hundred? I requested half that amount."

"Only half are yours," Professor the dragon Ondir cut in. "The rest are ours."

"What do we want with pyria?" said Spira. Even without maternal memories, they had a reflexive horror of the stuff. It had been the Goreddi knights' most potent dragon-slaying weapon for centuries. In this era of peace with humankind, it was appalling to think the oily substance still existed in great enough quantity to fill barrels.

"I expect it will have nautical applications," said Ondir. "It burns underwater. You could douse the Polar Serpent with it, unless you've formulated some better plan to kill it?"

Lord Hamish was physically incapable of turning paler, and yet Spira could smell that the blood had drained from his face. That was a sign of upset; Spira filed it away.

"I've made no such plan," said Spira, eyes widening ingenuously for Lord Hamish's benefit; Ondir wouldn't notice. "I must have misunderstood your orders."

This was a lie; they'd understood the professor perfectly well. Spira kept one eye on Lord Hamish, however, and noted his look of relief and gratitude.

It was a map to where a wedge could be driven.

"How else are we to study the serpent?" said Ondir slowly, as if explaining to a hatchling. "It gets too cold at the pole for us to live there for any extended period. Did you hope to bring it home alive? I don't see how. Perhaps you'd send in a team of hardy quigutl to observe it in its natural environment? They're unreliable; they'd forget to report back."

Ondir had another reason for wanting the serpent dead. If Spira could goad the professor into saying it aloud, Lord Hamish might become upset enough to quit the expedition. The pyria would still be aboard—it seemed to be Ondir's pyria, ultimately—but at least Spira wouldn't have to babysit an irritating human stranger for the entire voyage.

"The serpents are reputed to be sentient beings," said Spira. "Surely

I should try to find a way to communicate with it. Wouldn't we learn more by talking to it than by cutting it up?"

"These serpents should not exist," cried Ondir. "We've run the equations; they're impossible. Unless and until we understand how they work, none of us can call ourselves knowledgeable. None of us are safe. If nature makes exceptions to its own rules, then what can we rely on? Unless you think this animal has a grasp of higher mathematics and can explain itself on that level—and why would it have language at all? Whom does it have to talk to?—we're much better off studying it in pieces."

"Do you mean to say," said Lord Hamish slowly, "that when you come across something bigger, older, and mightier than you, all you can think to do is destroy it?"

"You seem not to care about all the theories and paradigms *it* has destroyed," said Ondir.

Only a dragon would think an argument like that carried any weight. Spira, born ignorant of so many things, was more accustomed to humiliation than most dragons and didn't take the serpents' existence personally.

Lord Hamish looked ill. Good. Spira was poised to nudge him overboard, metaphorically.

"You seem upset," Spira said. "Perhaps ours is not the right ship for you to—"

"It absolutely is," said Lord Hamish, while Ondir cried, "Of course he must."

The double reaction took Spira aback. There was a miscalculation somewhere.

"Lord Hamish," said Spira, "I need to speak with my supervisor in private."

The little man bowed and showed himself out. Spira sniffed; his lordship stood just on the other side of the door, likely listening in.

"Why have you burdened me with this human and his cargo?" said Spira in soft-mouth Mootya, the draconic tongue as spoken by saarantrai. Lord Hamish likely wouldn't understand it.

"He won't be a burden," said the professor. "You've assessed incorrectly. He's Count Pesavolta's enforcer of southern treaties and has traveled the Archipelagos extensively. He knows the region well. His expertise will save you a lot of time."

"You sought him out on purpose?" asked Spira, sinking into Lord Hamish's vacated seat, wincing as their knees cracked.

"He sought us out. He needs pyria and transport south. It's mutually beneficial."

It seemed superficially reasonable, but Spira hadn't survived 134 years by taking anyone's word for anything. "Why would an enforcer of treaties need pyria?"

"He didn't say, and I didn't ask. It's his price for helping us."

"And he'll guide us all the way south? All the way to the Polar Serpent?"

Professor the dragon Ondir shifted in his seat. Here was the rub, apparently. "He has not yet agreed to it, no. He claims he's never crossed the sixty-fifth parallel, because the treaties forbid it, but I suspect he's gone farther. He knows too much; he may even have seen the creature."

"If he thinks we want to kill it, he'll never take us to it," said Spira. Making Ondir spell that out looked foolish in hindsight.

"Give him no choice," said Ondir, as if this were the easiest thing in the world.

Anything seemed easy if you had someone else to do it for you.

Spira felt suddenly exhausted. It had taken so much energy just to come here and complain—and for what? They were still stuck with Lord Hamish, and now they had to force him to lead them to the pole. How? If he was mistreated, it would be Spira's neck on the line.

The saar were bound by treaties as well. It wouldn't do to forget that.

"You look peaked," said Ondir, eyeing Spira dubiously. "Do you have enough medicinal herbs? Store them properly. You won't get far if you have another flare-up."

Tathlann's syndrome meant joint and heart trouble, ambiguous anatomy, autoimmune conditions, and what dragons called hyperemotionality—meaning any emotions at all.

Spira was feeling one now, in fact. *Patronized.*

Spira's last "flare-up" had been a conflagration—they'd almost died—and they chafed at the suggestion that their own carelessness had caused it. One of Ondir's human students, William of Affle, and his dreadful girlfriend had maliciously stolen and destroyed Spira's herbs. Spira had been ill for three months, during which time William absconded from St. Bert's, leaving his miserable girlfriend pregnant. Spira had assumed she'd be packed off to a convent, the usual practice among Southlanders, but she'd escaped that fate somehow.

The nefarious girlfriend—Therese? Tess? She'd gone by both names—had walked to Ninys, fallen down a hole (a fate Spira had very much wished upon her), and discovered the so-called Continental Serpent. Through dumb luck, she'd affirmed the existence of World Serpents, previously considered a quigutl delusion. Dragonkind had been forced to take action, of course, so in some sense it was *her* fault that Spira had been coerced into this polar expedition.

There weren't enough holes in the world for her to fall down—or William of Affle, either.

"Your graduate students are acceptable, I presume," said Ondir, breaking Spira's reverie. He was clearly checking off some kind of list.

The graduate students were absolutely not acceptable, but Spira was stuck with them and knew it would be pointless to complain—again—at this juncture. Still, the scholar couldn't help grousing: "It's a pity that Quaali couldn't get her second submersible design to work. I'd have preferred to travel to the pole alone, underwater."

"Don't be ridiculous. Where would you stow your medicines in a vessel like that? To say nothing of food and water," said Ondir. "Quaali is a gifted engineer, but she failed to take several important things into account. Our intern almost suffocated. I shudder to think what a deathtrap her first design must have been. Just as well she lost it.

"What you really should do," Ondir continued, "is fly south. That's the way we're meant to travel, the way we've dominated this world. You're being overly cautious."

It would have been unimaginable agony for Spira to fly all the way to the pole. Their natural shape was more painful even than their saarantras. Ondir never seemed to remember, no matter how many times he was told.

But that wasn't the only reason not to fly. "Flying would be suicide. I've explained this. The pole is ringed by volcanoes. Their gases poison you over time, or knock you unconscious—"

"And then hitting the ground kills you—I was listening," said Ondir. "If I disagree, it doesn't mean I didn't hear."

"It means you haven't done the research," grumbled Spira, planting their cane and rising to their feet again. "My whole life, everyone has mocked me for being pedantic; when will you recognize that the slow-but-thorough researcher always knows what they're talking about?"

"If it's recognition you're after," said Ondir, not rising to open the door, "I remind you that a successful voyage might go a long way toward convincing the hiring committee at the Mootseye that you're worth considering for a professorship."

His words were carefully hedged, but Spira had no illusions on this point. The committee could always find another reason to reject their application.

Professor the dragon Ondir did not bid Spira farewell or wish them good luck. No self-respecting dragon had use for such coddling; Spira grudgingly conceded that at least they were treated like any other dragon in that regard.

The corridor was disconcertingly dark, but Spira could still discern Lord Hamish. He'd moved a bit away from the door. "Scholar Spira," he said, his wafting scent indicating that he'd bowed. "Shall we walk to the ship together?"

Here was another who was welcome to fall down a hole.

Spira began picking their way down the stairs. It took some

concentration until their eyes adjusted. Each step felt like someone was trying to pry off their kneecaps with a hot knife.

"I appreciate your reluctance to kill the Polar Serpent," said Lord Hamish, at Spira's heels like a terrier. "You're right that it's a sentient being and should be approached as such."

Spira snorted. "I was pulling Ondir's tail."

"Still," the man insisted. "Humans long believed dragons to be mindless beasts, but we've learned better."

"I believe you have that backward," said Spira, pausing on the landing to let their knees recover; regrettably, this meant Lord Hamish paused beside them.

The pale man glanced warily up the stairs, then cupped a hand to his mouth. "You're wondering what the pyria is for. It's for my client in St. Claresse. He requested fifty barrels, but I'm sure he could use a hundred. What if I sold him all the pyria and split the profits with you?"

That left no pyria to kill the serpent with, Spira noted. Of course, the Continental Serpent had died of a ballista bolt through the eye; there was more than one way to do the deed.

Lord Hamish continued: "I think you'd like my client. Like you, he fits uneasily into this world and chafes at its injustice. Have you never wished to see it all burn? His cause is righteous. You'd be helping an indigenous island nation push back against Ninysh tyranny."

Spira did not give two snorts for injustice, but they did chafe at this human noticing how poorly they fit and intuiting that they'd like to burn everything down. That was surely a lucky guess. Observing that a dragon wanted to set things on fire was not a particularly deep insight.

And yet. Spira felt unexpectedly exposed.

"I accept your offer," said Spira. "Double the barrels, half the profits."

Lord Hamish opened his mouth, but Spira wasn't done.

"In addition, you will lead us all the way to the pole. None of this sixty-fifth-parallel nonsense. You've seen the serpent. You will take us to it."

The man hesitated.

"I'm voluntarily relinquishing the means of killing it," said Spira, hoping this would do in lieu of an actual promise. People tended to react badly to broken promises.

Lord Hamish inhaled shakily, then said, "I agree."

He thrust his hand forward. Spira looked at it distastefully and then shook it.

It hadn't been so difficult to persuade Lord Hamish after all. Spira was feeling slightly smug about this and was on the verge of congratulating themself when they caught the faintest whiff of . . . prevarication.

According to experts at the Mootseye, it was impossible to smell humans lying, but Spira's nose and experience said otherwise. You had to train yourself to distinguish it (by spending a disagreeable amount of time with humans), but it was there.

They'd first noticed it when William's horrible girlfriend had sat on Spira's lap and professed her (lying) love as cover for the theft of Spira's medicines. Underneath the acrid tang of anxiety had been something fainter. Something nameless that had given Spira a frisson of synesthesia. She'd smelled brittle, like a porcelain vase full of fine cracks.

Lord Hamish smelled that way now. They should've known better than to hope that anything about this voyage might turn out to be easy.

Well, two could play that game. Spira had prudently promised nothing.

In brooding silence, they gingerly descended the rest of the stairs and emerged into the glare of afternoon.

Two

Tess Dombegh went to sea feeling hale and hearty. This was new; once she had been like an injured animal, curled protectively around her wounds. But she'd walked across the entire Southlands, found a World Serpent, wrestled with her past and won. She'd healed so much and come so far that she finally felt capable of living up to Mother Philomela's injunction:

Walk on, but don't walk past people who need you.

She could do that. She was uncurled at last, ready to be the hero of her own story.

A hero who presently, unglamorously, lay sleepless in her hammock, listening to her brother-in-law snore.

None of her favorite childhood pirate stories had mentioned that ships were noisy. Jacomo's snoring was almost the least of it. The wind howled and the waves grumbled; the bosun's whistle shrilled; the sailors sang almost constantly; and every time the ship changed course, the sails had to be reset with all the attendant flapping of sheets and squealing of pulleys.

Belowdecks was no better: the whole ship groaned ceaselessly. Rats skittered; her quigutl friends, Pathka and Kikiu, skittered after them. There always seemed to be somebody walking directly above her—or running. Their footsteps felt disconcertingly close to her face.

Jacomo gave a sudden snort, like a cow sneezing, which set her teeth on edge.

There was no point lying here any longer. Sleep had fled and it wasn't coming back.

Extricating herself from her hammock in the pitchy darkness, without falling on Jacomo, was easier said than done. The two of them had been a late addition to the expedition, so there'd been no place to quarter them except the *Avodendron*'s tiny records room; they were probably lucky Countess Margarethe hadn't made them sleep in a coil of rope on deck.

Jacomo lay upon the sea lockers, with Tess's hammock strung mere inches above him. The room was so small that she could brace her hands against the opposite wall while lowering her—

"St. Masha!" cried Jacomo.

"Did I tread on you?" she whispered, as if there were any point in keeping quiet.

"Only a bit." He shifted position; he was too tall for the cramped space.

This had been his first vomit-free night since Mardou. Tess was a heel for waking him.

She felt responsible for his being here at all, honestly. He'd only meant to deliver a message—that Tess's twin, Jeanne, was pregnant and wanted her home. Tess could have thanked him and let him go, but no. "Let's go to the South Pole and look for a World Serpent," she'd said. "It'll be fun," she'd said.

Turning your stomach inside out for three days wasn't anybody's idea of fun.

Still, she considered as she felt around for the hanging oil lamp, he hadn't been clamoring to go back, finish seminary, and finally become a priest. Tess herself, given the option, would have chosen endless vomit over going home to her mother, without a second thought.

Home was what had hurt her in the first place; home was a lost cause. Maybe she felt a bit bad for her twin (who was stuck with

Jacomo's unbearable mother as well as their own), but Jeanne had made her choice. It wasn't Tess's job to help her live with it.

Tess opened the lamp and turned up the flame enough to see by. Jacomo threw an arm over his eyes. His bulky form was tangled in a wool blanket, which had evidently been fighting him all night; his dense hair, badly in need of a trim, made a dark corona around his head.

Tess had slept in her breeches and shirt; she fetched her boots from the corner and her doublet from a logbook shelf, hurrying so she could let Jacomo go back to sleep again. "I hope you're finally on the mend," she said, fishing in a drawer for her thnimi-brooch.

"Maybe? Argol gave me some ginger," Jacomo mumbled into his arm.

"Well, go back to sleep," said Tess, pinning the cheap-looking jewel to her doublet. "Nobody's expecting anything of you. The decks have been swabbed"—this was a little joke at her own expense—"and I've got this mission for the Queen completely under control."

The mission was not a joke. She felt in her pocket for the slip of parchment. She needed to read Queen Glisselda's note once more to make sure she'd understood everything.

Tess closed the records-room door behind her as quietly as she could, unsure why she bothered. The entire ship moaned in ceaseless complaint.

She paused, worrying the note in her pocket, debating where to go. There wasn't much privacy on a ship. The mess would be full of sleeping sailors. The head was not a pleasant place to read, and her presence in the hold would be hard to explain. Up seemed best. There'd be lanterns on the weather deck, and not many of the crew about at this hour.

Emerging from a hatch, she found the sea air bracingly cold. The sky was still dark.

"Dzeni ho!" called a sailor up the foremast, spotting Tess at once. She was one of only three cream-pale people on board. *Dzeni* meant "foreigner" in Porphyrian; it seemed to be her permanent title among the crew.

"Hide the mop," called another, helpfully speaking Ninysh so Tess would understand. Laughter went up through the rigging, like a chorus of birds.

Tess smiled wanly and waved toward her unseen admirers. She'd been enamored of the idea of swabbing the deck—deep down she was still eight years old—and so she'd gone at it for four hours the previous afternoon, to the amusement of all.

Four hours had perhaps been excessive. Her shoulders still ached.

Tess unhooked a lantern and climbed the ladder to the forecastle, one of her favorite spots on the ship; she liked grinning into the wind as it whipped her short curls around, another of her dzeni eccentricities. She set the lantern on the prow railing and began unfolding her note.

"Good morning," said a gravelly, inhuman voice near Tess's elbow, startling her, so that she almost knocked the lantern into the sea.

"Don't sneak up like that," she cried, swatting the big lizard lightly with her parchment.

Pathka's head spines twitched with amusement. "I was sitting here the whole time," he protested. "If anybody was sneaking up, it was you."

She should have thought to look; Pathka's favorite shipboard activity, besides basking atop the mainmast, was sitting on the railing with his feet tucked under him and his tail curling, like some enormous, scaly cat. She hadn't realized he had stayed out all night, though.

"Where's Kikiu?" asked Tess, glancing around for Pathka's offspring. Tess was supposed to keep an eye on both quigutl, Countess Margarethe had stipulated, lest their flaming tongues set anything on fire. Kikiu was by far the harder one to keep track of.

"Ko is probably ratting," said Pathka, stretching and then settling his chin back on the railing. "But don't let me interrupt whatever you're doing—unless it's something the sailors will laugh about for ages. Then you might want to be interrupted."

"Ha ha," said Tess, turning her attention to Queen Glisselda's note.

She'd found it the previous evening, folded inside the scrip she'd received as part of her payment. Tess's half sister, Seraphina, had recruited her to spy for the Queen; Seraphina had made it sound like a merry jaunt. The Queen's note painted a grimmer picture.

The wind had wrinkled the note; she smoothed it against the railing and read again:

Tess:

I'm certain Seraphina will have explained your task with her usual diplomatic understatement. Let me be blunt where she was delicate: we believe Ninys is at war in the Archipelagos. They deny it—Count Pesavolta has denied it to my face—but they've been usurping territory and killing the Pelaguese. What is that, if not war?

My grandmother, Heaven hold her, once learned of an entire island population slaughtered by the Ninysh. To her shame, she did nothing. If such crimes are continuing, Prince Lucian and I cannot leave them unanswered. Goredd is prepared to intervene, if we must.

Be discreet; Countess Margarethe is a scientist, not a soldier, but we believe her partner, Lord Morney, is involved in colonization efforts. You are likely to go ashore and see the colonies for yourself. Use your thnimi to keep a stealthy record of Ninysh aggression and mistreatment of the Pelaguese. That, and your insights, will help us gauge where and when our intercession would be most effective.

There was a further paragraph about remuneration, which Tess skipped. Service to the Crown had its rewards, but Tess wasn't doing this for the money, or even for queen and country. Wrongs were being perpetrated in the world; this was a chance to do something important, meaningful, and, above all, *good*. After years of needing help, she'd finally be the one helping.

Just like she was going to help Pathka.

She glanced at the quigutl dozing on the railing. The lamplight revealed every bump and divot in his scaly skin, scars left by bites from other quigutl.

The scars Tess had given him could not be seen. It was her fault that Anathuthia, the great Continental Serpent, was dead. Pathka's dreams had been entangled with the serpent's when she was killed; he'd almost died along with her.

Tess scratched behind his head spines. She'd apologized a hundred times; it never assuaged her guilt or brought Anathuthia back to life. Still, she couldn't seem to stop: "I'm so sorry, Pathka."

He didn't need to be told what for. It was always the same thing.

"I already bit you," he said sleepily. "Don't keep sticking your neck between my jaws."

He meant she was forgiven; quigutl practice was to bite each other and forget it—which was probably more effective if you were a quigutl.

"I will get you to the Polar Serpent," said Tess. "You will dream together again, I promise. And I won't let anyone kill it this time."

"Kapatlutlo." Pathka corrected her with the Quootla name. "And I know you won't."

If only Tess could have felt as certain. Countess Margarethe was a scientist—as Queen Glisselda had underscored—but even she might react in fear, faced with such a massive monster. And Tess knew there was a boatload of dragons, led by Scholar Spira, also searching. Dragons were hard to predict. If they decided to kill Kapatlutlo, how could she hope to stop them?

She couldn't think like that, or it would be over before it began. She'd find a way, or a way would find her. There was no path forward except believing that.

Pathka tensed oddly under her hand and said, "Mind of the World, open your eyes."

"What?" said Tess, recoiling.

"What?" said Pathka.

"You said something strange," said Tess.

"The name Kapatlutlo is not *strange*," said Pathka indignantly.

"No, after that. You said, 'Mind of the World, open your eyes.'"

"Did Kikiu put you up to this?" Pathka was bristling. "I'm not going senile."

Tess was completely lost now. "You're not old enough to be senile."

"That's what *I* said," cried Pathka, leaping down from the railing. "I'll thank you to take my side next time."

"I'm on your side," Tess protested to the serpentine twist of his tail as he skittered off into the shadows. Inscrutable quigutl. Pathka was the one who usually made sense, too.

Queen Glisselda's note was still in her hand, a liability if it was found and read by anyone else. The countess surely wouldn't take kindly to being spied upon, even for a just cause. Tess crumpled it and threw it over the leeward rail (never hurl into the wind—as Jacomo had dramatically illustrated the first time he was sick).

Someone was moving below, in the waist of the ship, a petite, plump figure with short, coppery curls a shade lighter than her complexion. It was Countess Margarethe, dressed all in funereal white, in a padded jacket and breeches. At first Tess thought the countess was dancing a volta—by herself, for some reason—until her blade flashed, reflecting the lightening sky.

Countess Margarethe was famous all over the Southlands. Tess had known her only by reputation—youngest master of the Ninysh Academy, most fashionable woman in Ninys, a widow, and one of just three counts to survive Count Pesavolta's purges. She was apparently also no slouch with a sword and moved well for her advanced age (over thirty, Tess guessed). Tess knew no sword-fighting terms, but each of the countess's moves seemed to suggest its own name: *goat-skip, swirly swisher, skewer-thy-neighbor.*

She was beautiful, in motion. Tess had not understood that previously.

That only made the idea of speaking to her more intimidating, because of course the logical first step in undertaking the Queen's mission was to ask Countess Margarethe about the Ninysh colonies—whether the *Avodendron* would stop at any on this voyage, what things were like there, what she knew about the Pelaguese.

Discreetly, of course. It wouldn't do to offend Her Grace. Tess had been allowed to come along at her whim; the countess could abandon her on a deserted island just as capriciously.

Tess climbed down the forecastle—noisily, reasoning that it was a bad idea to startle a woman with a sword. As she approached, the countess broke off from her drills; she was breathing hard, but her face was illuminated by an enormous grin, as if panting and sweating brought her joy.

Tess, who'd once worked on a road crew, had some inkling what that felt like, and it made her a little braver. She hesitated, measuring her tone—mostly guesswork at this point—and decided to err on the side of confidence. Flatter, but don't cringe. "That looked well done, Countess. Brava."

The countess raised her hilt to her chin in salute. "I was All-Segosh Fencing Champion—twice, before Count Pesavolta decided the women should only face each other. I took the hint and retired."

She sheathed her blade; her young, pale maidservant, who'd been hovering nearby like an anxious ghost, stepped up and handed the countess a towel. Margarethe dabbed her brow with it.

"But you two are settling in, I hope? Is Father Jacomo's seasickness abating, or does he need the physician?"

When they'd first come aboard, Tess had pretended that Jacomo had finished seminary and taken orders. Priests were wanted in the

Archipelagos, she'd heard, and she'd thought that might entice the countess to let them come aboard. His being the son of the Duke of Ducana had apparently weighed more in the balance of Countess Margarethe's considerations.

The countess still seemed to believe he was a priest; it was awkwardly late to correct her.

"He's doing better. I think he's nearly over it," said Tess.

The countess turned over the towel to use the drier side. "Seasickness is not something one simply gets over. It comes and goes."

That was thoroughly dismaying news. The countess accepted a bottle of water from her maid; Tess racked her brains for how to say what she really meant to say. "I realize we got off to a rough start when we first met," she began. "I appreciate your taking a chance on me now. I was hoping to speak with you about the voyage, and what my role in it will be. I have certain skills and knowledge that I think you'll find quite—"

"I know, and I haven't been ignoring you," said the countess. She took a swig of water. "I thought I should give you time to consummate your marriage to the ship."

"My . . ." Tess felt a blush creeping across her cheeks.

"Her decks have never been swabbed with such tender devotion," said Countess Margarethe. "You've made the *Avodendron* very happy."

Tess was never going to live that down.

A bell rang, indicating ten minutes until breakfast. "You're supposed to be below, helping Karus and Argol ready the mess," said the countess. She signaled to her maid, who started gathering her things. "Come to my stateroom afterward, and we'll talk."

"I'd like that, Your Grace," said Tess, giving full courtesy.

"Please," said the countess, sounding pained. "We are both naturalists, are we not? That makes us equals in science. You must call me Marga."

"Of course," said Tess with a smile. She'd met eccentric nobles during her time at court. They were never quite as revolutionary as they believed themselves to be. Tess gave full courtesy again and went belowdecks.

⚓

The day shift were still rolling up their hammocks when Tess arrived in the mess. She looked for Karus and Argol, the father and daughter pair who'd been given charge of her nautical education. They were easy to spot: Karus was a white-bearded dotard, almost too frail and scrawny to heave the lines; broad-shouldered Argol, by contrast, was strong enough to turn the capstan by herself, and so tall that she had to duck her head belowdecks to avoid braining herself on the beams. If Tess hadn't heard Karus call Argol "daughter," she might have mistaken her for a man (her braids notwithstanding; half the Porphyrian crew wore braids). The truth was something still more nuanced: Karus had told Tess that while the term for *she* was fine in Ninysh, Argol was to be spoken of using the point-neuter pronoun *psei* in Porphyrian. Tess spoke no Porphyrian, but it sounded similar in concept to *ko,* the word that quigutl used for each other.

It was Karus and Argol's task to lower the hanging tables, which had been cleverly raised to the ceiling with ropes and pulleys to make room for the hammocks. Tess tried to help but mostly slowed them down; she had enough muscle to help Argol lower the tables, but tying the right knot to keep them from swaying was beyond her. Karus kept making her retie them.

Sailors began lining up at the galley, carrying their own tin bowls and cups—another detail stories never mentioned. Tess had to borrow a set from the kitchen and return it afterward.

"Go ahead and queue up," Argol told her with a wink. "Bapa and I can finish the tables."

Karus's brows shot up, sending parallel wrinkles rippling across the top of his bald head. "No, no. Tess will do the tables with me,

Argolele. You'll be late with the countess's tea again if you don't line up now."

Argol lowered a table, ropes clamped in her fists, a furrow deepening between her brows.

"We don't have to hang back; the captain said so," Karus insisted.

"We're lucky," Argol whispered urgently. "Everyone knows we're lucky. Maybe you're past caring, but I have aspirations, Bapa. I can't have insubordination on my record."

Tess fussed over her knot, trying not to look curious. Argol and Karus always waited with a handful of others until everyone else had gone through the line. They were clearly at the bottom of some hierarchy, but not because they were new or inexperienced. Argol had a golden sun, moon, and star embroidered on her collar—a first-class seamanship rating (her father had eagerly bragged). Karus was the oldest person aboard; he'd been going to sea "since before it was legal," whatever that meant. And yet cabin boys and teenaged midshipmen elbowed ahead at mealtime while Karus and Argol waited with half a dozen other shipmates, looking at the floor.

"Lucky" was new information, but Tess could make nothing of it. Waiting to eat didn't seem particularly lucky to her.

The quiet argument between father and daughter had caused an unfortunate pause in setting up tables. Darvo, the thickset bosun, stood nearby scowling, steaming dish in hand, tapping his bare foot impatiently (all the sailors went barefoot; "That's how you listen to the ship," Karus had explained).

Argol put her head down and got back to work. She could lower and tie off a table all on her own if Tess and Karus weren't slowing her down.

"Could I take Countess Margarethe her tea?" Tess asked, realizing she could get out of Argol's way and be helpful at the same time. "I'm going to see her after breakfast anyway."

"Good. Yes. Get in the queue," said Argol, deft hands working. "Thank you."

Tess hurried to the line, got her food, and found a seat as quickly as she could—at a table of able seamen, who tolerated her presence, even if they didn't look up from their breakfast. This morning it was *baganou*, an eggplant stew, and *bikeki*, as they called their tack wafers. Tess dunked the bikeki in her tea like the sailors did and then snapped it into two half-moons.

A wriggling bug popped out.

She yelped in delighted surprise and tried to corral it with her hands. The sailor beside her, a pockmarked fellow called Glodus, wrinkled his nose.

"Oops," said Tess as the weevil made a dash for Glodus. He crushed it with his thumb.

"It's my first one. I just wanted to get a good look at it," she tried to explain. "Dozerius tales are ten percent weevil puns, at least. 'Hear no weevil, see no weevil.'"

Glodus showed no trace of recognition.

"You know, Dozerius the Porphyrian pirate and his valorous crew? Those were my favorite stories as a—"

"Never heard of him," said Glodus. He seemed unamused by her dzeni eccentricity.

Karus and Argol were almost through the line. Tess, feeling chastened, ate faster.

She returned her bowl and spoon in exchange for the countess's tea—which turned out to be a silver tray with a teapot, porcelain cup and saucer, pot of lump sugar, and tiny pitcher of milk (there was a goat on board; now she understood why). Somewhat brazenly, she asked for a second cup and got it.

She had to cross the mess to get to the stairs; she couldn't carry this tray up a ladder. As she navigated the crowd and the ship's constant sway, she heard skittering and jingling. Some sailors jumped up, exclaiming loudly. Tess froze. That had better not be—

It was Kikiu. Tess first glimpsed the iron horns strapped to the younger quigutl's head, then the goggles clapped over her eye cones. The hatchling whipped in and out, around the benches. Sailors pulled up their feet to avoid getting slashed. A flick of her tail set one table loose; dishes flew everywhere. Someone yowled as Kikiu's horns caught their shins.

Kikiu made a diving pounce, snapping up the rat before it disappeared down a hole. She darted up the wall and clung to the ceiling. A narrow tail, protruding between the steel teeth of her bite enhancer, flopped around as she chewed meditatively.

So much for keeping the quigutl under control. Tess looked for the sailor who'd been caught in the shins, or the ones who'd lost their breakfast, ready to make amends, but no one seemed upset. Sailors gathered around Kikiu, reaching up gingerly to stroke her bumpy back or scratch behind her head spines.

Tess was so distracted by Kikiu that she almost stepped on Pathka, who was lapping spilled baganou off the floor. He waggled his spines at her.

"They're killing rats left and right," said Karus approvingly to Tess as she passed. He and Argol were finally sitting down.

"They're stealing your dinner, Lucky," called Glodus. His mates laughed.

There was that word again. Glodus had said it like it had a capital *L*.

Karus didn't react but kept his eyes on his food, steadily spooning it into his mouth. Glodus sauntered closer and said something in Porphyrian; his body language was clear to Tess, even if his words weren't. *Aren't you going to laugh at my joke, Lucky?*

Karus's cringe and forced smile gave the flavor of his reply: *Oh yes, ha ha, very clever. It's funny because the Lucky eat vermin.*

The Lucky are *vermin*, his antagonist's posture said.

Karus tried to resume eating. Glodus gave his table a shove and made it bounce. Half the Lucky ended up with tea in their laps. They yelped, which was all the excuse Glodus's mates needed to leap up, fists clenched and lips curled. Tess, stuck holding a large tea tray with no place to set it down, looked around in alarm.

A booming voice cut through the din: "Sit. All of you."

Captain Claado emerged from the galley, a steaming cup in his hand, his braids bristling as if they were alive. He was not a physically imposing man, but he had an imposing basso voice. Everyone sat at his command.

Everyone but Tess, awkwardly caught out with her tea tray, her white face turning red.

The captain strode through the mess, tugging his clipped gray beard; he had no mustache to conceal or soften his frown. His bushy brows made him look like a disapproving owl. "No one is Lucky aboard this ship," he said in Ninysh, presumably for Tess's benefit. "We are all thoroughly *un*-Lucky here. We eat, sleep, and work together. We do whatever is asked of us because we are comrades-at-sea. Do I make myself understood?"

Captain Claado was so stern and disappointed that even Tess found herself nodding along, resolving to do better. Lucky and non-Lucky alike muttered sheepishly, keeping their eyes averted. Only Argol met the captain's gaze and gave him a small, sad smile.

Breakfast resumed, albeit somewhat solemnly. Tess hurried toward the stairs, teacups rattling on her tray. The countess was surely growing impatient, waiting for her tea.

A deep voice called after her, "I'm glad to see you taking my niece her tea. I dislike her squandering my best sailor on such frivolities."

It was Captain Claado, apparently headed in the same direction she was.

Tess gave a courteous nod and let him catch up. "I'm glad to help. But I didn't understand. . . . Why are Argol and those others called Lucky?"

The captain's mouth creased at the corners as they mounted the stairs together. "The Lucky were once a reviled underclass in Porphyry, but not anymore, officially. The designation was abolished two generations ago."

"But unofficially?" ventured Tess.

"Unofficially, old habits die hard." He stepped up onto the weather deck. "'The past keeps a stranglehold on the present,' according to the tragedian Raxenias. I am determined to break that hold, though. My crew must learn to pull together. I will accept nothing less."

Captain Claado left Tess at the door of the great cabin and ascended to the quarterdeck. She watched him go, recalling her struggles with her own past. She'd walked across the entire Southlands to get free of it, and she'd succeeded. It could be done.

Smiling, she raised her hand to knock at the future's door.

Three

*M*ind of the World, awaken. The snows have fled.
  Stretch, stir, grow, and bloom.

Who would not aspire to be a flower? It can take more courage than you might think, especially when you're already a perfect, gleaming marvel of a seed, queen of all the soil you survey. A seed must crack, shrivel, disintegrate, and then—bravely, foolishly—reach for sunlight it has never known and only believes is there.

Do not fear the cracks upon your surface. They might be the first step.

Once upon a time (*that is to say, in its proper season*), a countess saw an opportunity to pass along some of her hard-earned wisdom and felt unexpectedly elated at the possibility.

Her father, the old count, had always had protégés—young priests, mostly, some of whom became bishops or advisers to Count Pesavolta. It had never occurred to Marga that she might have a protégé of her own, or that she'd want one. But looking at Tess—curious and eager, smart enough to have taught herself Quootla, resourceful enough to have found the Continental Serpent on her own—was like looking at herself at that age. There were things Marga needed to tell that young self.

(William, when he came aboard, was going to laugh, kiss her nose, and tease her about wanting a baby. And she did want one, but this was a different desire entirely; it would be years before she could teach a baby anything interesting.)

She hurried back to her quarters after sword practice. While Darienne prepared her washbasin, Marga unbuckled her padded jacket and looked around the great cabin with the appraising eye of someone expecting a guest. The morning sky through the bay windows cast a rosy hue across her unmade bunk and wardrobe trunks, her sword case and insect collections. The specimen jars seemed to glow on their barred shelves; dust motes sparkled in the air. Her hats had absconded from their pegs, congregating on the chart table as if plotting a mutiny. The wicker birdcage, which she still hoped would house a talking magpie someday, held a bust wearing a froth of golden curls, her best hair.

It was a mess, honestly, but maybe an interesting mess? After her wash, she'd bring out some books and maps. She would order Darienne to put those hats away.

And dust. And pack up Giles Foudria's shirts, which were still piled on the sea lockers.

Marga dropped her sweaty fencing togs on the floor and went behind the privacy screen, embroidered with pomegranates, where her maid was still fussing with her wash water.

"Too much lavender, Darienne," said Marga, wrinkling her nose. "I'm going ashore at St. Vittorius, so I shall want a gown today, not sailing slops—dark wool, serious, so they know they can't cheat me. Nothing too fine, though; you'll be washing coal smoke out of it afterward."

Darienne curtsied and left the countess to wash. Marga, in a cloud of lavender steam, wrung out the sponge and considered what to teach her protégé first.

Sea life was a logical starting point: distinguishing whales, classes of fish, algae. When they went ashore, she could send Tess questing for starfish and crustaceans in the tide pools. Karus and Argol were teaching her nautical skills—which must continue—but Marga would expand upon that with currents, winds, weather. A little geology? She shouldn't schedule too rigorously, or she'd miss out on lessons gleaned from the natural abundance around them.

The countess dried herself, still daydreaming, and put on her chemise. When she emerged from behind the screen, she was dismayed to see her fencing togs still on the floor and Darienne dithering at a wardrobe trunk, paralyzed by indecision. It would take longer to correct the girl than to do what needed doing, so Marga picked up her padded armor, straightened the coverlet on her bunk, and placed her short sword in the case with her other blades.

The cascading pile of Giles's shirts was the straw, however. It had been three days since she'd pointed them out to Darienne. "When I said put these away before William comes aboard," Marga snapped, "I didn't mean 'anytime before St. Claresse, don't trouble yourself unduly.'"

Darienne scurried to deal with the shirts. Marga, teeth gritted, cleared hats off the table and started laying out maps. St. Vittorius wasn't on any charts, of course, but Marga could show Tess where they were now, between two large Samsamese islands, sailing toward the Sea of Holes. She'd tell her protégé about her first voyage in search of World Serpents, three years ago, when that terrible sea—a maze of whirlpools and waterspouts—had nearly wrecked the *Avodendron*.

St. Vittorius was nearer that dreadful sea than sensible people felt comfortable sailing—a great advantage for a place Count Pesavolta didn't want anyone to stumble across by accident.

After St. Vittorius (maybe she'd sketch it onto the map) they'd sail east to St. Claresse, the oldest Ninysh colony. William had spent the last few months there trying to locate Giles Foudria. Their route beyond St. Claresse would depend on Giles's advice.

Giles had been her navigator on that ill-fated first voyage through the Sea of Holes. He'd gone mad, demanded to be left on an iceberg, and given them no choice but to do it. Marga had been a wreck, believing she'd killed him; she still had nightmares. But last year she'd heard reliable reports that Giles was alive. He'd reached the pole and returned to St. Claresse. . . .

Marga hoped he'd come with them, of course, but a map would do. Even a description would help. Her second voyage, last summer, had hit dead end after dead end. Giles surely knew a way through.

A sharp knock—Argol, with tea—interrupted her thoughts. Darienne was still stuffing Giles's shirts into a trunk, so Countess Margarethe, sighing, answered the door herself.

Tess Dombegh, the tea tray in her hands, froze in apparent confusion. Only then did Marga recall that she was barely half dressed.

Very well, *this* would be the first lesson, taught by example: any situation may be salvaged with poise and quick thinking. Marga straightened her spine, threw back her plump shoulders, and said archly, "Why, Argol, how pale you look this morning. Are you well?"

Tess blinked blankly at first but then broke into a grin.

"Set that on the table—mind the maps!" said Marga, stepping aside to let Tess by. The tray held an extra cup, which struck Marga as cheeky and presumptuous and exactly what she herself would have done.

Years of sword training had taught Marga to read people. Half the art of fencing was developing a theory of mind for your opponent and anticipating them. That was what had convinced her to let this girl come aboard, in spite of their previous history—Marga had recognized something in her.

Even Tess's aesthetic, which might have perplexed others, was transparent to Marga. Tess wore an ugly striped doublet, threadbare at the elbows; her breeches didn't fit right; her boots, though well made, had seen a lot of road. She looked like a bumpkin in town for his first feast day, fresh from hopping the clods.

One might assume she didn't know better, and yet she'd spent years at court, dressing her sister prettily enough to catch the eye of the future Duke of Ducana. No, Tess dressed like this on purpose. She was trying to be a bit shocking, to show how unconventional she was.

It was another, surprising way they were alike. Marga had married a poet, become the first female master of the Academy, and searched for World Serpents before most people believed they existed. It was a heady, powerful feeling to do things your own way.

You might ride a backward horse (the Ninysh saying went), but there were times to let it run and times to rein it in. Knowing which was which was an art, and *that* was the lesson Tess needed to learn. That, in turn, would show her the point of dressing properly.

Marga wouldn't even mention her clothes. Tess was the one who would be shocked.

"How do you take your tea?" Tess was saying, placing the silver strainer over a teacup.

"Please, you're my guest. My maid will pour," said Marga. She stared pointedly at Darienne, adding, "And then she will dress me."

Darienne, abashed, prepared the countess's cup first—one milk, one sugar. At least she needed no reminder about that. Tess, contrary to Ninysh custom, took hers black, which made Marga chuckle to herself. Was it still unconventional if it was entirely predictable?

"Is this where we're going?" asked Tess, stepping around to the front of the map table.

Marga traced their route between green-tinted Samsamese territories. "Note that the micro-islands in this strait—St. Looli's Chain—are all Ninysh red and grow denser at the southern end. I suspect that the same geological forces that carved out the Sea of Holes—"

"But where are your colonies located?" interrupted Tess. "Which ones will we visit?"

"St. Claresse, in a few days," said Marga tolerantly. The girl was bright; of course her curiosity would outrun her manners. "St. Vittorius, where we'll stop today, is . . . a bit different."

"St. Remy, St. Fionnani," Tess read off the page. "Are they all named for Saints?"

"Missionaries often arrive first." The annoying slogan for Count Pesavolta's Three-Pronged Approach to the Archipelagos popped into her head: *Faith, Farms, and Force of Arms!* Marga resented his taking up valuable space in her brain, and didn't inflict the words upon Tess.

"Where do the Pelaguese live?" the girl was asking. She was like a child, all questions.

Marga's hand hesitated above the map. The Pelaguese were an awkward subject. She kept aloof from politics—science had to stay neutral, to avoid bias—but her uncle had many strong opinions on the matter, and Tess was going to hear them eventually. And he wasn't wrong, alas, even if he was stridently idealistic; the Ninysh had not been kind to the islands' original inhabitants. But what was done was done. What could one *do* at this point?

"There was never any great civilization in the Archipelagos, if that's what you're asking," said Marga, certain that that was not what Tess was asking. "We won't discover any lost cities. If you're interested in archaeology, though, my friend Lady Aemelia Borgo keeps a museum of Pelaguese artifacts in her palasho on St. Remy. It's out of our way"—and Uncle Claado would confront Lady Borgo again, which would be mortifying—"but maybe we could stop on the trip home."

"But surely we'll meet living Pelaguese in your colonies or on uncolonized islands?"

"I should hope *not*," said Marga, more snappishly than she'd intended. If they saw Pelaguese in the colonies, Uncle Claado would be insufferable about it. If they saw Pelaguese *outside* the colonies, that would almost certainly mean their ship was under attack.

The two bombards she planned to purchase on St. Vittorius—over her uncle's strenuous objections—would be some deterrent. She only hoped they'd be enough.

Darienne was approaching with a purplish gown, like an overripe plum or a bruise; Marga resignedly set down her cup and saucer. "We will definitely see whales, though," she said, trying to sound encouraging. "I have a framed print depicting different spout clouds and fin shapes. You may study it while I finish my toilette."

Tess wandered over to look at the picture while Darienne pulled the gown over the countess's head. The sleeves attached at the shoulders with ribbons. Marga kept talking while Darienne pulled puffs of pale chemise through slashes along her upper arms: "The abundance in these waters is astonishing—seventeen kinds of sea anemones, nine kinds of seals, salmon so thick during spawning that you could almost walk on their backs, penguins—"

"Is this a human bone?" asked Tess.

Marga turned to look, although she knew what Tess had found. The girl cared nothing for whale diagrams, apparently; the shelf of human artifacts had drawn her like a magnet.

That was a little disappointing.

"It's a scapula, a gift from Lady Borgo," said Marga, wishing she could snatch it out of the girl's hands and shut it away in a drawer, but Darienne was lacing her up and she couldn't move. "The primitive St. Remy Pelaguese hung human bones in trees to frighten their enemies. Aemelia claims it was ineffective—the bones merely clanged together like wind chimes."

"Maybe they were supposed to be wind chimes," said Tess, examining the carved surface.

"Don't be silly," said Marga.

Tess replaced the scapula in its niche. "You don't like talking about the Pelaguese."

That was a bit forward. Marga was tempted to correct her somewhat forcefully but decided that patience was the better part of valor. "They're not my area of expertise," she said, stretching her shoulders to make sure Darienne had left her enough slack to move around.

Not that she planned to use her sword on St. Vittorius, but she always felt better knowing that she could.

"Forgive me," said the girl. "But Pathka's stories helped lead us to the Continental Serpent. The Pelaguese, I've heard, told myths and legends about a Polar Serpent called Aachi Zedelai, if memory serves. I sort of hoped we might hear some of those stories, see if they hint at the serpent's whereabouts, but you make it sound like there will be no one to ask."

Marga felt herself relax. "It's not a terrible idea. You must speak to Lord Morney about that, however. He's the keeper of the legends; he speaks quigutl as well. You two will have a lot to talk about."

She felt a stab of envy as she said it. Tess was supposed to be her protégé, not his.

Marga found herself trying to see Tess through William's imaginary eyes. There was a certain charm to her self-inflicted, lopsided haircut, and the way she fidgeted with her ugly brooch (maybe it had been her mother's). Her face was not entirely unbeautiful.

Marga would *not* be advising Tess to dress better; this clinched it.

That said, no good ever came of envy, and jealousy was even worse. Marga banished both from her heart at once. They were all on the same side, an unparalleled team of scientific minds (especially if Giles came aboard). She wasn't in competition with William; they'd both teach Tess, and Tess would teach them in turn, and they'd all be one big happy—

The door was flung abruptly wide. "Your uncle requests your presence on the forecastle, Your Grace," cried Karus, panting. "That ship is back again."

Marga downed the dregs of her tea. "Darienne, my sword belt," she cried, and then, "Not *that* sword belt, the strappy one with the silver studs."

Her maid buckled it on while Marga selected a blade, her father's rapier with the enormous basket hilt, visible from afar.

Tess asked, "What ship is Karus talking about?"

"The one you warned us of." Marga donned a tricorn hat. "The dragon expedition."

Tess paled, which was interesting; she'd blithely threatened to join that expedition back in Mardou. There was no time to wonder about it now.

"Bring that chart," Marga said, nodding toward the table. "I can teach you geography at the same time."

Countess Margarethe strode across the deck, ostentatiously well armed, even if this muted purple was not as imposing as she would have liked (although it was acceptable for St. Vittorius; Darienne had done well there). Marga looked around but saw no ship nearby. Her uncle awaited her on the forecastle, a spyglass in his hand.

"The *Sweet Jessia*?" she asked upon reaching him.

"Behind that islet," he replied. "You can see the topgallant mast through the trees."

"These micro-islands, Tess," said Marga, taking the glass and peering through it, "are St. Looli's Chain, which I mentioned previously."

Most were piles of rock crowned by a few twisted trees; the one her uncle had indicated was larger, with enough trees to make a grove. In the center they grew tall and straight, sheltered from the wind. At first Marga saw only fir branches and eagles' nests (great southern salmon eagles; she'd mention those to her protégé later), but then there it was, the *Sweet Jessia*'s mainmast, flying a tricolor Ninysh merchanteer's flag.

"That island should be . . . Frai Piscento?" asked Tess, squinting at the chart. "Why would anyone bother naming such a small island?"

"They must be named," said Marga, snapping the glass shut. "Sovereignty demands it."

"Translation: the grasping Ninysh claim every boulder," said Uncle Claado.

"If Samsam owned everything, that wouldn't be better," Marga retorted. She took back the chart, drew a charcoal pencil from her bodice, and scrawled *Here be dragons* across Frai Piscento.

"Have they been following us this whole time?" asked Tess, her brow creasing.

"They left Mardou before we did, in fact, but they stop frequently," said Marga. The ship was now easier to see through the trees; they'd raised topsails and were starting to move. "We pass them and then they pass us in turn. Being dragons, they're probably stopping to take pointless measurements of some kind."

"I can try to keep ahead of them, if it matters to you," said her uncle, relenting a little.

"Don't trouble yourself, Napou," said Marga, softening a bit in turn, using the Porphyrian term for *mother's younger emergent-masculine sibling*. "They surely must mean to cross the Sea of Holes, or else why come this way? We know how that ends, and I wish them joy of it."

"We should warn them," said Uncle Claado.

"We should *not*," said Marga.

The *Sweet Jessia* was moving again, pulling out from behind Frai Piscento into the open water of the channel. Marga considered giving some kind of sarcastic salutation, never mind that sarcasm was lost on dragons, but then she saw that their flagger was signaling the *Avodendron*.

Parallel to parlay, the message said—meaning the dragons wanted them to pull up alongside and talk. Claado signaled Darvo the bosun, who whistled out the order to the crew.

"Why are we approaching them?" asked Tess. "We should sail away."

Again the girl seemed unduly alarmed. "Would you really have joined their expedition if I hadn't let you come aboard?" Marga asked, eyeing her shrewdly. "Tell the truth."

"I'd have tried, for Pathka," said Tess. She looked grimly resigned; Marga believed her.

Marga led her protégé down to the waist as the ship drew nearer. The dragons aboard the *Sweet Jessia* were distinguishable by their bells; Marga counted five. The crew wouldn't be dragons, since the *Jessia* was a Ninysh ship, out of Mardou. Marga had probably met the captain, although she didn't recall him particularly.

On the quarterdeck stood a pale man dressed elegantly in white, wearing dark spectacles and an impeccable gravitas. At first Marga thought maybe that was him, but no, she'd remember an albino captain.

The ships pulled up about thirty feet apart, as close as they dared, considering that the strait was choppy and not very wide. A stout saarantras with mournful bulging eyes and bland mousy hair approached the railing, leaning on a cane, and called through a megaphone: "*Avodendron*, stop following us."

"That's Scholar Spira, my . . . acquaintance," Tess muttered at Marga's elbow.

Marga quickly gauged the postures of both. Not friends. Quite the opposite.

"Of course, following us was not the worst idea you could have had," the lead dragon was adding. "It's more sensible than following the advice of little girls."

That was clearly a dig at Tess, who turned so red she seemed in danger of catching fire.

Marga answered the impudent saar as soon as her uncle passed her the megaphone: "This 'little girl' found the Continental Serpent single-handedly, Scholar. Show some respect. And we're not following you—you're not even sailing in a straight line."

"We're taking depth readings."

"Of your own ignorance?" she cried. Her napou elbowed her, but it was worth it.

The saar seemed not to register the insult, of course. "Don't follow us. Find your own way to the pole. This is your only warning."

The scholar raised a signaling hand, and two subordinate dragons scrambled with equipment out of view on the forecastle. There was a snapping sound, and then a clay vessel, like a round gourd, shot into the air and arced lazily over the *Avodendron*'s prow, just missing it. The pot slapped the face of the sea, shattering into shards that quickly sank and a viscous, oily substance that floated—and then caught fire.

Flames leaped and danced upon the surface of the water, beautiful and horrifying.

It was pyria, the liquid dragon slayer, a sticky oil made to cling and burn, and the *Avodendron* was in imminent danger of drifting into it.

"Give those dragons credit for nerve," Marga muttered.

"Ready to port," Claado called to his crew. "Await my mark."

Marga knew what grim calculations he must be doing in his head. There wasn't much room to maneuver; timing would be everything. The *Jessia* blocked their port side; skirting the oil to starboard would take them close to a jagged sea stack (Frai Leporello, per the map). If they waited too long to choose their course, they'd slowly plow into the flames.

The captain of the *Sweet Jessia*—bearded and stocky; she did recognize him—was tearing around his quarterdeck, screaming at the dragons, apparently appalled that they'd used fire (naive, if you thought about it).

The dragons ignored him. His bosun, the calmer head, directed the crew to set stunsails and get under way with all speed. As the *Jessia* pulled ahead, Claado gave his signal and the *Avodendron* maneuvered in behind her. They cleared the pyria by several yards.

Tess rushed to the starboard rail and watched the water anxiously. Marga joined her and saw that the pale man now stood at the *Jessia*'s stern, never taking his eyes off the flaming sea. His spectacles glinted orange.

Claado stormed around the deck, pulling his braids and looking wild. "I can't believe they tried that. A merchanteer. In peacetime. What the devil were they thinking?"

"I hope *you're* now thinking that buying bombards on St. Vittorius is a reasonable idea," Marga said to her uncle, but her eyes were on Tess. The girl was trembling. Marga lowered her voice. "Was that warning meant for you? What on earth did you do to this Spira?"

"Something cruel," said Tess. "To impress a boy I liked."

Marga, trying not to laugh, gave herself a fit of coughing. "Oh dear," she gasped. "I wish I could say . . . I had never, but . . . I believe we've all been there."

Tess's smile was gruel-thin. "I owe ko an apology—but even that wouldn't be enough."

"You may still get your chance, if the Sea of Holes doesn't tear their ship to pieces."

"The warning may have been for me," said Tess, "but they didn't bring pyria in hopes of running into me. They surely mean to kill the serpent with it."

"It burns underwater; I expect it could do the job," said Marga. "But we won't let them. Giles will show us the fastest way to the pole, and if the dragons manage to catch up to us, we'll stop them with our bombards. You'll see. All will be well."

Tess nodded shakily, seeming not quite convinced. Marga, on the other hand, was feeling a familiar and welcome exhilaration. The expedition was a race this time, and she could not lose. Her ducks were not merely in a row, but alphabetized. Third time was indubitably the charm.

Her people were all in place, or would be soon.

And this one, her new protégé, was like an empty vessel waiting to be filled. "Come now, dear girl. Chin up. Before we reach St. Vittorius, I'll teach you where wind comes from."

Countess Margarethe, effervescent with knowledge and with hope, took Tess's arm and began to lecture on meteorology.

Four

Half a day's sail southwest of St. Looli's Chain, out of sight of all other land, lay St. Vittorius, the island that wasn't on the maps.

Tess saw nothing special about it. In fact, it looked utterly dismal—treeless, bare rock, what meager soil there was held in place by spindly, tenacious shrubs. As they sailed along the coast, the countess pointed out the tin mine, the saltpeter refinery, the smoke-farting chimneys of a dozen other smelters and furnaces. She didn't mention the ditches, stake walls, and watchtowers, Tess noted.

St. Vittorius looked like a scab on the face of the sea.

There were no towns. The island's one hospitable landing, a small harbor fronted by a sprawling castle of burnt brick, came into view. The *Avodendron* dropped sail at the harbor mouth and signaled the harbormaster with flags; two longboats rowed out to tow her to her berth. Five other ships were already docked—including the *Sweet Jessia*.

"What business could they have here?" cried Marga, clamping her hat down with one hand. The wind gusted from all directions in fits and starts. "I can't deny, it really does look like we've followed them."

"They'd better not be here to buy bangers," said Tess. *Bangers* didn't sound like the word the countess had used, now that she'd said it out loud.

Marga laughed, and then laughed again, longer and harder, clutching the ship's railing. She laughed so hard the shoremen stopped heaving the lines to stare at her.

"Bangers?" she gasped, dabbing her eyes with a lace handkerchief when she could finally speak. "I assume you mean *bombards*."

"I evidently don't know what I mean," Tess confessed.

"Look to the castle wall," said the countess.

Tess looked. Between each merlon a cylinder of black iron protruded, like a pig snout.

"The bombard, or cannon, is one of the Seven Deadly Devices of St. Lars," said Marga, "designed for St. Jannoula's War but never built. His design was flawed, but Lord Aveli and his technicians have perfected it here in the last few years. Pesavolta is fitting our navy with them."

"What do they do?" asked Tess. They looked like drain spouts.

"They fire projectiles at high velocity, an iron ball or a burst of grapeshot. If the castle opened fire on us, they could sink our ship—all these ships—in mere minutes."

Tess felt her stomach clench. If bombards could sink ships, they could kill a World Serpent. Marga's idea for stopping the dragons apparently involved making *herself* capable of killing Kapatlutlo. A risky plan, surely. Even if she didn't intend to harm the serpent, hammers had a way of finding nails.

"Napou hates the idea," Marga continued, "but we must be realistic. You saw what the dragons thought they could get away with. Things only get more dangerous as we go south."

"Has the danger . . . increased since last time you were here?" said Tess. That sounded relevant to Queen Glisselda's interests.

Marga's brow furrowed slightly. "There have always been conflicts, but the cannons are new. You don't want to be the only person without a blade when everyone else is carrying one."

The shoremen had finally secured the lines; now the gangplank was being lowered. Marga drummed her fingers on the rail. "We are a neutral research vessel. We don't take sides, but to be left in peace, sometimes we must appear fierce."

Tess pondered that last statement as a philosophy, while the countess descended to the main deck. She was still wearing her sword belt—a sling of elaborate leather straps holding a slender, elegant scabbard. The sword hilt glittered with silver and gold inlay. Her negotiations on St. Vittorius apparently required a bit of fierceness as well. Tess had to credit her consistency.

On the quay, a gaunt woman wearing a heavy brown apron over a workaday homespun kirtle hailed the countess with a wave. Tess, chin in hand, watched Marga descend the gangplank and attempt some laughing banter with this person. The taller woman nodded solemnly, hands clasped behind her back. She looked a drab bird beside the countess's rich plumage.

Tess heard the tinkling bell before she saw it; the tall woman was a dragon.

Tess switched on her thnimi, aimed it at the burnt brick facade of St. Vittorius Castle, and repeated what Marga had said about St. Lars's deadly device. "They've 'perfected' bombards here, and they sell them—since we're buying a couple." Tess spoke into her thnimi. "I would guess, given all the smokestacks, that they make them here as well."

"They're small enough to put on ships?" said a crackling voice from the device.

"Seraphina?" said Tess. "Sorry, I must've hit the wrong switch. I meant to record a message to send later, not impose myself upon you now."

"Do mind the switches," said Seraphina dryly. "I spent half an hour watching you swab the deck the other day before realizing you hadn't intended me to."

Of course she had.

"But Lars's original design had a forty-foot barrel," said Seraphina, back to bombards. "It was meant to shoot dragons out of the sky."

"The Ninysh are equipping their navy with them," said Tess, staring at a cannon on the castle wall. It stared back, a beady black eye.

"Are there shipyards? Where are you, exactly?"

"St. Vittorius, which is probably not on your maps. I see no shipyards, no sign of the fleet," said Tess, looking around. There were no other islands on the horizon. "The countess said they didn't want the Samsamese finding this place."

"The coming and going of the Ninysh navy would certainly attract Samsamese scrutiny," Seraphina mused. "They must be equipping their ships elsewhere. But this is significant news. With bombards, the Ninysh could take on anyone, even the Porphyrians. They could lay siege to coastal cities. You need to find out how many bombards have been made and who they've been sold to."

"Oh, sure, I'll just infiltrate the castle, shall I?" said Tess.

"Only if you can do it safely," said Seraphina. "No unnecessary risks."

"Cluck-cluck, mother hen," said Tess, switching off the device and wondering, not for the first time, what her sister must think of her if she was ready to believe that Tess could infiltrate a castle. Not that this brick monstrosity was a real castle. It might have crenellations, but the front gates stood open, no guards visible.

She could always pretend she was looking for the countess and got lost.

The sound of hammering broke her reverie, and she turned to see the *Avodendron*'s crew erecting a large wooden crane on the deck, complete with treadmill, which had been stored in pieces in the hold. Nearby stood Jacomo, his pale face making him look like a tall, fat, raven-haired ghost. Tess waved at him. He waved back and began picking his way toward her.

She descended the forecastle to meet him halfway. "You're back among the living."

"For now," said the student-priest, inclining his head.

"Come ashore with me. I want to have a look around," said Tess, tapping her thnimi brooch significantly. She'd told Jacomo about her royal mission, figuring it couldn't hurt to have one human ally on this ship. He'd seemed more awed by Tess's sister, St. Seraphina, than by Her Royal Majesty; his father was the Duke of Ducana, third in line to the throne, which must've made Queen Glisselda seem less impressive.

"Are we shadowing the countess?" said Jacomo out of the side of his mouth, which was less subtle than he seemed to realize.

Tess herded him toward the gangplank. "She's long gone. Went off with a dragon, of all things."

"The technician, you mean?" said Jacomo. "The one who's built the engine for Lord Morney's contraption?"

Tess bugged at him. "Where did you hear that?"

Jacomo pointed back at the crane. "I talked to the sailors. They're preparing to haul the contraption out of the hold so the engine can be installed. I'm told it's a *submersible,* but I don't know what that means, in practical terms. A boat that sinks? What's the point of that?"

He'd asked and they'd answered. Just like that. Seraphina had recruited the wrong spy.

"Yes," said Tess. "That's what I meant. Glad I don't have to catch you up on everything."

At the top of the gangplank, Jacomo looked worried. "I hear it takes time for your sea legs to readjust to solid ground. You feel like you're still moving, even though you're not."

Pathka and Kikiu came tearing out of nowhere, whipped around his ankles, and bounced down the plank, which clattered and jiggled and looked terribly flimsy. Jacomo swallowed hard.

"There's no such thing as landsickness," said Tess, trying to distract him from the swaying gangplank. "Going ashore will teach your stomach that there's always solid ground on the other side, however rough the crossing. You'll never be seasick again."

She had no idea if this was true, but surely belief was half the battle.

Belief, however, didn't stop Tess's sea legs from overcompensating her first few steps ashore and pitching her sideways into a coil of rope.

Jacomo offered her a hand up, clearly trying not to laugh.

There were no guards in front of St. Vittorius Castle because the courtyard was intended for visitors. It had a variety of amenities: a sparkling-clean tavern called the Traveler's Rest; some outdoor tables, in use despite the cold wind; and a few shops, which sold mostly ship supplies in bulk, hand-knit woolens, and paper, for writing home. Jacomo seemed interested in browsing, but Tess had no patience for that. She circled the yard, trying to find a way into the castle proper. The iron-strapped double doors on the north side of the courtyard were guarded, as were smaller doors presumably leading to the east and west wings. The courtyard-facing windows were shuttered.

Tess asked for latrines at the Traveler's Rest; an armed guard arrived to escort her. She bit her tongue and followed him, seeing no other way to penetrate the castle. The guard led her out the back of the pub and up a whitewashed corridor lined with closed doors. The six-seater latrine had a narrow, barred window, its only view a stretch of strand beyond the harbor. Tess saw rocks, sky, and tufts of waving seagrass.

Her guard considerately waited for her.

Tess returned to the courtyard and found Jacomo at the money changer's kiosk, digging through his satchel. He extracted a frayed, filthy slip of parchment with his father's seal on it. He'd probably been banking with it since his seminary days. The money changer peered at the seal through a lens and grudgingly handed over a small stack of coin.

"I want a hat," said Jacomo to Tess's questioning look. "Maybe some socks. It's only going to get colder as we go south. I've heard there are places where the ice never melts."

Tess had heard that, too. She'd been trying not to think about it.

She waited while Jacomo shopped, keeping her eyes on the double doors to see if the guards ever moved; they didn't. Jacomo ended up with a hat, as well as several pairs of socks and some gloves, which he stuffed into his satchel. He went ahead and wore the flat-topped midnight-blue hat, tying the earflaps under his chin; his longish hair stuck out in dark tufts all around.

They returned to the harborside. The wind was bitingly cold, making Jacomo's hat purchase seem prescient.

"Are those the weapons the countess is buying?" asked Jacomo, pointing to the iron snouts protruding from the facade. "What are they, bombards?"

"You've heard of them?" asked Tess.

"I took Advanced Theological Ballistics at seminary," he said. Something in Tess's face must have said she was seriously considering this, because he hastily added, "I'm joking. My brother Heinrigh got hold of the schematic. You recall how mad he is for hunting. He had some notion that he could build a bombard in miniature and use it to hunt bears."

"That sounds rather clever, for Heinrigh," said Tess.

"Never underestimate his ingenuity for killing things," said Jacomo. "He got our smith to make some tubing, but the formula for black powder defeated him, thank Allsaints. The last thing the world needs is Heinrigh blowing the heads off bears."

Anyone with that power would be frightening—to say nothing of an entire navy. "The Queen wants to know how many of these things they've made, and who they've sold them to," Tess said. "There are surely records here somewhere."

Kikiu suddenly appeared, atop the battlements, leaping from merlon to merlon, jingling like a horse in winter harness.

"Do you need a way in?" said Pathka, startling Tess. He'd apparently sneaked up while she was watching Kikiu. "There's an entrance to the warehouses around back. Just one guard. No place to hide on the approach, though. He'll see you coming, unless he's asleep."

"Or distracted?" said Tess.

"He'd have to be astoundingly distracted."

Up on the battlements Kikiu gamboled and clinked.

Pathka's head spines twitched. "I suppose that might do it."

They hailed Kikiu, concocted a hasty plan, and then sent her back up the battlements. The rest of them strolled along the eastern wing of the castle, like tourists going to the seashore. Jacomo, twenty feet ahead of Tess and Pathka, rounded the easternmost tower and disappeared from view. Tess peered cautiously after him. He was crossing a plain of bright white gravel toward a perpendicular wing of the castle. The builders hadn't bothered with crenellations or other affectations back here; this part looked exactly like the blocky brick warehouse it was.

Jacomo was impossible to miss: a big, dark cipher against the pale glare of the gravel. There was not one boulder or shrub, no place to hide until near the arched entryway, where two ponderous bombards squatted like malevolent toads.

They were aimed diagonally across the gravel field, toward a crumbling stone wall a couple hundred yards away. It took Tess a minute to guess what that was for.

This was surely where they demonstrated their cannons' firepower for customers. Tess flipped on her thnimi and whispered, "See where the stones and brick have been crushed? That's what this weapon could do to a city wall. It would pulverize a ship."

Or Kapatlutlo. Saints' bones.

Jacomo's scream startled her, even though she'd known it was coming. Kikiu had leaped from the roof and was chasing him across the gravel, snapping her jaws. "Help me!" Jacomo screamed, stirring up a cloud of dust as he bolted toward the arched entryway. The guard took two steps out of the shadows, trying to understand what was going on. Jacomo veered away from him and ran toward the pulverized wall; Kikiu, hard on his heels, snapped and spit fire.

The hatchling was also shouting: "Can I jump the guard? If he won't leave his post, I could bite his face off. . . ."

The guard, unwittingly wise, left his post and went to Jacomo's aid.

Tess dashed toward the unguarded archway, trying not to let the antics on the gravel field distract her. She crouched behind the bombards and then ducked into the darkness.

In the distance, Jacomo was shouting, "Hold on now—I didn't ask you to kill it!"

That didn't sound good. Tess glanced back, but Pathka, scuttling on the ceiling above her, said, "Kikiu can handle koself. The bigger worry is that ko might really bite the guard's face off."

Tess's eyes adjusted; she was in a vaulted tunnel large enough to pull a wagon through. The ceiling was whitewashed beveled brick, stained with soot. Large doors lined both sides of the passageway. Tess tried one and found it locked. There was a strong smell of must and metal and . . . something burnt? She couldn't identify it.

She switched on her thnimi.

Halfway along she found a set of unlocked doors. She put her shoulder against one, expecting such a heavy door to scream protest, and was surprised when it glided open easily and silently. Inside was an enormous room, lit by tiny grated windows, stacked floor to ceiling with barrels. The floor felt gritty underfoot; a layer of grime seemed to cover everything.

Pathka, at her ankles, muttered "Bad" in a muted voice.

"What's in these casks? Can you smell it?" Even she could smell it, but what was it?

"Out," said Pathka, nudging her toward the door.

"Why so tight-lipped?" said Tess. "Just tell me."

Pathka kept his mouth clamped shut.

Tess heard voices and turned to see two men coming through the silent door: a short, balding workman in a leather apron, and a younger soldier, tall and sharp-featured, with a poleaxe slung across his back. They stopped short at the sight of Tess.

There was a moment of mutual staring while Tess's mind reached for plausible excuses.

The man in the apron spotted Pathka and went white. "St. Masha's stone," he cried, backing into the axeman. "You can't have that thing in here!"

"Stay calm," said the soldier, cold eyes on Pathka. "Don't startle it."

It was a bit late for that. Pathka was bristling all over.

Tess, struggling to sound calm herself, said, "The quigutl is my friend, and he's calm. I hope you will also stay calm, gentlemen. We mean no harm. We were looking for Countess Margarethe and got lost. We were just leaving."

The axeman's face suggested that he found each sentence less plausible than the last.

He was not a guard-for-hire like the one at the tunnel entrance, but a career soldier—a lieutenant, if Tess still knew how to interpret Ninysh rank ribbons (it had been a while since her etiquette lessons). He had brown hair tied in a queue, a decisive nose, and a deep scowl. His nose, in particular, was disconcertingly familiar, but Tess could not identify it.

"You've brought your fire-breathing pet into a room full of explosives," said the lieutenant. "Would you call that sabotage or stupidity?"

That was why Pathka had been so taciturn: he'd smelled the danger.

"*Explosives*, meaning"—Tess racked her brains for Jacomo's term—"black powder?"

Neither man answered. The workman tugged on the lieutenant's arm like a child. "Kill it! We can't let it go. It's too dangerous."

"Not here. Its death throes would send sparks everywhere," said the lieutenant.

"Harm Pathka, and Countess Margarethe will want to know why," said Tess. "It would be wiser to let us return to our ship."

The men exchanged a look, and then the lieutenant opened the silent door to usher her out. That explained the well-oiled hinges— they couldn't risk a single spark.

As soon as they were out, the workman locked the heavy door and hurried away up the corridor. Pathka began frantically scouring himself all over with his tongue-flame. Tess had often seen quigutl clean themselves this way, burning off parasites and dead scales, but this was different. Traces of powder flared up, sparking bright white as they burned off. A shocking amount of flammable dust had clung to Pathka's skin in a short time.

The lieutenant drew his poleaxe from its back holster—he'd also been worried about sparks, maybe—and Tess finally got a good look at it. It had a vicious spike on the end, and a butterfly-wing blade with something resembling a meat tenderizer opposite it. He swung the weapon lazily so the point was aimed at her heart, or more precisely, at the eye of her thnimi.

It was still recording. If he didn't kill her, mother-hen Seraphina most certainly would.

"Michel is fetching this countess of yours," said the lieutenant, "and then we shall see what we shall see."

They waited. Tess tried once or twice to ask about black powder; the lieutenant was having none of it. Jacomo had made it sound so simple—ask and voilà, people answer—but it never seemed to work that way for her. She glanced toward the egress, wondering how Jacomo and Kikiu had fared. The guard wasn't at his post. He couldn't still be chasing them around, surely?

She listened carefully and heard talking, punctuated by occasional laughter.

The lieutenant had also noticed the empty guard post; he scowled at it. "Hands on your head. Move," he said, goading Tess and Pathka toward the gravel field. The distant voice became clearer as they walked. It was Jacomo, and he was . . . telling a story?

"The seas only rolled harder," he was saying. "So St. Polypous said to his companions, 'Maybe we're going about this all wrong. Maybe we should stop trying so hard and let the sea have its way.' So they went below, took the ballast from the bottom of the ship, and moved it to the top of the ship. And then—would you believe—the sea flipped their ship upside down!"

The erstwhile door guard let out a peal of laughter.

"And do you know what St. Polypous found on the other side?" Jacomo said. "The world reversed, like inside a mirror. The sea was the sky, and the sky was the sea, and the undersides of islands were green and mossy and full of upside-down people in upside-down towns."

Tess could now discern Jacomo and the guard sitting in the shade of the cannons, eating together. She emerged from the tunnel, blinking in the glare, and then stumbled forward as the lieutenant gave her an unnecessary shove.

The guard dropped his bread roll, hastily scrambled to his feet, and saluted.

"Am I interrupting your picnic?" said the lieutenant in a low, dangerous voice.

The guard's throat bobbed. "No, sir. Weren't no picnic, sir. Only this fellow had a bit of a scare, see, and he fainted, so I thought he could do with a bite to eat—"

Tess raised her eyebrows; Jacomo shrugged, as if to say, *Sorry, I had to improvise.*

"Saints and onions, what kind of scrape have you overeager young people gotten yourselves into?" called a laughing voice from atop the east tower. Countess Margarethe was striding onto the battlements, a well-dressed young man scrambling to keep up with her.

"Put your hands down, Tess; you're not his prisoner," the countess commanded. "Sirrah, I demand to know why you've apprehended my people. This won't do."

The lieutenant sheathed his axe and bowed curtly. "I beg your pardon, Your Grace, but your . . . girl?" He looked Tess up and down as if to double-check. "She let a quigutl into the powder store, endangering the lives of everyone on this island."

"Is this true, Tess?" called the countess, looking exaggeratedly stern.

"We got lost looking for you," Tess called back. "Pathka realized the danger right away, even if I did not. He would not have let a single spark pass his lips."

"There, you see? An innocent mistake," said Countess Margarethe, almost aggressively cheerful. "Tell your man to release them, Lord Aveli, and let us forget all about this."

This last utterance was directed toward the young man beside her on the battlements—an aristocratically phlegmatic fellow with slick, dark hair, his doublet all epaulettes and buttons. Lord Aveli sniffed disdainfully and said: "Lieutenant Robinôt is no hireling of mine, Your Grace; he won't answer even to one as elevated as yourself. He's Sixth Division."

Luckily, Tess wasn't positioned directly between the two men, because they were staring daggers at each other. The countess, for her part, fell suddenly serious. Tess didn't know what Sixth Division was, but she found Marga's new solemnity a little unnerving.

"I know your name, Lieutenant," Marga called, sounding conciliatory now. "My partner—Lord Morney—speaks admiringly of you in his letters and says you've helped him greatly on St. Claresse. I trust he has mentioned me to you."

"He has, milady," Lieutenant Robinôt said with a cordial nod.

Tess was staring at him anew. His familiar nose had been joined by a somewhat familiar name, but she still couldn't place it.

"Then I hope you might indulge me, for friendship's sake. These rapscallions"—they were rapscallions now, apparently—"are *my* people. Whatever nonsense they and their quigutl have gotten up to, I vouch for them. They will cause no more trouble, you have my word."

"I'll hold you to that, milady," said the lieutenant, giving the countess full courtesy. He waved Tess and Jacomo along. Pathka had already scurried out of sight.

The erstwhile door guard, it seemed, was to be left to Robinôt's discretion; Lord Aveli said no word on the poor man's behalf as the lieutenant marched him back indoors.

"Your people may sit in my salon while we finish our business," said Lord Aveli to the countess. His scrawny chicken's neck was red, as if he'd scraped too hard shaving it.

"Tempting, but that one has trouble sitting still," said the countess. Tess, knowing full well whom she meant, made an innocent face and pointed at Jacomo. Marga ignored this and continued, "Perhaps they might look for starfish along the shore? The girl is a naturalist and has been itching to get her hands on some specimens."

Tess bit her tongue, trying not to laugh at this transparent ploy to educate her about invertebrates. As much as Tess loved animals, she wasn't as keen on the ones without faces.

The countess seemed convinced they were fascinating. Very well, she'd won this round.

"They may," said Lord Aveli, scratching his chin. "But they're not to go inland."

"They won't," Marga assured him, glaring at Tess and Jacomo. They gave Lord Aveli full courtesy; apparently satisfied, he turned to go back indoors.

Marga leaned between the merlons and waved Tess and Jacomo closer. "I vouched for you," she said when they'd drawn near enough to hear her stage whisper. "Don't make a fool of me, and do as his lordship asks, for Heaven's sake."

Tess was wondering whether to ask the obvious question when Jacomo asked it for her: "What's inland, besides mining and metalworks?"

The countess glanced over her shoulder, then turned back and hissed urgently: "Fences, traps, and vicious dogs. This is a penal colony. Criminals do the mining and smelting. Now please—keep to the shoreline!"

She turned on her heel and followed Lord Aveli back inside.

Five

"I'm actually kind of excited—I've never seen a starfish," said Jacomo as they picked their way down the rocky trail to the shore.

"The countess has a bizarre affinity for the slimier sea creatures," Tess replied.

"To be fair," said Jacomo, gravel skidding underfoot, "you did join her expedition on the pretext of caring about such things."

"I'm more of a megafauna person," said Tess, nearly running into him.

"Anyway," said Jacomo, "bringing back some specimens seems a small price to pay for her saving us from being interrogated by Sixth Division."

Marga had stood up for them—however catty Tess was feeling about starfish—and Jacomo was making it sound significant. "What is Sixth Division, exactly?" Tess asked.

Jacomo shrugged his big shoulders. "Count Pesavolta's not-so-secret police?" He glanced back at her. "No? Maybe they're a bigger secret than my father always made them out to be. Pesavolta is technically a usurper, having overthrown a king and killed off as many rival nobles as he dared. That's a precarious position to be in. You have to keep what's left of your landed gentry in line somehow. Keep them scared, keep them guessing. Lieutenant Robinôt is probably here to intimidate Lord Aveli."

The narrow trail ended at a broad plateau of rock, exposed by low tide. The quigutl were already there, chasing each other, driving clouds of screaming gulls skyward.

"Would Robinôt have arrested us? I hear there's an extremely convenient penal colony," said Tess, craning to look over her shoulder toward the smoky, scarred interior of the island, recalling the ditches and stake walls.

Jacomo followed her gaze. "I'm not sure who's being held here. I hadn't even heard of this place until today."

They picked their way along the strand. The exposed rock was slippery with algae, so Tess stepped on clumps of barnacles and mussels, feeling mildly guilty about it.

His ignorance of St. Vittorius notwithstanding, Jacomo had clearly received a broader political education than Tess. He might be able to elucidate some things from Queen Glisselda's note that Marga had thus far been reticent about.

"Do you know anything about the Pelaguese?" said Tess, lowering her voice as if the rocks had ears. "I'd hardly heard of them in Goredd. My vile ex-boyfriend cited 'ancient Pelaguese myths' as proof of World Serpents' existence, but the people themselves seemed mythical. Queen Glisselda claims the Ninysh are fighting them here in the Archipelagos."

"I don't know much," said Jacomo, staring out to sea, his brows drawn. "I may have read some legends once as well. At seminary, though, we used to get Ninysh recruiters trying to persuade us to come south and convert the heathens. I'm not sure whom they could have meant, if not the Pelaguese."

"Father Erique suggested I go on a mission like that, Heaven slap him," cried Tess. That was one part of her travels she'd just as soon forget. A terrible village priest had been abusing his maid; she'd helped the girl escape.

Jacomo was snapping his fingers, clearly trying to remember

something. "What about that other churchy fellow you met, the monk . . . Frai Moldi! He was originally a soldier in the Archipelagos, wasn't he? Didn't he lose an arm fighting the Pelaguese?"

Of course. She should have thought of that before. "He threw himself under a horse, rather than spend one more day fighting."

"Faith, Farms, and Force of Arms," said Jacomo. "That's what the recruiters used to say. It's alliterative and it rhymes, so you know it's good policy."

Tess glanced over her shoulder again. No farms here.

Here, the Ninysh seemed to be subduing the earth itself.

When they reached the edge of the tidal plateau, where the surf pawed at the rocks, they paused to look for the fabled starfish in the clustered tide pools. Their search was abundantly rewarded: there were dozens, orange and pink and a shocking purple. Tess reached into a cold pool to gently touch one and found it rough as a cat's tongue.

There were green crabs, sea pickles, and clinging anemones that closed up like fists at a touch. A tiny crayfish tried to pinch Jacomo's finger, to his absurd delight. The quigutl splashed each other and seemed to be getting along for the moment.

An hour slipped away, and the cold spray of the encroaching tide began herding them back toward dry land. Tess gathered some starfish—one of each color—which Pathka permitted her to place on his back between his dorsal arms, and they headed for higher ground.

"Look!" cried Kikiu, pointing out to sea.

Tess looked, but the sea was flat and featureless.

No, wait. There was something to the northeast, near an outcropping, picking its way on long legs, wide wings spread for balance. A bird? It was enormous, if so.

Pathka raised his nose into the breeze and sniffed. "It's an old woman."

"It's destiny," said Kikiu. Without warning, she scampered toward the outcropping; the figure was just disappearing behind it. Tess and the others followed Kikiu up the ridge and (following her example) pressed themselves to the ground and peeked over the top cautiously, so as not to startle the bird-woman or frighten her away.

On the other side was a semicircular cove, the rock weathered into a cavelike overhang with a beach of crumbled shale beneath it. The winged figure standing in the dark water was unquestionably human, viewed up close. Knotted strands of yarn dangled in a fringe from the edge of her deep hood, obscuring her face; her leather tunic was covered with mother-of-pearl medallions. She wore breeches and soft boots and a pair of wide, membranous wings stretched over willow frames. Her tall heron-legs were stilts.

Around her, five long milk-white creatures swam. They had four limbs and broad heads, like salamanders, but were bigger than quigutl.

They were visible even when they dived deep. Their pale skin glowed faintly blue.

Anathuthia, the Continental Serpent, had glowed that same color.

"What are those?" Tess whispered to Pathka, but got no reply.

The woman began to sing. The words, to Tess's astonishment, sounded like Goreddi:

> *Brother, come out and be blessed!*
> *Brother, your struggles are over,*
> *Your stories will soon come home,*
> *For I have brought you sabanewts.*
> *What the Snow Lords have forbidden*
> *The True Priests will permit.*
> *It is our joy, granted by the Lights,*
> *To be the bridge between worlds.*

Those must be the sabanewts, then, in the water. Tess could see the *newt* part, anyway. She'd heard such creatures mentioned in a lecture once, by an explorer who'd glimpsed one near an iceberg. He hadn't managed to bring it back, so no one had quite believed him.

In the cove below, a man was picking his way out from under the overhang; the shale shifted in mini avalanches under his weight. He scuttled like a crab to keep his balance. His hair and beard were long and red; he wore only boots and breeches. His bare back and shoulders were freckled and sunburned, wiry with muscles.

"How is he not freezing?" Jacomo muttered into his hat flaps.

The man squatted at the water's edge. One of the sabanewts approached. He extended a hand as if to touch its slick head, but it reared out of the water and snapped at him, giving a glimpse of long, vicious teeth. The man threw himself back, exclaiming loudly in a language Tess couldn't understand.

She exchanged a look with Jacomo, who mouthed the word *Pelaguese?*

That was Tess's guess, too, although she'd assumed the Pelaguese would look . . . she wasn't sure. Different, in clothing if nothing else. Those were Southlander breeches. She scrutinized the man's skinny frame; he looked Ninysh, with his red hair. It was a bit matted . . . well, no, he'd braided sections of his hair and beard, and adorned them with beads.

The old woman was laughing. "You know better than to touch without permission," she said, still speaking Goreddi.

She was the one Tess would've guessed was Pelaguese, so why was she speaking Goreddi? Tess and Jacomo spoke it only to each other these days, using Ninysh everywhere else.

In the water, the sabanewts began squeaking and crooning, singing almost.

"How much of that do you understand?" the old woman asked.

The man shrugged as if to say: *Some, but not all.*

The woman sighed hard, making her fringe billow. "They say they can't do the ritual here. This island is a Dead thing, overrun by the Dead. They want to go to your home island."

The man spoke again in his own tongue; he sounded pleading now.

"The Dead will only kill you if they can find you," said the woman in a correcting tone. "But we know someplace near your home where you can hide, an islet sacred to the Little Lights. That's where it must happen. Not in this haunted nightmare place."

The man bowed his head.

"I must go; the Greater Lights have told me a True Priest is coming, and I must be there to meet them. I will leave one sabanewt with you, though." The woman turned to the creatures in the water. "Who will stay? Who will guide our brother to the place of his destiny?"

One pale form separated itself from the others. The old woman gave a satisfied grunt, spun deftly on one stilt, and began walking away. The other four sabanewts circled their erstwhile companion, then followed the old woman out of the cove, toward the open sea.

"What are they?" Tess whispered to Pathka. "Dragons, like you?"

"Perhaps a subspecies," said Pathka, whose whisper was not particularly quiet. "But I've never heard of Mindlets."

"Mindlets?" asked Tess. "She called them sabanewts."

"No, she called them Small Pieces of the Greater Mind," said Pathka. "*Mindlets* is my own innovation; it seemed less awkward."

The man hadn't looked up, preoccupied with the creature in the water. Hands on his hips, like a frustrated parent, he hummed tunelessly, chirped, and squeaked. The sabanewt didn't respond. The man whistled; the sabanewt lifted its tail out of the water and wagged it teasingly.

He laughed and then said in perfect Ninysh, "It's my fault. My mother taught me, but I never practiced. I never believed I was going to need it." He knelt again, gazing into the water. "My clumsy mouth can't make the chirps right. It barely makes Shesh right."

Shesh. That must be the language he was speaking. He—

Jacomo was elbowing Tess in the ribs. "Where are the quigutl?"

Tess glanced around. She'd just been talking to Pathka, not ten seconds ago. She looked back toward the water, and there were Pathka and Kikiu, climbing down the crumbling overhang. They leaped down to the shale beach and approached the water's edge, muttering together. Pathka, absurdly, had three starfish still clinging to his back.

"Stay back. Shoo!" cried the man, darting toward them, flapping his arms. The quigutl ignored him; they had eyes only for the creature in the water.

The sabanewt submerged, but Tess could still see its outline.

Pathka put an exploratory claw in the water, and the man cried, "Back off!"

Pathka ignored him. The man scooped up a rock and threw it; it knocked a starfish off the quigutl's back. Pathka, apparently unconcerned, kept his eyes fixed on the water.

Kikiu, however, turned her baleful gaze on the man and flared her head spines. She bared her steel bite enhancer and shook herself, so that the metal strung to her back flashed and jingled. She began creeping toward him, as if she were too strong to be in any kind of hurry. *Here comes Death,* the crocodilian sway of her tail seemed to say.

The man drew a knife. It was not knife enough to take on the likes of Kikiu. Tess decided she had better intervene.

"Kikiu, stop!" she cried, launching herself over the top of the ridge and skittering down the slope on the other side, barely keeping her feet. What she lacked in dignity, she made up for in breaking the tension (she hoped). Everyone had turned to stare; even the sabanewt had surfaced and was peering at her with one fathomless black eye.

Tess brushed herself off and addressed the man in Ninysh: "Put the knife away, sir. Please. And, Kikiu, step back. Shake it off. He's not going to hurt either of you."

Kikiu grumblingly returned to her mother's side. The man kept his knife out and now seemed to be sizing up Tess, calculating his odds.

"Sir," said Tess, stepping back as he stepped forward. "We mean you no harm. The quigutl are curious about your sabanewt. As am I, I must admit. It glows."

"Sabak," said the man.

"Pleased to meet you, Sabak," said Tess, giving him quarter courtesy, because why not? Good manners cost nothing.

He shook his red head. "Don't say 'sabanewt.' They're called sabak."

"All right," said Tess gamely. "But the stilt woman called them sabanewts."

"I'm sure it sounded like that to Ninysh ears," the man sneered. "You probably thought she was speaking Ninysh."

"Goreddi, actually," said Tess, perplexed.

"Goreddi?" said the man, wrinkling his sunburned nose. "Is that what we've come to? Are Ninysh invaders not enough—now Goreddis are piling on? How many of you are there?"

"Two," said Tess, gesturing behind her. Atop the ridge, Jacomo had come out of hiding and was poised to fling himself down the slope to her defense, probably.

It was the man's turn to look confused; his sunburned brow furrowed. "No, how many total? Give the number of ships, if that's simpler."

"It's just us," said Tess, beginning to understand. "We're not . . . *invaders*. We're on a voyage of scientific discovery." It seemed wisest not to mention that it was a Ninysh expedition.

The man put his knife away and ducked back under the overhang. Tess could see a bedroll and the stones of a small cook fire; he'd been camping here, waiting for the stilt woman and her sabak. He started piling his things into a little black coracle.

His talk of invaders had fully convinced Tess that the man was Pelaguese. Tess switched on her thnimi so she could document this meeting for the Queen, because who knew when she'd get another chance? Marga had made it sound like they could sail all the way to the pole and never see a living Pelaguese.

"What is your name, sir?" called Tess.

She wasn't sure he'd heard her, but he finally said, "Fozu."

"And are you Pelaguese?"

He looked up at her balefully, the whites of his eyes flashing, but did not deign to answer.

She couldn't very well blurt out her mission from Queen Glisselda, and how would she have brought it up, anyway? *Would you mind telling me how the Ninysh are mistreating you? Where do you think Goredd could best intervene?*

So she asked the only other thing she could think of: "Is it true your people tell myths and legends about the Polar Serpent? Aachi Zedelai, I'm told it's called in your language."

When Fozu turned toward her again, his eyes were wide. "What?"

"I'm asking because we're searching for the Polar Serpent, who the quigutl call Kapatlutlo," Tess continued. "I believe your myths might help us find it. Quigutl stories led me to the Continental Serpent, after all, and—"

"If you know the serpents exist," Fozu cried, coming out from under the overhang, "then why call our stories myths? Myths aren't told about things that exist. Are your Saints' tales myths—especially now that it has been revealed that there are living Saints who walk the earth?"

"I . . . all right, that was a poor choice of words," said Tess.

"You know what's an even poorer choice of words?" said Fozu, who was apparently just getting started. "*Pelaguese* means 'Islander'; I might as well call you a Continental. Who do you mean when you say 'Pelaguese'? Your fellow Continentals who've settled here and become Islanders, or any of the numerous, distinct nations you're actively stealing the islands from?"

Tess cringed; she'd meant the latter but disliked the accusation bundled with it.

"We're not here to steal islands," she said. "Goredd would like to help, in fact."

Fozu ignored her protestations. "Furthermore, do you know which nation calls the Polar Serpent Aachi Zedelai?"

Tess had no idea. She knew no other name but the Pelaguese one.

"Is it the Ggdani?" said Jacomo, who'd descended the slippery slope to stand behind her.

Fozu looked like he'd been slapped with a wet fish, hearing that word from Jacomo's mouth. For a moment Tess hoped that the Goreddis were finally making a good showing, but then Fozu burst out laughing.

"No," he said, falling serious.

"I saw that word in a book once," said Jacomo with an apologetic shrug.

Fozu wiped his eyes. "The Ggdani exist," he said, stressing the double *G* in a way Jacomo had not. "They live at the pole itself. You know the name of the nation farthest from you, but not the one you're trampling underfoot at this very moment."

Tess looked down at her feet, as if expecting to see bones amidst the shale.

"What happened here?" said Jacomo quietly. "The stilt woman called it 'a Dead thing, overrun by the Dead.'"

Fozu licked his lips, white with salt exposure.

"Were they your people, living here?" Jacomo persisted. "Were they killed?"

Tess recalled the blighted landscape of the interior—a scab on the face of the sea—and shuddered. She hadn't considered that more than vegetation might have died here.

Fozu sighed. "These people were the Jovesh. My people, the Shesh, are descended from Jovesh who intermarried with early Ninysh colonists. The Ninysh insist we're Ninysh, of course. Twenty years ago, to punish us for an unsuccessful rebellion, the Ninysh decided to teach us a lesson by pruning this side of our family tree, our Jovesh cousins. Ten thousand lived here."

He stared out the inlet mouth, toward the featureless sea.

"What happened to them?" Jacomo asked.

"What do you think happened?" said Fozu. "When an island is set on fire, there's nowhere to run. A few fled in boats to Paishesh, where we took them in and hid them. Some adapted and are now productive Ninysh citizens, but some fell into despair and did not survive. The unluckiest lived but were discovered and sent back here, to mine their own island and fill their lungs with coal smoke alongside the worst criminals from the mainland."

"Surely it's better to be alive than dead," said Jacomo.

"Sometimes it is, sometimes it isn't," said Fozu.

Tess was glad she'd switched on her thnimi. If Glisselda wanted to know how the Ninysh were treating the . . . the Shesh and Jovesh, she was getting an earful. "Twenty years ago," Tess muttered to her brooch. "Is this the atrocity you mentioned, the one Queen Lavonda ignored?"

"Queen Lavonda knew what happened here," snapped Fozu. Tess must not have spoken as quietly as she thought. "I petitioned her myself. She did nothing. There was no consequence to Ninys, from either Goredd or Samsam. So breathe deeply as you walk around this island: some of the stink is yours.

"And now you're here—why? To buy munitions? You're giving money to murderers and thieves, acquiring the means to become murderers and thieves in turn."

Fozu ducked under the overhang and emerged dragging his coracle, a round boat of tarred hides stretched over a frame of slender twigs, with all his gear heaped in it. There was barely room for him, but he climbed in, pushed off with a plank-like paddle, and whistled for the sabak, who languidly rolled in the water and turned to follow. The tide pressed inward; Fozu had to paddle frantically to make headway against it. The sabak nudged him in the right direction with its broad white head.

"Give Countess Margarethe a message from me," he called over his shoulder as he cleared the inlet mouth. "Tell her to turn back. The serpent is forbidden to you; the islands are forbidden. Your voyage will end in misery and death."

The open water tossed and spun the coracle, but he made skilled use of his plank and grew steadily smaller.

Tess watched him go, the tide lapping at her boots, certain that she had never mentioned the leader of their expedition by name.

Six

As they hiked back, Tess found her eyes drawn again and again toward the interior of the island. She'd understood *penal colony* to mean that prisoners were sent here from elsewhere, but the former inhabitants of this island were still here, some of them. They were being forced to make munitions for the destruction of other islands. It was grotesque; it made her ache all over.

At the top of a rise, she could make out a cluster of small fires far away—the cook fires of some encampment, maybe. Jacomo paused beside her and said, "You know this is too big for us, right? We can't storm the interior and free everyone, even with two doughty quigutl—"

"I wasn't thinking that," snapped Tess, only then realizing that her heart had longed for just such a release. To do *something*.

Her thnimi was still on. "If the Queen wants to intervene, she could start right here," she said to it. "But the castle has an awful lot of bombards." She switched the device off.

It was fully dark now, with clouds obscuring the moon. Pathka and Kikiu took the lead through the rocky landscape, the former keeping his tongue lit, the latter jingling.

A glow appeared on the horizon, and Tess soon saw it was torches, lining the eastern wing of the castle. Dark silhouettes milled around;

she heard a snatch of viol music when the wind shifted. It looked like a party under the (not-shining) stars.

A few droplets hit her cheeks; the clouds were ready to burst open at any moment.

And then thunder crashed.

Tess and Jacomo froze.

"How close was that? It sounded close," Jacomo whispered.

"I didn't see lightning, did you?" Tess asked, glancing around. This would be a terrible landscape to be stuck in during a storm.

"We're almost there. Quick, before it gets bad," said Jacomo, grabbing her hand.

They ran, and soon Tess saw the broken wall looming ahead of them; from there it would be a short dash across the gravel field to shelter. The people near the castle were chatting unconcernedly, the viol scraping away, as if they hadn't heard the thunder.

Tess slowed as a terrible realization dawned, and she pulled Jacomo to a stop with her.

Across the field, someone yelled, "Fire!" and the thunder roared again.

Everything seemed to happen impossibly slowly and fast. Jacomo tackled her to the ground. The wall, which had already withstood so much battery, half collapsed in a spray of sand and stone chips as a great cheer went up.

It took Tess and Jacomo some minutes to find the courage to rise. Tess, realizing Jacomo had shielded her, asked, "Are you all right?" He nodded, spitting sand, but let her help him up. They were both shaking so violently they could walk only by leaning against each other.

Jacomo waved a white handkerchief as they crossed the gravel field. "We surrender!"

Gasps went up from the assembled guests—Lord Aveli's prospective customers, Ninysh lords and merchants. Countess Margarethe rushed to Jacomo and Tess, alternately hugging and swatting them, laughing and scolding. "You could have been killed! What were you thinking?"

"We brought you some starfish," said Tess, teeth chattering almost too hard for her to speak.

"Countess, aren't these the people you vouched for earlier?" cried Lord Aveli, hurrying toward them, epaulettes flapping. "I'm not sure we can do business if such disruptions continue."

"*You* told them the seashore was safe," Marga said to Lord Aveli, with a pointed laugh that made clear (to Tess's ear) that she was utterly fed up with him.

"*Safe* isn't the right word for any part of this island," muttered someone in the crowd, a short, pale man with tightly curled white hair. It was the man Tess had seen aboard the *Sweet Jessia;* he'd worn dark glasses then but had now removed them. He seemed to be some sort of minor lord, to gauge by his bearing and his doublet—years at court meant Tess knew quality tailoring when she saw it.

Why was he with the dragons? Maybe he was a master of the Academy, like Marga.

Marga didn't seem to know the small, pale man, however. Or if she did, she took no notice of him. She was leading Jacomo toward the bombards. "When they fire again, cover those earflaps with your hands. I'm warning you."

Lord Aveli, still disgruntled, seemed to be looking for someone to fuss at. His gaze lit upon Tess. "There you are," he said. "I've considered your request to visit the interior of the island. The answer is no."

Tess balked in confusion until she heard the pale man say, "Might I inquire as to why?"

Lord Aveli hadn't been talking to Tess at all; he'd been looking just past her shoulder. She tried to get out from between the two men by stepping toward the refreshment table, but Lord Aveli moved in the same direction. He took up two glasses of wine, handed one to the pale man, and then stood with his back to Tess like she didn't exist.

"You have no jurisdiction here, Lord Hamish," said Lord Aveli, lingering on *Hamish* to underscore their relative ranks. Tess's courtly education was paying off again: Hamish was a given name, not a place name like Aveli, which meant that the pale man was a younger son or cousin of someone more important. It didn't matter as much for nobler titles—Countess Mardou could go by Margarethe; she was still a countess—but if you were merely a minor lord, every little bit of elevation helped.

"I showed you my authorization from Count Pesavolta," Lord Hamish began.

"Yes, but what treaty could the enforcer of southern treaties possibly be here to enforce?" said Lord Aveli. "King Moy's treaties, if they're really still applicable, were with the Pelaguese. We've no Pelaguese here."

Tess remembered Fozu's account of the Jovesh and felt a chill.

"No Pelaguese convicts?" said Lord Hamish. "I'll want to check your rosters."

"We prefer to call them *conscripts*, not *convicts*, and you're welcome to check," said Lord Aveli, his smug voice grating on Tess's ears. "Of course, the paperwork is kept back on the mainland, at Mardou, ever since our records office caught fire."

"So your original records were conveniently destroyed," said Lord Hamish.

"My father perished in that blaze," said the younger lord. "I do not take that lightly."

"Forgive me," said Lord Hamish in a gentler tone. "I meant no disrespect. But the welfare of Pelaguese, ah, *workers* of any kind would be within my purview. There was a Pelaguese nation centered upon this very island at one time. Most were massacred, but it's possible—nay, likely—that any survivors were put to work in your mines or refineries."

"You're misinformed, sir," said Lord Aveli with a crispness that made Tess look up from the refreshments to make sure he hadn't drawn a sword. "My father built this industry from nothing. There was no one on this barren, smoking rock heap when we arrived. I remember the very day; I was six years old."

Tess peered around Lord Aveli's epaulette as subtly as she could and as directly as she dared, her curiosity renewed. Lord Hamish had affirmed the basics of Fozu's story—but what kind of enforcer of southern treaties confessed his government's crimes?

One who had regrets, presumably.

Lord Hamish's tone was conciliatory now, almost pleading. "One couldn't simply tour your facilities in an unofficial capacity, as a civilian interested in black powder production?"

"You expect me to believe you won't be surreptitiously spying?" scoffed Lord Aveli. "It's bad enough that Sixth Division is breathing down my neck. I'm not sure what I've done to deserve all this sudden scrutiny, but I suppose envy is the price of success."

"Sixth Division is here?" asked Lord Hamish, glancing around.

"Over there," said Lord Aveli, pointing out Lieutenant Robinôt talking to Marga and Jacomo near the bombards. "I'm given to understand Count Pesavolta has become touchy about the sort of language we put in reports. There are words he does not wish to hear. That word you just used, for example—*massacre*—sounds distressingly one-sided, as if ruthless aggressors were slaughtering innocents, which we all know is not the case. I merely mention it."

"I appreciate the warning," said Lord Hamish. He polished off his wine, drew himself up, and gave half courtesy. Lord Aveli gave an eighth back (*Rude*, Tess thought) and stalked off.

Lord Hamish set off at a quick pace harborward, presumably returning to the *Sweet Jessia*. After a moment's consideration, Tess went after him. This might be her only chance to talk to a member of the dragon expedition who wasn't Spira; there were things she wanted to know about their intentions.

"Lord Hamish!" she called. "Hold on a minute."

The pale man let her catch up. "Do I know you?"

"Tess Dombegh," she said, giving full courtesy. "We haven't met;

I'm with Countess Margarethe's expedition, on the *Avodendron*. I saw you aboard the *Sweet Jessia* when your dragon comrades threw pyria at us."

"Ah," he said, his mouth puckering.

"I just want to know whether you're equipping the *Sweet Jessia* with bombards in addition to pyria?" This was met with stony silence. Tess continued, pigheadedly, "I ask because I'm concerned for the well-being of the Polar Serpent. Do the dragons mean to harm it?"

Lord Hamish licked his lips with a wine-stained tongue. "The well-being of the what?"

This took her aback. Was he ignorant of what the dragons were up to? Surely he was bluffing. "I know what the saar are searching for. We're looking for it, too."

"Then you're chasing a fable," he said, turning away.

She dogged his heels. "I found the Continental Serpent. The quigutl tales are true."

He kept walking.

"And I know the serpents can be killed," she said, hating to utter her guilt aloud, but seeing no other way to impress the reality and urgency of her concern upon him. "It's my fault Anathuthia is dead. I can't let it happen again. I will stop you and your comrades from killing Kapatlutlo if I have to stand in front of the bombard and take the blow myself."

As if in answer, someone called, "Fire!" and the cannon thundered.

Lord Hamish stopped and looked back at her, some incomprehensible emotion in his face. "You're quite serious," he said at last.

"I am," said Tess stoutly, simultaneously praying that it would not come to that.

Lord Hamish stepped nearer, narrowing his pale eyes at her. "Then I will tell you this: we're not here to buy bombards. And you need not fear a repeat of the pyria stunt. We'll be rid of it soon. As for . . ." He made a gesture, possibly meant to indicate the serpent. "You and I are of the same mind. It must not come to harm. I'll deal with the dragons, but you must stop your expedition. Turn back now. Tell your countess that what she seeks is forbidden to her."

Tess frowned. "I can't just abandon the search. I have obligations. I promised Pathka—"

"That's not my concern," said Lord Hamish. "You do your part, and I shall do mine."

He set off again. Tess watched him go, her heart in her boots.

He was right about one thing, as much as she hated to hear it: the only sure way to stop the serpent from coming to harm was to stop her expedition—and any others—from reaching it. But she'd promised to take Pathka to Kapatlutlo. How was she supposed to do that without a ship and people to sail it? Without Marga's determination, expertise, and funding?

Surely she could get Pathka there and still keep the serpent from harm. Surely these goals weren't diametrically opposed if she could contrive to be clever enough.

If. There was a lot of weight resting on that small word.

Tess returned to the gathering and found Marga and Jacomo, along with Captain Claado, discussing practical gunnery matters with Lieutenant Robinôt. "The worst mistake people make," the lieutenant was saying, "is forgetting to swab the barrel to cool it before reloading. A hot barrel will set off your charge prematurely. That's how you lose an arm."

"Here's our most enthusiastic swabber," said the countess, extending a hand to welcome Tess into their circle. "Would you like to add gunnery to your list of skills, Tess?"

"No," said Tess more sharply than was advisable when speaking to a countess.

Marga was apparently too buoyant to take offense. "You'll be missing out. Skilled gunners will be in high demand, I predict. You'd be getting in on it early."

"The girl is being sensible for once; don't discourage her," said Captain Claado.

"She did try to blow us all up this afternoon, taking a quigutl into the powder store," said Robinôt, smiling wryly. "Then she wandered through a bombardment demonstration, and not a scratch on her. Clearly, she leads a charmed life."

"Clearly," said Tess, irritated by his ribbing and by the fact that she still couldn't work out why his pointed nose looked familiar.

"Do take care with those sparking quigutl, now that you've got bombards aboard," said the lieutenant. "You must absolutely keep them away from the powder barrels."

"Yes, thank you, I understand what safety is," said Marga, suddenly prickly. She forced a smile and clapped Tess on the shoulder. "That's Tess's responsibility, since she won't go near the cannons. I hope you won't be too frightened to sail with us now, Lieutenant?"

"Only a little," said Robinôt, rubbing the back of his neck. "But you're doing me a favor, and if your ship explodes, perhaps I'll reach St. Claresse all the sooner, by air."

Marga laughed. "I look forward to it. And you must tell me every bad thing Lord Morney has been getting up to in my absence."

"He's been a scholar and a gentleman," said the lieutenant with a sardonic bow.

"That's less reassuring than you might think," said the countess.

"Ouch, he warned me you were wounding," said Robinôt, pressing a hand to his heart as if hurt. He clapped Jacomo on the shoulder. "She's too high and mighty for us third sons, eh? We must stick together and form a defensive pact against her."

"Ha. Ha?" said Jacomo.

Tess's fixation on Robinôt's nose was almost unbearable now. The answer was on the tip of her tongue. She blurted out: "Don't third sons usually join the church?"

"I almost did," said Robinôt, his smile becoming as hard and sharp as glass. "I spent three years in a monastery, if you can imagine. My elder brother, designated soldier of the family, was thrown and trampled by his own horse—which takes some doing! But I believe that horse was saying, 'Send Moldivian to the monastery, and let his valorous younger brother take his place!'"

Moldivian? Not . . . Frai Moldi? It had to be. Tess knew that story. Of course, in Frai Moldi's version, he'd thrown himself under a horse on purpose. But that answered the riddle of Robinôt's nose. It was the same as his brother's. Tess should have known it at once, but the face around it was quite different. The hair was longer, the chin more stubborn, and the mouth more sardonic than self-deprecating—but none of that should have thrown her entirely off track.

It was the eyes that were all wrong. Moldi's had been deep and mournful, whereas the lieutenant's eyes were hard and cold as diamonds. The more he joked, the more chilling the difference seemed.

What was it Moldi had said about his brother? *If the Archipelagos catch fire, it will be Robinôt who did it.* Tess felt her stomach tense. The countess was taking another powder keg aboard, and maybe she didn't even know.

On the other hand, maybe Robinôt's presence aboard would have its uses. Tess had been charged with documenting Ninysh aggression, after all. It was awfully considerate of Robinôt—a Ninysh aggressor, according to his brother—to put himself right where she could watch him.

She tried not to fret that he was Sixth Division and likely to be watching right back.

Seven

Mind of the World, open your eyes.

We see—have seen, will see—every thread of this story, its warp to its weft. We untangle them so that your heart (the Heart of the World) may feel what needs to be felt, and your hands (the Hands of the World) may do what needs to be done.

With gentleness and conscience, we set you down again.

Once upon a time (*time is where we dutifully put you*), Spira set out just after sunset, up the large heap of stone that Lord Hamish had insisted on calling a mountain. The dragon Aganat, who'd refused to go farther than her laboratory, had warned them to keep to the southern and eastern slopes, not because these were the most scalable, but precisely because they weren't.

"Patrols go up there sometimes, for a view of the whole island," she'd warned, flicking ash from her smoking stick. "But the dogs can't climb the jagged side."

"I appreciate your help." Lord Hamish had bowed cordially. "We'll be back by dawn."

Spira knew mountains, and this was no mountain, but reaching the summit and returning by dawn was beginning to seem wildly optimistic. The southern slope was so steep and rocky that Spira would've thought twice about attempting it even in broad daylight. Lord

Hamish, sensing this—or hearing Spira's labored breaths—circled east toward a clearer trail. It was no less steep, but the chunks of stone made reasonably sized steps.

There was a moon, at least, the rain having finally cleared that afternoon just after the *Avodendron* had set sail.

Spira's knees required rest every twenty minutes or so—ten if the gradient was particularly steep. Lord Hamish showed no impatience; it was Spira who grew steadily out-of-ard angry. They'd been given a choice, and they'd chosen to accompany Lord Hamish on his fool's errand, and that had been a mistake.

Were they so easily manipulated? One flattering remark—"I need your help, and I don't trust the others"—and they were following this man up a mountain in the middle of the night without any real explanation why.

It hadn't even been that flattering. He hadn't said, *I trust you,* after all, just implied it—barely. Which, if Spira was being honest with themself, probably showed good sense.

"Do you want water?" said Lord Hamish, removing his pack. It was an enormous leather monstrosity with straps over both shoulders, large enough to contain a second Lord Hamish, if you folded him up a bit. Spira had never seen anything quite like it.

"No," said Spira sulkily.

Lord Hamish dug around, found his waterskin, and drank some himself, as if to demonstrate that the water was real and offered freely.

It wasn't the flattery, Spira suddenly realized, but the patience. The relentless kindness. Spira didn't trust it, and yet it seemed to call them like a flame called to moths.

Surliness was assuredly their best bulwark against it. They turned their back on him.

Another hour, punctuated by pauses, and they were halfway up. Spira, beginning to get thirsty in earnest, felt reticent about asking for water. Had they been too rude and burned that bridge? They'd just made up their mind to ask when Lord Hamish said quietly: "You agreed to let me sell all the pyria, so what were you doing, flinging it at another ship?"

"It won't happen again," said Spira, startled into contrition, and then startled by the contrition itself. That wasn't very draconic.

"Your associates built a catapult," said Lord Hamish. "That's a lot of work for a one-off."

"They needed something to do," said Spira. "You don't know what it's like to supervise graduate students. They get destructive when they're bored."

These particular students seemed also prone to scorn and to questioning their supervisor's authority. There was some chance that the grad students were, even now, mutinying and sailing off without Spira and Lord Hamish. Spira wouldn't have put it past them.

The dragon scholar felt a flicker of rage in their belly, and only then did they realize what should have been obvious several feelings ago: they were overdue for destultia. Spira carried a small satchel; where Lord Hamish's pack held enough practical provisions to outfit a whole camp, Spira's satchel held nothing but medications. Two weeks' supply. They would never be caught flat-footed again.

Lord Hamish, seeing what Spira was about, offered the waterskin wordlessly. He didn't wait for Spira to finish, but hefted his pack and moved on. His mouth was pressed into a straight line, as if Spira's answers hadn't reassured him, or he was worried about something else.

Spira swallowed their destultia and hurried to catch up.

At the next stop Lord Hamish asked, "Why didn't you tell me that the ship you attacked was a rival expedition?"

"We don't consider humans rivals, exactly," said Spira. "More like buzzing flies."

"You wouldn't waste pyria on a mere annoyance," said Lord Hamish.

He had a point. Spira took another swallow of water.

"How many expeditions are out there?" he asked.

"How should I know?" said Spira. "I only know about Countess

Margarethe because she's searched for the serpent before. She's famous for it. Anyone with enough money and a wild gleam in their eye might do the same, however. Ever since the Continental Serpent was found, it's only been a matter of time. You know Southlanders: they'll see it as a race."

"I do know Southlanders," said Lord Hamish grimly. "And you're right. They will."

Spira had intuited more than once that this man was not what he claimed to be. Count Pesavolta's trusted agent shouldn't be selling pyria to indigenes, most obviously, but there was more to it than that. He wasn't merely greedy or a traitor. Spira, accustomed to observing everyone closely, had hypothesized that he wasn't Ninysh at all, and now he'd all but confirmed it: he spoke of Southlanders as if he didn't consider himself one.

No Ninysh enforcer of treaties, even a corrupt or treacherous one, would talk like that.

Spira was tempted to call him on it—it could be leverage for making him lead them all the way to the pole—but something gave them pause. Lord Hamish had convinced Ondir that he was who he said he was; he couldn't have done that if he were prone to careless gaffes.

The man was no fool. If he was tipping his hand in front of Spira, chances were that this was something he wanted Spira to figure out.

But why?

The mystery gave Spira a strange feeling, a not-unpleasant tingling in their stomach, like indigestion except . . . That was wrong. The destultia hadn't kicked in yet, probably.

Lord Hamish hefted his pack and they set off in silence again, up the little mountain, toward some end Spira did not yet understand.

After Lord Aveli had denied Lord Hamish's request to see the interior of the island, Spira had assumed the little man would give up on whatever he'd come here to do. The next morning, however, Lord Hamish had lit upon the idea of soliciting the dragon Aganat's help. He'd enlisted Spira to speak with her. Aganat was a busy engineer and could get in trouble for taking a stranger inland against Lord Aveli's express wishes; Lord Hamish had anticipated that she'd be more likely to accept such a request from another dragon.

Spira had very much doubted this but had agreed to (pretend to) try. It had seemed the quickest way to get their expedition moving again.

Spira had found her at the dry dock, where a shiny metallic vessel— like a pumpkin with a pointed nose—was on the blocks. Aganat was directing crane operators to lower an engine into an open hatch in the back. Spira scrutinized the surface of the contraption, noting windows, propulsion vents, rudder.

It was a submersible. Of all the indignities. Quaali couldn't be troubled to design a working one for Spira, but here was one already built for someone else? Had Aganat built it?

Aganat stared at Spira, chewing the end of what looked like a smoldering black twig. She inhaled smoke and exhaled it at Spira. It was sickly sweet and irritating to the mucous membranes.

"You must be Spira," she said before they could speak. "I've heard of you."

Spira blinked in confusion, eyes watering from the smoke.

"You've got Tathlann's syndrome," she observed.

"Yes," said Spira resignedly. She must've smelled it; it was surprising that she could smell anything over that smoke.

Spira perfunctorily conveyed Lord Hamish's request—could she take him to the big hill in the center of the island tonight?—but Aganat hardly seemed to be listening.

She ran her tongue over her teeth. "Will you be coming along?"

Lord Hamish had asked Spira to accompany him. Spira had been so certain Aganat would refuse that they hadn't thought about how to decline the offer. It was important to consider such things in advance, because Spira was terrible at spontaneity. Either they froze up or—

"Yes," they squeaked, which was not what they'd intended to say at all.

Aganat nodded once. "Then I'll do it. But I can only take you as far as my lab, and I can't leave until I've finished installing this engine for Countess Margarethe."

"How did the human expedition acquire a submersible?" asked Spira.

"I built the engine; some exile in Porphyry built the shell. The real question is, where did they steal the plans?" said Aganat. "Don't get too excited, though. It will probably run, but I'm not convinced it's safe."

Still, Spira brooded on it all day, stopping by the dry dock to check its progress, watching the crew return the contraption to the hold of the *Avodendron,* staring after the *Avodendron* (now with chasers installed at the bow) as she sailed away.

Late afternoon, Spira and Lord Hamish met Aganat on the west side of the castle. She shook hands with his lordship, looming over him like a smoke-breathing camelopard. "It's not out of bounds for me to show you my lab," she said. "If you wander farther than that without my noticing, well, I don't see how I could have stopped you. Just a warning: if you try to free prisoners and get caught, they will hang you. That's what happened to our last priest."

The three of them crossed the rolling, rocky landscape, Spira always lagging behind. Aganat explained that this was the only route to the interior without checkpoints, dog patrols, spiked wire, and pit traps. She'd left herself a path so she could escape the tiresome humans at the castle, with their endless demands. Lord Hamish laughed self-deprecatingly at this.

Spira, puffing and sweating uncomfortably, struggled along the uneven path.

The laboratory was—to be draconically honest—a shack full of hoarded junk. Spira bit their tongue as Aganat gave a "tour" of all her favorite pieces of scrap metal; Lord Hamish managed to look politely interested.

His lordship declared that he needed a nap, since he meant to be up all night. Aganat cleared a patch of floor, while Lord Hamish extracted a tight bundle from his pack—a sealskin, fur side inward, that fit him like a mitten. He pulled it on, curled up, and fell asleep.

This left Spira sitting on a pile of rusty chains; Aganat sprawled across what looked like a lobster trap, lighting another of her noxious smoking sticks.

"So," she said in Mootya, waggling her eyebrows in undraconic fashion. "You've said nothing, so I assume this will surprise you, but I've got Tathlann's syndrome, too."

"Impossible," said Spira. "Only three recorded cases ever survived past childhood—"

"Right," she said. "Tathlann, you, and me. Come sniff my wrist if you like. I don't bite."

That was a joke. She'd made a joke. Maybe she wasn't lying.

Spira sniffed her bony wrist anyway. *Trust but verify* was their motto, minus the trust.

Their nose confirmed what her ceaseless smoke had masked. The records had called the third survivor by another name, however. She'd renamed and gendered herself.

Spira was suddenly bursting with questions—dizzy with them—the most urgent of which they quickly shoved to the bottom of the pile. *Never ask a question you don't want to know the answer to* was another rule that had served them well for a very long time.

"Isn't it difficult to get your medicines here?" asked Spira. That was a safe question.

"No trouble at all," said Aganat. "But then, I'm important—and very rich." Her broad gesture encompassed all the junk in the room. Spira must have looked skeptical, because she hastily added, "Not this. This is for comfort, the place I come to think. I have real money, lots of it, because I've made crucial discoveries. It was I who perfected black powder, made it strong enough. St. Lars had the principle, but the crumbly Zibou gray— used at children's parties and to flush out pheasants—couldn't propel iron.

I also invented the way to refit naval ships with cannon. I can't show you that; our shipyards are far from here."

Spira nodded absently; this was interesting but a far cry from what they wanted to know. "You seem to have less inflammation than I do."

"It's under better control—but my genius has served me here as well. I inhale some medicines this way." Aganat flicked her smoking stick. "I use a salve of my own invention on my knees." Her gaze grew distant, as if she was remembering pain. "And my hands. And feet. Shoulders and back. It spreads to all your joints, over time. At two hundred and seven, I'm starting to feel it in my jaw."

"I don't like hearing that," said Spira.

"Hearing what? That I've outlived Tathlann by five years already?" She licked her teeth. "I can give you a pot of salve to try. Can't spare much—I'm waiting on a shipment of lard—but if you stop back at the end of summer, I'll have more mixed up. We'll work out a fair price."

"That's very generous," said Spira warily, mistrusting the salve, distrusting the fairness.

Aganat took a drag on her herb stick and exhaled through pursed lips, letting the smoke curl around her head. "So," she said. "Why haven't you adopted a gender presentation?"

There it was, the question Spira had been grimly determined never to ask—but in reverse.

"It's a human affectation," they said, rubbing their suddenly cold hands together. "I don't see the point."

"But we're the most humanlike of all dragons," said Aganat. "Think about it. We were torn directly from our mothers' oviducts, not hatched. We have no maternal memories, so we had to start from nothing. We're comparatively frail, more emotionally volatile, and we find this wingless shape more comfortable than our own." She paused like she was recollecting pain again. "There's not enough lard and herbs in the world to keep my wings from aching."

"But . . . what is it for?" asked Spira, determined to get an answer now that the subject had been broached.

Aganat looked down at her kirtle and spread the skirt with her hands. "What is what for? Gender? It's for communication. It helps people understand who I am."

"And who is that?" sneered Spira.

"Myself! I can't explain better than that. I've tried both, and I've tried neither, and this one is correct. This is how I look most like myself."

Aganat had been so glib that it was a shock to hear her voice quaver with suppressed emotion. She was touching upon another pain remembered, something worse than arthritis.

A pain Spira knew very well.

She had to be wrong about the remedy, though. How could putting on a gown make anything better? It seemed insultingly facile. Spira felt a rising rage, even through the destultia.

"You're a shallow, cynical panderer," they said. "You're not expressing some inner truth: you want admirers. You want . . ." The word *friends* wouldn't come out; it cut too close to the bone. Furiously, Spira changed tack. "Humans hate what they don't understand, so you drape yourself in a nonthreatening costume to make them comfortable."

"Alienating everyone is morally superior, I take it?" said Aganat.

"It's honest," cried Spira.

"Indeed, you honestly don't want friends—I'm beginning to appreciate that," said Aganat, stubbing out her smoking stick in a shallow dish of sand. "You should get some rest before you follow your nonfriend up the mountain. A night is a long time to spend with someone who despises you."

She turned away and did not say another word to Spira, although they noticed later that she'd sneaked a jar of salve into their satchel.

It was handy, possibly, to have something to brood about while climbing the little mountain. Spira needed a distraction from their knees and from Lord Hamish's disappointed questions; rehashing their argument with imaginary Aganat did the job quite nicely.

What she hadn't understood—what they wished they'd had the wherewithal in the moment to explain—was that they weren't trying to alienate anyone. Spira was simply being Spira, and surely it was up to other people (dragon and human) to accept them as they were.

One shouldn't have to change for anyone else's comfort; to demand such was tyranny.

(*Fine, don't take other people into consideration,* said imaginary Aganat. *As you die alone, you can rail about what intolerant monsters they all were.*)

People were monsters, though. The humans bristled with derision and mockery, fear and poison; the saar were, unexpectedly, harder to take. Maybe your own people's scorn cut deeper. Dragons treated Spira like a curious piece of furniture that had inexplicably taught itself to speak and reason: They might let you talk, just for the novelty of it, but they weren't listening. They were calculating how heavily they could sit on you before you would break.

At least humans were sometimes too polite or embarrassed to be cruel. Lord Hamish was that sort. He made no snide remarks, never let his face crumple in repugnance when he thought Spira wasn't looking. He sort of smiled in Spira's general direction sometimes.

And as a result, Spira was following him up a mountain (whatever doubt they'd had about this pile of rocks meriting the title, their knees had come down firmly with Lord Hamish and would accept no contradiction).

It was pathetic.

"Here we are," said Lord Hamish, interrupting Spira's self-pity. They'd reached the bald, stony crown of the hill (*Mountain,* insisted Spira's knees). Lord Hamish took off his pack and turned in a circle, taking in the moonlit landscape, his pale face flashing by like a lighthouse.

Spira, winded and aching, plopped down on a boulder.

Lord Hamish stilled at last, looking down into the broad valley to the north. Spira followed his gaze; cook fires punched intermittent holes in the darkness, illuminating clusters of tents. That must be where the miners lived.

The prisoners, rather. This was a penal colony. Spira saw no reason to be coy about it.

Lord Hamish began taking bundles out of his pack. He unrolled a small mat on the ground and laid objects around its perimeter—south, north, west, east—same order every time. Spira couldn't tell what they were. A shallow bowl went in the center of the mat, and then his lordship sat back on his haunches, hands open on his knees.

Spira had been watching so intently that they hadn't noticed the cold gradually creeping up through the boulder. Suddenly it shot along their spine, up to their neck and shoulders, and they began to shiver.

Lord Hamish glanced back. "Are you cold? You can use the sealskin. We'll be here a while, and it's only going to get colder."

"W-what are we doing here?" asked Spira through chattering teeth.

Lord Hamish rose to fetch the sealskin, giving Spira a clearer view of the objects on the mat. Some looked like stones, some like pieces of ivory carved into different shapes, geometrical and figurative. It almost looked like a game board, but no one set up a game that reverently (unless it was a sacred game—Spira hadn't survived by discounting far-fetched possibilities). To their scholarly eye, it looked like he'd constructed an altar.

Other dragons wouldn't have noticed; other dragons disregarded the irrational, and religion was one of the most irrational things humans did.

The sealskin, which had fit Lord Hamish so snugly, surely wouldn't hold Spira, who was stouter, but his lordship unfastened a concealed row of bone buttons and opened it up. He spread it across Spira's shoulders; tail flippers stood up behind their neck like a high collar. Spira rose slightly, despite their knees' sharp protestation, to tuck the end between the rock and their bottom, and then they were completely, surprisingly warm.

Lord Hamish crouched before Spira. "I'm sorry to drag you out here," he said in a half whisper, "but I have an obligation that requires a witness."

"A ritual," Spira guessed.

"That's not entirely the wrong word for it," said Lord Hamish, smiling sadly.

"Who are you? Not Pesavolta's man." There was no point dragging it out any longer.

Lord Hamish's face registered no surprise at the assertion. "My name is Hami, and I'm a Watcher for the Ggdani. Retired Watcher now. I have two final obligations to fulfill—this is one—and then, after thirty-three years, I'm finally going home."

Spira, who had not anticipated a straight answer, was too startled to reply.

"You'll have a few more questions, I expect," said the pale man.

"A Watcher is . . . some sort of spy?" ventured Spira.

Lord—Hami inclined his head, his mouth crimped into a not-quite smile.

"And Ggdani is . . . ?"

"My nation. Closest to the pole. Protectors of the One."

Spira opened their mouth, then closed it again. They had a dozen more questions, but Hami's short answers did not invite deeper inquiry. The One was surely the Polar Serpent, anyway. The rest could wait. It was a long way to the pole.

"What do you need me to witness?" said Spira.

Hami's pinched expression relaxed. "This is a ritual of contrition," he said. "I confess my crimes aloud and promise restitution. My witness holds me to my word, in principle, although you shouldn't take that as a binding obliga—"

"Will you be confessing in Ninysh?" said Spira. "I can't be much of a witness if I don't understand what you're admitting to. You might be reciting a recipe for sausages."

Hami said, "I suppose it serves me right, choosing a pedantic dragon for this task."

"It does indeed," said Spira, feeling an unaccustomed spasm around the edges of their mouth. What were their lips trying to do? Not smile, surely? Was there any reason to smile?

There was, though. Lord Hamish was smiling—a real smile this time. Spira must have been experiencing some sort of mirroring reflex.

Hami seated himself before his portable altar once more, opened his hands to the sky, and closed his eyes. He stayed silent for long stretches and only occasionally spoke.

Even in Ninysh, Spira didn't grasp the significance of most of it. There were long lists of ancestors, invocations of Lights (both great and small), references to events and laws, to historical or mythological persons. None of it sounded like a confession, particularly.

Finally Hami picked up a vial from the southeast corner of the mat, unstoppered it, and held it above the bowl. "I harmed this place and her people through my arrogance and inflexibility. Island, souls—accept my sabaggatg. All of it." He emptied the vial into the bowl; its contents shimmered silver in the moonlight, like dragon's blood.

Spira, downwind, sniffed unobtrusively. It smelled fishier and oilier than dragon's blood.

"Island, souls—accept my blood," Hami said, cutting his wrist with a chip of obsidian from the southwest corner of the mat. He let the wound trickle into the bowl for the span of sixty heartbeats before binding up the wound.

Spira could smell his blood almost without having to inhale; it smelled comforting and delicious and made them a little dizzy. They covered their nose with the end of their sleeve.

Hami looked back. "I can't say the next part in Ninysh because it's a specific prayer."

He prayed aloud until the moon had set, and then lifted the bowl and got to his feet. He raised the bowl above his head, once, twice, releasing it on the third rise. The bowl flew up, turning end over end, and Spira ducked, expecting to be spattered.

"Look up," said Hami as the bowl clattered to the ground. "Witness my wealth and my health as they catch fire and disappear."

Spira cautiously craned their neck and looked. A thousand new stars seemed to blaze in the night sky, each an inexplicably flaming droplet of blood and oil. They hung suspended for a moment, and then one by one began to fall back toward the earth like shooting stars, burning out before they hit the ground. All around, Spira heard the soft patter of cinders landing.

Spira could not fathom what any of it was for, but felt awed nonetheless.

"What happened to this island?" they asked as Hami packed up. "What did you do here?"

"It's something I did elsewhere," said Hami, looking away. "I invoked Ggdani law—and obscure Ninysh treaties—and persuaded the Ninysh governor of Paishesh to execute two people for harming sabak. Sabanewts, Southlanders call them. I don't know what dragons call them."

Dragons called them nothing: sabanewts had been proved (mathematically) not to exist. Spira, as another factual counterfactual, should have known better.

"There are rules about sabak," said Hami. "Only five nations may keep them. A Shesh woman smuggled one to Paishesh, where a Ninysh soldier killed it. According to Ggdani law, both the woman and the soldier deserved death. I considered my verdict evenhanded, judicious, and fair.

"But the Ninysh soldier was nobody, whereas the Shesh woman was their Speaker, a leader of their people. The Shesh revolted after her death. The Ninysh quashed their rebellion and decided to break their spirits by slaughtering their cousins, the Jovesh, who . . ." His voice broke. "This island was covered in trees twenty years ago. The Jovesh were as numerous as the trees.

"And where was I? I'd returned to Ninys, congratulating myself on justice served."

Spira handed back the sealskin, wishing they knew some comforting word to deliver along with it. Even a human, surely, would have had trouble thinking of one.

"It wouldn't have looked like much to you, but that sabak oil was a real sacrifice," Hami said as he rolled up the sealskin. "My entire inheritance from my teggdi parent's side. Five generations of judges and archivists, scrimping and saving—"

"Which parent was your teggdi parent?" asked Spira.

"The one who wasn't my mother," said Hami, buckling the straps of his pack.

"So—your father," said Spira.

"No," said Hami patiently. "There are women, and men, and teggdi—the third kind. Like you, I believe. Your professor told me about your syndrome."

Spira boggled at him. Their breath seemed to have gotten stuck in their chest.

"Maybe it's why I trust you," said Hami. "Teu was my favorite parent. One doesn't meet teggdi very often in the Southlands, nor among dragons."

"No," said Spira thickly. "One doesn't."

One might in Porphyry, presumably, but that's where dragons went into exile. Spira wasn't ready to be banished. Not yet.

Hami extended a hand; Spira took it and let him pull them to their feet. Their knees, stiff from sitting so long in the cold, straightened under extreme protest. Hami waited until Spira seemed able to stand, and then he fetched their cane, which had fallen behind the boulder.

The stars were shining as they made the long trek back to Aganat's lab.

Eight

St. Claresse, where the *Avodendron* would pick up Lord Morney and drop off Lieutenant Robinôt, was a mere two days' sail away, if the wind held.

Tess was up early on the second morning, thanks to Jacomo's snoring. She went above and stood on the poop deck (it was real; her inner eight-year-old had reacted as you might expect). The first inklings of dawn played upon the eastern horizon. The ship's wake glistened like the trail of some cosmic snail.

She descended to the quarterdeck and heard voices in the great cabin below, speaking emphatically. Suddenly the countess burst onto the main deck, Lieutenant Robinôt at her heels. She was dressed to go ashore again—in vibrant reds this time, golden curls pinned up under the brim of an audaciously plumed hat. "Argol!" she called. "Come settle an argument."

"*Argument* isn't the right word for it," Robinôt protested as Argol descended the mainmast. The lieutenant was dressed up, too, to Tess's vague amusement; the Ninysh dress uniform had puffy, riotously colored sleeves.

"Describe to this doubting lieutenant the nature of our ex-navigator Giles Foudria," said Marga haughtily. "Would you say he was devious, and if not, why not?"

"He was the opposite of devious," said Argol. "The captain ordered us not to play cards with him anymore, or he'd have no shirts left. He had a readable face." Argol fiddled with her beaded earring, considering further. "Sometimes he lost on purpose, though. I once mentioned wanting to buy Bapa a down quilt, and five hands later I had the money."

"Yes, yes," said Marga, waving this story away. Losing on purpose was a bit devious, in fact; she evidently wanted proof to the contrary. "But he was never violent or angry."

"Oh, never," said Argol, coming down on the correct side of the argument this time. "I'd have called him tenderhearted and melancholy."

"Then he's a changed man," said Lieutenant Robinôt. "His gang—the Shesh Nine—plotted insurrection and terrorized civilians. We caught and executed eight of them, but Foudria got away. The governor wants him hanged."

The word *Shesh* caught Tess's ear; she descended to the main deck, listening intently.

"I don't believe it," Marga was saying.

"Don't, or won't? I can provide witnesses. Or ask your paramour. Foudria thrashed him the time they met face to face. His black eye has healed, but he has scars he could show you."

Countess and lieutenant stared at each other for some moments.

The breakfast bell rang. "Pardon, Your Grace," said Argol, "but I need to—"

"Of course. You may go," said Marga, her eyes still locked on Robinôt's.

Tess knew she should go, too, and help set up tables, but she didn't want to turn away from this silent battle of wills.

"You should've told him that the navigator was once your lover," said Robinôt quietly.

"That is none of your business," said the countess. The plumes of her hat twitched in the wind like living things, snakes itching to strike.

Robinôt finally broke eye contact with a shrug. "It's just a pity he had to learn of it during that fight. The shock distracted him and gave Foudria an opening."

"So it's my fault Giles got away," said Marga.

Robinôt gave half courtesy. "I've offended you. Forgive me. But please also consider that I've done you a favor. He's going to have questions—*you*, at least, have been forewarned."

The lieutenant bowed and went to breakfast. Tess imagined Marga's glare physically propelling him away.

"St. Claresse ho!" called the watch, high up the mainmast.

"Good," said the countess. "Come, Tess, let's have our first look at it."

Tess, surprised and then chagrined that the countess had noticed her lurking, followed Marga up the forecastle and joined her at the rail.

"I realize the *Avodendron* is quite a close space, but try not to look so eager to eavesdrop, hm?" said Marga.

"Sorry," said Tess.

"To be fair, we got a bit loud." Marga sighed, guarding her hat against the thieving wind.

Tess cast her gaze ahead, where an island was rising from the flat face of the sea. Several islands, in fact. "Is St. Claresse the entire cluster or the largest one?"

"Both," said Marga dully. "As well as the name of the town."

The big island had a port, Tess could now discern, but there were many more ships moored around the smaller islands. "Is this where they're retrofitting the navy for cannon?"

"No," said Marga, sounding unaccountably cross. After a moment's pause, she burst out, "A pox on his jealousy! I have nothing to answer for. Does Lord Morney account for all his previous lovers to me? Indeed he does not, and I care not a fig. If I'd been dueling some villainess who claimed she'd had him, I wouldn't have become so upset and distracted that I lost the fight. I'd have laughed before stabbing her in the throat."

That sounded a bit jealous to Tess, but she shut her mouth and nodded.

The countess sighed again. "We've been apart for months. I was so looking forward to seeing him again, but now I'm all in knots."

Tess considered: she had two exes, one good and one evil, so surely she could think of something useful or sympathetic to say. "If I were you," she said at last, "I'd ignore that lieutenant. He's a vicious, meddling gossip—they probably all are, in Sixth Division."

This made the countess laugh, so Tess continued, "And then hold your head up, no defensive cringe. If Lord Morney has some complaint to make, he can say it to your face."

"Facing me is far more perilous than facing down Giles," said Marga, turning morose again. "It makes no sense. I've known Giles forever—and yes, we were involved, so to speak, after I was widowed. It lasted all of two months, and then we were merely friends again.

"But that's my point: we were *friends*. I know him. He was born in St. Claresse but always scorned everything to do with the islands. He never mentioned the Shesh except to criticize the very idea of them. The Shesh were originally Ninysh colonists, you understand; we settled this island a hundred and fifty years ago, but then our forces were recalled to fight the dragon wars. The abandoned settlers 'went native,' as it were, intermarrying with Pelaguese. They had to, to survive, and no one begrudges them that, but—Giles himself used to say—at some point you have to stop being contrary and admit that you're Ninysh."

Marga tapped her fist softly against the railing. "I left Giles on that iceberg—at his insistence—but I should have tied him up, for his own good, and made him see sense. Maybe I can make up for that error by taking him away and breaking this delusion that's gripped him."

"But if the governor of St. Claresse wants him hanged," said Tess, "and if Lord Morney is jealous and wants to avenge his honor—"

"The latter remains to be seen," said Marga, smiling slyly underneath her hat. "Being a countess doesn't make you all-powerful, Tess, but I believe I can be reasonably persuasive."

Down on the main deck, Argol arrived with the countess's tea tray, looking both anxious and irritated. Tess cringed; that was supposed to be her job now. The countess, however, hailed Argol merrily, climbed down, and disappeared into her stateroom.

Tess watched St. Claresse's slow approach, counting the men-of-war moored around the outlying islands, getting repeatedly stuck at thirty-three. The harbor of St. Claresse town held only one naval vessel—the *Indomitable,* flying a Ninysh tricolor flag as large as a carpet—disgorging armored soldiers onto the quay. They marched up the hill in gleaming units of twenty.

It was hard to imagine anyone attempting insurrection with so many Ninysh troops here.

Spring came late this far south; the piers wore ragged skirts of ice, and there was still dirty snow along the spit of land leading to a spindly lighthouse. Fishing shacks and warehouses fronted the harbor, but inland and uphill loomed the massive walls of the garrison fort, the clock tower of the Governor's Hall, and the scaffolding-wrapped spire of a cathedral under construction.

Docking was a busy, buzzing process. Slender lines, their ends knotted around lumps of lead, were thrown toward the quay, where harbor workers scrambled to catch them. The shore folk reeled in these light lines, which hauled in the much heavier mooring ropes; once they had these heavy ropes in hand, a cry of "Heave!" went up all round. The *Avodendron* was pulled by hand the last several yards toward shore—warped, the sailors called it—until the ship was close enough to the wharf for the mooring lines to be tied.

Countess Margarethe, emerging again, called: "Tess! Why are you still standing there? Go fetch your things. We'll be staying here for a night or two while Lord Morney tests his submersible and we sort out this beastly business with Giles."

Tess gave a little wave and descended to the main deck. The crew were lowering the gangplank; Darienne, pink-cheeked, was flitting around four sailors who were hauling the countess's trunks. Lieutenant Robinôt and Jacomo had their bags and were ready to go ashore.

People had crowded onto the quay to greet the ship: stevedores, snack sellers, fisherfolk, merchants, soldiers, and stray children. The countess prepared to descend the gangplank first, as was her prerogative. Someone ashore was waving for her attention.

Jacomo suddenly appeared beside Tess. "Do you remember what I called you at your sister's wedding?"

Tess blinked at him. "You called me a whore, and then I broke your nose."

Jacomo went white, and she was half afraid he was going to throw up again.

"Not *that*," he said, swallowing. "The other thing, earlier. 'Lord Morney's Little Bit'?"

Tess stared blankly. She didn't remember that, but she'd had an awful lot to drink.

"You scoffed at the name," said Jacomo miserably, "so I assumed the rumor was wrong, or I'd misunderstood, but now here we are, and I just want to make sure . . ."

Tess stopped listening and looked shoreward, where Countess Margarethe was rushing down the gangplank into the arms of Lord Morney. He looked younger than Tess had guessed—in his early twenties—tall, blond, generically handsome. As he bent down to kiss Marga, the cold wind tossed his hair about and made the ends of his long coat dance.

His hands were unsettlingly familiar.

". . . that's not anyone you know?" Jacomo's voice seemed to travel from far away.

That couldn't be right. It couldn't.

Instinct or luck prompted Lord Morney to raise his face and look directly at Tess with those knowing blue eyes. The eyes she still saw sometimes in nightmares. That arrogant mouth cocked into a mirthless half-smile . . .

And then Tess was in the records room, sprawled across the sea lockers.

Pathka was beside her, his soft finger pads upon her cheeks. "Teth," he was saying, but it was his breath that brought her back and made her eyes water, and ye Saints, she was over this. She was better, it was done, this didn't still happen to her, couldn't still happen. She'd worked so hard to heal herself.

"Teth, nest-friend, what is it?" said Pathka. "You went into your mind, like you used to."

"No, no, no," said Tess, voice and heart breaking together.

"Don't be embarrassed," said Pathka, stroking her face, his throat pouch pulsing encouragement. "Jacomo told everyone you were seasick. You can greet Lord Morney when you're feeling bet—"

"Lord Morney!" Tess cried, and burst into tears.

A lifetime ago, in some other story, she'd called him Will.

Nine

Tess must have drifted out of herself again, because the next thing she knew, Kikiu was sitting on her stomach, breathing horrible quigutl breath in her face and saying, "Do you want me to kill him for you? I could make it look like an accident."

"You'll do no such thing," said Pathka, nipping his offspring's tail.

Kikiu's back arched like she was about to pounce on her mother, but Tess cried, "Stop! Let me sit up at least, before you start fighting like cats right on top of me."

"You didn't answer my question," said Kikiu, leaping down.

"*No,*" said Tess, rubbing her head. "But I appreciate the offer."

"How did you grow up to be so violent?" asked Pathka, head-butting Kikiu.

"You're the one who named me Death," said Kikiu, head-butting him back.

"Would you squabble somewhere else?" cried Tess, pressing the backs of her wrists against her eyes. There was a lot of noise at once as the two quigutl scuttled up the walls and out the air vent, clawing each other as they went, but then it was blissfully silent—except for the usual slapping waves, creaking timbers, and muffled screams of gulls.

Tess emitted a few sobs, so harsh they hurt, then breathed until they were under control. She didn't want to cry; she was furious. She wanted to scream at someone. With trembling fingers, she plucked the thnimi from her doublet, aimed it at herself, and switched it on.

"Tess," said Seraphina a few seconds later. "How pleasant to see your beauteous visage. Have . . . have you been crying?"

"Why didn't you warn me about Lord Morney?" barked Tess.

Tess couldn't see Seraphina but knew what face she would be making. Inscrutable owl.

"About whom, sorry?" said Seraphina cautiously, as if Tess were a feral animal.

"The countess's lover and co-conspirator?" cried Tess. "You must have known it was Will."

The pause was deafening.

"Hold on." Seraphina's voice was strained. "I'm scared that you'll switch off and hate me forever, but please give me a moment. I deduce that Will was your ne'er-do-well boyfriend—"

"The one who ran off when I was pregnant?" said Tess.

The rapist? she couldn't quite bring herself to say. Surely there would never be an easier time to tell Seraphina than now, but the word caught in her throat like a fish bone.

"William of Affle, he called himself," Tess continued. "Mama said you searched high and low, turned the world upside down and shook it, trying to find him."

"Oh," said Seraphina. "Did I indeed."

"How can you not remember?"

"I remember everything," said Seraphina. "For example, I remember Anne-Marie saying he was trash. Certainly not a lord."

"He wasn't a lord back then—I don't think," said Tess. He'd lied about lesser things. The hamlet of Affle stood close by Castle Morney. Maybe he was a bastard sired off some milkmaid down the village, only learning of his inheritance when the old baronet died.

It was the kind of romantic story she would have believed about him once, so she rejected it out of hand. But then, some Morney family crisis might indeed have taken him away from her. Maybe she'd finally have a chance to learn why he'd disappeared. She could just . . . ask him.

She wasn't sure she wanted to know. Nothing he could say could undo what he'd done.

"Anne-Marie specifically asked me *not* to search for him, dearest," Seraphina was saying. "She said you never wanted to see him again, and good riddance."

Tess's heart pounded. "That can't be right," she said, but she knew, even as the words came out of her mouth, that it could be. Of course Mama hadn't wanted Seraphina to look. Of course she would have lied to stop Tess's taking matters into her own hands.

This was a new wrinkle, after all these years. How was it that you could never seem to know all the myriad facets of history, even if the history was your own?

"You don't have to stay with someone who's hurt you," said Seraphina, her voice low. "Selda will be irritated, but I'll handle her. If you need to leave, for safety or sanity, go."

"I appreciate that," said Tess. "I need to think it over, though."

Seraphina spoke a little more, probably; Tess had stopped listening. When the call ended, Tess repinned the thnimi to her doublet, flopped back, and stared at nothing.

She would not be quitting the expedition, that she knew for sure. Will had already taken so much from her. He didn't get to take this, too, not without a fight—a metaphorical fight, that is, although getting drunk and punching people had a certain nostalgic appeal.

Anyway, what was the alternative? Give up and go home to the other people who'd hurt her? Seraphina wasn't terrible—they were learning not to step on each other's toes—and Tess had promised to try with Jeanne (although she wasn't trying very hard; Tess hadn't called once since Mardou). But her mother? The woman who'd scapegoated her at every opportunity and cudgeled her with the scriptures? Whose repression and abuse had driven her into Will's arms in the first place, and who'd considered it a blessing when Tess's baby died?

Tess was never going back to that. Not ever.

There was a tentative rap at the door, and then Jacomo opened it a crack.

"No need to knock," said Tess. "My closet is your closet."

He kept his mouth shut until he'd closed the door again. "Pathka told me what happened. I'm sorry I wasn't wrong about Lord Morney."

Tess untangled the apology. "I'm sorry, too. But since when can you understand Pathka?"

"He wrote a note," said Jacomo, pulling from his sleeve a rumpled scrap of fine paper, probably stolen from the countess's personal stash. "The spelling requires some imagination."

Tess felt a flash of nostalgia as she read:

see is sik wis hateen hem
hee was her mait hee hurt her

(ink spatter, possibly intended as punctuation)

kiquu has iren chaws i merly menson it

Pathka had taught her to understand Quootla using this same astonishing orthography. It seemed like centuries ago. Tess handed the note back.

"Lord Morney hurt you, but what happened, exactly?" asked Jacomo, lowering his voice to a whisper. He leaned against the shelves of ship's logs, arms folded.

A haziness drifted over Tess. She couldn't tell him; she'd go under again. She'd never managed to tell anyone but Josquin, her good love, whom she'd left behind in Segosh.

"You seemed pretty sure of the story when you called me Lord Morney's Little Bit," she said, suddenly cross. Being angry was a relief—it helped her feel more present—and she did remember him saying that now. She'd thought it sounded like a horse's name.

Jacomo turned red. "I was quick and eager to judge you. I'm not judging you now."

"Good, because you can't," said Tess. She still couldn't say it out loud, the crux of the thing, although there was one bone she could throw: "Will abandoned me when I was pregnant. I had a baby, Julian Dozerius, who lived for three days. I was fourteen years old."

"I had no idea," said Jacomo. He seemed to shrink inside his clothes.

"You couldn't have," said Tess, sitting up and rubbing her eyes with the heels of her hands. "My parents took great care that no one should know. Papa had concealed his half-dragon daughter for sixteen years, after all; he had the means, the skill, and lots of practice."

"Tess," said Jacomo. "I'm so sorry."

Tess's chin quivered. "It's all in the past."

"But it isn't," said Jacomo with surprising vehemence. "Because here he is again, popped up like the devil in a parable. When you saw him on the gangway, you . . ." He pressed his lips together. "You turned and walked away. You didn't respond when I spoke; you looked haunted. I don't know how you think you can travel together on this claustrophobic ship, but I want to help. Tell me what you need. Anything."

His sympathy was making her eyes sting. That was the kind of thing a friend would say, and she needed a friend. She couldn't think of anything to ask that wasn't stupid or homicidal, though, so she said, "Just don't leave me alone with him."

Jacomo said, "Of course."

That was some small reassurance, but then, what was she so afraid of? That Will would try to hurt her—or she would try to kill him? Surely neither of them could pull that off on a crowded ship. Was she afraid she'd fall to pieces? She wasn't a child anymore; she knew how to take care of herself.

Will might decide to slander her preemptively—maybe even get her kicked off the expedition—for fear of the terrible things Tess might tell Marga about him.

Or what if he wanted to pick up where they'd left off? That was a grotesque thought, but it led her one step further: What if he thought that's what *she* wanted? He was vain enough to think that, and he'd want her gone before she could spoil his chances with the countess.

Jacomo was watching her patiently. Tess ran a hand over her eyes and took a shaky breath. "All right, I should get this over with. Is he above, or . . . ?"

"Everyone went up to town—hours ago," said Jacomo. "It's almost evening."

"Sweet Heavenly home," said Tess, appalled at herself.

"We're staying at the Limpets, the countess's favorite inn—also the only inn, which is a perennial joke, it seems." Jacomo's calm voice was helping keep her calm. "The governor is giving an elaborate welcoming fete tonight, and tomorrow Lord Morney plans to test the submersible. If you want to hide in your room the entire time, you can. I said you were taken ill."

Tess smiled weakly at this, then rose and started organizing her travel satchel. Jacomo hefted her bag onto his shoulder, and she let him.

He set a leisurely pace, which Tess appreciated. One step after another, the way she'd walked back to herself before. Down the gangplank; across the quay, where fishnets were hung out to dry and gulls fought over scraps; up the winding road between the houses. Smoke curled from chimneys. Low, lingering clouds spit drizzle; the breeze off the water was ice cold, but Tess rather liked it. It made her feel alert and awake, senses at the ready.

All of her at the ready.

By the time they reached the square at the top of the hill, Tess felt like herself again. She could do this, with Jacomo like a bulwark at her back. All he had to do was loom largely.

The Limpets, a grand inn, took up almost the entire south side of the square. Across from it squatted the hulking garrison fort, while west and east stood the Governor's Hall and the half-built cathedral, respectively. An equestrian statue of King Moy, last of the great Ninysh kings, had been erected off-center in front of the cathedral. Market stalls were being dismantled at the end of the day, their canvas tarps flapping in the wind.

Jacomo had already been to the inn and back in the time it had taken Tess to recover from her shock, so he was able to lead her upstairs, directly to her room. He dropped off her bag, let her get cleaned up, and was waiting in the hallway to escort her to the fete when she emerged.

She could do this. She was feeling greatly fortified now.

The smell of roasted meat wafted up as they came downstairs, along with murmurs of conversation and the scrape of stringed instruments being tuned. Tess and Jacomo entered a spacious hall, where the upper echelons of St. Claresse society milled about in their nicest clothes, selected tidbits from the sumptuous tables, and paired up for dancing at the far end.

Tess thought (hoped, really) that she'd never find Will in this crowd, but she spotted him almost at once near the tall windows, talking animatedly to a large, admiring group. At least Tess could observe him from a distance, at her own pace. His fair hair was longer than she'd seen it; his shoulders had grown broader, and his face less boyish. He'd always been handsome, but he'd gotten even better-looking in the last four years.

It was appalling, frankly. Why couldn't his outsides give some preview of his insides? How was anyone to know what a monster he was, looking like that?

"There you are!" cried a voice to Tess's right. It was Marga, beaming, arms extended, but for a moment she had looked like a stranger. "Jacomo said you were ill. I was worried." She took Tess's hands. "If it's your bleed, I've got—"

"It was nothing," said Tess. "A fit of light-headedness. I'd missed breakfast."

Tess was light-headed now, in fact. She swayed on her feet, gripping Marga's hands a bit too tightly, as if she could keep this moment and not move on to the next one, where Marga inevitably introduced Lord Morney.

"Eat a little here," said Marga. "We'll have actual supper in my suite, a simple meal, after I've paid my dues. The townsfolk like to take what occasion they may, but I'd have preferred a quiet evening." She extricated herself gently from Tess's lobster grip. "You're still a bit clammy. Would you prefer something sent to your room?"

Tess wiped her hands on her doublet, considering, but then someone began tapping a crystal goblet with a spoon. The room quieted as an old, stocky gentleman stepped onto a dais at the far end. He wore a stately maroon robe, a thick chain of office, and what was plainly a wig.

"Governor Boqueton," Marga whispered to Tess.

The governor cleared his throat. "Friends, neighbors, I bid you welcome. Tonight we honor Countess Margarethe, who graces us with her noble presence yet again."

Marga smiled and raised her hand, to applause.

"She's headed south," the governor continued, "preparing to brave storms, volcanoes, and wild Pelaguese in the cause of Ninysh exploration. Heaven hold her, and all our brave sons and daughters who venture forth, spreading civilization to the dark corners of the world."

Around the room people kissed their knuckles toward Heaven.

"Before she departs," said the governor, "let us show her a merry evening, island style."

The crowd spontaneously burst into song:

> *Brighter than the eastern sky*
> *When morning comes and gulls do fly,*
> *Inviting as a young girl's smile,*

Welcome to our peaceful isle.
Cease, O traveler, from distress,
Cease and pause and rest
In the bosom of St. Claresse.

Countess Margarethe sang along; the governor clasped a hand to his breast, moved to tears. Jacomo rolled his eyes at Tess, in an apparent attempt to make her laugh; she couldn't, quite, but she rolled her eyes right back.

The governor moved aside, and Will stepped onto the dais, beaming handsomely.

Ugh. Tess's eyes rolled to the floor.

"As some of you know," said Will once the crowd had quieted, "I sail south with Countess Margarethe. My time in St. Claresse is at an end." Some gasps went up among the applause. "I'm sorry to go. This place feels like home, and all of you, like family. I'm glad I could give something back, and trust you're sleeping more soundly than you were five months ago."

The citizenry laughed and cheered at this. Tess, still not looking, wished he would stop talking. His voice hadn't changed at all. She felt its timbre and cadence viscerally.

"I didn't do it alone," Will continued (Tess squirmed). "Without Lieutenant Robinôt, the Shesh Eight would still be at large. Where are you, Robbie? Take a bow."

Tess peeked up through her lashes; the lieutenant bowed with a great show of reluctance.

Through the applause, someone shouted, "I thought they were the Shesh *Nine*?"

"Their leader has fled St. Claresse," said Will. "He won't be back."

He had to mean Giles Foudria. Tess glanced at Marga to see how she was taking this news, but her expression remained fixedly neutral.

"I know you want to get back to the main business of the evening— drinking and dancing." Will paused for laughter, smiling sweetly.

What a lie. Everyone seemed to be falling for it. "But I have one last order of business. My dear countess, when do we sail?"

The crowd parted a little so Marga could speak across the room; she was short, but her voice carried. "If your submersible trials go well tomorrow, we'll leave the day after."

"Could we stay one day more, and leave the day after that?"

"I suppose you have some amusing or compelling reason to delay us?"

"I rather think I do," said Will. He laid a hand upon his heart; it was disgusting, really. "Margarethe, Countess Mardou, would you marry me the day after tomorrow?"

Marga gave a shriek and clapped her hands to her mouth. Cries of delight and surprise (and possibly dismay) arose from the crowd, which became a sort of tide, buoying her along toward the dais. Will took both of Marga's hands and went down on one knee.

She probably said yes and kissed him, or some such. Tess couldn't see, didn't care to see, and didn't try. She turned away and found Jacomo behind her, a quizzical look on his face.

"All right?" he said quietly. "I hope it's not painful to see him propose to—"

Tess cut him off with a scoff. "Hardly."

That part didn't hurt at all. In fact, it was a relief. A newlywed Will was surely a safer, tamer Will, not trying to pick up where he'd left off.

That was one less thing to worry about, although—Tess realized almost at once—it raised another question. Did she have some sort of obligation to tell Marga what he'd done? Would she herself, in Marga's shoes, have wanted to know?

She didn't have to figure this out now. Surely she was allowed to focus on getting through the rest of the evening, however she could. Will would still be terrible tomorrow.

The happy couple worked their way through the crowd of well-wishers toward Tess's end of the hall, shaking hands and fielding congratulatory kisses. As she waited for them to reach her, Tess paced, rocked on her heels, and puffed out her breath; she kept one eye on Will, as if he were a spider in the corner. She took a few morsels from the refreshment table but didn't drink.

She'd have loved to credit her own forbearance for that, but really there wasn't time to get properly drunk, and halfway seemed worse than not at all.

Her evil ex-boyfriend ambled, inexorably, toward a reunion more than four years in the making. Tess, all horror and impatience, made crumbs of a cheese pastry on a tiny plate.

And then there he was at last, looming over her, that handsome devil, tossing his fair hair off his forehead. Tess forced herself to meet his blue eyes unflinchingly.

She had assumed—quite taken for granted—that he must have recognized her the instant she recognized him, when their gaze met, ship to shore. But no, she saw recognition hit him now, coursing through his body in a wave. It came with a fleeting glimpse of—anger? Fear?

He squelched the emotion before she could read it, plastering on a careful blankness.

She knew that blankness. She'd been cultivating it all evening in herself.

Countess Margarethe was hanging on Will's arm, face aglow. "You met Father Jacomo this afternoon," she said to him.

Jacomo bowed. Tess was next. Her hands were ice.

"This is my protégé, Tess Dombegh," said Marga. "Tess—my fiancé, Lord Morney."

Tess gave half courtesy, no more, no less. Marga would notice sarcasm.

"This one is trouble, Will," drawled Lieutenant Robinôt, gliding up to poke his decisive nose into the conversation. He hovered behind Marga like a vulture. "And the priest is no better. You should hear what they got up to in St. Vitt's."

"All a misunderstanding," said Marga breezily, edging away from Robinôt. He took the opportunity to fully enter the circle.

Will was still staring at Tess. "I didn't catch your name, Miss . . . ?"

Is that how he wanted to play this? Like they'd never met? That was fine with Tess.

"Tess Dombegh," she said, trying to enunciate and finding it hard with such a dry mouth.

"You look like someone I used to know," he said.

Cack. Tess's mouth felt like she'd swallowed sand.

Then Jacomo wedged himself into the gap between them, stepping on Tess's foot and bumping her to one side. "Maybe you can answer a question for me, Lord Morney," he was saying. "Who are these military fellows in the gaudy sleeves?"

Will looked after Jacomo's pointing finger; when his gaze shifted, it felt to Tess like the hot sun finally going under a cloud. For a moment she could breathe easier.

Quick thinking, Jacomo. She'd have to remember to thank him later.

It was Lieutenant Robinôt who answered Jacomo's question. "They're from the Ninysh Pelagic Legion, stationed at the garrison fort."

"But then who are those other soldiers in maroon?" Jacomo kept pointing; a duke's son could be casually rude. "Are those ones mercenaries?"

"The Governor's Guard," said Will, an edge in his voice. "A division of local lads."

"Mongrels," offered Robinôt.

He must mean they were Shesh. Tess felt some curiosity about this but was disinclined to peek out from behind Jacomo.

"It keeps them on the straight and narrow," said Will. "Until it doesn't."

"They're prone to violence, these Pelaguese," said Robinôt.

Tess suspected this was a reference to Giles Foudria. Marga's frown suggested she was thinking the same thing.

The countess cleared her throat. "Won't you join us for dinner in my suite, Lieutenant?"

"Alas, I must decline," said Robinôt, inclining his head. His brown queue flopped over his shoulder. "I've still got to debrief with Governor

Boqueton. Foudria's trail went cold in St. Vittorius; I'm sure Boqueton will have opinions about what we do next."

"I hope he'll forgive my absence," said Will.

"On your betrothal evening?" cried Robinôt, clapping him on the shoulder. "He would shoo you away if you showed up. Don't give it another thought."

The lieutenant bowed himself away, and then Tess, Jacomo, and Will followed Countess Margarethe toward her suite. Tess maneuvered herself so that Jacomo eclipsed Will at all times. If she couldn't see him, maybe she could pretend he wasn't there.

It was a childish strategy, and obviously unsustainable for an entire voyage, but it would do for tonight. She would find some other way to tolerate his presence and coexist aboard the ship; she had to.

Marga's suite was a warren of little rooms; she led them past a parlor and into the dining room. The Limpets had gone all out for their favorite guest, laying the table with crisp linens, gilded flatware, and a cut-crystal vase of hothouse flowers. Candelabra winked and tinkled in every corner; a silver tureen shaped like a caravel under full sail dominated the sideboard. Three servingmen, each with his own bottle of wine, had been sent to attend on four guests. Marga, irritated by the fuss, shooed them out and let Darienne do the serving.

Tess considered her options and then sat across from Will, hoping the flowers would block her view. Instead, his face was framed by forget-me-nots.

Was that funny? In a better state of mind, she was pretty sure she'd find it funny.

"Quiet at last," said the countess, holding her goblet for Darienne to fill. There was a new, fat ring on her finger. "My love, you're wonderful, but I wish you had forewarned me."

"And spoiled the authenticity of your response?" said Will. "Your shriek was my gift to the people of St. Claresse. They'll be telling the story for generations." He reached for her hand.

Marga, with an exaggerated sigh, allowed him to kiss her fingers.

Tess was pleased to note that she was not even a little bit jealous. That was about all she could say for herself.

Will's gaze turned toward Tess. "So how did you come to join our expedition, miss?"

Tess's eyelid twitched.

"I told you, darling. She's the one who found the Continental Serpent," Marga interjected. "She's an expert on all things quigutl—like you. Two of the little monsters came aboard with her. They take some getting used to, although the crew seem amused by their antics. You two will surely enjoy comparing notes."

Will refocused on his soup, looking like he would not enjoy comparing notes, in fact. Unless he'd spent the last four years learning Quootla, his "expertise" had been handed to him by Tess. She didn't gloat; it was just one more secret the countess could never learn.

One of many.

Ye Saints, so much for being Marga's protégé. Farewell to the open, easy rapport they'd been building. Each secret between them was a pit trap leading to the sharp spikes of *Your fiancé is a rapist who left me pregnant*. It didn't leave much room to maneuver.

Will was talking again. "Is Tess short for something? Therese, perhaps?"

He was determined to keep picking this scab, it seemed.

Jacomo came to her rescue again: "Tess was named for her grandmother, I believe. Lady Therese Dombegh, now deceased."

"So not your Belgioso grandmother?" pressed Will, as if it had been Tess who spoke.

His tone stayed carefully neutral, but there was nothing neutral about these questions. He was calling out her lies. Therese Belgioso was the false name she'd given him so word would not get back to her family that she was sneaking out to St. Bert's at night.

"I forgot your mother's a Belgioso," said the countess, jarringly cheerful and apparently oblivious. "Is old Count Julian still alive and kicking?"

"As far as I know," said Tess, happy to follow any conversational path that led away from Will's attention. "Mama always said he was too mean to die."

Marga chuckled, scraping the bottom of her bowl. "I never met the man, but my father used to make him sound terribly wicked. Of course, Papa claimed all the executed and exiled counts were devils, and that our family's singular virtue had spared us Count Pesavolta's purge."

"He might have been right about Count Julian," said Tess. "In exile, he became the Count of Crime. My cousin Kenneth ran off and became an astronomer, but he used to tell the most appalling stories. Count Julian would have had him out breaking fingers if he hadn't escaped to St. Bert's."

Oops, that hadn't led away from Will at all; her cousin had been there when she first met him—at St. Bert's. Will would think she'd brought up Kenneth on purpose, to goad him.

Marga was looking thoughtful. "It sounds like your mother escaped, too. Good for her."

Tess could tell this was a powerful insight, but she didn't have the wit to appreciate it right now. She wasn't even managing to eat. Her full soup bowl was whisked away; a crown rack of lamb took its place.

"But I was making a point about my father," Marga continued, taking the conversational reins more firmly in hand. "Over time, I realized that his 'singular virtue' was his ability to remain neutral— almost religiously so—and keep out of politics. In private, he'd say, 'I don't support Pesavolta, but I can't oppose him from the grave.' And indeed, unlike many of his generation, he died in his own bed."

"Heaven hold him," said Jacomo, raising a glass to the old count. Tess took only a minuscule sip; Heaven would know she meant no disrespect.

"I mention this because I think there's a lesson for us, here and now," said Marga, raising her knife. "We've entered a complicated political milieu. Things will only become more complicated as we approach the edge of civilization. It would behoove us to remember that ours is a voyage of scientific exploration, and that science must be apolitical if it is to progress."

Will set down his cutlery, eyes flashing. "If you have something to say, say it."

He seemed to be taking this personally. Tess stuffed a forkful of lamb into her mouth.

Marga pursed her lips. "Simply that I wish you had not thrown yourself so entirely into island politics, my dear. We might have had a map to the pole if you hadn't taken it upon yourself to help Lieutenant Robinôt solve St. Claresse's Pelaguese problem."

Tess's eyes darted from Will to Marga and back. She'd told the countess to keep her head up, but Marga was taking it a step further and going on the offensive.

It was probably wrong to feel satisfaction in that. Anyway, Will was not likely to sit there and take it.

"Robbie helped *me*," Will was saying. Here it came. "I'd never have gotten near Foudria without him. And you might have warned me what a menace your ex-navigator was. Should I have let him keep terrorizing everyone?"

"We might have smuggled him aboard the *Avodendron*—quietly removed him from St. Claresse—thereby solving the island's problem at the same time as our own," said the countess, holding up her goblet for more wine. "Now we can't."

Tess suddenly had a vision of these two arguing ceaselessly for the entire voyage. That might not be so bad. It would keep Will's attention focused elsewhere.

"You can't really think helping a wanted man escape is an apolitical act?" cried Will.

"He is not just any wanted man. I know him. I could have talked him out of this fanaticism," said Marga. "He trained at the Ninysh Academy. He should know better, and so, quite frankly, should you."

Maybe Marga would notice Will was terrible and break off the engagement. Maybe Will would decide she was a hectoring harpy and leave.

"He's not the only explorer who's ever been to the pole," said Will.

"Crackpots and madmen with no cartographic skill? I've heard they eat their own boots."

"I'm just wondering whether you have other reasons for wanting to save Giles Foudria specifically," said Will.

"If *you* have something to say, say it," said Countess Margarethe, plainly unafraid of him.

"Are you sure you want to talk about this here?" said Will. His voice was quiet now.

Tess knew that quiet-angry tone. It made her guts contract. That, right there, was reason enough not to hope they kept arguing for the whole voyage. Maybe Marga could take it, but Tess couldn't bear to listen to his voice for one more minute.

Exhaustion landed like a lead blanket; she thought she might fall out of her chair.

"Excuse me," Tess mumbled, staggering to her feet. "I need to go to bed."

"But Darienne is bringing out the cheese course next," said Marga, signaling her servant, who bustled over to the sideboard. "They make a marvelous little bleu on St.—"

Tess swayed. Jacomo rose beside her, propping her up. "I'll see her back; neither of us have been sleeping well on the ship," he said.

The countess's brows drew together. "Very well, if you must. I hope our little dispute hasn't put you off, is all. We could contrive to be congenial through dessert, I should think."

Jacomo said something conciliatory or reassuring. Tess couldn't listen. She bobbed her head in lieu of courtesy and trudged stone-footedly out of the room, Jacomo at her elbow.

"All right?" he said quietly when they were halfway down the corridor.

"I will be," said Tess. "I just need not to have his voice in my ears for a—"

"Therese!" called that very voice from behind them. It hit Tess like a bucket of ice water.

Will was hurrying to catch up with them. Jacomo drew himself up to his full height—he had maybe an inch on Will—and planted himself a little in front of Tess with his arms crossed.

"*She* sent me," said Will, pointing back toward the countess's suite with his thumb. "To apologize for being such an argumentative boor." He eyed Jacomo warily. "And I'd like a word with Therese alone, if her eunuch wouldn't object too strenuously."

The epithet did nothing to deflate Jacomo. He jutted his chin.

"Anything you have to say to me can be said in front of him," said Tess.

Will's eyes narrowed. "And who is he to you? A new lover?"

"Her brother-in-law, merely." Jacomo's ears went pink, which undermined his glowering.

"Well, take care that you don't end up her next victim," said Will. "When I met her, she called herself Therese Belgioso and passed herself off as sixteen. I learned too late that she was thirteen. And I surely wasn't her first—she seduced me with a lustful cunning beyond her years."

So much for coexistence. If he could have kept pretending they had no history, that might have worked, but if he was going to tell brazen lies about her . . .

"You *were* my first," said Tess, her voice so dark she hardly recognized it, "and I didn't seduce you. You took me when I was sleeping, without my permission and against my will."

Will barked a short laugh. "Right. If you say so."

He might as well have slapped her, she was so stunned. In her imagination he'd always wept or raged—a flippant denial had never occurred to her. How could he not take this seriously? Was she wrong about what had happened? The solid ground of fact and experience seemed to warp beneath her. The earth tilted.

But no—no! She wasn't misremembering. *He* was lying. Or else—

What if the moment that had shattered her entire life had been so insignificant to him that he didn't remember it? What if he truly believed he hadn't done anything wrong?

Saints above.

"Why did you follow me here, Therese?" Will was saying. His mirthless smile had eroded into a frown. "If you want me back, you can't have me. If you're here to play the woman scorned and poison my future happiness with your lies—"

"It's not a lie!" she cried. She felt like her words were disappearing down a hole.

"*Right,*" he repeated, a hard edge in his voice now. "It's your word against mine, though, isn't it? And what lasting harm was really done to you?"

"You left her pregnant," interjected Jacomo. "She bore your child."

The color drained from Will's face. His mouth opened and closed like a grouper's.

He clearly hadn't known about the baby.

And Tess, now that the words were spoken, realized she hadn't wanted him to know. Julian Dozerius was hers and hers alone; Will did not deserve to know the first thing about him.

Jacomo, perceiving that he'd scored a hit, loomed over Will menacingly. "I'll tell you another thing: My father, Lionel Pfanzlig, Duke of Ducana, is third in line to the throne. He keeps scrupulous records of all noble births, deaths, and successions in Goredd, lest someone bring forth an obscure claim to unseat him. I remember the discussion when your grandfather died. After a dispute, the title and estate went to his daughter Epzibah. *Lady* Morney, your aunt. The grandson— bastard of the younger daughter, now a prioress—received a tidy sum and an injunction to ride off into the sunset."

That answered the question of his new title. Tess didn't have it in her to take joy in Will's crimson cheeks, however. Jacomo was giving her a dozen more things to worry about.

"Return to your countess," said Jacomo. "She won't learn of this from us as long as you do Tess no mischief. Let that be the truce that enables us to continue this expedition together."

Will turned sharply, fists clenched, and stalked back into the countess's suite.

Jacomo crowed after him, "That's right. Run off with your tail between your legs."

This was not victory; Jacomo was wrong to imagine that. Will's revenge upon Spira for insulting him—and for just generally being Spira—had taken months. Will would bide his time until he found a way to get rid of this troublesome priest, and then Tess would be all alone, without even her big, foolish brother-in-law.

Her overbearing, overstepping brother-in-law. She was growing steadily angrier at him.

Jacomo chortled as they walked up the corridor. "He'll think twice before undermining us now."

Tess could bear his self-satisfaction no longer. "No, he won't. You've given him an incentive to see you removed from the expedition."

Jacomo scoffed. "And how is he going to persuade the countess—"

"He doesn't have to persuade anyone; he only has to make something happen. It will seem to have nothing to do with this. You'll fall overboard, or get an emergency message from home. I wouldn't put anything past him."

"I think you're being a bit paranoid," said Jacomo. "He's a fraud, not a monster."

Ye Saints. Her head was going to explode.

"Were you not listening?" cried Tess. "'Without my permission and against my will'? Was that not clear enough for you? That was rape, Jacomo."

Jacomo looked stricken.

"You told him about my baby." Her voice was rising. "You had no right. And did it ever occur to you that I might *want* to warn Marga about him? That it might be the right thing to do?"

"How do you think she'd take it?" said Jacomo. "She'd kick you off the ship."

"We'll never know now!"

Jacomo's voice was growing strained. "I was trying to help you. You asked me for help."

"I asked you not to leave me alone with him, not unilaterally make decisions for me."

Jacomo threw up his hands. "Unbelievable," he said. "I step up and stick my neck out and this is the thanks I get."

"Oh, is that why you came along on this voyage?" said Tess. "For the *gratitude*? Shall I kiss you, you hero?"

His face went white and shocked-looking, and Tess realized she needed to stop right now. She'd punched him at her sister's wedding and, by some feat of unexpected grace, he'd been able to forgive her. Now she saw exactly what shape of hole she could tear into him and that he would not be able to forgive her if she went much further.

He'd intended to be kind, even if he'd failed to think it through. If she lost sight of that, she was lost. She didn't have so many friends that she could afford to scuttle this one.

"I shouldn't have said that," she mumbled. "I know you meant well."

He grew even paler; it was hard to understand how.

Tess could think of nothing to say that wouldn't make everything worse. She went into her room and closed the door behind her, closed it on everything.

Ten

In her previous life at court, Tess had stashed away a bottle of plum brandy for times like this, times when she felt like an open wound. She had wanted to hurt the whole world, so hurting herself had seemed the more humane option.

She could have sent down to the Limpets' kitchen for a bottle of something; it would be a lie to say it didn't occur to her. Left to her own devices, she might eventually have done just that. When she entered her room, however, it became quickly evident that she was not alone. The bed, illuminated by a single oil lamp, was full of large, wiggling lumps.

Tess threw back the coverlet to reveal a pair of quigutl trying to get comfortable.

"Teth!" cried Pathka, while Kikiu said, "Pile in, pile in. Be nest."

Tess, well acquainted with quigutl body heat and breath, opened a window first and then gingerly climbed in. The bed was mercifully wide, and soft enough to offset her scaly co-sleepers. Tess found a spot in the middle, claiming the pillow for herself, and held still while Pathka and Kikiu settled around her.

The quigutl had to sniff, turn in place, heap and reheap the blankets. It was like sleeping with two scaly, spiny dogs, each five or six feet long. Kikiu had considerately removed her metal accoutrements, except the bite enhancer, or else the feather mattress would have been in shreds. They finally settled with Pathka's head across Tess's knees and Kikiu's nose in her armpit.

Tess was too exhausted to care that this was uncomfortable. She'd nearly drifted off when Kikiu yanked her back into consciousness by saying, "Could I bite him, at least?"

"Who?" asked Tess. Awkwardly, she'd thought of Jacomo first. Whatever he deserved, it wasn't *that*.

"Lord Morney," said Kikiu, grinding her forehead into Tess's side.

Tess groaned, aching for sleep. "Please don't. It wouldn't help."

"Help is the second intention of the universe," said Pathka from Tess's knees.

"What?" asked Tess, struck by the oddness of it. She propped herself up on her elbows.

"Don't mind ko," said Kikiu. "This happens at night lately."

"Mind of the World, open your eyes," Pathka mumbled.

Tess sat all the way up. She'd heard him say those words before, that early morning on the forecastle, but then he'd denied it. She studied him closely now. His eye cones were shut tight, as if he was asleep. She stroked his head spines, but he didn't wake.

Kikiu rolled onto her back. "Ask ko a question. Go on, it's funny."

Tess grimaced. "Pathka, are you well?"

"That's a tedious question," fussed Kikiu.

Pathka, however, replied, "All is right and shall be right and has been right and . . ."

"My theory," interjected Kikiu, "is that Anathuthia left an echo of her thoughts in Pathka's mind when she died, and they resonate when ko is sleeping. Or else ko is going senile."

"But he's not . . . ill or something?" said Tess. The pulse at his throat felt as hot and strong as ever; whatever this affliction was, it didn't resemble the so-called splitting death he'd suffered after Anathuthia died.

Kikiu whapped her tail against the coverlet in apparent unconcern. "Muttering about cosmic spookiness never hurt anyone. Probably."

"Moons," said Pathka. "Hope is memory, but backward."

"Ko always returns to normal by morning," Kikiu assured her.

"All right," grumbled Tess. "I won't be able to sleep if he's talking all night, though."

She was proved wrong almost the instant she laid her head down again.

⚔

Tess was awakened by Kikiu getting up to hunt rats. There were surely several ways the hatchling could have extricated herself from their "nest" without bothering Tess, but for some reason she'd preferred to crawl right over Tess's face.

Pathka followed soon after, treading on Tess's bladder.

Tess decided she might as well give up and get up.

The bath was down the hall; Tess charged it to Marga's account, hoping that was correct. She returned to her room, tiptoeing past Jacomo's, and was combing her damp hair when Pathka crawled back in the window and snarled, "There's nothing wrong with me."

His offspring had apparently said something. "You were talking in your sleep," said Tess, trying to sound soothing. "That's all. Lots of people do it."

"Unnatural, Kikiu says. *Unnatural!* You know what's unnatural? All that metal ko wears. Running away from the nest." Pathka was bristling and sparking with indignation.

"*You* ran away from the nest," said Tess, treading on a corner of the rug that was beginning to smolder. "Let's ignore Kikiu and go see when the submersible test is happening."

The test was today, the wedding tomorrow, and they'd sail the day after—presumably without Giles Foudria. It wasn't clear to Tess how they meant to reach the pole without the navigator or his map, but if she knew Will (and she did, alas), he wouldn't let a little thing like that stop him. "Where there's a Will, there's a way," he used to say, full of boundless confidence.

She couldn't remember ever seeing fear or doubt on his face before last night.

"Is the thumerthible that contraption in the hold?" Pathka interrupted Tess's thoughts. "They'd better not take it too deep. It has structural flaws."

"I guess they'll learn that when Will tests it," said Tess, leading the quigutl out into the corridor. An image popped into her head of Will drowning inside the metal sphere, his face squashed grotesquely against the window.

That was unworthy of her; she pushed the thought away.

No one answered the door at the countess's suite, but not because no one was there. Tess could hear voices. Will and Marga seemed to be arguing—had they been at it all night? Surely they'd slept and then gone back to fighting first thing?

Tess pressed her ear to the door. It sounded like they weren't in the anteroom, but deeper in the suite—the parlor, most likely, but maybe the boudoir. Morbid curiosity spurred her to open the door a crack.

"Darienne?" she called softly, but the maid did not reply. Maybe she'd been sent to fetch breakfast.

Tess closed the door silently behind her and crossed the anteroom, knowing full well she shouldn't. Pathka followed. The parlor was empty, the dining room cleared of any trace of last night's meal. Marga and Will were arguing in the boudoir with the door closed.

Tess knew she should turn around and leave, and she would, absolutely.

But what if Will was quitting the expedition? What if he couldn't stand the idea of traveling with *her*?

". . . do you really believe, after all these years—" Marga was saying.

"He plainly still has feelings for you. And you've kept his things—explain that!"

"I kept his things *for him*. Because I wanted to believe Giles hadn't died out there, and that maybe I could give them back to him someday."

"Why not leave everything on the ship, then? Why are his shirts in your trunk?"

Will was furious. Was it wrong to enjoy that? Probably. If Marga could handle herself—and she certainly seemed able—did that absolve Tess of having to tell her the worst? Surely Will couldn't hurt a countess the way he'd hurt Tess? She tried to put herself in Marga's shoes, to work out whether she'd want to know, but imagination failed her.

"They mean nothing to me," Marga was saying. "Darienne, gather them up and take them away. And bring us some breakfast."

The bedroom door opened and Darienne, rushing out with an armload of linen shirts, almost ran into Tess and Pathka. To her credit, she didn't shriek at the sight of the quigutl, although she did drop half the shirts.

"Sorry," Tess whispered, helping her pick them up. One had landed on Pathka's snout. "I'm just going to leave and come back later. Let's pretend I wasn't here."

Darienne nodded, casting a wary glance back toward the bedroom. Tess followed her out of the suite, and they parted ways in the corridor.

Once the maid was out of sight, Pathka began bouncing around like an oversized kitten. "Oh, Teth," he said. "Teth, Teth, Teth. Who is this *Zhileth* the countess was talking about?"

It took Tess a moment to understand that Pathka was trying to pronounce *Giles*. "Her old navigator, Giles Foudria," said Tess.

"I just learned who else he is, by sniffing his shirt," said Pathka, head spines waggling saucily. "You met him already, on St. Vittorius. The redheaded man with the sabak, who called himself Fozu. He's been everywhere on this island."

Tess went downstairs for breakfast, mulling this new information.

Fozu's Segoshi accent now made sense—he was Marga's old friend from the Academy. He could easily pass for Ninysh. He hadn't paid attention to his mother's sabak-speaking lessons, because he'd never meant to use them; he'd renounced and denounced everything about his Shesh upbringing . . . until one day he'd asked to be left on an iceberg.

Maybe he hadn't gone mad, Tess considered, spreading goat cheese on toast. Maybe he'd gone *penitent*.

She was on her third cup of tea before she realized something else: she knew where Fozu was. Well, she sort of knew. The winged woman had said the sabak would lead him to an islet near his home island (Paishesh, he'd called it—that was surely the Shesh name for St. Claresse, and the name Fozu would want her to use). He should be offshore, not far away. Pathka could probably sniff him out, if the wind was right.

They could quietly find him and smuggle him away, just as the countess had hoped.

Except Will was almost certain to be an ass about it.

Tess was still brooding on this when Will and the countess walked past, arm in arm. Getting rid of Fozu's shirts must have ended their quarrel for the time being.

"Tess, come watch the submersible testing," called the countess, holding out her free arm, plainly hoping Tess would take it. Will looked unhappy about this.

"In a minute," said Tess, not getting up. "Just . . . I'll go fetch Jacomo, shall I?"

Marga seemed content with this; she urged Tess to hurry, and then they were out the front doors. Tess slowly folded her napkin, laid it on her plate, and went upstairs with heavy steps.

She'd been pretty hard on Jacomo last night and felt embarrassed now that a full night's sleep had dissipated her anger. He'd been trying to protect her, however clumsily, and while she'd been in the right, she couldn't forget his last look of bafflement.

She was standing at his door like a fool, hand raised to knock, when he opened it.

"Oh," squeaked Tess. "Um, going to the ship? They're testing the . . ."

Jacomo nodded and closed the door behind him.

They walked down toward the harbor, not speaking. It was breezy and cold, but the sun was out, which was surely all anyone could hope for on an early-spring day this far south. Tess shivered from the biting breeze, or possibly from nerves.

The *Avodendron* was in sight when Jacomo stopped short. Tess looked back and was shocked to see tears in his eyes.

"Oh no," she cried, certain that this was it, their friendship was over.

"I want to say something before we're face to face with Lord Morney again," said Jacomo. "I gave myself a stern talking-to after we parted ways last night. You were right. I didn't listen, and I overstepped."

"Y-you did?" This was not what she'd anticipated him saying.

"Thinking it over last night," he said, beginning to walk again, "I was reminded of the time your sister St. Seraphina gave a talk at my seminary."

Tess couldn't help rolling her eyes. "Sorry," she said, in case he'd noticed. "I have a low tolerance for hearing my sister called a Saint."

"That's reasonable," said Jacomo, finally smiling a little. "But she said something that I think applies here, and I want to explain what—"

"Dzenia ashore!" called a booming voice from the *Avodendron*. Tess and Jacomo looked up to see Captain Claado. He waved his megaphone. "Get aboard, unless you mean to watch from there."

Tess and Jacomo hurried up the gangplank. "You don't need to explain," Tess said quietly when they reached the deck. "You didn't even need to apologize. I'm not mad anymore."

Jacomo inclined his head, and that seemed to be the end of it. They were friends again. Tess hoped it really was that simple.

The deck buzzed with crew, some erecting the crane, some hastening to stow the gangplank, some preparing to turn the capstan and kedge the ship away from shore. The anchor had been taken aboard the ship's dinghy, rowed as far out as its chain allowed, and dropped. As Argol and the other strongest sailors heaved the capstan around, the *Avodendron* would be pulled toward the place where the anchor had landed.

Local dignitaries had been invited to watch from the deck of the *Avodendron*, including Governor Boqueton, his wife and two teenaged daughters, the bishop, some officers of the Ninysh Pelagic Legion, and Lieutenant Robinôt. They sat upon a bank of improvised seats—crates with cushions on top—shivering under a newly erected sunshade. Marga sat among them, speaking with the governor's family; old Karus, bobbing and smiling, served snacks and drinks.

There were no seats left. Tess was content to stand at the rail with Jacomo and feel the sun on her shoulders.

Once the crane had been reconstructed, hatches down to the hold were thrown open. The ship had kedged a good fifty yards, leaving a gap between ship and shore where the submersible could be lowered in sight of the citizens gathering on the pier. Argol left the capstan for her next task: walking with two companions in the treadmill. They lowered the hook into the depths of the ship, where other sailors attached it to the submersible.

Will was directing things down in the hold; Tess could hear his voice.

Captain Claado approached the landward rail and stationed himself beside Tess and Jacomo, acknowledging them with a curt nod.

"We missed you at the fete last night," said Jacomo.

"You couldn't pay me to attend one of Boqueton's fetes," said Claado. "I dislike these colonial towns. Everything one might find mildly annoying about Ninys is exaggerated here, as if they have to be Ninysh as loudly as possible to drown out the other voices."

"Do you mean the Shesh?" said Tess. "Which ones are they?"

A couple hundred people had crammed onto the quay, workaday people—fisherfolk, net menders, salt packers, warehouse workers. They all looked plausibly Ninysh to Tess—but so had Fozu. If there was some visual marker, she wasn't picking up on it. The men wore slops and smocks, grain-sack hats and clogs. The women were in kirtles and aprons.

Captain Claado said, "They're here, among newer settlers from the mainland. The women tie their kerchiefs to the side—see there? And the men wear mustaches with their beards, which seems a bit . . . unhygienic." He rubbed his bare upper lip; Porphyrians and Ninysh agreed on this point, apparently.

"They're half this crowd, if you're right," said Jacomo.

"You won't see that acknowledged by Governor Boqueton, not now, not ever," Claado said. "The Ninysh pretend they aren't even there, but the past never disappears. It coils like a snake until it's ready to strike."

Karus tapped on Claado's shoulder at just that moment, startling him.

"Case in point," said Captain Claado before following the elderly crewman up the forecastle.

Someone shouted, "Keep clear!" and the crane began hoisting the submersible out of the hold. Argol and her comrades strained in the treadmill; a clanking ratchet ensured that the massive weight would not slip and spin them wildly in the other direction. Everyone—crew, crowd, the special guests under the sunshade—cheered when the shiny metal gourd cleared the deck, its pipes gleaming brassily in the thin sunlight.

Will, for maximum drama, stood atop his machine as it rose, grasping the cable with one hand. The sea breeze tossed his fair hair around. Robinôt's shouted encouragement was snatched by the wind; under the awning, everyone chuckled.

When the submersible had been raised high enough, the crane operators slowly pivoted the beam landward, pausing above the ship's rail so that Will could climb off the contraption first. He gingerly eased himself down, keeping tight hold of the rigging, and stood perched on the *Avodendron*'s railing.

The beam kept turning until the submersible hung over the water; the whole ship tilted in response. Jacomo's knuckles turned white against the railing.

Countess Margarethe emerged from under the awning and swung herself up beside Will. The plump, petite countess seemed more at ease among the lines than he did, but then, he'd grown up landlocked, like Tess. She wondered whether he could swim.

"Don't let it fall," called Marga. "It might crack like an egg, and that would be half Lord Morney's fortune drowned."

Will circled an arm around her waist. "That's nothing. My treasure is all right here."

He bent his fiancée back over the water, carefully daring, and kissed her. The guests under the awning cheered and stamped; the Porphyrian crew, not as Ninysh in their enthusiasms, still grinned and looked charmed.

Tess would have had a particularly good view of the kiss if she could have brought herself to look up. It was galling to think Marga could be happy with him. Tess preferred them arguing.

That gave her pause. It wasn't that she wanted him back—she absolutely did not. She wanted him miserable, even if it meant Marga was miserable.

That was mean. The countess didn't deserve that.

Marga cut the kiss short, pulling herself upright with the lines and returning to practicalities: "You're submerging it empty first?"

"Just to make sure the seals hold. Your uncle was unwilling to let me drown one of his sailors," said Will. Marga swatted him playfully, as if that had been funny, then hopped off the railing and returned to her seat.

The crane, ratchet clanking, lowered the sphere in jerky increments toward the water.

"He's a true man of genius," said a deep voice in Tess's ear as a muscular arm was thrown across her shoulders. Lieutenant Robinôt had crept up without her noticing. He casually draped his other arm around Jacomo as if they were old comrades.

"He's told me some interesting things about the two of you," said Robinôt. "I'm half inclined to come along and help you find that pesky serpent. Wouldn't that be fun."

Tess shot a glance at Jacomo; his eyes were round, as if the lieutenant's strong arm was making him realize unpleasant possibilities he had previously dismissed.

Up on the railing, Will raised his hand and everyone quieted, both ship and shore.

"Friends, compatriots—enemies, even," Will cried, gracing everyone with his infectious grin. "Having given you the gift of safety, having seen the Shesh Eight hanged and order restored, I have the great privilege to bestow one last gift upon St. Claresse before I leave.

"You will soon witness the maiden voyage of a vessel the likes of which the world has never seen. It's a boat of my own design that travels underwater, enabling us to see what has hitherto been unseeable, to explore environments that were hitherto too hostile. The dragons said it was impossible, because they lacked the imagination to achieve it. Ninysh ingenuity has found a way. What a glorious day to be Ninysh, citizens!"

He paused for applause.

"And who knows what new life we will find beneath the sea? What strange creatures and lost civilizations? We Ninysh shall go—dare I say *boldly*?—where no one has ever gone before."

The shipboard dignitaries seemed particularly impressed by this turn of phrase. Will had a talent for persuasion, Tess had to admit. He'd been the best debater at St. Bert's back when she knew him, able to make even the most noxious position sound sweet and reasonable.

The enthusiasm of the crowd on the quay was muted, just a smattering of applause. Tess tried to gauge their mood. These were not the upper echelons of St. Claresse—Ninysh mainlanders all—whom Will had addressed at the Limpets last night. The Shesh among them (the ones Tess could discern, anyway) kept their eyes down and faces neutral, as if they were trying not to react to Will's bald-faced provocations nor draw the attention of the Governor's Guard, lurking among them in maroon livery.

Will continued: "My imminent departure has worried some of you. The fugitive Giles Foudria is still at large, so how can you feel safe? I assure you, he will be found. Let this submersible impress upon you that there is no place left in this world that Ninys cannot reach. We have the right. . . ." Pause; applause. "And we have the might."

The loudest cheering came from the deck of the *Avodendron*. Tess ventured a look back, even though it meant pulling against Robinôt's arm. There was something she needed to see.

The countess sat among her peers, clapping perfunctorily, her mouth pressed flat in irritation. Tess knew better than to suppose that a countess, of all people, disagreed about Ninysh right and Ninysh might—she was the living emblem of both, after all—but Marga wouldn't like Will politicizing a vessel meant for scientific study. She was consistent in that.

There would be more arguing tonight. Tess, who was a bad person, looked forward to it.

Robinôt, beside her, directed a comment at Will: "We may see Foudria as soon as tomorrow, Saints willing."

Will grinned down at Robinôt just as Tess looked up, and she was caught in the cross fire, like getting a sudden sunbeam in the eye. She scowled and turned toward the water.

Four long, pale shapes were swimming in ominous, slow circles around the nearly submerged vessel. The dark water distorted their forms, but Tess knew them at once: sabak. Maybe even the same four that had left with the stilt walker.

Was she here? Tess scanned the crowd but saw no one with hide wings or a fringe of knotted yarn in front of her face.

On the pier, someone noticed the sabak and cried out—with joy or dismay, Tess couldn't tell. The Shesh in the crowd moved cautiously away from the water, while the Ninysh pressed forward, pointing at the creatures and exclaiming excitedly.

Will, noticing that he was no longer the center of attention, leaned as far over the water as his grip on the lines would allow, trying to see what the fuss was about.

"What are those, Robbie?" he called. "Sharks?"

"Devil pinch us," muttered Robinôt, pushing between Tess and Jacomo to get a better look. "Governor, Countess—you need to see this."

Governor Boqueton was clearly put out that he had to get up; Marga took his arm, smilingly cajoling, and they stepped forth together. Tess, glad to extricate herself from under Robinôt's arm, offered her place at the railing.

The governor took one look at the sabak and seemed to wilt on Marga's arm. "I haven't seen sabanewts here in twenty years," he cried. "This is a terrible omen."

"What can we do about them?" said Robinôt. "I brought my crossbow—"

"Don't touch them!" barked the governor. "Mardiza's Rebellion started with the death of a sabanewt. I've learned my lesson."

Mardiza's Rebellion might be the failed Shesh uprising Fozu had mentioned, the one that had led to the slaughter of the Jovesh. Tess met Jacomo's eye; he nodded minutely.

"Could we capture one?" Will called down from his perch. "Sabanewts and their oil are specified in our mandate from the Ninysh Academy. No one has ever brought one back, dead or alive. Pelaguese legends claim they're eerily wise and intelligent, and that their oil is a panacea."

The sabak swam closer to the ship, as if drawn to his voice.

"Is it true? Are you as intelligent as you are elegant?" Will called down to them. Then he turned back to the crowd. "I think we may discover, upon closer examination, that these are a new subspecies of dragon."

"That's a neat trick—discovering what other people already know," said Kikiu's gravelly voice from an unexpected direction. Tess looked up and saw both quigutl curled around one of the mainmast spars above Will's head. Kikiu hung upside down, clinging to the furled sail, tail twitching.

Tess gave the hatchling a warning look.

"You never said I couldn't mock him," Kikiu objected.

The sabak began circling the submersible, which was now almost entirely submerged. They thwacked it with their tails, and it made a hollow sound.

"Ahoy!" Will cried. "Come back, my beauties. Leave that alone."

"They're testing for structural deficiencies," said Pathka from on high. "I expect they'll find a few."

Tess cringed, although she knew no one else understood. Even Will—the supposed quigutl scholar—hadn't reacted to a single word they'd said.

There was a devastating crack, and then huge bubbles started glugging out of the water. The sabak had broken one of the windows. Will gave a shocked, inarticulate cry and shouted, "Haul it in quick, before it takes on too much water!"

The sailors in the treadmill began straining in reverse, but they were battling a great deal of inertia and the additional weight of water.

"It was good-looking but fragile—like your face," Kikiu crowed from above. "It was expensive but a waste—like your face!"

And then, without warning, Kikiu came hurtling out of the sky.

Tess wasn't looking up, so she didn't see how it had happened, whether Kikiu had lost her grip, taken the leap, or been pushed. All Tess saw was 150 pounds of lizard hitting Will's handsome, fragile waste of a face and bowling him backward into the sea.

They fell together.

Kikiu twisted like a cat in midair, reached out with her sticky toes, and managed to grab the barnacled side of the ship.

Will struck the sea flat on his back. His eyes met Tess's for a fraction of a second, the kind that stretches to eternity.

"He can't swim!" screamed Marga as he went under.

He surfaced briefly, arms flailing frantically, and then did what any drowning person might have done: he reached for anything nearby that might keep him afloat.

Reached without permission.

The sabak swarmed him. He didn't have time to scream before they pulled him under. The water roiled and churned, foaming white and then pink and then red.

Eleven

Shock kept the world at arm's length. No, farther away than that. Tess watched it all through a backward spyglass.

Pathka, from the sail spar, dived into the sea.

Marga would have dived in, too, to save what was left of Will, but her uncle and Jacomo held her back. She struggled in their arms, bellowing.

Someone tossed out a sad, futile life preserver. A sabak snapped it in half, scattering shards of bobbing cork across the surface of the sea.

Lieutenant Robinôt fired his crossbow once, twice, thrice. A slick of iridescent oil and silver blood oozed across the water.

Out of nowhere, Spira and Lord Hamish came rowing across the harbor in a dinghy. In the distance a bell was ringing.

On the docks, the crowd began to shout and throw things. A warehouse caught fire.

Later, Tess would not remember how they'd lifted the submersible or recovered the bodies of the two dead sabak.

She would not remember soldiers descending from the garrison fort to suppress the rioting citizenry, or what words had passed between Lord Hamish and Governor Boqueton.

"Where's Pathka?" she would remember asking. And Jacomo saying, yet again, that he didn't know.

Soldiers subdued the docks and put out the fire, with the help of a squall that moved in as the sun was setting. It was quite late before the *Avodendron* was permitted to tie up at the wharf. The *Sweet Jessia* followed suit. Governor Boqueton, his family, and as many other dignitaries as would fit crowded into his carriage and lumbered up the hill. The two dead sabak were hauled up to the fortress in a wagon; Lieutenant Robinôt accompanied it. Tess and her friends made slower progress, climbing to the Limpets on foot.

Captain Claado had come ashore for his niece's sake; she leaned heavily on his arm. Tess watched their silhouettes; the countess was crying.

She had a good reason to cry. Tess did not.

When they reached the square, the cold evening air began to bring Tess back to herself. She looked to her left—that was the statue of King Moy, and beyond it, the cathedral. She looked right—that was Jacomo.

He was looking back at her, his brows raised in concern.

She didn't like his concern; it made her feel something, which made her steps falter. Jacomo stepped up as if to take her arm and steady her, but backed off when Tess shied away.

If she let him touch her arm, the last of her shock would dissipate. She'd be entirely here, and she still wasn't ready.

Alas, she was steadily growing more present whether she wanted to or not. The damp, chill wind on the back of her neck was bringing her round.

A dark shape scuttled down from the roof of the inn—Pathka. The quigutl carried something long and slender in his mouth. He raised his chin, presenting it to the countess.

It was Will's sword, still in its scabbard, dripping seawater.

Countess Margarethe took it gingerly.

"It's all that was left," said Pathka, and you didn't need to speak Quootla to understand.

Marga drew the sword, and Tess took a reflexive, protective step forward. The countess held the scabbard upside down, letting the salt water drip out of it, but then she pointed the blade directly at Pathka's nose. Pathka didn't flinch.

"Your comrade killed my fiancé," said the countess.

"I'll bite ko myself," said Pathka.

"If I ever so much as glimpse her again," said Marga, swishing the sword, "I will skewer her with this very blade. Her head will hang on my wall."

"Enough, Marga," said Claado, placing a hand on the countess's outstretched arm, urging her to lower the weapon. "It was an accident. Killing the quigutl won't make it right."

"Don't tell me how to make it right," cried Marga, pulling out of his grasp. "You never liked him. You're not even a little bit sorry he's dead."

Captain Claado looked so chagrined that Tess suspected the accusation was true.

"I'm sorry he's dead," said Pathka. "Tess, translate."

"I'm . . ." No, she wasn't. She couldn't say it. "*Pathka* is sorry he's dead."

"You won't want to bite Kikiu, but I have another idea," said Pathka. "Your navigator, Fozu, is still nearby. What if we sniffed him out and helped him escape the gallows? Could saving his life make up for the other one's death?"

Tess translated, saying *Foudria* instead of *Fozu*.

Marga shrugged. "I—I don't know. I can't think about this now." She sheathed the sword and went up the steps of the inn; her uncle followed doggedly.

"*Was* it an accident?" said Tess after the doors had closed behind Marga.

Pathka squirmed. "Accident-*utl*," he said, using contradictory case. It was and it wasn't.

"What do we do if she won't forgive Kikiu?" asked Tess.

"One thing at a time," said Pathka. He slipped away into the darkness.

"Shall we go inside?" said Jacomo. "You look exhausted."

He shouldn't have said that, shouldn't have sounded so sympathetic, because here came everything she didn't want to feel, leaking out of her face, and there was no stopping it.

"Oh, Tess," he breathed. "I'm so sorry."

She pressed her face against his shoulder, bawling, a fount of snot and tears. Tentatively, then more determinedly, he wrapped his arms around her and let her sob all over him.

"I—I'm not crying . . . for *Will*," she hiccuped. "I'm not even . . . sad." *Hic.* "He doesn't deserve . . . one single . . . tear from me. . . ."

"It's all right if you are sad," said Jacomo. "I'm sure it's not the only thing you are."

Tess sobbed into his chest, pounding her fist against his heart. He stood and took it like a bastion wall. Like a friend.

No part of her had still loved Will.

But how *dare* he be dead?

Twelve

Mind of the World, who carries your doubts?

Let us now show you one close to our heart, whom we loved from boyhood. He was riddled with doubts—and it was good. He wasn't wrong. Someone has to ask the hard questions.

The stronger the destiny, the more crucial it is to push back.

Once upon a time, a small Ggdani boy tried to evade his destiny.

When he arrived at the archives, only Archivist Oggmi was there. She'd spread her little fur mat upon a block of ice and was repairing the cords of a broken book. She looked stern at his approach, but her weathered face softened when she recognized him. Hami quickly knelt on the frozen floor before her; a student should not remain standing while his teacher was sitting.

He even felt unmannerly standing when she was standing. He was twelve and small for his age; Oggmi, propped up by her walker, was even smaller.

"Do your parents know you're skipping the Scrying?" she asked, not unkindly, as she deftly knotted a tendon cord around a slat of inscribed baleen.

"Scrying's over," said Hami, a little breathless from running. He removed his obsidian goggles to wipe sweat out of his eyes, then carefully replaced them.

Oggmi raised her gray head and looked toward the doorway, sternness returned, as if expecting an imminent stampede of children. "Nobody else is coming," Hami reassured her. "They went straight for their sleds and slings. A few took the deep tunnels."

"But you came here," she said, eyes twinkling cannily. "Do you need help researching something for your quest? I know many legal precedents by heart; that could save time."

"I'm not questing," said Hami, raising mittened hands. "I don't want to be the Watcher."

"That's up to destiny," said Oggmi, gnarled fingers pulling another knot tight.

Hami disliked the idea of destiny; in songs and stories, it never seemed to lead any place good. However much you revered the laws, you would have to break them if that was your destiny. Destiny was how you ended up killing what you loved.

Hami loved home.

That cold rill of thought threatened to erode his composure. He would not fear destiny; he was pushing back against it. "I actually thought I might retake my ice-layer test."

The old archivist blinked at him. "*Now?* Three years after your age-mates? When a strange notion pops into your head after a Scrying—"

"I'm not questing," Hami reiterated—in Tshu-veit this time—then flinched under Oggmi's glare. "Apologies for interrupting. But I'm trying to avoid the prophecy, not fulfill it."

"That," said Oggmi tartly, "is the surest way I know to fulfill one."

She gestured toward the book-hook in the corner; Hami fetched it and rehung the book she'd repaired. (Books hung from the ceiling like rope ladders, each page a rung, and were read bottom to top so you'd grow, metaphorically, while reading; adult Hami, decades later, still got nostalgic for the way a Ggdani library swayed and chimed, something Ninysh books never did.)

Archivist Oggmi gripped her walker, a sturdy antler frame, and hauled herself up. Only one of her thin, bowed legs could bear her weight; she got around well, if not exactly quickly, with the walker. Its pointy feet jabbed into the ice floor, *tchk-tchk-tchk*. Hami walked behind his teacher, as was meet, not minding how slowly they went.

Surely procrastination could foil destiny. He'd waste time in the testing tunnel, giving others ample opportunity to fulfill the sabak's prophecy. Someone was bound to eventually.

"What impossible task was foretold this time?" Oggmi asked as they traversed a forest of hanging books. "My generation had to find a way to have our Voorka and eat it, too."

Hami made an annoyed sound through his lips. "All the sabak said was 'You will discover a monster,' which is ridiculous. There are no monsters in nature; it must be a metaphor for something. A storm. A betrayer or oath breaker." He paused, imagination failing.

"What about the monstrosity of your own ice-ignorance?" said Archivist Oggmi. "Haven't you come here explicitly to slay it?"

Hami bit back his first reply; sarcasm was not an option, not to a teacher. "I'm not questing" was all he dared say, in Murkhee this time.

"We shall see," said Oggmi, opening the tunnel door for him. There was no lock—the door was a leather curtain—but Hami would never have brazenly opened it himself. A closed door was the first law every child encountered, and he'd been raised to respect it.

Hami took up the oil lamp and pickaxe from the alcove at the entrance and trudged up the tunnel. It had lengthened since the last time he'd taken this test. Fresh ice chips littered the floor at the end; the testing wall had quite recently been rehewn.

He wasn't unobservant; he just wasn't very interested in ice.

He didn't really need the lantern; the chamber was close enough to the surface of the glacier for blue light to filter in. Hami took off his obsidian goggles, blinking until his oversensitive eyes adjusted. He knew from hard experience that he'd need their acuity here.

A square had been carved into the lower half of the wall, where the layers were distinct; higher up was all a refrozen jumble, without discernible strata. Hami's task was to identify the kinds of ice inside the square, bottom to top. With goggles on, he'd spotted four types; now he could make out six. That wouldn't be all. Layers that looked alike might crumble differently under his pick, might taste or even smell different. He wouldn't know until he dug in.

This was why the tunnel kept growing: taking the test destroyed the testing wall.

Hami chipped off flakes, crumbled them to gauge their strength and texture, and tasted them for salt, sulfur, or oily residue. He pretended the wall was a book in a strange language that he was trying to read.

Languages, he liked. Too bad they were so little use on the ice.

By the time he'd found every layer, he'd dug well into the wall and was sweating in his fur suit. He sat down to catch his breath, count the layers again, and recite their names, bottom to top. He'd identified eight and was feeling rather smug. He would pass, at long last. He'd be permitted to abseil down ice cliffs on his own—something most of his age-mates could already do, something he didn't really care about. Oggmi would be astonished.

She'd be even more astonished if he came back with something intelligent to say about the anomalous refrozen mass above the testing square. It was as big around as his circled arms, gleaming glassily, full of black flecks.

Hami had no idea what might have caused it, but he needed an excuse to linger here, away from any possibility of questing, and so he began to hypothesize. Maybe someone had built a fire atop the glacier; a mere campfire wouldn't have melted through so many layers, though. A volcanic rock? The volcanic ring wasn't near enough for the stone to have still been hot when it fell. A star-stone? Even the very small ones supposedly left enormous craters.

He stood and pressed his nose against the glassy whorl. It was nearly transparent, but for the black specks, and full of distortions. He thought he could discern a dark shape behind the ice. He brought the lamp up, but that only exacerbated the crystalline glare.

There was an air bubble behind the refreeze, he suddenly realized. That was why he couldn't see; the refraction changed. Desperately pleased with himself for noticing (he'd pass with a commendation; he wasn't the useless lump they all thought he was), he took up the pick again and struck the center of the whorl, hacking until he had to stop and catch his breath.

He was going about this all wrong. The uppermost layer of the testing square was murri, which crumbled easily. He could dig past the refreeze from below and look behind it.

Hami took a hard swing at the murri, and another.

The wall cracked and then shattered. A cascade of falling ice bowled him over.

His first thought was that he'd found a way to fail his test after all. Not only had he not anticipated that the wall would collapse, but the testing square was destroyed, and his tumble had knocked the carefully memorized layers right out of his head.

His second thought was that he was the greatest fool who'd ever lived.

The icefall had uncovered a massive reptilian head almost as big as he was. Its jaw was dislocated from the pressure of the ice, making its long teeth jut out at grotesque angles; its solid white eyes stared at nothing. The rest of the creature was still buried in the ice.

There was his monster. Hami sighed resignedly and sat on the cold floor to wait.

It took the sabak several hours to reach him, tunneling through the ice with her claws (he could have gone to her pool in the Hall of Winds and saved her the trouble, but he'd still had hope, absurdly, that this wasn't what he knew it was). The sabak was white, except for the fringe of pink gills around her neck—retracted now, out of the water—and her small obsidian eyes.

Hami respectfully covered his face with both hands.

Open your eyes, she whistled. *You may touch me.*

Hami didn't want to touch her. He racked his brains for a law that said he shouldn't.

Touch me, she whistled, a command this time. There was no getting out of it or pretending he didn't understand. He'd worked out sabak chirp-speak when he was five.

He'd never touched a sabak before, but he'd seen how it was done. He removed his mitten and pressed his palm between her wide-set eyes.

He expected wild, unbridled visions—that was what children who'd touched sabak by accident or mischief always reported—but she had words for him: *You are the one we foresaw.*

"I'm not so sure," said Hami, who'd had time to think things over. "You said the next Watcher would find a monster. This is merely a dragon."

In what way could it be considered a monster? said the sabak.

Hami opened his mouth and closed it again. That was the question he'd planned to ask next, confident that whatever the sabak might answer could be refuted. Now he was stuck answering it. Size and appearance didn't make a monster; many animals had horns, fangs, or scales, and the One was far larger. In the Land of the Dead, it was believed that dragons were monstrous by nature, but Deadlanders were superstitious and didn't know better.

The Land of the Dead was where he would be sent if he couldn't wriggle out of this.

It wasn't a monster. There were no monsters. He resorted to a proverb as proof: "The only monster is one who scorns the law."

As he spoke the words aloud, though, he understood: this dragon had scorned the law. Dragons were not allowed at the top of the world. That wasn't mere human law, but the law of the One. This dragon had been punished for its transgression—poisoned by volcanic gases, frozen by polar winds, or shot down by the Murkh.

"But what if the dragon came here by accident?" he said in a small voice, a last-ditch effort to deflect the inevitable. "What if it was lost?"

It was not, said the sabak. *And you are quite the little skeptic.*

"I don't know the word *skeptic,*" said Hami in some surprise. He knew all the civilized languages, plus Aftishekka.

It's a word from your home-to-be, said the sabak. *It has come to mean "doubter," but originally it meant "one who looks closely." You are already a Watcher; you always have been.*

"That sounds like destiny," said Hami. The word tasted like tragedy.

Call it duty, if you prefer, said the sabak. *It's less grand but every bit as necessary.*

The sabak told him more: he would learn Ninysh from a retired Watcher; he would receive a suit of sabak skin (an honor usually reserved for priests and judges); a noble family in the Land of the Dead would foster him and teach him their ways, for a price; he would protect the One, his people, and the laws; and after thirty years he could come home again.

Hami barely listened. Despite his best efforts, he was afflicted with destiny. He would kill what he loved, like the tragic bootmaker, Vulkharai.

Unless he was lucky, and what he loved contrived to kill him first.

⚔

Thirty-three years later, Hami was not dead, but he was very, very tired. He would never be retired from Watching. Duty or destiny would follow him forever.

Hami awoke at the crack of dawn, dressed, and prayed, and then lingered in his cabin, trying to contact Fozu. Each of his cocoon-like earrings was an eyu, spun from semitransparent fibers of sabak spittle, and each connected him—via the Worldmind—to someone else.

Fozu was not responding. Hami spoke anyway: "I'm in Paishesh harbor with your pyria, but there's been an unfortunate incident. The place is crawling with soldiers, and I see no way to unload inconspicuously. We'll need to meet somewhere else."

Hami paused, dreading what he had to say next. "Two sabak were killed last night. I have every reason to believe you are responsible, that you went against my admonition and asked a Katakutia to bring them here. Your mother was hanged, on my orders, for exactly this crime. Maybe you're gambling that I won't do the same to you. . . ."

He paused again; he was getting emotional. He thought about ice.

"And you're probably right. But you need to understand the mess you've made. The dead sabak have been taken to the garrison fort. They were shot with arrows, and they're leaking oil. The Ninysh are a hair's breadth away from learning everything I was sent to prevent them learning. Your selfishness may have undone the work of six generations of Watchers.

"Whatever you think you've gained, it was not worth scorning the laws."

That was mean. He felt a bit bad about it. It wasn't Fozu's fault Hami had failed.

He had been destined to fail; he'd felt it in his bones the moment he uncovered that frozen dragon. Being a Watcher was like trying to hold back an avalanche with your mittened hands (the mittens, in this analogy, being the law—indispensable and yet futile).

Hami put on his soft boots and smoked glasses, strapped on his sword, and went above. All was quiet aboard the *Sweet Jessia;* he would slip ashore, run his errand, and be back before anyone knew he was gone.

"Were you able to contact your buyer?" said a soft, familiar voice behind him.

Hami stopped, drumming his fingers on the gangway railings and considering how to answer. Honesty was probably best; he was already lying to Spira about so many things that his conscience would buckle under the weight. No point piling on more unnecessarily.

"He didn't answer," said Hami, turning to face the dragon scholar. "I'll keep trying."

Spira stepped toward him, leaning on teur cane, teur eyes on some circling gulls, preparing a question and clearly trying to convey that Hami's answer would be of absolutely no consequence. "Would you . . . should we go ashore and find some breakfast?"

Hami's stomach did a little flip, plausibly from hunger (although he knew better). Here was this lonely being—maybe the only person lonelier than Hami himself—not daring to hope and yet trembling with hope. Teur transparency was beautiful and devastating.

They should have been friends—more than friends—but of course they could not be. Hami still had work to do (it would never end), and Spira, alas, was on the wrong side of the law.

Teu was doomed; teur whole expedition was doomed; Hami had sown the seeds of its destruction, as the law required. The dragons would not make it to the One.

It turned out you could follow the laws and still be a monster. Hami felt the irony keenly.

He shouldn't take Spira with him to deal with the dead sabak—the saar knew too much already—and yet if teu was doomed, what difference could it possibly make? Who was Spira going to tell?

"There's something I must do—as the enforcer of southern treaties," said Hami carefully. "Come along, if you wish. Afterward, we can find something to eat."

Spira nodded with endearing solemnity and followed him off the ship and up the hill in silence. They walked near each other, but not too near. Hami could almost feel the scholar vibrating with anxious excitement beside him.

Oh, to be someone else. Someone allowed to love you.

Being fully retired from Watching wouldn't have solved it. Dragons had their own laws regarding humans—all humans, not just Deadlanders. And then there was the law of the One.

Hami was so preoccupied that he arrived at the garrison fort without having given Spira any explanation or instruction. It was too late then. Soldiers escorted them to a corridor in the basement.

They weren't the first to arrive. Countess Margarethe had risen with steely determination from her bed of mourning and was already there with her two young attendants—the tall, fat priest and the girl who'd spoken to Hami about the One on Paji-Jovesh.

He'd told that girl to halt their expedition. She'd failed; maybe she hadn't tried.

Hami wished, not for the first time, that he had the luxury of not trying, that he could lie back and let the avalanche roll over him instead of standing with his stupid, hopeless mittens pressed uselessly against the impending wave of—

"I understand you're one of the Tacques-Moutons, Lord Hamish," Countess Margarethe said, interrupting his thoughts. She was attempting a smile. "Any relation to the great sword master Bartomeo Tacques?"

There was no one she could have mentioned (except perhaps the One) who could have snapped the cord of Hami's self-pity and restored him so quickly to his duty. He was Lord Hamish Tacques-Mouton, enforcer of southern treaties. He was here for a purpose.

He drew himself up to his full height (still shorter than the short countess), inclined his head respectfully, and said, "Master Tacques was my foster uncle, Your Grace."

"He was my teacher for three years when I was a girl," said the countess. "He must've been close to eighty then."

"Ninety, Your Grace, unless you're older than you look," said Lord Hamish. Behind him, Spira snorted; dragons could sniff out exactly how old someone was.

"I'm thirty-two," said the countess, sounding pleased, "but thank you."

She was a plump, handsome woman. She didn't look like a fencer—*exactly the sort to watch closely*, Uncle Barto would've said. She had a rapier buckled on; Hami should have spotted that at once.

Governor Boqueton arrived at last with an entourage of soldiers in maroon livery—the Governor's Guard. Hami remembered this division from twenty years ago—local boys, collaborating with their colonizers. No one kicked the Shesh as viciously as the Shesh themselves.

The governor had circles under his eyes and a haunted expression.

"We've kept the bodies on ice for your inspection," said Boqueton, acknowledging Lord Hamish with a bow. "I ordered that no one should disturb them."

"And the killer?" said Lord Hamish, eyeing the Governor's Guard coldly.

"He'll meet us there. Please, this way."

Governor Boqueton led them up the corridor. The countess—unacknowledged and clearly insulted—hurried to catch up with him. Lord Hamish bowed to the young priest (who outranked him, he seemed to recall) and let him walk ahead.

The girl (Tess?) had lingered behind and was speaking to Spira with quiet urgency. Spira had folded teur arms, refusing to meet her eye.

". . . Will hurt me, too," the girl was saying.

"And yet you were traveling with his expedition," said Spira.

"If I'd known he was a part of it, I wouldn't have. I'd grown to hate him."

"Is that a fact," said Spira. "So did you push him overboard yourself?"

"No," said the girl, plainly horrified.

"Then I'm not particularly inclined to believe you," said Spira, moving away from her.

"Spira, please. I'm *sorry*—" the girl cried after teu. Lord Hamish positioned himself between them and gave her a warning look. Her lips trembled, but she didn't call out again.

They arrived at a large, open hall, an indoor training area for the Ninysh Pelagic Legion. Racks of swords and pole arms lined the walls;

straw dummies stood at attention. At the far end was an enormous hearth; two of the Governor's Guard were dispatched to build a fire, per Hami's instructions. Under a wan skylight in the center, the two dead sabak lay upon a heap of dirty snow, their gill frills tangled, their pale flesh withering. They stank of fish.

Hami resisted the urge to cover his face, although it hurt him.

Someone was already here—the soldier who'd killed the sabak, presumably. He leaned over the bodies, using his dagger to prod at one of their wounds.

"Governor, get him away from those corpses. They're poisonous," said Hami, his icy tone betraying no inkling of the panic he felt. "You assured me no one could get near them."

"You were told not to approach the sabanewts, Lieutenant Robinôt," said the governor, whose panic was pretty plain.

The lieutenant looked up, and Hami recognized the man Lord Aveli had identified as Sixth Division. No wonder he hadn't obeyed the governor. Those bastards considered themselves above the law, and alas, they weren't entirely wrong.

That said, Lord Hamish Tacques-Mouton would not have lasted thirty years in Ninys if he couldn't work around Sixth Division. For the second time today, one of Uncle Barto's fencing precepts came to him: *It's not the stronger arm that prevails, but the stronger mind.*

"Don't wipe that on anything you mean to use again," Hami called to the lieutenant, who'd been about to clean his dagger. "It must be scoured with flame."

Governor Boqueton directed one of his Guard to collect the dagger; Lieutenant Robinôt handed it over with a show of reluctance.

"Governor," Hami continued, clasping his hands behind him, "you will recall, from last time, that two things must now happen. The bodies must be burned, and the perpetrators of this crime—whoever brought the sabak here, and whoever killed them—must be punished."

Lieutenant and countess both burst out talking at once, their volume increasing as they tried to shout over each other. Hami permitted this for some moments, then interceded: "Countess Mardou, I would hear from you first."

She outranked the lieutenant. Hami was quite content to let the man sweat.

"I request that the sabanewts be donated to the Ninysh Academy in Segosh," said the countess. "I can't preserve them properly, but they might be sent—"

"Your request is denied," said Hami. There was no point pretending he could consider it.

"You don't understand," said Countess Margarethe, voice rising. "They ate my fiancé—the least they can do is make themselves useful to science!"

There had never before been a case of sabak eating anyone, as far as Hami knew. They gave you bad dreams, refused you knowledge, administered a mild shock at worst. Killing Lord Morney had been a judgment; Hami shuddered to think what they must've glimpsed in his mind.

Six generations of Watchers had prevaricated, manipulated, and even assassinated to keep the sabak (and the One) if not exactly secret, then entirely uninteresting. If the Deadlanders considered sabak a threat, that was all the excuse they'd need to come hunting.

In his heart, he asked forgiveness for what he was about to say. "You're understandably upset, Your Grace, but they're dumb animals, acting on instinct. They aren't aggressive. The water at these latitudes is so warm that they were likely disoriented."

The countess was not placated; her priest muttered something, trying to soothe her.

Perhaps she could be soothed by the law. Hami extracted a folded copy of *King Moy's Treaty with the Five Polar Peoples* from his doublet and handed it to Countess Margarethe. It was a real treaty, although most Ninysh seemed not to have heard of it.

As the countess perused it (Robinôt reading over her shoulder),

Hami said, "These creatures are 'sacred,' as it were, to five tribes of the polar regions." He hated portraying his own people as superstitious primitives, but he had to be a believable Ninysh lord. "King Moy agreed to respect their quaint beliefs. No one may hunt, imprison, or injure sabanewts—properly called sabak. The only people who may keep or touch them are the five polar nations—" Ah, Lights, he'd said *nations* instead of *tribes;* he might as well name them properly now. "The Ggdani, the Murkh, the Tshu, the Katakutia, and the Wandering Cities.

"Not the Shesh," he added, in case Fozu's misbehavior had given any of the Governor's Guard ideas. They remained impassive; maybe they didn't consider themselves Shesh anymore.

"Is this still valid?" asked the countess, but Hami sensed her resolve crumbling. "When Count Pesavolta ended the line of kings, did he not renegotiate their treaties?"

"Not all of them," said Hami. The count had almost certainly forgotten this one existed.

"Treaties are made between sovereigns," sneered Lieutenant Robinôt, "not with ragtag bands of pirates and savages."

It was time to deal with this villain. Hami, satisfied that the law had made an impression on the countess, turned his attention to the thornier problem.

Twenty years ago, two people had been hanged for the crime of harming a sabak—a lowly Ninysh soldier and Mardiza, Speaker of the Shesh. Hami's conscience balked at executing Mardiza's son, Fozu. If this lieutenant were hanged all on his own, however, and nothing happened to the Shesh who'd brought sabak to the harbor, there would be trouble. The Ninysh settlers might decide to punish their Shesh neighbors themselves. They didn't need much excuse.

Hami thought he saw a way around this, however.

"Governor," he said, "we have a problem. Lieutenant Robinôt should be hanged for his crime, but I glean he is a member of Sixth Division, and not under your jurisdiction."

The governor, who looked like he'd been staring into the flames of twenty years ago, seemed to wake up at this pronouncement. "Why, so he is."

"Then let him be returned to the mainland to face judgment there," said Hami.

"You have no authority to send me back," cried Robinôt.

Hami was startled by his vehemence. Surely the lieutenant understood that this was the mildest consequence he could receive? The captains of Sixth Division had so much discretion in the matter that they probably wouldn't bother with a court-martial; they'd read Governor Boqueton's letter, read the treaty (maybe), have a laugh, and ship him back here.

It barely fulfilled the law, but it was the only way Hami could see to keep Paishesh from going up in flames again. He'd done enough harm here in the name of the law.

If this lieutenant objected to such mild treatment, there was something else going on. Maybe he didn't want to be brought to the attention of his own captains.

"Your superiors will surely be lenient," Hami prodded, keeping close watch on Robinôt's expression. "Who's your supervisor? Captain Roux?"

Fear crossed Robinôt's face and disappeared again so quickly it would've been invisible to an untrained eye. Perhaps he would be in some sort of trouble if he went home.

Before Hami could prod further, Robinôt took the offensive: "The treaty says any person who brings sabanewts into harm's way must also be punished. I know it was Giles Foudria. What will you do about him? And why are we obligated to do anything you ask, Lord Hamish?"

This unimaginative attack on his authority was easily countered. Hami drew out Count Pesavolta's letter of dispensation (unlike the treaty, this was technically a forgery).

"You arrived here with pyria," the lieutenant was insisting. "How much? I think we should really be asking ourselves what you intend to do with it."

Hami froze as he realized that he'd failed to take something important into account: the countess and lieutenant knew each other. They'd talked. She must have told him about the dragons' foolish stunt with the pyria.

The pyria that Hami had, in fact, brought here at Fozu's request.

Suddenly it all seemed to catch up with him, the impossibility of his task, the weight of his failures. His longing for the home he would never make it back to. Hami felt his blank expression, so carefully refined over years, crumple minutely.

Lieutenant Robinôt saw his opening—how could he not? It was as wide as the sky—and pressed his point home: "You meant to sell it, didn't you? Perhaps to Giles Foudria and his Shesh co-conspirators."

He'd guessed right. Hami grasped for any plausible alternate explanation, but he was too tired. His wits failed him. Governor Boqueton looked like he was vacillating; the countess and her companions looked shocked. Hami felt himself teetering on the edge of a precipice.

Then Spira stepped forward. Hami stared as if teu had appeared out of the very air.

"That pyria is the lawful property of the Tanamoot," said the scholar with unimpeachable gravitas. "It is for one purpose only: to destroy the Polar Serpent. We calculated the precise amount required, to the nearest thousandth of a percent, and have none to spare for your interisland squabbles. Our permits are all in ard, and I can produce them if you require."

"How much is that, exactly?" asked Governor Boqueton.

"What units would you prefer?" Spira replied. "Quarts? Cubic feet? It takes surprisingly little to coat the entire surface of a serpent."

"But are you carrying enough to endanger our harbor?" asked the governor.

Spira looked scandalized. "Of course not. That would be foolish."

Hami, who had apparently stopped breathing, inhaled at long last and tried to thank Spira with his eyes, but teur frank gaze was still leveled at the governor.

Boqueton seemed satisfied with teur sincerity. He ordered the Guard to burn the dead sabak and to throw Lieutenant Robinôt (protesting loudly) into a cell until he could be transported back to the mainland. Countess Margarethe looked like her sleepless grief was finally catching up with her; she departed on the arm of the young priest. The girl, Tess, glared daggers over her shoulder at Spira.

It all washed over Hami, who felt only gratitude at being saved, and the warmth of Spira's reassuring hand upon his elbow.

The ways Hami had still managed to fail hit him only later, as he sat on the steps of a bakery waiting for Spira to come out with breakfast.

He hadn't prayed for the dead sabak (he said the words now, in his heart). He'd come closer to giving himself away than ever before. And Fozu was still out there, possibly in possession of a live sabak he was not entitled to touch, let alone keep. A good Watcher would continue looking; Fozu's punishment might be deferred, but the sabak must be returned.

A good Watcher would not be so tired, or so doubtful that Watching had done any good.

What gnawed at him the most, though, was the way that girl had looked at Spira. She would be trouble if she was convinced that Spira meant to destroy the One. She'd never turn back, but would be more determined than ever to find the serpent before the dragons did, believing wrongly that she could protect it.

How was he supposed to stop two expeditions at once? Even if he stopped these, there would be more next year (he was so tired; he would never make it home). The Continental Serpent had been the beginning of the end; the Deadlanders thought it was a race now, and they would keep going for the One until they found it.

Hami suddenly realized—and wished he could unrealize—that he probably could stop the countess, in fact. He'd have to leave the dragon expedition to self-destruct on its own, though. That it *would*, he had no doubt; seeds of distrust grew among Spira's subordinates, and all he'd had to do was water them. There was no need for him to stay on, except . . .

He glanced back through the open door of the bakery. Spira was leaning on teur cane, speaking earnestly with the baker's girl. "But is there any special *Shesh* pastry we could try? Maybe you don't offer them to Ninysh, but we're not Ninysh. I'm a saar, and my friend—"

"You're with the Ggdani?" said the girl.

Hami turned away, smiling slightly. Sadly. In some other world, they should have been more than friends. In this world, he was never even going to be retired.

He plucked an eyu from his ear. Long ago, he'd given its mate to a bereaved boy and told him, "I'm sorry about your mother. If you ever need my help, you shall have it. Anything."

He'd never dreamed the boy would ask for a sabak and fifty barrels of pyria.

"Fozu, answer me," he said softly.

"Hami!" came the reply through a crash of waves. Fozu was by the sea somewhere. "I heard you this morning—I'm sorry, I was occupied and couldn't reply."

Occupied with an illicit sabak, no doubt. Hami bit his tongue; he needed to find Fozu, not drive him deeper into hiding.

"You're right—we should meet somewhere else," said Fozu. "I'm thinking Edushuke. The Ninysh call it St. Fionnani, but I've been trying to get them to call it Little Bitch Island. That's a rough translation of Edushuke, and it sounds just insulting enough that the Ninysh will think they thought of it themsel—"

"Edushuke is way over in Aftisheshe territory," Hami cut in. He could hear the baker's girl counting out change now.

"It's out of your way, I know, but you'll understand when you see it. Also, I have a contact there—Berekka—who you can leave the goods with if I'm delayed."

"Berekka on Edushuke," Hami repeated. Spira's three-beat gait approached. "I need to go."

"Lights lead you," said Fozu. It was something a Katakutia would say.

Hami rose, replacing his earring, and turned to face Spira. The saar stopped in teur tracks, and Hami realized belatedly that he was frowning.

"Everything all right?" said Spira.

"Our contact wants us to meet him in . . ." What was the Ninysh name? "St. Fionnani. I'm not happy about that. It's a long detour east."

"We'll still get you home," said Spira.

Hami tried to smile as if he felt reassured. That only made him sadder.

Spira would be all right. It might be better this way: the mutiny could happen on Edushuke, instead of the high seas. After Hami scuttled the countess's efforts, he might be able to make his way there, find Spira again, and—

Why was he still wrestling destiny after all these years? He never learned.

Spira picked teur way carefully down the steps. "I acquired a Voorka-flipper pie," the scholar said, brandishing a large turnover. "Last one. We'll have to split it."

"It smells lovely," said Hami, his heart breaking a little.

"Do your people eat these?" asked Spira, making two steaming halves.

"We have Voorka seals," said Hami, accepting a piece, "but not pastry."

They descended the hill slowly in deference to Spira's knees, eating in silence. Halfway down, Spira tugged Hami's sleeve, pointed toward the lighthouse, and said, "What's that?"

A winged figure was picking their way through the surf on stilts like a fishing heron—a Katakutia, probably the one who'd brought Fozu his sabak. Hami was seized by an irrational, incandescent rage at the Wind Kin—for sowing chaos where he'd been charged with keeping the laws, for making his life harder.

He quickly quashed it. There was no point getting mad at Katakutia; they dwelt so far beyond law that they were almost a law unto themselves. They were even allowed to kill—the way a tempest was "allowed" to kill. You might as well scream at the sea.

"That's a sort of wandering priest," Hami told Spira. "Sometimes if a person is dying in childbirth, their life may be saved with a tincture of sabak oil—but the child will be born a Katakutia, speaking the Language of Winds and communing with the Lesser Lights."

"They wander—on stilts? Between islands?" asked Spira.

"They travel with wild sabak, who build them roads, of a sort," said Hami. "And I assume the wings help, although I've never seen one fly."

"If this Katakutia brought the sabak here—"

Why should Fozu be punished and not the Wind Kin? Hami anticipated. A fair question, but hard to explain to outsiders.

But Spira was asking something else: "—do you think they could lead us to wherever Fozu has hidden himself? Then you wouldn't have to follow him to St. Fionnani."

It was an unworkable proposition: the Katakutia would never cooperate. And yet Hami felt a weight drop from his heart. It wasn't St. Fionnani he was dreading—he wouldn't be going, after all—but the necessity of leaving Spira for the countess's expedition. That had to happen in any case, but maybe it could be delayed by one day, while they looked for Fozu here.

Maybe—knowing a day was all he had—he could make it one to keep close. One to sustain him as he tried (and failed) to make it home.

"I don't know whether the Katakutia would deign to talk to us," he said, smiling. "But it couldn't hurt to try."

Spira's hair blew tenderly against teur soft, round cheeks; teur eyes were as deep and varied as the sea. "M-may I take your arm? The lighthouse spit looks rocky."

"I was just about to offer," said Hami, giving full courtesy. Full like his heart.

They descended arm in arm as a soft drizzle began to fall. Hami drank everything in—the kindly gray sky, the glistering droplets on Spira's cloak, the gulls caught laughing as they tried to fly against the wind. He would remember every detail, would hold and love them always. Whatever duty or destiny might bring, this day, at least, would live.

Thirteen

Tess emerged from the garrison fort ahead of Marga and Jacomo, who were moving slowly. The cobblestones of the square were slick with drizzle; market stalls huddled stubbornly with their backs to the wind.

"How is this fair?" the countess muttered, leaning on Jacomo's arm. The moisture on her cheeks might have been drizzle or tears. "Why must we submit to far-off polar peoples who will never know what happened here? We might've kept the creatures and sent along a note of condolence: 'Sorry about your enormous ice newts, but we absolutely burned them, per your reasonable requirement—'"

"Did you sleep at all last night?" asked Jacomo. Tess was glad for the interruption; she'd been gritting her teeth at Marga's every word. Were the Ninysh always so scornful of their own treaties? The islanders deserved better. The sabak deserved better.

Marga said, "Is that your polite way of telling me I'm ranting?"

Before he could answer, someone called her name. Governor Boqueton, waving, rushed out of the fort after them. His Guard followed in formation.

"Countess," said the old man, his face flushed from exertion, "I'm sorry he wouldn't accommodate you. He's a stickler, is Lord Hamish. I'm just relieved it was settled indoors, out of sight of our more volatile elements." He glanced around apprehensively, as if the shoppers who'd braved the weather were a riot waiting to happen.

Marga pursed her lips and turned away. Boqueton followed doggedly. "I'm organizing a funeral for Lord Morney, tomorrow at sunset. It would mean everything if Your Grace would stay one more night and mourn with us."

Marga turned back toward him with a softer expression, her eyes glittering. Her voice caught when she tried to speak, but she managed to nod. Governor Boqueton bowed, smiling.

He departed for the Governor's Hall; Marga watched his retreating back.

"Saints above," she said when she'd recovered enough to speak. "I hate funerals."

So do we have to go? was the question that popped into Tess's head. Of course she would never say such a thing out loud. Jacomo was bugging his eyes at her to no purpose.

"I'll get through it," said Marga, glancing from one to the other and apparently deciding their mugging was out of concern for her. "I'm the closest thing William has to family here. Someone's got to place the keys on the Golden House."

Marga resumed walking toward the Limpets. "And it will be nice to hear the eulogies," she added. "He was so lovely. Clever, kind, and good. I was blessed to have had as much time with him as I did."

Tess felt her entire body go hot. *Kind? Good?*

"Life can be distressingly brief," said Jacomo, who seemed to be in full priest mode.

Marga, encouraged, launched into an anecdote about Will. He'd rescued puppies, or donated a library to Pelaguese orphans in St. Remy, or nursed plague victims with his own two hands, or some superhuman nonsense.

She was talking about Will the rapist. *That* Will. Tess couldn't listen.

At the door of the countess's suite, Tess pulled Jacomo aside and whispered, "I can't take one more beatific story about Will. I can't."

"I'll provide the shoulder to cry on. I don't mind; I actually have some training," said Jacomo, looking determined. He unclasped his gold necklace and handed it to Tess; she recognized the square pendant thnik dangling from it. "Here. You promised Jeanne you'd be in touch, and you haven't even tried. That's your excuse to leave."

Tess took the device gratefully and returned to her room. Talking to her twin was its own flavor of difficult, but infinitely preferable to hearing another word about Will. She flopped onto her bed and flipped the switch.

A merry, masculine voice answered, "Jackie?"

It was her brother-in-law, Jacomo's older brother. "Hello, Lord Richard," she said.

"Tess—how nice!" cried her brother-in-law. His enthusiasm surprised her; she'd ruined his wedding night, after all. Maybe a year was long enough to forgive and forget.

"I wanted to speak to Jeanne," said Tess.

"Ah, well . . . she's sleeping, I'm afraid. Bad night. Apparently unborn babies can cause indigestion. Is it urgent, though? Should I wake her?"

"No, no, it's fine," said Tess, unsure whether to feel disappointed or relieved. "I only needed to hear that she was well."

"Everything all right?" asked Lord Richard. "How's my rascally brother?"

"Jacomo's fine. He finally stopped throwing up," said Tess, answering his second query. The question of whether "everything" was "all right" felt too deep and vast for her just now.

"I hear you're rooming together," said Richard. "I hope all the vomiting hasn't ruined his prospects." Tess could all but hear the wink and nudge.

"I hope you're not implying what I think you're implying," she said.

"Forgive me, little sister," he said, not sounding particularly contrite. "I'm getting ahead of myself, clearly. But you've no idea what a relief it is to his brothers, at least, that he's followed you on this expedition. I believe it's an encouraging sign. Heinrigh and I used to joke that he went to seminary for the celibacy, since he clearly wasn't there for the religion."

Tess blinked incredulously at the thnik, glad it wasn't a thnimi, so Lord Richard couldn't see how pink her cheeks had gone.

"I don't think that's why he's here," said Tess's mouth, but her mind was replaying how pale he'd gone when she'd sneeringly offered to kiss him. How his arms had felt around her yesterday, while she was weeping.

Ugh, none of it had meant anything. She was too suggestible.

She extracted a promise from Lord Richard to tell Jeanne that she'd called, and then she switched off the thnik, satisfied that she had fulfilled her promise without having to actually talk to her sister. All the credit, none of the pain. If only things could always go that smoothly with her family—she might almost have been tempted to go home.

She couldn't go home, though. She had a mission from the Queen and a duty to Pathka—and the latter was suddenly in peril. Spira intended to kill the Polar Serpent. The dragon expedition feared no consequences, but they'd underestimated Tess's determination.

Pathka would get another chance to commune with a World Serpent, whatever Tess had to do to make it happen.

Speaking of quigutl, how were they progressing toward finding Fozu? Tess dug around in her satchel for the palm-sized thnik Pathka had made for her out on the road last year. It looked like a moon, or possibly a bug. She found it wrapped in one of her socks and switched it on.

"I know what you're going to ask," rasped Pathka. "The answer is yes. We found him."

"That was quick," said Tess.

"You shouldn't be surprised," cried Kikiu in the background. "Quigutl have the keenest olfaction in nature."

"Keener than the great dragons?" Tess couldn't resist teasing.

"How do you think we survived so long in the nooks and crannies of their caverns? We won a centuries-long war of smeller versus smellee."

"Unstoppable force versus immovable object," Pathka affirmed. "The immovable object wins, provided it has the sense to keep moving."

"All right," said Tess. "But where is—"

"Don't say his name," said Pathka. "We're in a public place, and many people are looking for him, I glean. He does not yet know he's been found. I can take you to him, but we have to go at low tide. Meet me in a couple hours beside the equestrian statue in the square. The one covered in delicious guano."

Tess lay back and pondered whether any guano wasn't delicious for a quigutl, and the next thing she knew, she startled awake. She'd slept so soundly that for a moment she didn't know what day it was. She dragged on her boots, hoping she hadn't missed Pathka, and opened the door to see Jacomo, whose knock was apparently what had awakened her.

"How's the . . . whatsit?" asked Tess, still disoriented. The countess, she meant.

"Feeling guilty for wasting her fiancé's last day arguing," he said. "And feeling cursed. If they hang Giles Foudria, every man she ever loved will be dead. She's a widow, you know. Her husband died of a rosebush."

Tess had been about to announce that Fozu was found, but death by rosebush gave her pause.

"She promised to sleep, but I don't have much confidence," Jacomo was saying. "She was sharpening her sword when I left."

"They're not all dead yet," said Tess, glancing up the hallway for eavesdroppers. "We have a chance to save the last one. The quigutl have found him. Pathka's going to take me there. Come with me?"

"Wouldn't miss it," said Jacomo. "It's not every day you get to save someone from the noose and partially unbreak a good woman's heart."

"We probably should ask her to come along with us," said Tess.

"Then she'll never get that nap," said Jacomo. "Besides, I kind of feel she's earned a pleasant surprise, don't you?"

The weather had worsened, drizzle giving way to a blowing sleet that slapped your cheeks, and yet there were more people in the square than previously. A large group had gathered, arms linked, before the statue of King Moy—where Tess was to meet Pathka. They'd draped oilcloths over themselves against the weather, so it was hard to tell if their kerchiefs were tied Shesh style, but Tess definitely glimpsed some mustaches. The people were singing in a language Tess couldn't understand. She recognized a few words in the chorus, though: *Shesh Paishesh, me nai Jovesh eshu!*

It gave her shivers.

The shoppers at the market, a bit better dressed than the singers and not a mustache or kerchief in sight, were trying to ignore the song. The Governor's Guard were standing around in small clusters, talking among themselves and looking anxious. A squad of foot soldiers from the Pelagic Legion marched past in formation, heading for the fortress; their commander hung back, hands on his hips, scowling at the dithering guardsmen.

"You!" he finally barked at one, whose plumed cap identified him as the ranking officer. "That language is forbidden in public. Get your people under control, or we'll do it for you."

"Governor Boqueton said they may, this once," said the officer of the Guard, approaching the Legion commander and speaking quietly. "They're paying respects to the dead sabanewts."

"Pagan hogwash," said the commander, not lowering his voice at all. "And you're lying. I heard them say 'Shesh Paishesh.' That's a traitorous, nationalistic song."

Tess had stopped to listen to them, imagining several ways this could end badly. Jacomo tugged her away, around the singers, toward the statue, where Pathka should be waiting.

"Finally," said a raspy voice on high. Kikiu curled around the bronze horse's neck like a spiky ruff. She crawled down its leg toward Tess and Jacomo.

She'd removed her metal horns, and her goggles, but she still wore her bite enhancer.

"Where's your mother?" asked Tess, glancing back. The Shesh singers were still singing, but the Ninysh shoppers had stopped to watch the commander and the guardsman. The soldiers and the Guard were staring each other down.

Kikiu swiveled her eye cones. "Pathka is having a fit of strangeness. I stowed ko in a safe place, but I don't know what to do. It hasn't happened in broad daylight before." She paused and sniffed. "We should get off the streets. I can smell the tension rising. This is going to get ugly."

Abruptly the officer of the Governor's Guard broke off from his staring match, turned angrily, and began shouting at the singers, waving his arms like he was shooing crows out of a garden. "Break it up. Go home! Boys, help me clear them off."

Tess switched on her thnimi.

The singers didn't budge; some began singing louder. The shoppers, rather than minding their own business, began shouting in turn—"Ninysh might, Ninysh right! Do the Shesh like we did Jovesh!" The legionnaires spread out, ostensibly to keep the sides apart, but their weapons were drawn and it would only be a matter of time before—

A burst of sleety wind blasted the square, bringing a person with it. They glided out of the sky on wide wings, stilts dangling underneath like the long legs of a wasp, their face obscured by a knotted fringe hanging from their hood. Shock and amazement stilled the crowd.

Then it was the Katakutia's turn to sing.

Fourteen

*M*ind of the World, our sister has arrived. We know, better than most, that a Katakutia can be difficult to understand, and so we'll tell you this: she has trouble with proper nouns, and she'd rather sing than speak. She is a bridge between worlds. No page can hold her.

Sing, Sister. You are the song that sings itself.

For a Daughter of Winds, it is always now.

It is a beautiful, sleet-spattered day—all days are beautiful to the wind—and she is frolicking with her herd (the living sabak, the remembered dead) in the shallows beside a lighthouse. Its light is not real, but there are real Lights upon the water and inside her mind.

Soon, the Lights say. *The priest is almost here.*

She's never visited this island before—it's too far north for sabak. Too warm. She only came because the Sad Brother summoned her (there are ways; he must have spent time in colder parts of the world, to know them). His mother was a Speaker, he said. That is surprising. Why would a people forbidden from keeping sabak know their speech?

One of the Wandering Cities was banished generations ago; its people could no longer keep sabak, and so the Worldmind lost track of them. Maybe this is where they went.

She laughs in wonderment at how the world goes round.

The sabak swim around her stilts, like stars.

Sad Brother is carrying the stories of his people. He didn't say so, but a Daughter of Winds can tell these things. That's why he needs sabak—he's afraid he will die and the stories will be lost. He wants the sabak to hold his ancestors and keep them safe.

Suddenly upon the strand, a Snow Lord and a dragon appear. They are friends, which is both unexpected and enchanting.

Wind Kin, says the Snow Lord, making the obeisance of his people. *You recently brought sabak to a man of this island. I need to find him.*

"You do not," she answers, and her voice is wind. It becomes clouds and drizzle and fog.

You know sabak are forbidden to him and his people, the Snow Lord says in that icy way they have.

"That is a human law," she says, "not the will of the Lights. The Lights decide for themselves."

What an unfathomable person, says the dragon, and the Daughter of Winds laughs because that is exactly the right nuance. People seldom get it right.

Un. Fathomable. Too deep to measure.

They scatter, but she doesn't notice where. She has things to do.

Up the hill, say the Lights. *A True Priest awaits.*

She spreads her wings.

<hr/>

Her mind is not like your mind. It is much, much larger, and has better ventilation.

<hr/>

She lands in the square, where a crowd has gathered. There are people, and there are People. She sees the difference instantly, although she cannot see the priest, which surprises her.

Beside the Dead Horse, say the Lights.

She sees two of the northern Dead there, and a lizard. This is very confusing.

Around her, the crowd roils like a tempestuous sea, and she realizes that she has stepped into the middle of something. A fight, perhaps. Here, on one side, are the Dead, and here, on the other side, are the People. Between them are . . . the word *collaborators* drifts into her ear and then her mind. She hasn't met that concept before, so she has to taste it to understand.

The taste almost bowls her over backward, it's so sad.

What choice do you have, though, when the Dead have come to kill you? You make yourself Dead, as best you can, and try to keep the living as quiet as death.

Maybe this is why they need the priest.

The Wind Daughter lifts her chin and begins to sing:

> *O priest, I know you're here.*
> *Arise! Tell us a story—true*
> *In depth of meaning and*
> *Your heart's intention.*
>
> *The Lights call you True Priest,*
> *But how? If you have come*
> *From the Land of the Dead,*
> *I am surprised but open.*
>
> *Arise and speak, O priest—*
> *The Lights impel you.*

Beside the Dead Horse, a man stands up. He is tall and stout—and Dead—and yet she perceives a heart in him. Can a True Priest come from the north? There's always a first time.

Behind him, the lizard says, "I can't think of a story." She laughs appreciatively; the creature is unsettling but beautiful. It reminds her of a sabak.

The man is about to tell a story. She opens the ears of her heart and listens.

It's a parable (*he says*). Two parables, actually, but the second one depends on the first to be understood. The first is the more famous, though: St. Vitt's lesson of the mole holes.

(*The names of saints blur in her ears, but you will need them, to understand.*)

Once upon a time, one of St. Vitt's followers asked, "O holy one, how can we best fight the devil?"

St. Vitt, not known for optimism, said in answer: "Ye must fight ceaselessly, sinner, for there is no lasting victory against the devil. Envision a vast field of mole holes. The devil pops out of one, and ye beat him down. He pops out of another, and ye beat him down. However many times ye beat him down, always and forever shall he rise again to mock and torment ye."

"Then why do we even try?" cried his disciple in frustration.

And St. Vitt said to him in answer: "Would ye rather be overrun with devils? It is our lot to struggle against the world's corruption in vain. But I assure ye, there is virtue in the struggle, and rest for the virtuous in the hereafter."

I know, I know, I don't really like that story, either (*he says, because the People are grumbling*). But it's context for my second parable, the response of St. Polypous, the divinely devious, to St. Vitt's lesson.

St. Polypous's companion, St. Asparagus, told him the story you just heard, to which St. Polypous replied, "My friend, there are always more options. I have at home a field full of holes. Let us go see whether we can't find another way to deal with the devil."

So they went to St. Polypous's holey field, and when the devil inevitably popped up, St. Polypous did not whack him down, but grabbed him under the armpits and pulled him out. Then the Saint tossed an apple core into the hole, which sprouted at once into a stout sapling. The devil, indignantly, disappeared in a puff of smoke.

"That's one," said St. Polypous.

It should come as no surprise that the devil popped up again, from a different hole this time. St. Polypous hauled him out and found something else to fill the second hole. Soon the Saint was preemptively filling holes, faster than the devil could contrive to pop out of them, until finally there was just one hole left.

As was his nature, the devil popped out of it. And as was St. Polypous's determined philosophy, he grabbed the devil under the armpits and pulled him out. St. Polypous filled the hole with one of his own legs—he had several to spare—and then he was finished. The field was free of holes.

"But look what you've done," said St. Asparagus, pointing over his friend's shoulder. St. Polypous turned and saw the devil still standing there, scowling and snorting brimstone. The fiend couldn't disappear, for there were no more holes.

"Now the devil will be with us forever!" cried St. Asparagus despairingly.

"He was always going to be with us forever," said St. Polypous. "He was my devil all along, and these were my holes to fill. Better to acknowledge him as mine than to keep futilely denying him and never repair my field."

St. Polypous took that devil and made a new leg out of him, and that is how one of St. Polypous's legs came to be the devil. He never lost sight of that truth as long as he lived.

The Daughter of Winds has heard a lot of stories, and she knows what makes a story true.

This one is true—or at least the second part is. She can hear the echo inside his heart as he tells it. She is pleasantly surprised to learn that there are true stories among the Dead.

"Well told," she says. "Hear this true story, O People, and see the heart of this priest."

The crowd is grumbling again. The story didn't sound true to everyone who heard it, but this is always the case. Not everyone can hear the words behind the words.

A Daughter of Winds can hear *only* the words behind the words. Sometimes that's too much knowledge.

Now soldiers are coming out of the fort to apprehend her. They look frightened. The Dead are always frightened. She would pity them if their fear didn't make them so dangerous.

"True Priest, farewell for now," she says, spreading her wings. "I will find you again."

She runs three steps on her stilts, catches an updraft, and glides down to the harbor, high above the houses. Arrows arc through the air around her, whistling, and she laughs, delighted by the musical accompaniment.

She sings:

Arrows—fly with me
Away from death!
Fly like sabak, swift
Beneath the waves.

I'll teach that priest
To swim the sea of mind—
He'll cease to be
An instrument of death.

Fifteen

"We should get out of here," said Tess, tugging Jacomo's sleeve.

He was staring at the spot where the Katakutia had disappeared. The soldiers were staring, too, but surely it wouldn't be long before they decided they'd lost her and came after her story-telling accomplice instead.

Tess pulled Jacomo down a narrow side street away from the square, following Kikiu.

"Are we going after Giles Foudria?" asked Jacomo, snapping out of his fascination.

It took Tess a moment. "Fozu! Yes. Sorry. I'm not used to Giles, since I was introduced to him as Fozu first."

"Maybe we shouldn't get used to it," said Jacomo. "Maybe we should call him what he calls himself."

That sounded like a sensible policy across the board. Maybe she could start sending back helpful advice for Queen Glisselda: *To do better than the Ninysh in the Archipelagos, at the very most basic level, start by not imposing your own names over the names that are already there.*

Kikiu swiveled an eye cone. "We're not going after Fozu yet. I'm taking you to my mother first. We can't just leave ko all alone in a strange place."

There was another example: Pathka had laid the egg Kikiu had hatched from, and liked to be called Kikiu's mother (Tess had confirmed this). But then Pathka had undergone thuthmeptha, becoming male, so now—

Wait.

"Should I have been calling you both 'ko' all along?" Tess asked Kikiu, who had taken a small detour through a trash bin.

"Mmr?" Kikiu popped up with a mouth full of fish heads and took a moment to chew them. "Only if you're speaking Quootla."

"That's what I thought—"

"You should have *asked* before now, though," said Kikiu, giving Tess a *fthep* across the shins with her tail for emphasis.

Fair enough. She'd make a point to do better going forward.

Kikiu led them to the harborside and made for a broad building clad in gray, peeling planks, not far from the warehouse that had burned when the sabak were killed. An elderly watchman leaned back in his chair beside the weathered door, ostensibly napping.

"Pathka's in there?" whispered Tess, afraid to wake the old man. It seemed a strange place for quigutl to hide.

Kikiu didn't answer, but nudged the watchman's knee with her snout. He opened one eye and gave a familiar nod. Kikiu bobbed her head back at him.

"Friends of the quigutl, are you?" he asked Tess through his stringy mustache.

"We are," said Tess.

He reclosed his eye and waved them along.

Kikiu led them into a busy fish-salting house, where workers were scaling and gutting the day's catch before packing it into barrels of salt. One man tossed Kikiu some fish guts, and she caught them on the fly. At the back of the room, another sentry guarded a set of narrow steps. He tipped his hat to Kikiu, barely glancing at Tess and Jacomo.

"Everyone seems to know you," said Tess as they started down the stairs.

"Some Shesh saw me knock Lord Morney overboard," said Kikiu. "He was, shall we say, not popular. They hid me here, away from the countess's wrath. I'm something of a folk hero."

"They wanted him dead?" asked Tess.

"He caught the Shesh Eight," said Kikiu, "and saw to it they were hanged."

At the bottom were doors labeled SALT ROOM and ICE ROOM. Kikiu opened the latter. Her tongue-flame revealed a glistening wall, blocking their way. The hatchling ducked through an almost-invisible gap near the floor. Her flame shone through the semi-transparent wall like a will-o'-the-wisp. "Follow," she cried. "There's a passage through."

A winding tunnel had been built into the stacked ice. The low entrance was awkward for human-sized people, but Tess and Jacomo managed to squeeze through. Behind the initial wall, they could stand. Kikiu led them back and forth (the maze wasn't hard; the room wasn't large) until they reached another door.

This opened into a wide chamber lit by oil lamps—a natural cavern, domesticated. The rough walls and ceiling had been evened out with chisels, and the floor was hard-packed earth. Four other entrances had been fitted with doors. Someone's priority had been to ensure that there were many ways out; comfort had come a distant second. Low, hard benches lined the irregular perimeter (a snoring, lumpen shape in the corner had apparently found them comfortable enough to sleep on). At the far end roared a hearth with a kitchen set up around it—two stewpots, a washtub, pantry shelves, and a cupboard full of glassware.

Only one of the pots held stew; the other, farther from the fire, was warming something alcoholic. Tess's nose hairs prickled at the smell from across the room.

A stout, middle-aged woman knelt by the hearth; she looked up at the sound of the door. "We're closed," she said, rising and wiping her hand on her apron. The other hand still grasped a ladle. "You'd rather drink somewhere with windows and daylight, surely? I'll show you the fastest way back topside."

The ladle twitched as if she might beat them about the ears with it.

"We just came for our friend," said Tess, raising her hands. "We'll be gone directly."

Tess looked to folk-hero Kikiu to smooth things over, but the hatchling was nowhere—no, there she was, crawling all over the sleeping person. "Wake up, wake up."

"You're with the quigutl?" said the woman, her expression softening. "I gave the sick one a cup of okush, thinking it might settle him, but it put him straight to sleep."

Tess should have recognized the snoring. She rushed to where Kikiu was pawing at Pathka's face.

Behind her, Jacomo was asking, "Is that okush?"

"It is. Want some?" This establishment suddenly wasn't as closed as first supposed.

Pathka stirred, feebly pushing Kikiu away. "I'm fine. You're overreacting."

"You went strange again," said Kikiu. "You've never done it in daytime before."

"Who can tell if it's daytime down here?" Pathka muttered.

Tess palpated Pathka's throat, feeling for his pulse, as if its speed or irregularity could give her knowledge she'd know what to do with. She'd seen him injured and ill. This was different; she couldn't gauge how worried to be.

"You told me you'd take me to you-know-who," said Tess, avoiding Fozu's name and trying not to sound too irritated. She should have known locating the navigator couldn't be as easy as it had seemed. "You're in no condition to go after anyone right now."

"Not because I'm *strange*," said Pathka sullenly. "It's that fermented seal milk."

"If you spray it through your lips and ignite your tongue at the same time, you can make quite a large flame," said Kikiu. Tess hoped she hadn't tried it.

Jacomo arrived with a steaming mug of the stuff. "The proprietress found you a bit rude, ignoring her offer of okush," he told Tess. "So I took a double portion."

"Drink that slowly," warned Tess. If it was flammable, it was stronger than anything she'd ever seen him drink.

Other people had begun trickling in—stevedores, fishermen, sawyers, sailmakers. Some looked askance at Tess and Jacomo but then seemed to find their proximity to the quigutl reassuring. Tess listened to the low conversation around her; some was in Ninysh, most was definitely not. Studying their firelit forms, Tess began formulating her own theories of how to tell the Shesh by sight, beyond what Claado had told her. She'd worked as an embroiderer, so it was their embroidery that drew her eye. She'd hardly noticed it at first, because it was hard to see: blue embroidery on blue fabric, green on green. Here in the firelight, the texture change was visible, and a bit of the pattern—sunbursts and whorls, stars and shells.

It was subtle, but it had to be. They couldn't even speak their language in the street.

Pathka tried to rise and almost fell off the bench. Tess sat on her hands, trying not to fume with impatience. Pathka had said they had to go at low tide, and surely they'd already missed it. By the time Pathka was sober, Jacomo was going to be drunk—

Before either thing could happen, though, the Katakutia blew into the room.

It was not a metaphor: the wind arrived with her. The hearth fire roared and oil lamps winked out. Cries of dismay went up as drinks spilled.

"Lights touch all here," said the old woman, as if she hadn't extinguished half the light in the room.

Dismay became laughter once the patrons realized what had happened; they raised mugs to her. Jacomo, somewhat unsteadily, joined in.

The Katakutia wasn't wearing wings or stilts now, and she'd thrown back her fringed hood, revealing short white hair and a face as creased and wrinkled as the sea. The mother-of-pearl medallions adorning her tunic winked like a hundred eyes.

"Welcome, Light Mother," said the proprietress, filling a mug for her. "You honor us. I don't recall that Paishesh has ever been visited by one of your nation."

The Katakutia barely glanced at the proffered drink; she was scanning the benches. "Where's my priest?"

In this confined space it was easier to hear what was odd about her speech. Tess still understood it as Goreddi, although the specific sounds seemed to blur and change the harder she listened. Maybe the Katakutia was speaking not any language, but something else entirely, something everyone understood as their mother tongue.

"You found us!" cried Kikiu. The hatchling leaped from the bench and capered like a kid.

"Of course, my love," said the Katakutia, who apparently understood even Quootla. She scratched Kikiu's head. "But where is the story-teller from the square? I need to find him."

Jacomo rose, swaying from okush but maybe also from nerves. Tess planted herself at his elbow, trying surreptitiously to steady him. The old woman pressed her knobby hands to Jacomo's cheeks and proclaimed, "The Lights said I would find a True Priest. They must have meant you, although you are foreign and very young. What do you think, my love?"

My love seemed once again to refer to Kikiu, who cried, "Yes! I don't know! Maybe!"

The Katakutia laughed like wind chimes. "I can't discern his heart just now, but I suspect he may be drunk."

"My abject and humiliated apologies for appearing thusly in this state," said Jacomo with the painfully excessive formality of one who is not sure how much longer he's going to be able to maintain a standing position. "I am unaccustomed to strong drink, and this . . . oshu . . . ogu . . ."

"Okush!" called another patron.

"It tastes like feet," said Jacomo, head wobbling. "And it kicks like . . . like feet."

Laughter and saluting mugs went up around the room.

"Don't apologize," said the old woman. She elbowed in front of Tess to help him sit down.

"I'm Jacomo," said Jacomo.

The old woman smiled wanly. "I'm me."

"Mee?" said Jacomo.

Tess thought she understood. If Katakutia spoke in meanings, not words, maybe she couldn't say her own name. All they'd hear was what she meant—*me*.

"Are you able to hear our names, or do they also sound like *me*?" Tess asked.

The Katakutia ignored her. "The Lights told me to find the True Priest—presumably so I could teach you their ways. I know you don't see the Lights in the Land of the Dead."

Land of the Dead seemed unnecessarily harsh, but Tess kept her mouth shut. The old woman only had eyes for Jacomo, clearly.

"I hate to disappoint you, Mee," Jacomo was saying, "but I'm not actually a priest. I ran away from seminary before taking orders."

The chiming laughter again. "What's that, a place to make priests? A priest workshop? A priest kitchen? No wonder your northern priests turn out wrong. Priests aren't crab traps; you can't build one out of sticks. Priests are people who *know*."

Kikiu, at her feet, did an interpretive dance in the firelight.

"I heard the truth of your story," said Mee. "I know you. I am, myself, a priest."

"More like a priestess," muttered Tess.

"I'm not a false, exotic priest," said Mee. Of course she wouldn't ignore Tess this time.

"A *priestess*," Tess said a little louder. "A female priest."

"Is that all the word means to you?" said Mee. "Are you quite sure? I hear echoes of *ineffectual. Seductive, deceitful, unserious.* In your heart, it means 'false, exotic priest.' That is not what I am. I am a True Priest."

Jacomo handed Tess his mug; there wasn't much okush left, but a little went a long way. Tess downed it at a gulp and found it was not the worst she'd had. It blunted her annoyance.

Had she meant the word that way? If she was being honest, yes.

Mee refocused on Jacomo. "A priest understands stories, which one is needed and when."

"Pardon me, Light Mother, but I heard his story in the square," said another patron, a tall man in sailor's slops. "It confounded me. Did you mean, sir, that we shouldn't knock the crap out of these usurping Ninysh devils? Because I can't agree."

The Shesh began discussing among themselves, some echoing the sailor, others claiming Jacomo had meant the story for Ninysh ears. Maybe the Shesh were the devils in his story, nothing but a "leg" of Ninys in the end.

"Oh, no, that's not . . . no," said Jacomo. He had the look of a man who knows he's too drunk to give a sensible answer but is nevertheless determined to cast a net and fish for it in the broad, dark ocean of his mind.

Mee cut in, "This is your first lesson, my son: stories land differently in every ear that hears them. You may tell a true story, but others must measure it against themselves. Sometimes they find it false. It can be hard to accept that they're not wrong."

"They're not?" said Jacomo, eyes bugging. "Doesn't it matter what *I* thought I meant?"

"It matters," said Mee. "Just not in quite the way you think it does."

"Then why did you call it a true story?" cried Jacomo, visibly upset. Tess would have handed back the okush, if there'd been any left. She settled for squeezing his elbow.

"You told the truth about *yourself*," said Mee. "You showed us the messy imperfection of your heart. That is a priest's job. Someone here must have needed to see it. *You!*"

The word and her gnarled finger were pointed at a scrawny fellow with peach fuzz on his cheeks who immediately choked on his drink; the woman beside him slapped him on the back.

"You were there, considering whether to become a collaborator," Mee said.

Gasps went up. Someone spit on the floor.

"Yes, Light Mother," the scrawny fellow managed to cough out.

"Martu, how could you?" said the woman beside him.

"Oh, let us not pretend he is alone." Mee's stern gaze swept the room; patrons seemed to wilt before it. "The Dead governor surely makes life pleasanter for those who cooperate. I won't ask what tempted you, only what you thought the story meant."

"I . . . I thought it was about shame," Martu mumbled, turning his mug in his hands. "I've been ashamed of being Shesh and tried to . . . beat it out of myself. I thought the story meant that I could fix the holes—the ones I tore and the ones they made. Plant a tree there. That's all."

His friend put her arm around him and pressed her cheek against his head.

"You can tell who someone is and what they've been through by how they understand a story," said Mee, addressing Jacomo again. "When you travel—as every priest must—you'll hear the same tales told quite differently. There are five essential stories among these islands, told by every nation. Who can tell 'The Tiger Lover'?"

"'Vulkharai'?" said Martu's friend, looking up. "I keep my mother's version, but it's more song than story."

"Sing, then," said Mee, settling back in her seat.

The woman stood, to applause and encouragement; her name seemed to be Reta. Martu reached under his seat for his instrument, a miniature viol with two strings. He droned a minor interval with a short bow while she sang:

Vulkharai loved a fierce ice tiger,
Though he was a bit of a fool.
He didn't pause to sharpen her claws,
But made her some four-year boots.

A year hunting Voorka, a year tanning hides,
Sewing the seams, embroidering the sides—
Such boots the world had never seen.
Even an ice tiger might be intrigued.

    O Vulkharai, Vulkharai,
    Then you laughed until you cried.
    Did you know that was but half?
    Soon you'll cry until you laugh.

He gave the boots to his fierce beloved,
Laced them tight upon her feet.
The tiger could tell that he meant well,
So Vulkharai she did not eat.

Bright queen of the ice, she slips and slides.
The boots get no traction;
She can take no action.
She falls in a hole and she dies.

    O Vulkharai, Vulkharai,
    Brokenhearted Vulkharai,
    The time has come for you to cry
    Until one day you reach the other side.

Martu ended with a flourish, and applause went up all around.

"Well told," called Mee. "I'd never heard that version. Usually it's either tragic or comic, but you've made it both."

"Perhaps that's what it means to be Shesh," said Reta, smiling slyly. "We're both. From the continent and from the sea, the dead and the living. We're like islands ourselves, between."

"Shesh Paishesh!" cried the sailor, and everyone drank.

"So what are the other essential stories?" asked Jacomo, and Tess groaned inwardly.

Mee, apparently, could talk about stories forever, and Jacomo seemed utterly smitten with the idea of being a True Priest.

Tess found it unaccountable. He'd run away from seminary; he hadn't seemed religious.

In any case, he had clearly forgotten all about finding Marga's ex-navigator and was still pretty drunk. Tess didn't see how she was going to drag him out of here.

Pathka, on the other hand, was struggling to his feet again. "Come, Teth," he said, staggering sideways. "I'll show you where he's hidden."

"Good, yes, let's go," said Tess, eyeing Pathka uncertainly. He didn't look quite steady.

"Are we off?" said Jacomo, trying to rise.

"Stay!" cried Mee, grabbing his arm. "You have more to learn."

"It's fine," said Tess, waving off his concern.

"I'm staying, too," said Kikiu, though no one had asked.

Tess and Pathka left through the ice maze. They'd stayed in the hidden tavern so long that the fish-salting house was deserted; the last rays of sunset shone through the windows, making the great heap of salt sparkle like diamonds. The watchman let them out, with a nod at Pathka. Tess and the quigutl climbed toward the square, their breath misting in the cold.

"You seem crabby that Mee likes Jacomo so much," said Pathka at last.

"I don't see what's so special about Jacomo," Tess burst out with a bitterness she hadn't quite realized she felt. "I've told a few good stories in my time."

"You used to tell me Dozerius stories," Pathka affirmed. "But if I know you—and I'm pretty sure I do—you don't want to be stuck in a cellar talking all night. You'd rather be out here, making a new story."

She had to admit it was true.

"Well then," said Pathka, tail twitching, "let's find Fozu."

Tess, grinning, followed him onward and upward.

Sixteen

Tess insisted that they fetch the countess on their way through town. Adventuring alone with Pathka, just like old times, appealed to her, but with age came a certain respect for practical considerations. Fozu hadn't seemed to like them much when they met him on St. Vittorius, whereas Marga was his dear old friend. Will had believed Fozu still loved her.

Fozu himself, on the other hand, had insisted that the countess turn back. This could go almost any way, but Tess still thought it best to have Marga along.

Marga, as it happened, was wide awake and pacing her suite. "Widow's insomnia," she said, with what was meant to be a smile. "A regrettably familiar condition. Going after Giles will take my mind off it, at least."

Nine minutes later, they were following Pathka across the deserted town square, heading north. Marga, who'd dressed with lightning speed, buckled her sword belt as they walked.

The houses of St. Claresse got larger and nicer north of town, built from imported limestone instead of local planks; they passed the governor's mansion, as well as shippers of fish and timber. Beyond these were farmsteads, and then they reached the logging operations, sawpits and piles of logs and planks. The air was ripe with cedar dust.

Over a ridge was a vast moonscape of tree stumps, some of them breathtakingly huge. One might have held a country dance on top.

Pathka skirted the giant-tree graveyard, heading toward where the land grew rougher, covered by scrubby shrubbery, which the wood-cutters hadn't bothered to clear. Nearer the sea stood a glade of un-touched cedars, twisted and stunted by the wind. Beyond that was a rocky shore, where the bones of the earth seemed to have broken through its skin at an angle. Black ridges, cracked and worn over cen-turies, sloped toward the pounding water. Pathka trotted along a jut-ting stone buttress. Tess almost lost her footing twice, misjudging how slick the striations could be; Marga was sure-footed as a nymph.

If the countess was surprised to look for Giles in such a wilder-ness, she gave no hint.

Across a rough channel stood an islet, little more than a precarious stack of rock. Tufty plants grew out of any likely crevice.

"Is that where he's hidden himself?" asked Marga, eyeing the micro-island as if calculating whether she could swim there. "No won-der nobody could find him."

"It has a cave, enlarged by human hands," said Pathka, per Tess's translation. He scratched his hide against a barnacled outcropping. "Its natural entrance is underwater, but there's another, high on the seaward side, invisible from shore. It's an easy climb once you reach the islet. It's getting there that's hard."

As if to underscore his point, a wave lashed the outcropping where they stood and sent cold spray high into the air. It fell around them like a rain shower.

"How did Giles cross this strait?" asked Marga.

"He has a coracle in the cave," said Pathka. "I'd steal it for you, but he sleeps in it. If you want to wade across, you'd better go now."

"Wait—what?" cried Tess. He hadn't mentioned wading. She was going to get water in her boots.

"In a quarter hour, you'll have to swim," said Pathka. "The tide is rising."

"Right. In we go," said Marga after Tess had explained.

Tess did not feel so sanguine. "This won't survive the water, will it?" she asked, pulling Pathka's ungainly homemade thnik out of her doublet.

"I can keep any devices dry," said the quigutl, opening his mouth.

The countess had a Saint-medallion necklace for Pathka to carry. Tess took the opportunity to subtly unfasten her thnimi. Pathka held everything in his throat pouch.

Marga braved the surf first. The dizzying tide sucked and tugged at her legs; she wobbled slightly at each buffet but didn't lose her footing.

Tess stared at the white water, heart quailing.

"I'm with you," said Pathka. "It'll be over before you know it."

Tess grasped one of his dorsal hands, and he kept her upright as the waves tried to steal her feet from under her. The water was bone-bitingly cold; she had to clench her teeth to keep from cursing loudly and warning Fozu of their approach. Fifty yards seemed to stretch to fifty miles. On the other side, Marga gave her a hand up onto the rocks.

"An easy climb, the quigutl said?" the countess muttered, looking up. The sheer rock face had only spindly shrubs for handholds. Pathka squeezed past her toward the seaward side; Tess and Marga followed him around until they reached a set of steep steps carved by human hands.

Marga led the climb, grasping the stubborn, hapless brush for support. Tess's boots, waterlogged, squelched dismally. Near the cave mouth, Marga crouched and gestured Tess to do the same. The moon shone brightly enough that Tess could discern the coracle. There was no movement. They crept up, moving when the surf crashed, pausing in the lull. Marga drew her sword slowly and then sprang forth to pin Giles Foudria into his makeshift bed.

The coracle was empty.

Marga cursed. Pathka ignited his tongue so they could see to the back of the chamber. It was lucky they hadn't gone deeper into the cave in the darkness, because there was a large hole in the floor, as deep as a well. It echoed and gurgled, water flowing into it from below with the rising tide.

There were blankets in the coracle, the embers of a fire (he'd banked the ashes so it could not be seen easily by ships), a sack of dried food and spare clothes, a pan, and a fishing line.

"He was here earlier," said Pathka a little defensively. "I didn't scare him off. There's no human excrement in this cave—maybe he's gone outside to defecate."

"Then he can't have gone far," said Marga after Tess had translated. "And by now he'll have glimpsed the quigutl's light and realized we're here."

"Should I have let you fall down the sabak hole?" said Pathka.

Sabak hole? Tess peered into the pit. It glugged ominously. In the depths, something moved, a familiar eerie blue glow.

Marga drew nearer to look. "Well, well," she said, mouth flattening. "Giles has been keeping sabanewts after all. Pathka, I need my thnik back."

At her feet Pathka deposited a St. Capiti medallion, which Marga used to contact her uncle: "Have Argol bring the plaion around to us." She gave some complicated nautical directions. "She'll see our light. Tell her to signal with a lantern, and don't let the flood tide push her too close; it's rough here."

Marga returned the device to Pathka and announced, "Let's kill the sabanewt."

"What? No!" cried Tess, struck with a vertiginous sense that she didn't know this woman at all.

The countess, approaching the cave mouth, signaled for quiet with one finger and continued: "We'll pack its corpse in salt and donate it to the Academy for dissection."

Someone came hurtling out of the darkness.

Marga, ready for him, dodged. He skittered past, almost to the edge of the hole. Her sword was already drawn; all she had to do was press the point to his throat.

They stared at each other, their shadows flickering across the wall of the cave. Giles Foudria—erstwhile navigator, properly called Fozu—rose slowly, hands raised. His long red hair was tied back; his beard was, if anything, more feral than before. He'd found a shirt somewhere.

"You won't touch her," he said. "You'll have to kill me first."

"Calm down. I've no intention of killing either of you," said Marga, lowering the point.

Tess exhaled, a little embarrassed that she hadn't seen the ruse. Apparently Tess was willing to believe the countess capable of terrible things. Was it because she'd loved Will?

Was it her fault, if no one had told her the truth about him?

"My apologies for greeting you with a sword, but I'm told your time in the wilderness has turned you quite ferocious," Marga was saying.

"They lie about me in town. The troops need an excuse to kill me on sight," said Fozu.

"Lord Morney, my fiancé, said you attacked him."

"Then Lord Morney is also a liar."

The sword tip was at his throat again. "He's dead. Sabanewts tore him apart."

Something seemed to break in Fozu then, some pose or pretense. He looked shocked. "Oh, Marga, I'm so sorry," he breathed, although her blade prevented him from coming closer.

The countess took a shaky breath. "Thank you, Giles. Now—truce? If I put my sword away, will you attack me?"

Fozu shook his woolly head. The countess sheathed her weapon, and suddenly Marga and Fozu looked like two old acquaintances, trying to figure out what to say to each other.

"You survived the iceberg," said Marga at last.

"You survived the Sea of Holes," said Fozu, his beard-shrouded smile like moonlight behind clouds. "That was every bit as uncertain, by my reckoning."

The countess scoffed lightly, then fell serious. "We're going after the serpent again."

"So I've heard," said Fozu, nodding toward Tess, who cringed. She almost certainly should have told Marga about meeting a strange man on St. Vittorius.

The countess let that pass. "Come with us, Giles. We need your expertise—and a map, if you can draw one from memory—and you need—"

"I'm not joining your expedition," Fozu said. "The serpent is not yours to find."

There it was, the argument Tess had known he would make, the one Lord Hamish kept making. She couldn't even consider the possibility of giving up; it meant breaking her promise to Pathka. And yet the more they said it, the more it bothered her, buzzing and biting like a gnat. She turned her back on Fozu and looked out to sea, arms folded.

Marga was saying, reasonably, "Well, you can't stay here."

"I can, and I will, unless you mean to kidnap me?"

"The word you're looking for is *rescue*," said Marga. "Boqueton means to hang you."

"He'll have to find me first," said Fozu.

"Lord Hamish Tacques-Mouton," the countess persisted, "claims you endangered the sabanewts by bringing them here. That crime may also incur hanging, I understand."

"I know what penalty it bears." His voice had grown quiet.

"Lord Hamish is friends with dragons," said Marga. "If our quigutl could sniff you out, it's only a matter of time before his dragons do, too. You've got to come with us."

"I can't leave the sabak. She's just beginning to trust me," said Fozu.

At the back of the cave, Tess heard the creature surface, blow spray from her nostrils, and shrill. Fozu whistled back.

Out at sea, a lantern flashed. "Argol is here," Tess announced.

"We're not debating this, Giles," said Marga. "We have to get you aboard the *Avodendron* before the sun comes up, before anyone else realizes we've got you."

"Not coming," said Fozu.

"You are. I'm overruling you, for your own good. I still regret not tying you up when you demanded to be left on that iceberg," said Marga. She fetched her thnik medallion. "Argol, I'm sending the quigutl out to retrieve the towline. Prepare to haul us in."

Pathka obligingly ran out of the cave and leaped into the sea. Tess saw that it had risen a lot; they'd come up fifteen carven steps, and now there were just six above the waterline.

"You would never have tied me up," said Fozu in a small voice.

"I'll tie you up now if you don't cooperate," said Marga, tucking her thnik away.

Fozu threw himself at her again, and this time she wasn't ready. Marga landed flat on her back, the air knocked out of her. He pinned her arms to the floor with his knees; his hand, possibly raised to strike, froze above his head, as if he couldn't quite make up his mind to do it.

Tess took her opening and shoved him over. He swatted her head as he lost his balance. She tumbled over him, but now Marga was on her feet again. The countess wrenched Fozu's arms back and slammed him belly-first onto the cave floor.

"You said you wouldn't attack me," she said, holding him down with her knee. "Tess, I need that rope he's got stowed in his coracle."

Tess rushed to the coracle, grabbed the rope, and . . . hesitated.

Marga really meant to tie him up. It wasn't a bluff this time.

"Tess!" Marga shouted.

Tess jumped. Her hand overrode her vacillating conscience and decided for her.

She passed Marga the rope and then immediately felt a roil of nauseated regret.

The countess bound Fozu's wrists behind him—without his

permission and against his will. His face was pressed against the floor; his eyes flashed balefully at Tess.

She'd made a mistake, reacted before she'd finished thinking. This was wrong. Maybe she could undo it. "Marga . . . ," she began, but then Pathka materialized, dripping, with the towrope clamped between his teeth, and Marga was barking at her to help get Fozu into his coracle.

We need Fozu's help and Fozu needs our help, Tess repeated to herself, trying to rationalize it. The ends were good, so don't think about the means.

They lifted him into his coracle. He made it difficult by going limp. Tess still felt like vomiting, but she gritted her teeth and ignored it. Marga tied the line and carefully slid the coracle toward the water. It held only one; Tess and Marga would have to hold on to it while it was pulled through the frigid water. Pathka was dispatched to the dinghy to let Argol know it was time. Tess hoped she hauled quickly.

"Don't let go," shouted the countess over the roaring surf. "This water is rough enough to drown a porpoise, and cold enough to turn your limbs to stone."

Tess's limbs couldn't be as heavy as her conscience.

The coracle gave a lurch and dragged them in. Tess's scream was swallowed by the crashing waves. The coracle tossed about like a leaf. Waves slapped Tess's face, and her boots, full of water, seemed determined to pull her under.

When they'd nearly reached the dinghy, the coracle's stiff, tarred rim cut into Tess's palm like a serrated knife and she couldn't hold on. With nothing to keep her afloat, she flailed about; she could swim, but not in angry water like this. She heard Argol shouting, then nothing as water closed over her head—then she broke the surface and screamed along with the countess and the wind, then silence again under the waves.

The current was hauling her down into darkness. That wasn't all bad. She wouldn't have to look any closer at what she'd just participated in.

A blue light was rising toward her fast—the sabak, emerged from her grotto. Tess thought dimly, *What if Will and I die the same way? Maybe we deserve to.* The sabak butted Tess with her broad white head and pushed her toward the surface.

Tess tried not to touch her with her hands, since that seemed to be forbidden, but the sabak had hands of her own. She grabbed Tess's face with soft, padded fingers tipped in needle-sharp claws.

Tess's head filled with cacophony, a thousand images, a thousand thousand voices. Ice floes and volcanoes and ice tigers and cities and the ceaseless sky and and and

We looked for the intersections of their stories and found several easily: how these two had been lovers; how he'd left (it was easiest) when her cousin told him her true age and who her father really was; how the child, Dozerius, had died after three days, taking half her heart, and she'd raged like the sea until she found herself again; how shocked he had been to see her after so many years; how he'd spent the last hours of his life with hollow eyes, haunted by ghosts but never truly believing he'd done wrong.

The girl, though, was all remorse. She felt sick with it even now, as well she should.

We told her: You, too, did what was easiest. Don't let that be all you do.

Big hands reached under Tess's arms, pulling her out of the water and into the dinghy. Tess lay in the bottom of the boat, gasping like a fish; her mind was her own again, and yet it wasn't. Argol grinned down at her.

Above them, the ceaseless sky was beginning to dream of dawn.

Seventeen

Tess, all remorse, sat wrapped in a blanket, trying to look at anything but Fozu.

Having only spent time aboard a baranque, which lumbered through the waves, groaning and mooing like an aurochs, Tess had not appreciated that sailing could be quick and nimble. The *Avodendron*'s dinghy—more properly called a plaion—had a sail as well as oars, and a sailor of consummate skill in Argol. She could always find the wind, whether it gusted or barely breathed, and persuade it to send her in any direction she wished. Under her steady hand, they rounded the lighthouse horn before the sun was even a glimmer on the horizon.

The sabak, swift as a porpoise, kept pace. Sometimes she headbutted the coracle, which they were towing behind them. She chirped at Fozu, who whistled back, shrilling over the wind. He'd gotten better at speaking to her, or at least the sabak wasn't mocking him anymore.

Now she was mocking Tess, inside her head: *You, too, did what was easiest.*

She had, though. She'd handed over the rope the moment Marga shouted; she'd helped put Fozu in his coracle. That had been the path of least resistance, much easier than telling a countess no.

Don't let that be all you do.

That was easy to say, but what else *could* she have done? Refusing to hand the rope over wouldn't have accomplished anything.

That's just it, said the imaginary sabak in her head. *You'll never know. You didn't try.*

"The sabak is concerned about me," Fozu announced. "She offered to sink your dinghy. I declined, but I don't know how she'll react when you take me aboard your ship. She could sink it, too. She has powerful claws."

"I don't respond well to threats," said Marga, holding her gaze aloof.

"Speaking of threats," said Pathka from under Tess's seat, "ask whether she still plans to kill my offspring, Teth. Reminding her, of course, that Kikiu helped find her navigator."

Tess translated; the countess frowned deeply and then answered, "Very well. I relinquish my claim to Kikiu's head, but I can't have her on my ship. She stays behind in St. Claresse."

"Or I sneak ko aboard and make sure no one ever sees us together," grumbled Pathka.

Tess did not convey this message.

Argol carefully maneuvered the plaion into the harbor and drew up alongside the *Avodendron*. The crew cast down a sling for the prisoner, whose hands were still bound, and a rope ladder for everyone else (except Pathka, who climbed directly up the side of the ship). Fozu docilely let himself be bundled onto the sling; it swung and bumped as the sailors hauled him up.

The sabak was swimming in agitated circles. She raised her snout above the water, teeth flashing, and began to keen—a sound like nothing Tess had ever heard before. A sound you could feel in your bones and upon your flesh, that could have peeled the paint off a man-of-war.

"Oh dear," said Fozu languidly. "That's terribly loud, isn't it?"

Marga, jaw clenched, gestured to Tess to start climbing.

"In the wild, they can summon each other from fifty miles away." Fozu kicked his heels idly against the side of the ship. "Lord Hamish will hear that, wherever he's staying, and know exactly what it is. It will be audible at the governor's mansion, although Boqueton might not recognize it. He'll certainly send troops to investigate, though. What will happen when they discover you've taken the leader of the Shesh Nine aboard?"

Marga, helping Argol lower the plaion's mast, cried, "What do you want, Giles?"

"I *want* you to let me go," he said crisply, "but I will settle for your bringing the sabak aboard with me. I've worked too long for this. We must not be separated."

"So I should take her aboard and blithely break the law?"

"You're already blithely breaking the law, harboring a fugitive."

"You promise she'll stop screaming?"

"I'll speak to her."

Marga stood with her hands on her hips, her booted toe tapping. Tess, halfway up, finally ventured a glance at Fozu. If she really regretted her role in his capture, maybe this was her chance to make up for it. She called down, "Maybe it would be best to let Fozu go?"

Marga didn't react. Tess had spoken too timidly, perhaps, her voice lost beneath the sabak's keening. Fozu, hanging right beside her, seemed to have heard, however. He darted a glance her way, blue eyes glinting with interest. Tess felt unpleasantly warm.

Marga threw up her hands. "Fine! Let us haul the creature up."

Fozu whistled. The sabak quieted, then gave two short chirps.

"Cradle her gently in a net," said Fozu as he was lifted over the ship's rail. "Take care not to tangle her gills. I will direct you in how to keep and feed her."

He graced Tess with a full smile now, looking perfectly contented, as if he'd planned this all along and Marga was inadvertently doing his bidding.

Did that mean she didn't have to feel guilty about his capture? Somehow she still did.

Everything suddenly felt like too much. If Fozu refused to draw them a map, how would the expedition go forward? And how was Tess supposed to go forward with reporting Ninysh aggression to the Queen when she'd arguably just participated in it?

She was wet, exhausted, and shivering. She didn't wait for them to haul up the sabak and plaion, but took off in search of a nap and a change of clothes. Only when she reached the records room did she remember that her dry clothes were up at the Limpets.

Tess stared stupidly at the door, too exhausted to decide what to do next.

A hand on her shoulder jarred her out of her daze. It was Karus, who said, "The countess has sent for your things. You've earned the ocean's promotion, as they say. Follow me."

Tess mutely followed the gnarled old sailor toward the aft end of the ship.

"I'm sure his soul will rest the easier," said Karus, opening the door to Lord Morney's cabin, "knowing that you and Father Jacomo will be a bit more comfortable now."

Tess didn't think Will's soul would be placated in the least. "He . . . he didn't use this bed, did he? He was sleeping up at the Limpets?"

"It's all clean," said Karus, sounding mildly miffed. He bowed and left her to settle in.

It would be foolish to refuse a cabin such as this, directly under Marga's stateroom and half as large. Unlike the records room, it had a proper bunk (clean, supposedly, but still unsettling), natural light, a writing desk and chair, glass-chimneyed oil lamps, gauzy curtains, plump cushions atop the sea lockers. In the corner, a hulking, well-sealed trunk looked like it might possibly contain a dry shirt, or a blanket at least.

It turned out to be full of journals, papers, and knickknacks. Everything smelled oddly like . . . him. She flipped open a journal to make sure, recognized the blunt, square hand, and tossed it back into the trunk.

These were Will's things. Records and souvenirs of the years since he'd left her.

The *years*. Tess sat down heavily on the floor.

The sabak's words—thoughts? feelings?—came back: *Will left (it was easiest) when your cousin told him your true age and who your father really was.* The cousin could only be Kenneth, whom she'd long considered her lone ally in the family, who had apparently lied to her face about whether he knew anything about Will's disappearance.

Will had left to avoid trouble with her father, because she was so young. Not because he felt guilty for what he'd done. Not because he knew she was pregnant.

How could the past still find new ways to hurt her? Will was dead; you'd think it would all be over.

But no, the sabak had delivered one final twist of the knife and confirmed what she'd suspected when Will brushed off her accusation: Will had not truly believed he'd done wrong.

And now it was too late for him ever to admit it to himself.

She wasn't sure why that mattered to her, but it did. Immensely.

Tess slammed the trunk lid shut, leaned her head against it, and wept.

When she finally ran out of tears and her mind was in that silent, still place on the other side of crying, she was able to consider more calmly. The sabak had been trying to make a connection between two things. Tess, too, had done what was easy instead of what was right. She felt remorse—where Will had not—and that mattered, but it wasn't enough.

Don't let that be all you do.

She had to make amends to Fozu.

Tess woke up an hour later with the trunk lid's texture imprinted on her face and a panicked sense that she'd misplaced Jacomo. She'd left him listening to stories—it felt like weeks ago. Surely he'd returned to the Limpets and gone to bed like a sensible person?

Jacomo had surely forgotten what day it was (Tess herself had half forgotten) and that there was a funeral to attend that evening. Someone should fetch him back to the ship.

Tess went above and scanned the harborside. The stevedores were returning from the Limpets with her things, but there was no tall, stout student-priest tagging along. When they came aboard, she asked the hindmost carrier, "Did you see Lord Jacomo at the inn?"

"No," said the man, as if she'd accused him of taking the wrong luggage.

Cack. Had her fool brother-in-law stayed out all night? She trudged down the gangway and along the quay toward the fish-salting warehouse, which was surely where he'd be.

The old, half-asleep watchman recognized Tess and let her pass with a nod. Piles of fish—the morning's catch, some still twitching and flopping—covered the salt house floor. She slipped and skidded her way around them to the stairwell and descended to the secret Shesh tavern.

It was still half full, although the storytelling seemed to have ended. She found Jacomo, Kikiu, and Mee where she'd left them, Jacomo speaking animatedly.

"I have to write these stories down," he was saying, his eyes feverishly bright. "I'll never remember them otherwise. I can already feel them slipping out of my head."

"You can't write them down," said the Katakutia.

"I could compare different versions, then," said Jacomo. "Line by line. Really understand how the Shesh variants differ from the ways other nations tell them."

"You'd understand nothing," said Mee. "Stories require breath to live. Writing them down turns them into something else, something dead. You might as well call a pile of autumn leaves a tree."

"Or a pile of bones a seal," added Kikiu. The Katakutia scratched behind her head spines.

Jacomo persisted: "Writing preserves stories. They would disappear otherwise."

"They're meant to disappear. That's the point," said Mee, beginning to sound cross. "You have the heart of a priest—I've heard it beating—but your people have taught you the wrong things. It's a pity that I have to leave you now."

"I'll see you . . . you know where," said Jacomo.

"Don't speak of it in front of the Dead," said Mee, glancing cagily at Tess.

Tess folded her arms and bit her tongue.

"I won't," said Jacomo. "Tess doesn't count, though; you can trust her."

Mee frowned. "Doubtful. But the Lights are calling. Are you ready, little one?"

"Ready," said Kikiu, shaking herself like a dog.

"Don't go too far," Tess said hastily to Kikiu. "We sail right after Will's funeral—"

"I won't be sailing with you," said Kikiu. "I'm traveling with the Katakutia."

Tess stared into a corner of the room as this sank in.

"Does Pathka know?" asked Tess, suspecting she knew the answer.

"Ko will figure it out," said Kikiu. "And our paths will cross again. Ko will hardly have time to miss me."

They followed Mee out the door she'd come in and up a long, dark passage, emerging on the shore beyond the lighthouse, well away from the harbor. Mee clambered down a rocky incline to a cave hidden behind some tangled brush, where she'd stowed her things—a traveler's pack, a pair of broad canvas wings, and her telescoping stilts.

She tightened straps, buckled buckles, and then mounted her stilts by catching the wind with her wings. Kikiu gamboled around her in the shallows.

"Now you see the other side of priesthood," said the old woman, addressing Jacomo one last time. "We come where we are needed, do what is required, and then we go."

Jacomo smiled wryly. "Lights lead you, Katakutia."

Mee pivoted on one stilt and picked her way through the breakers, like a spindly-legged plover looking for sand crabs.

Kikiu, it seemed, intended to swim—metal gear and all—to wherever they were going next. Pale shapes cut through the water nearby, the last two sabak of Mee's herd. Kikiu slapped the water with her tail, and then she and the sabak were swimming together, chasing each other, breaching and splashing and playing. Mee's laugh carried shoreward on the wind.

Tess and Jacomo watched until they passed out of sight, beyond the next islet.

"When did you say we're sailing?" asked Jacomo. He had dark circles under his eyes.

"Not until after the funeral. You have time for a nap before then—we have a new cabin, with an actual bunk," said Tess, suddenly realizing she had a lot to tell him.

She took his arm in comradely fashion and steered him back toward the harbor, telling him all about finding Fozu, omitting her ignominious abetting of Marga as well as the sabak's words. They passed the lighthouse point just in time to see the *Sweet Jessia,* out beyond the breakwater, setting sail for parts unknown.

Tess watched it go and did not flinch from recalling that there was someone aboard that ship she also needed to make amends to. She silently wished Spira safe travels.

Eighteen

Mind of the World, consider love.

Love can change the world. Alas, it often doesn't. A wily heart, one that moves but is never moved, can easily elude it. Death can cut it short. Love persists, however. It hopes; it believes. Are you the fool who will tell love to stop trying?

Once upon a time (*that timeless time, where love resides*), a portly Ninysh count and a tall Porphyrian admiral, with little in common but their hearts, against all advice eloped and against all odds lived in each other's eyes until they died. Their greathearted daughter, Margarethe, grew up believing that with love, anything was possible.

And it was, or would have been, if there had not been death in the world.

The evening of Lord Morney's funeral, Marga stood on the quarterdeck under an overcast sky, buckling her sword belt. She was beginning to regret not napping. Her limbs felt leaden, and the tension in her neck threatened to become a headache.

Funerals always brought Albaro back and reminded her what a sleepless, weeping wreck she had been for months afterward.

She could not let that happen this time. If she fell apart, this voyage fell apart.

A nap would have helped. It wasn't as if she hadn't tried. She'd delegated the sabanewt's tank construction to the crew. She'd dismissed Darienne for an afternoon ashore, to the girl's great delight. She'd drawn the blinds and even managed to lie down.

But sleep had eluded her, just as it had when Albaro died, except back then (had it really been fifteen years?) there were nightmares. This time she felt itchy, like crawling out of her skin. Lying still was not an option. She'd paced her cabin and ended up obsessively polishing William's rapier, salvaged from the sea, the one she'd given him as a gift. It was all she had left of him, and she felt compelled to make sure there was not a stain or blemish on it.

She'd wasted his last day on earth arguing about Giles. The sword must be what her conscience was not.

Marga, standing on the quarterdeck, looped the long end of her sword belt over and down, so it hung parallel to her silver pomander. Her gown, the finest she'd brought, was of black silk embroidered with silver and pearls; she wore white-gold curls pinned up under a plumed hat. It was not typical funeral attire, but she hadn't begun this voyage expecting to be widowed again before the end. She was an optimist, despite everything—

"Papa, I'm going to marry Albaro des Fleris," she announced definitively upon her seventh birthday, over a heaping bowl of brandied cherries.

"It would be wiser to marry his elder brother, Theodez," the old count said fondly. "Theodez has his own horse already, and he'll have the whole estate—"

"Albaro wrote me a poem about stag beetles," she retorted, with every ounce of hauteur she possessed. Her father, humoring her, conceded that stag beetles were indeed lovely, but then she married Albaro ten years later to the day—

Marga blinked and saw that she'd drawn the rapier in one smooth, silent motion, a reflex against ghosts. Its swept hilt caged her hand in an elegant whorl; the blade glinted even under the overcast sky. She swung it—a test, merely—cutting the air with a satisfying swish.

That almost made her smile. She'd whetted it diabolically sharp.

How sharp did a sword have to be to slice the rough edges off the past? *Swish.* To shave off guilt and pare away regrets? *Swish.*

Her next cut was fierce.

Swish.

Maybe she wasn't exhausted after all. Maybe she needed to move. She couldn't do a proper Blystane drill in this gown; silk abhorred sweat. But what if she moved very slowly? She brought the hilt to her chin in salute, then posed with a dancer's grace, en garde.

The wisdom of Master Tacques came to her: *Do not bring violence to the sword. Do not bring heartbreak or anger or passion. You hold in your hand the steel of rationality.*

Excruciatingly slowly, she performed a lunge simple, recover, parry sixth, riposte, lunge Pinabresca—and little by little the world contracted, focused itself to a single point, the point of her sword. Here was calm; all else was noise. She could endure this funeral. It wouldn't take all night, and anyway, she needed to leave before the tide turned. Afterward, she'd drill to her heart's content, until she was so tired that even widow's insomnia couldn't—

"Countess?" said a voice behind her.

Marga whirled, faster than thought, her blade at the interloper's throat.

It was only Father Jacomo, benignly rumpled, looking more surprised than terrified. He raised his hands as if in surrender.

"Forgive me, Father," said Marga, sheathing her weapon. "What's that St. Wilibaio says? 'Go ye not armed to a funeral, lest ye bring about a second'?"

"I know that sword has sentimental value. It'll be all right," said Jacomo, folding his hands behind his back.

Not a single line of scripture in return? What were they teaching at seminary these days? In Marga's experience there were two kinds of priests: the sort who spouted scripture, and the sort who was just a little too handsy. Some were both. Father Jacomo managed to be neither; he hadn't mentioned the will of Heaven once, and when he offered a pastoral shoulder to cry on, she'd quickly learned, he meant it figuratively. It threw her off balance.

"Are we ready to go? Where's Tess?" said Marga, taking up her silver pomander and flipping it open. It wasn't the usual kind, full of aromatics, but a timepiece that had belonged to her father and was correspondingly eccentric. It seemed to have stopped. She started winding it.

"That's what I came to tell you," said Jacomo, glancing toward the gangplank. He had dark circles under his eyes, as if he wasn't sleeping well, either.

Marga followed his gaze and saw several things at once: Boqueton's carriage waiting on the quay; Tess at the top of the gangway with her arms folded; and a soldier in dress uniform, his sleeves a riot of colorful puffs and slashes, facing off with Tess.

It was Lieutenant Robinôt.

Marga's first thought was that she was caught, that he knew she'd found Giles and was coming aboard. Goose bumps rose on her arms.

But how could he know? He didn't, surely. Lack of sleep made her paranoid.

She was not entirely surprised to see Robinôt again. Yes, he should've been imprisoned, per Lord Hamish's directive, but the younger brother of Lord Modera—and one of Pesavolta's pets in Sixth Division, besides—was never going to stay locked up for long. Marga considered it poor taste to have him strutting around free so soon after the *Sweet Jessia* had sailed, but then again, was she not also disregarding Lord Hamish's rules? At least she was doing it secretly.

Secrets were Robinôt's stock in trade.

"We thought you wouldn't want him aboard, in light of . . . you know," Jacomo muttered.

"Indeed. Well done," said Marga, snapping her pomander watch shut and descending from the quarterdeck. Jacomo followed like her shadow.

"You're supposed to be in the lockup!" Tess's shrill carried from thirty feet away.

Marga's protégé had no tact (and what was she wearing to the funeral? It was too late to regret not addressing this). Marga prepared to sweep in as the voice of moderation.

Robinôt scoffed. "Boqueton saw sense at last. He knows there's no point prosecuting me for an archaic law no one cares about."

"I bet the Shesh care." Tess was nearly snarling.

"Tess, enough," said Marga, fully expecting her gravitas to end the matter.

Tess backed off, but Robinôt couldn't resist a parting shot: "I hope they do care. I hope they try something."

"I hope you don't mean tonight, at your dear friend's funeral," said Marga, giving Lieutenant Robinôt a stern glare.

That seemed to cow him. "Forgive me, Your Grace. Of course nothing should disturb the solemnity of the occasion." He gave full courtesy, as full as he could upon a narrow gangplank.

"Governor Boqueton sent me to escort you. I fear I've arrived early."

Politeness dictated that she invite him aboard and offer him a drink—she had some excellent spirits, although she didn't care for them herself. That was what he'd expect.

That was out of the question, though. There was no telling when Giles might start shouting again about being shut up in the records room. He'd been audible all the way from the great cabin. And the sabanewt was housed right on deck, in a bin that had once held spare sails. Robinôt wouldn't care that she'd captured it, probably, but it might start him wondering where she'd found the creature, and in whose company.

Harboring a fugitive could be a hanging offense—it depended on the fugitive and on who was harboring them. She was taking a terrible risk, and for what? She might not even get a map out of this if Giles kept refusing to cooperate. He was lucky she cared what happened to him. Saving his life might have to be enough, in the end.

And then what? No map, no William—Marga felt herself teetering at the edge of a vast chasm. She grasped her sword hilt to steady herself.

Deep breath. Steel of rationality. She had to endure this only for a few hours.

Marga made a show of taking up her pomander watch and looking at it. "We should go, Lieutenant. It's closer to sunset than you think. It can be hard to tell, with this overcast."

Lieutenant Robinôt did not argue, but led the way down the gangplank.

Governor Boqueton had arranged for the carriage to be flanked by an honor guard. A trumpeter seated beside the driver played Count Pesavolta's personal fanfare, all the way up the hill. It was excessive and in poor taste. Marga clenched her jaw and tried to tolerate it; Governor Boqueton was mourning Lord Morney in his own way.

She would, too, when she had a chance. Preferably with a blade in her hand.

When they reached the square, Marga was surprised to see the plaza packed with people. The carriage had to stop at the edge because the crowd was too dense to pass through. As she descended from the carriage, Marga felt all eyes upon her, expecting a show of grief.

At a smaller, semiprivate service, she might have felt free to shed some tears. She did not care to have the whole town watching her fall apart—

at the foot of St. Ida's, asking, begging, "Why Albaro? He never harmed a soul. He was sweet and kind, if a bit prone to versifying. Lockjaw is a fencer's affliction, so why didn't you take the fencer? How does any of this make sense?"

Her father's protégé, Father Erique, had been sent to counsel her; he was the one priest she'd tolerate, and only because they'd practically been raised together.

"It is not for mortals to question the will of Heaven," he said, quoting some Saint or other. He drew nearer and put his hands on her shoulders, trying to knead away her tension.

"A pox on Heaven!" she cried, shoving him into a candelabrum—

Father Jacomo bumped into her; apparently she'd stopped walking. "Are you well?" he whispered. "You look a bit . . ."

She probably looked embarrassed—that's how she still felt, years after venting her pique on poor Erique, who'd only been trying to help. Had she ever apologized? She couldn't recall.

"I'm tired," said Marga. "I'll get through it."

"You don't have to get through it alone."

Ah, but she was never alone at a funeral. That was the entire problem.

She motioned Jacomo and Tess nearer and muttered, "Stay close. When it's time to leave, I shall want to go right away. There won't be time to search for you in the crowd."

"How long do we have to—" Tess began, but Jacomo elbowed her. There was some kind of nonsense going on between these two, and Marga felt quite sure she didn't want to know.

"How long do we *have,* that is?" The girl amended her question.

Marga opened her watch; it was running smoothly. "Two hours until the tide turns."

If they missed the tide, they'd be stuck here overnight with a wanted man aboard. Uncle Claado had told her in no uncertain terms that that was a risk he was not prepared to take. He'd gotten unnecessarily loud about it.

"Countess Margarethe, this way!" Governor Boqueton's voice cut across the crowd. Marga saw him waving from the portico of the Governor's Hall. That's where the service was being held? Not the cathedral? Marga changed course toward him, her shoulders tensed almost up to her ears.

Boqueton helped her up the steps and seated her in the colonnade with the other guests of quality. From there, Marga could see that the

Golden House—the model of Heaven at the heart of any cathedral—
had been brought outside and set before the Governor's Hall.

They really meant to do the whole service right here in the open
under these rain clouds. Marga glanced up apprehensively, worried for
her silks.

The maroon-liveried Governor's Guard were herding the citizenry toward the edges of the square, creating an open area in the
center. Into this space marched a pipe and drum corps, followed by
three units of pikemen, who paraded in formation and saluted smartly
toward the hall.

Martial pomp was unexpected; William had not been a military
man. Marga sat solemnly, itching to open her watch but knowing how
rude that would look. Beside her, Tess didn't even try to conceal her
squirming; Jacomo seemed to be trying to yawn without opening his
mouth.

The pikes and pipers finally marched back into the fort, and then
the crowd refilled the square and began singing hymns—late. The sun
had surely set, although there were so many blazing torches that it was
hard to tell. Marga managed a surreptitious peek at her watch and
was relieved to see it was not as late as she'd feared.

There were hymns to St. Brandoll, William's patron, Saint of hos-
pitality, and to St. Jobertus the Physician, patron of natural philosophy.
There were many to St. Claresse, patroness of this island, and one to
St. Kathanda, lady of beasts—possibly in reference to the sabanewts.

It had all been songs to St. Ida when Albaro died. He'd always
loved—

"What time is it?" Tess hissed.

Marga peeked at her timepiece. "We have half an hour," she whispered back.

In the absence of a body, it was customary for the closest grieving
relative to climb to the top of the Golden House and deliver the Keys
to Ascension, a set of symbolic keys provided by the bishop. It would
be Marga's duty, as the bereaved fiancée. As the hymns wound down,

she rose expectantly. There was just enough time to place the keys before she had to go.

Governor Boqueton rose at the same instant and cried, "Who wishes to deliver eulogies for Lord Morney?"

Marga, in confusion, sat down again.

Several townspeople stood forth; the governor let them come up the steps by turns to speak. William had touched many lives here: singing like an angel, stacking sandbags ahead of a storm, rescuing lost souls shipwrecked on an islet. A young couple had even named their baby Morney, after William had saved the father's life.

Marga had been looking forward to the eulogies, but she found herself biting the inside of her cheek, hardly listening. She didn't dare let herself be moved to tears now. It would be hard to stop weeping once she started, and there just wasn't time. The tide would soon turn. If the *Avodendron* was stuck here until morning, her napou would never forgive her.

"What time is it *now*?" Tess whispered, like a child on a long carriage ride.

Marga cracked open her watch. "Half an hour."

Except . . . it had said half an hour ten eulogies ago.

Marga snapped the watch shut, cursing inwardly, weighing her options. She still had to place the keys. It was her duty and her right.

She beckoned to Jacomo, who leaned across Tess. Marga put a hand on his shoulder and bowed her head, trying to look like she was praying with her personal priest.

"You two go back to the ship," she whispered. "Tell Napou I'm delayed and to engage maneuver fourteen." The ship would get out before they lost the tide, at least, and leave the plaion for her.

"Should one of us stay and help extract you?" Jacomo whispered back.

"I'll be fine," said Marga. "Go."

They rose and edged out of the colonnade. That was one small weight off her mind.

Now she just had to end these endless eulogies. Marga stood, rudely cutting off the next speaker, and announced, "I will place the keys now, and see my beloved on his way up the Golden Stair."

She expected the bishop to approach (where was he?), but Robinôt, of all people, got to his feet. He fished three jewel-encrusted keys out of his pocket. Marga was not pious—she'd buried most of her belief along with Albaro—but still, it seemed profane and wrong for a mere soldier to be brandishing holy relics. What good was ritual if the correct forms weren't followed? The forms were the entire point.

Robinôt whispered as he handed her the keys, "Where's Foudria?"

The back of her neck prickled. Surely he didn't suspect she'd found the navigator; she'd given him no reason. "I don't . . . How should I know?"

"Let her perform her duties, Lieutenant," Governor Boqueton interceded across Marga's fluster. "Perhaps she hasn't been visible enough."

Visible enough? Who was supposed to see her—Giles?

Sweet Heavenly home.

They must believe he was still in love with her, enough that he would risk everything to attend his rival's funeral—to gloat? To get a glimpse of her? That would explain why they'd held the funeral outdoors, and why they'd made it drag on so long.

Marga determinedly climbed the steps of the Golden House, where William's body should have lain. There was a bowl-like depression on top, full of stars, where his head—

rested, swathed in a white shroud, forever invisible to her. She would have liked to look upon him, to have her last memory be of Albaro at peace, no longer screaming or spasming with such violence that he broke his own bones. Father Erique had insisted that she didn't want to see him like this, but she was getting awfully tired of people telling her what to want—

She pushed the memory away. Now was not the time. It was never time.

She steadied herself against the gilded wood, took a breath, and said in a clear voice, "St. Eustace, my beloved is at your door. Let him in, and lead him across the threshold. May he dine at your table." She laid the keys gently in the starry bowl. "Accept these keys; they are his heart, mind, and body. You already have his soul."

She climbed down. Governor Boqueton kissed both her cheeks, then announced, "Now let us recite the Departing Prayer together."

Marga didn't have time for this; Uncle Claado was going to be leaping out of his skin with worry and anger. She began sidling along the steps of the porch, trying to leave without disrupting the prayer. Suddenly Robinôt was blocking her way.

He ducked under the plumes of her hat to whisper in her ear: "You're not going anywhere."

"My visible presence hasn't flushed Giles out, if that's what you were hoping for," Marga whispered sharply back. "He's not an idiot—"

"Boqueton's the idiot," said Robinôt. "When your wedding was canceled, he thought a funeral could serve the same purpose. But Giles Foudria was never going to come into the light, was he? He's been on your ship this whole time."

Marga went cold, but not with fear.

She went fencer cold, looking at him with clear, appraising eyes. He was bluffing, hoping she knew something and would tip her hand. If he really believed Foudria was aboard her ship, he would have searched the *Avodendron* when he had the chance.

"You're coming with me," said Robinôt, taking her elbow. "I have questions that need answering."

She didn't have time for this.

"Giles Foudria!" she shouted.

Governor Boqueton broke off his prayer; every eye in the square turned to stare at her.

"Giles Foudria!" she shrieked, louder. "I see him, over there!"

A ripple passed through the crowd—fearful, skittish, eager— the way a flame travels along a fuse. Somebody shouted at Marga— "Ninysh might, Ninysh right!"—and a hundredfold answer roared back from every corner of the square: "Shesh Paishesh!"

The Shesh had come in great numbers to William's funeral, and not because they loved him.

The first blows were thrown, two yards from where the countess stood; a man landed at her feet and leaped back up to join the fray. The riot that had been brewing two days ago had only been deferred, it seemed. Neighbor pelted neighbor. The Governor's Guard, who at least were armed, hesitated to skewer their own and were overrun by screaming Shesh. The garrison fort quickly disgorged a battalion, and then another; cries and clashing filled the air.

Marga had thought to break away and lose herself in the crowd, but the fighting escalated too quickly; only a fey fool would run through the middle of this.

"Now you've done it," Robinôt growled. "I'm going to charge you with harboring a fugitive *and* inciting a riot."

On this thin pretext, he grabbed her arm and twisted it behind her. It was an insultingly insecure hold. She could have stepped right out of it—but then what? He was surely faster; if she bolted, he'd catch her before she reached the harbor.

A little arrogance might just goad him into taking her where she needed to be. Marga said, with all the hauteur at her disposal, "I was trying to help you by pointing out where Giles might be, since he is certainly not aboard my ship."

"We'll see about that," said Robinôt.

He forced her around the perimeter of the square toward the harbor road, dodging thrown fists and other objects. Robinôt spotted some people he knew in the crowd, twenty feet and several brawls away, and shouted to them. Two soldiers shouldered their way toward him through the melee—a beefy pair, a crossbowman and a glaivier.

One had been holding Robinôt's poleaxe for him during the service. He tossed it; the lieutenant caught it inches from Marga's head.

Marga had figured she could escape Robinôt—he was bound to underestimate her—but she had no idea what to do about these two lugs. An eddy of panic began to stir in her heart.

Her left hand bumped the scabbard of her sword and then grasped it tightly, the way a shipwrecked sailor clutches any stick of wood in a stormy sea. Her blade was no use to her until she reclaimed her right arm from Robinôt, but the caress of steel at least reminded her to breathe.

It's not the stronger arm that prevails, but the stronger mind. She'd have an opportunity to test that precept, it seemed.

Robinôt marched her down the harbor hill, his thugs lumbering behind. They passed dozens of people running in the other direction, who'd apparently heard the commotion and were rushing to join the revolution—or thwart it. Marga's mind raced to devise a plan before Robinôt realized the *Avodendron* was already gone.

"I told Will you'd be trouble," the lieutenant was saying. "That you'd get in the way of our plans, that you were using him to get an heir. He seemed to think your fortune was worth it. Did you shed one tear for him at that service?"

He was trying to rattle her; she would not rise to such obvious bait.

"As soon as I learned Giles Foudria had been your lover, I knew you'd try to save him. Softhearted women always sympathize with the wrong people."

"You don't know me," said Marga.

"I don't have to know you," said Robinôt. "It's enough to know your kind."

He wrenched her arm again to remind her who was in charge. His clanking comrades closed in on either side.

The harbor now opened before them, deserted and poorly lit by intermittent lanterns. Marga scanned the line of ships for the

Avodendron's figurehead—a mythical eggplant tree—and breathed easier. Uncle Claado had made it out before the tide changed. And the plaion? It bobbed in the middle of the open harbor, well away from the docks.

She had her uncle to thank for that overabundance of caution, she felt sure.

"You've sent your ship away," mused Robinôt, noticing its absence as quickly as she had. "That looks like an admission of guilt to me."

As they approached the gap where the *Avodendron* had been moored, Marga watched the plaion. Tess and Jacomo had spotted her. They were gesturing frantically, clearly urging Argol to act. Argol, still as a heron, had eyes on the countess, awaiting instruction.

Most Porphyrian nautical hand signs had a one-handed variant, in case of emergency, but Marga had never been good with her left. She managed, *Circle past.*

Understood, Argol signed back.

Good. Timing would be everything, though.

"Will insisted you were intelligent," Robinôt was saying, "but did you overlook that half our navy is here? The *Avodendron* will be pursued and captured. You'd have done better to send Foudria away in your dinghy and let me search your empty ship—"

Marga took a graceful step forward, simultaneously twirling clockwise, as if she and Robinôt were dancing a bourrée right there on the docks. With a snapping twist toward his thumb, she yanked herself free of his astonished grasp and drew Will's rapier from her scabbard.

For a moment, the only sound was the lapping waves. Robinôt grinned.

"She drew a weapon on *me*," he said to his two companions. "We all saw that."

Robinôt hefted his poleaxe in both hands and stepped left; the glaivier stepped right to flank her. Marga did not like her odds against either of those weapons, let alone both together, but the crossbow worried her most. The bowman had stepped aside and begun turning the cranequin; its ratchet ticked like a clock.

Once it was cocked, he'd aim it at her heart. If the plaion wasn't near enough by then, she'd be forced to drop her weapon and it would all be over.

She glanced back. The plaion had just begun to move.

The cranequin clanked.

"It would be a pity if you died resisting arrest," said Robinôt.

"You won't kill me," said Marga. "You've too much sense for that."

"Oh, it would be an accident—just as Will's death was an accident." His eyes glittered. "Who gave that quigutl its orders? Perhaps this conspiracy goes deeper than we know."

She almost laughed—the accusation was so ridiculous—but the animosity in his eyes seemed real. What had she ever done to him?

William wouldn't have stayed friends with a man who hated her that much, surely? Grief or strategy was making him say cruel things.

Marga backed toward the edge of the pier. She kept her sword pointed at Robinôt, but her eye was on the glaivier. He carried a seven-foot pole with a cleaver at the end; she'd be lucky to parry a blow from that thing with this slender rapier, let alone touch the brute wielding it.

Robinôt, on the other hand, had a slightly shorter pole arm and wasn't wearing gloves.

The cranequin stopped; Marga felt her heart stop with it.

The crossbowman raised his weapon and fired. Marga felt a breeze as the bolt whipped past her cheek. She thought he'd missed, until she heard a thunk and a cry of dismay. She glanced back and saw the bolt embedded in the plaion. Tess and Jacomo were taking up oars, while Argol tried to tack farther from shore. They would not be circling past after all.

They were right to back off—it was their only move—but that left Marga . . .

Robinôt and the brutish glaivier swung at her in quick succession—

one, two. The glaive sliced her skirts, just missing her leg; the point of the poleaxe popped a single pearl off her bodice. It was as she'd suspected: Robinôt talked big, but he wasn't trying to kill her—not yet, anyway. He was letting her know that he could, if he really meant to, and it would be no accident. That kind of finesse took exquisite steel-sense, as Master Tacques used to call it.

Marga could not afford to feel terrified, but she let herself feel momentarily impressed.

And then she braced herself for what had to come next.

"I am going to give you the benefit of the doubt," she said, speaking slowly and calmly, as to a cornered animal. She took another step back. "You are plainly distraught over William, as well as massively paranoid—"

"It's my job to be paranoid," said Robinôt, stepping after her. She didn't dare take her eyes off him to see what his glaivier was doing.

The cranequin begin to clank again.

"—but you dishonor his memory, accusing me," Marga continued. "I am going to leave this island and pretend none of this ever happened." She felt behind her with one foot. She was at the edge; there were no steps left to take. "Don't follow me. Find something constructive to do with your life, Lieutenant. That's what Lord Morney would have wanted for his friend."

Robinôt struck, a hooking move intended to disarm her. Marga whisked her blade away before the blow could land, and then spiraled in to sting his uppermost ungloved hand. The tip of her sword pierced the triangle of flesh between his thumb and forefinger.

She could have taken his thumb off, but she had to pull back and parry the blow she knew must be coming from the glaive. There was no time to look; she prayed he hadn't swung for her knees.

She glanced the blow away, but Will's rapier shattered in her hand.

There was no time to mourn its loss. She flung the hilt at Robinôt's head and launched herself off the edge of the pier. She heard the crossbow go off as she jumped, heard her comrades in the plaion shouting, and then heard nothing as cold water closed over her head.

Her dress turned to lead almost at once, pulling her under, wet silk binding her legs together. Marga struggled against the clinging feeling, kicked and thrashed and—

For months afterward, she wouldn't touch a sword. Father Erique had half convinced her that Albaro's lockjaw had been Heaven's punishment, even though she'd never once persuaded the dear, sweet lad to spar with her. It was her friend Giles, upon her return to the Academy, who finally convinced her to practice with him, enter a tournament, try again.

"I'm not so arrogant as to say it wasn't a sign," he said, leaning against a low wall by the practice yards, pulling on his ratty gloves, "but maybe you read it backward. Maybe the message was that life is short, for poets as well as swordswomen. That the people and things we love will disappear, so we'd better just love them now, as fiercely as we can"—

Her silk-tangled legs were a mermaid's tail. She kicked them together in one strong motion and finally broke the surface, close enough that Argol could throw her the towrope. Marga grasped it tightly with her left hand. Her sword hand wouldn't close quite right; that last parry must have wrenched her wrist. It was beginning to swell.

Marga looked toward shore while Tess and Jacomo hauled her in. Her hat and her best hair bobbed on the waves like two sleeping pelicans. The crossbowman took another shot—it struck the water alarmingly close—and then resumed cranking; the glaivier was wrapping Robinôt's hand in a length of linen.

The towrope jerked; the sails had finally caught the wind. She'd be out of range before the crossbowman got another shot off. Marga grinned at this, but only for a moment. A glow in the sky behind them arrested her eye and made her breath catch in her chest.

Something up the hill was on fire, something large—the Governor's Hall or maybe the Limpets. Robinôt looked up, too; maybe the smoke had reached him, or cries she was too far off to hear. He called a halt on the crossbow cranking, and the three men rushed off.

She hoped it had merely been grief talking, but if Robinôt harbored half as much resentment as he'd seemed to, she should not assume he was giving up on her for good.

Jacomo and Tess hauled the countess aboard with difficulty. Her right wrist was well and truly sprained (she hoped not broken), and her legs were tightly cocooned in wet silk. Finally her skirt tore (cursed seawater) and she got one knee up. She flopped into the bottom of the boat like a seal, and the stress of the last two days—finding Foudria, enduring the funeral, fighting Robinôt—rolled off her as waves of laughter.

Tess's eyes bugged at the ruined gown. "I've been an embroiderer," she said. "Do you have any idea how many hours of work you've destroyed?"

Marga did not, but it only made her laugh harder. And she knew this was the wrong response to everything that had happened and was happening—the town really was on fire, she could see clearly now, which was far grimmer than the death of her dress—but she couldn't stop. She laughed until she choked and gasped for air, and she couldn't stop because there was a terrible, bottomless sorrow that had been trying to eat her all day, and even the laughter wasn't going to stave it off, because maybe she was actually crying and would cry forever because—

The last day Albaro was able to speak, before the rictus grin became permanent and the dragon physician stupefied him with opium, he tried to explain. "Do you remember the sunset at our wedding? The color of the clouds? It blooms that color."

"You should've worn gloves," she said, hating to scold him when he was suffering, but unable to stop herself. "Or made the gardener plant the damned thing."

"It was supposed to be—" A spasm cut him off. He grimaced, sweating,

until it passed. "A surprise. The breeder . . . named it after you. 'Centifolia Margabella.'"

Tears rolled down her face, unheeded. "It's exceptionally thorny, Albaro. I'm inclined to take that personally."

He laughed, but the laugh turned into a screa—

"Countess?" Someone was patting her cheek lightly. "Are you still with us?"

She was at the bottom of the plaion, in the bilge. Tess was in front of her, struggling with the tangled laces of her ruined bodice, fighting the shriveled silk to get her some air. Jacomo was behind, propping her up, holding her hand; Marga let her head fall back against his shoulder.

"She hasn't slept." Argol's voice wafted from the stern. "Not since yesterday."

"Are you hurt?" Jacomo's sparkled in her ear. "We couldn't see what was happening."

Tess wrapped the unstrung laces around her knuckles, like a pugilist. "We're finally away. On to the next place. I hope we can leave him . . . leave this grief behind us."

Marga let out a little sob-hiccup, a scoff. She had tried for years to leave him behind. Every time he'd come back to her, she'd quieted her mind with sword drills. It had worked, and yet it cut both ways—he was never really gone.

And then she was crying again, because she suddenly realized Tess had meant William, and she'd been thinking about Albaro. She'd been thinking about Albaro during most of the funeral, and then she'd been fighting Robinôt. She'd hardly begun to mourn her fiancé.

Poor William. It all had happened so fast—romance, betrothal, death—and nothing she'd done or felt was pure. She'd loved him, in her broken way, but Robinôt wasn't wrong: she needed an heir. She couldn't quite believe William was gone. Some part of her was half convinced they'd catch up to him in St. Remy or . . .

She lay, laces undone, heart exposed to the starry sky, and the truth tumbled out. "What if . . . what if I didn't love him as well as he deserved?"

"You did," said Tess with unexpected vehemence. "I'm certain you loved him more than he deserved."

She was overstating it, probably, but Marga appreciated the effort. That kind of stouthearted loyalty was everything one could wish for in a protégé, even if she was a terrible dresser. Jacomo, at Marga's back, was soft and warm. The boat bobbed upon the waters, rocking the sorrowful countess firmly, finally to sleep.

Nineteen

Tess's whole face felt chapped and she could practically hear the salt gritting between her teeth by the time the plaion caught up with the *Avodendron* the next day.

The countess had wanted her uncle to "engage maneuver fourteen," whatever that meant, but he'd moved the ship before Tess and Jacomo had even reached the harbor. "We're well past fourteen," Argol had said when they asked her. "And there's a navy to evade. This is forty-two."

Meaning, apparently, that the *Avodendron* was well under way and the plaion was going to have to catch up as best it could.

The rendezvous point was east-southeast, a pip of an island called Sora Regina, chosen not for its isolation but the opposite—there were a dozen islands around it to hide a ship behind. Once the plaion was in position, Argol drew a flimsy yellow sail out of the plaion's kit, and Marga helped affix it to a folding frame. It caught the wind and rose into the air, tethered by the thinnest of lines—a signal kite, Argol called it—and soon it had done its job. The *Avodendron* rounded the horn of a neighboring island, her prow cleaving the waves. Tess had never seen anything so majestic. The cheering from both vessels outroared the ocean.

Whatever scolding Marga had anticipated didn't materialize. Her uncle silently wrapped her in his arms and held her. Tess smiled wistfully at this, then went below for a nap.

She slept so soundly that when she woke—in an unfamiliar cabin, after sunset—she had no idea where she was or what day it was. A single lamp illuminated Jacomo, hunched over the writing desk, scribbling away. The room smelled enticingly of lentils.

"I saved dinner for you," said Jacomo, glancing back when she stirred. He turned over whatever he'd been working on (bad poetry, Tess was forced to conclude) and handed her a bowl of stew. "When you're done, go talk to the countess. She's got a task for you."

"Is it learning to distinguish kinds of seaweed?" asked Tess. "Because I—"

"I suspect it's to do with our prisoner," said Jacomo, lowering his voice.

Tess, who'd taken a mouthful of lentils, swallowed with difficulty. "Is he still being held prisoner? I figured she'd untie him, at least, once we cleared St. Claresse. *Paishesh*, I mean."

Jacomo grinned at that and nodded.

It would be hard for Fozu to draw a map with his hands bound, though. He'd already refused once within Tess's hearing. What would happen if Marga couldn't change his mind?

"He wasn't untied at the meeting," said Jacomo. He had a brassy Saint medallion that he was worrying between his fingers.

Tess had apparently slept through something important. "Meeting about what?"

"Our next heading," said Jacomo. "The countess drew a weapon on Lieutenant Robinôt, if you recall. She anticipates that he will send out a warrant for our search and seizure, and that limits where we can go to have the submersible repaired."

Tess had nearly forgotten the contraption's broken window, with all that had happened since. "We can't let that thing go?" she asked, picking at a chunk of carrot in her stew.

"The captain asked the same question," said Jacomo, absently tapping his medallion on the desk. "The answer was no. It's Lord Morney's legacy, and the countess seems to think that once we make it to the pole—with or without Fozu's help—we'll need it to locate the serpent in the murky depths. We're going to St. Remy and we're getting it fixed."

Tess had seen the maps—and she hadn't forgotten the decorated human scapula among Marga's collection of artifacts. "St. Remy isn't exactly forward toward the pole."

"It is not, and also Captain Claado detests the island's governor, Lady Borgo—these arguments were made," said Jacomo. "Fozu argued for someplace with three different names—so of course the only one that stuck with me is Little Bitch Island. That was another no; apparently the rest of the Ninysh fleet is docked there. My vote tipped the balance toward St. Remy, on your behalf."

"On *my* behalf?" cried Tess.

"Because if the countess insists upon both repairing the submersible and evading that warrant, the only other viable alternative, besides St. Remy, is to go home and have it fixed there." Jacomo paused, flipped his medallion, and tucked it into his pocket. "I figured the person who'd made a promise to a quigutl wasn't ready to give up on that and turn back yet."

He'd figured right. Tess's heart had flipped during that pause, along with his medallion.

"To say nothing of your mission from the Queen," he added.

"Good point," said Tess, feeling mildly guilty.

"And your general disinclination to be anywhere near your family."

"You can stop now," said Tess.

She lingered over her lentils, not entirely anxious to finish eating and go confront the countess about leaving Fozu tied up. A soup bowl is only so deep, alas, and after Tess had scraped it with her spoon and licked as much of it as her tongue would reach, she had no choice but to return her bowl to the mess and climb, lead-footed, to the weather deck.

All the lanterns were lit for the countess, who was practicing swords on the poop deck. Tess hauled herself up; Marga spotted her and smiled but did not stop until her drill was finished. Darienne handed her a brimming cup of water.

"You found a replacement sword," Tess noted, while the countess sipped.

"I brought five of my own," said Marga, wiping her brow with a proffered towel. "It was William's that broke—the only thing I'd kept to remember him by. I'd already donated his clothes to the poor on St. Claresse."

Tess bit back a comment (*You didn't think to keep a single shirt?*), realizing she knew something the countess didn't. "There's a trunk full of his things in our—er, his old cabin."

"What things?" asked Marga, brightening.

Journals, Tess almost said, but she suddenly wondered how far back those records went. Had he kept a journal at St. Bert's? Was her false name, Therese Belgioso, in there somewhere? He'd all but called her that on Paishesh; Marga would surely remember. Tess had made it this far without having to admit that she'd known Will previously. It would be unfathomably awkward if Marga found out now.

"It looked like junk, honestly. I don't know that any of it is worth saving," said Tess. "But Jacomo said you had a task for me?"

"Yes," said Marga, pulling off her gloves. "There are three species of terns on St. Remy, distinguishable only by the color of their eggs, and—" Here she burst out laughing. "Oh dear, you should see your face. That's not the task, forgive me. I learned my lesson after that starfish-gathering errand, when you tried to end it all by walking across a firing range."

"That's not exactly what happened," said Tess.

Marga leaned back against the gunwale. "I've spoken with Father Jacomo about that day, trying to understand why you failed to inform me that you'd stumbled across Giles."

So she had been paying attention to what Fozu said, even if she'd let it pass in the moment. Tess sighed. "He called himself Fozu. I had no idea he was your navigator."

"I'm not blaming you," said Marga. "But here's what I'm thinking: Father Jacomo says you have a particular interest in the Pelaguese. I've observed it myself. I can already tell I'm going to have a devil of a time getting a map out of Giles—"

"Fozu," said Tess.

The countess frowned slightly. "He'll hardly talk to me, except to scold me, but maybe he'll be more open with you. You might persuade him to help us and learn some things about the Pelaguese at the same time."

It was time to speak up. Tess felt her pulse quicken. "I will if you give him his liberty."

Marga's face fell. "I can't, not until he's himself again—*Giles Foudria,* not this desperate Fozu. Not the madman who demanded to be left on an iceberg. I need assurances that he's not going to have a knife to my throat—or yours—demanding we go to St. Fionnani."

"Little Bitch Island?" Tess guessed.

"*St. Fionnani,*" said Marga sternly. She was accepting no alternative names for anyone or anything, it seemed. "Going there would end this voyage. Even if Giles escaped the navy as miraculously as he escaped that iceberg, we certainly would not."

Marga turned toward the railing, folding her arms upon it. Tess leaned beside her; the *Avodendron*'s wake glittered in the moonlight.

"Believe it or not," said Marga at last, "I'm trying to help him. He was my friend through some terrible times. I'm certain he's going through something now, if only I knew what it was." She lowered her voice: "Find out what has led to his sudden embrace of this . . . *Shesh* side of himself, and how we might bring him back from this crisis."

"What if it's not a crisis?" asked Tess. "What if this is who he really is?"

"I don't accept that," said the countess.

Tess pursed her lips, smarting as if she'd been swatted. It must be nice to be a countess, seeing only the clear, pure essence you want to see, and never the messy, complicated slob in front of you. Tess was suddenly glad she had never told Marga what Will had done. Imagine pouring your heart out, revealing the excruciating truth, only to be told, *I don't accept that.*

"Is he allowed to come out and enjoy the sunshine, at least?" asked Tess.

"Provisionally, with Argol's supervision," said Marga.

"And may I let him see the sabak?" Tess pressed.

"Absolutely not. We have little enough leverage over him. He can see it when he draws us a map." Marga's jaw was set, her eyes iron, but then something seemed to make her waver. "I suppose withholding his freedom is also leverage. I might consider untying him if he's open with you about what he's going through. I am not an unreasonable person."

It was not a promise, but Tess gleaned that it was as close as she was going to get.

She took Fozu breakfast in the morning. Glodus, the pockmarked sailor, was on shift guarding the room. He unlatched the door, muttering, "Watch your fingers. He bit the barber."

Tess appreciated the warning—not about the biting, but about Fozu's having seen the barber. He was almost unrecognizable. His hair had been slashed to stubble, his mustache uprooted; of the wild thicket that had been his beard, only a small, cultivated garden remained.

She had no right to feel a pang for his hair, but couldn't they have simply combed out the braids and removed the beads? Ninysh men often wore a queue. Her dear Josquin, in Segosh—

Ah, but that was it. Fozu looked quite a bit like Josquin with just a chin beard.

How long had it been since she'd thought of Josquin? It was a pity to lump him in with all the things back home she resolutely wasn't thinking about, but lumped he had been.

"You look like you've seen a ghost," said Fozu. He was seated on the sea lockers, watching her from under heavy lids.

Tess shook her head carefully, as if it were fragile. "No more than usual," she said.

Unexpectedly, that made him smile.

"I'm not supposed to untie you," Tess began—intending to explain that she was willing to untie him anyway so he could eat, as long as he promised not to escape and to let her retie him afterward. Fozu, however, curled and contorted himself until he'd threaded his body back through the circle of his arms. Now his hands were in front of him.

"Don't tell Marga I can do that," he said, winking. "I'll put myself back when I'm done."

Tess watched him eat; he managed the spoon surprisingly well. "I'm supposed to make you tell us how to get to the pole," she said after a while.

"I figured," said Fozu, crunching a piece of bikeki. "You seem like a clever girl. I'm sure you remember what I told you on Paji-Jovesh."

Paji-Jovesh, the "clever girl" concluded, must be St. Vittorius. "You said the serpent is forbidden. The islands are forbidden."

"Correct," said Fozu with his mouth full. "But your countess, like any entitled lout pinching the barmaid's bottom in a tavern, has difficulty taking no for an answer."

If he was trying to horrify Tess, he could not have chosen his words any better.

She couldn't take no for an answer, either; she had a promise to keep.

"You've been on the receiving end of such a pinch, I glean," said Fozu, appraising her with a shrewd eye. "Never dreamed you might someday be doing the pinching, did you?"

She sat beside him on the sea lockers; there was nowhere else in the tiny room to sit. "Can there be no extenuating circumstances?" she said. "I promised Pathka, the quigutl who helped us find you, that I would get him to the Polar Serpent. . . ."

"Then you naively made a promise you can't keep," said Fozu.

"I . . . maybe. But please listen," said Tess, and she told him everything: how she and Pathka had searched for Anathuthia; how it had been like a pilgrimage for Pathka; how quigutl joined their dreams with the serpents'; and how Pathka's mind had been entangled with Anathuthia's when she died. "He almost died with her, and he has not been the same since," she said. "The strangeness is overtaking him more and more. I don't know how else to help him but to get him to Kapatlutlo."

The quigutl name for the serpent seemed to give Fozu pause. "A name is a claim," he said at last. "Here's the thing, though: I can tell you to stay away, but I can't give you permission to approach. Only a Ggdani can judge your worthiness."

"The Ggdani live at the pole?" asked Tess, trying to remember what Fozu had said when she first met him.

"They do, and they're judgy, all of them." Fozu got a strange look. "I know one, in fact. I'm supposed to meet him on Edushuke—or Little Bitch Island, if you prefer—and—"

"*Edushuke*," interjected Tess, repeating it so she would remember. A name was a claim.

Fozu's face cracked into a grin. "Brava," he said. "Anyway, I need to get there, and soon. You'll have a chance to impress a real, live Ggdani if you can help me."

Tess's heart sank. "We can't sail that way. The countess—"

"Wants to see her horrible friend, Lady Borgo, in St. Remy. She explained it. I couldn't not ask," said Fozu, his smile turning sad. "There is one other thing you could do for me, though. Check in on the sabak and make sure my instructions are followed. Her water must be changed daily so she stays cool—*cold* may be too much to ask at these latitudes. A bucket of fish, thrice daily. If the water's cloudy, or her gills start turning green, you must tell me at once. Obviously, don't touch her without permission unless you want the very devil of a headache."

"Or to be eaten," said Tess, gathering his empty dishes.

"Lord Morney wasn't eaten," said Fozu, sticking his feet one at a time through the loop of his arms. He stood awkwardly and then shimmied upright until his hands were behind him again. "You'll never believe me, since you saw it with your own eyes, but you misunderstood what you saw. The sabak tore him up and spit him back out. The fish ate him, if anyone did."

"Why did they kill him?" asked Tess. "Because he touched without asking?"

"Because they saw the contents of his heart and found him wanting."

They'd been right. At least someone had seen Will clearly.

"I told you"—Fozu cut across her thoughts—"they're judgy at the pole."

Judgy they may be, Tess considered as she took his dishes back to the galley, but Fozu had given her hope. Not that she might impress his Ggdani contact on Edushuke—that seemed a lost cause—but that there was a way to persuade the ones at the pole who guarded the serpent.

Worthy was a goal to aspire to. If there was a way to make herself so, she would find it.

Taking care of the sabak seemed like a good place to start. Tess went up to the weather deck to have a look at her. The ship's carpenter had cleverly converted a large wooden bin, originally for sail storage, into a tar-sealed tank. The bin had had a scupper drain already, or else it would have filled up with water anytime it rained; he'd only needed to add a sluice gate and a grating, so the creature couldn't escape while her water was being changed. The box's wooden lid had been replaced with another grating, a hinged metal lattice fastened with a padlock.

When Tess arrived, they were refilling the tank, which involved hauling buckets of water directly out of the ocean. Even with a block and tackle, it was backbreaking, repetitive work. Three sailors hauled the line, and two more coordinated pouring through the grate, singing all the while in Porphyrian.

Tess approached cautiously, worried about getting in the way, and saw that Karus was there as well, feeding the sabak by sticking individual herrings through gaps in the lid.

The sabak wasn't the only creature he was feeding; when Tess reached the grating, she saw that Pathka was in the tank as well, cheerfully accepting fish from Karus's fingers.

"Hello, Teth!" Pathka cried, wagging his head spines.

"So this is where you've been hiding," she said, shading her eyes to see better into the shadowed tank.

"Not hiding," said Pathka. "It's not our fault you never visit."

"Stand back," said Karus, stepping between Tess and the splash of another bucket being poured into the tank. "That's enough, lads," he called. "It's full."

The sailors dispersed to their next task, whatever that was; there was always more work to do aboard a ship, it seemed. Tess glanced around. The sabak tank was tucked out of the way, between the forecastle and the plaion. She could almost have brought Fozu up here to see her without anyone noticing.

Except for any sailor who happened to be up the mainmast. They'd have a clear view, and there was almost always someone up there.

Tess turned back to the tank and pressed her nose against the grating. The inside was black with tar, making the white sabak stand out vividly. Tess got a good look at her pale, smooth skin and fathomless jet eyes. A ruff of branching, delicate gills extended to either side of her head like pink antlers; Tess had heard of amphibians with similar structures, although she couldn't name one. The countess probably had pictures of them in her books. Amphibians didn't have teeth like that, though, or retractable claws at the tips of their fat, sticky fingers.

The sabak's gills weren't the least bit green, and Tess knew the water was fresh. There was something odd in a corner of the tank, however—a mass of translucent fibers, like an underwater cobweb.

"What's that?" Tess asked Pathka, pointing at it.

"A nest," Pathka replied. "Made of sabak spittle. It's a most re-markable material—she told me that they use it to make paths so the Katakutia can walk on stilts from island to island."

"She told you?" said Tess. "You've learned her chirp-language that quickly?"

"Not on my own," said Pathka modestly. "She wanted me to know, so she touched me and the knowledge went directly into my brain." He cocked his head to one side. "But you know what that's like. I saw pieces of you in there."

That revelation made Tess feel squirmy, and she decided she'd checked in on the sabak enough for one day.

It seemed inhumane to leave Fozu belowdecks for the entire fortnight it would take to reach St. Remy, so Tess, who had permission, brought him up that afternoon and gave him a turn about the weather deck, even though it was drizzling and breezy. Glodus unsubtly shadowed them and then deliberately blocked the path to the sabak tank. Those were his orders, it seemed. Tess led Fozu up to the forecastle, where he could at least look down at the locked tank and see the faint blue glow under the water.

The next day was sunny. Fozu kept vigil on the forecastle and didn't seem to care that his nose was turning red. After a time, Tess heard the countess down in the waist of the ship, speaking with Jacomo and Darvo the bosun.

"Let's walk past her and say hello. You could smile," she told Fozu. "Impress upon her that she can trust you enough to untie your wrists."

"So . . . *don't* try to take Darvo hostage and demand to be left on an iceberg again?" said Fozu. "This impress-the-countess scheme of yours is unworkably complicated."

Tess marveled that he could keep a sense of humor with his wrists bound.

As they approached, it became clear that something was wrong. Jacomo was holding one of Marga's natural history books—or rather, holding its almost-empty cover. Its pages were a charred, crumbling mess; the wind snatched up fragments and blew them over the port railing. Marga was irate: "It was irreplaceable. Hand-painted illustrations. And you found it where?"

"In the head," said Jacomo.

"So someone stole my book, read it on the toilet, and then set it on fire?"

"We've been finding fires everywhere, Your Grace," said Darvo. "Small ones."

He glared directly at Tess.

"It can't be Pathka," she objected. "He's locked in the tank with the sabak."

"They unlock the cage occasionally. How d'you think he got in there?"

Fozu cut in: "It's the ghost. My father's ghost. It followed me aboard."

Marga looked incredulous, but then she sighed and dismissed the bosun, saying, "Keep me apprised, Mr. Darvo. Keep watch on the powder kegs at all times, and I shall start locking my cabin. We'll flush out this 'ghost,' have no doubt."

The bosun plodded off. Marga turned to Fozu, not quite smiling. "If you weren't tied up, Giles, I'd suspect it was you who burned my mollusc book. Please take the remains away, Father Jacomo. Maybe say a few words over them as you throw them overboard."

Jacomo carried the ruined husk of a book aft toward the poop deck. Marga stepped up to the port railing and leaned her hands against it.

Tess thought they'd been dismissed, and tried to lead Fozu back to his cabin, but he seemed determined to approach the countess.

"I suppose this means you're keeping me tied up for the foreseeable future," he said.

Marga looked back at him and wrinkled her nose; she had a slight sprinkling of freckles, only really visible outdoors on a sunny day. "In fact, I've been considering whether you might like to take some exercise with me, doing sword drills." He opened his mouth; she raised a hand to cut him off. "With a wooden sword. I'm not a fool. But it was you who encouraged me to take up fencing again after Albaro died. I've told you before, I'm convinced that saved my life. It brought me back—*you* brought me back."

Fozu placed his bound hands on the railing beside Marga's. Tess suddenly realized he hadn't returned them to their original position behind his back after lunch; she hoped the countess didn't think about it too hard.

"Remember that tournament at St. Fustian's, when I beat Milo, Jan, and Alpheus the Unbeatable?" said Fozu. "Just for the privilege of losing to you. It was the first time you'd smiled since your husband died."

"I smiled to see my old Academy friend out of his depth. Those were good times." She laid her hand over his pale hands. "Whatever you're going through now, Giles—whatever gnaws at your heart—let me help you come back to yourself. I know the real you. 'Swords are more honest than words,' Master Tacques used to say. 'Show me a man's riposte, and I will show you his soul.'"

"You know that's poetic nonsense," said Fozu, gently extricating himself. "I faced your Lord Morney in Paishesh. If his swordsmanship matched his soul, then you're well rid of him."

There was a pause, during which Tess thought her heart might be the loudest thing on the ship. Fozu had some nerve. She wasn't sure if she was afraid for him or of him.

Marga's eyes flashed like a blade. "What did you learn? That he was direct and honest, unafraid to risk everything and seize his moment?"

"I suppose that's one interpretation," said Fozu. "I found him an unimaginative brute. He had two moves—overpower and intimidate—no subtlety at all."

"No deceit, you mean," snapped Marga.

"Fozu, we should get you back to your room," said Tess, trying to take his arm.

"Glodus will take him. Glodus!" called the countess, and then the pockmarked sailor was leading Fozu away and Tess had the distinct impression that she was the one in trouble.

"Has he agreed to draw that map yet?" said Marga, looking out at the cliffs and firs of the island they were passing, rather than at Tess.

"Not yet," said Tess.

"It's been two days. You have a job to do," said Marga. "Maybe do it, instead of borrowing my books without asking."

"You said I should borrow your books—and that wasn't me!" cried Tess, realizing too late which book the countess was referring to. "I am not even a little bit interested in molluscs."

Alas, her words seemed to bounce off the countess's retreating back.

Tess went straight to the records room, already lecturing Fozu in her mind: *Antagonizing the countess—though amusing—won't help you, and she has the power to make everyone's life miserable, so if you want me on your side, and I think you do . . .*

She entered quietly and closed the door behind her. Fozu was hunched over, his back to her, speaking in a low voice. He held a small, woolly cocoon cupped in his hands.

It looked like one of the earrings Lord Hamish wore, or like the sabak-spittle nest. It was glowing a pale blue.

"Hami, answer me," Fozu was saying. "I've found transportation, but not to Edushuke."

Was the cocoon . . . some sort of device? Like a thnik?

And whom was he talking to? Was Hami short for Hamish?

Lord Hamish would want to see them all hanged for illegally taking a sabak on board.

As if he felt her staring, Fozu looked over his shoulder. He went pale and guilty-looking.

Tess snatched at the cocoon device. Fozu ducked and rolled, trying to keep it out of her reach, but he was hindered by his bound hands and the closeness of the room. Tess got a hand on the thing, which was not as soft as it looked, and they played tug-of-war until its fibers tore and its light went out.

Tess had the device, ripped nearly in half. Fozu looked shocked.

"You broke it," he cried. "I hope you're happy."

Tess shoved it into her pocket, ashamed to have wrecked it. "Were you calling Lord Hamish? Are you trying to get yourself hanged?"

Fozu settled sulkily back on the sea lockers. "Lord Hamish is the Ggdani I was supposed to meet in Edushuke. I've been trying to tell him to meet us at Femefu-syu-la-Nutufi—St. Remy—instead, but he's not answering. It's inexplicable. He's an uptight, conscientious little bastard, usually. Of course, now you've broken my eyu, so that's the end of that."

It was a lot to take in at once. "You *want* to meet him?" asked Tess. "Isn't he out to punish you for keeping sabak?"

"Oh, he is, but not the way you think." Fozu shifted in his seat. "I asked *him* to bring me a sabak, in fact, but he wouldn't do it. We Shesh are still in exile, and a Ggdani would rather die than break a law, even if it's not their own law and there are extenuating circumstances."

"But what's it for?" asked Tess. "Why do you need a sabak so badly?"

"I have responsibilities," said Fozu. He stared at his hands, bound in front of him now; a shadow seemed to cross his face. "I killed my father—not with my own two hands, not deliberately, but as surely as if I'd tied the noose myself."

All of a sudden there was a ghost in the room. Tess wasn't sure how she knew, but she knew. She had ghosts of her own. She could barely breathe.

"Long ago," said Fozu, his eyes two wells of shadow, "the Wandering City of Bjoveh was exiled for making war on her sisters. She was stripped of her legs; her people were scattered to the ends of the world. For ten generations, they were forbidden to keep or touch sabak, who remember histories and lineages all the way back to the birth of the world. The Worldmind lost sight of Bjoveh, and so their history ended—a most grievous punishment.

"And yet their history didn't really end. The people—now called Jovesh—designated one to be the Keeper of their history and another to be the Speaker, preserving the sabak speech until they could give their stories to the Worldmind again. When some of the Jovesh intermarried with strangers and became the Shesh, the custom of Keeper and Speaker came with them.

"My mother, Mardiza, was our Speaker. She taught me what she could, but after she was hanged, I ran away from home and tried to forget I'd ever heard of Paishesh. I did not set foot there again until the summer I sailed with Marga to the Sea of Holes."

He paused to let Tess absorb all this, or to listen for the ghost stirring.

"I saw my father in Paishesh. He'd remarried but had no other children. He was glad to see me, and gladder still that I remembered most of the Generation Songs he'd taught me." Fozu stared at the ceiling, eyes glittering. "He was our Keeper. I was born to bear both burdens.

"Of course, he had thought he'd never see me again, so he'd been trying to teach some of the children, holding classes in cellars around town. The Ninysh claimed he was 'rabble-rousing.' Boqueton was ready to make an example of him. My stepmother begged me to take him away. She'd equipped a small boat, thought we could find a Wandering City and cast him on their mercy as a refugee. The songs prove kinship, many generations back.

"I argued against it. We were exiled, all of us, for three more generations; they wouldn't make an exception for him. And besides, how do you find a Wandering City? We might sail a year and not catch one. He was frail. He wouldn't last a year in a small craft on the open water.

"Finally," said Fozu, "I told her, 'Look, I can't. I'm the navigator for an expedition. People are relying on me. Maybe next year, on our way home?'"

Tess felt what was coming, the horrible logic of it.

"And so, of course, our expedition came across a Wandering City." There were tears in his eyes. "They usually avoid the Sea of Holes. I know five hundred stories, and none of them take place there. It was a sign: I'd been an arrogant fool. I could have brought my father with me on that voyage, saved his life without reneging on my obligations.

"That's why I asked to be left on an iceberg: it was the harshest penance my Bjoveh ancestors ever undertook. He was dead already, thanks to me, and I had a lot to answer for."

Tess swayed slightly on her feet. "Was he dead, though? You couldn't know for sure."

"I knew," he said, his voice suddenly harsh. "He was hanged that very same day."

He paused to regain his composure.

"There are things I want to do for my people—dangerous things that need to be done—but I can't risk myself, because I'm the only one who carries the Generation Songs. And when I've risked other people—you've heard of the Shesh Eight?—it's ended badly."

"Is that why you needed a sabak?" Tess asked. "So you could set down the burden of the Generation Songs? But aren't there still three generations to go?"

"By the letter of the law, yes," said Fozu. "But sabak, as manifestations of the Worldmind, are beyond mere human law. I'm hoping she might hear my plea, if I can figure out how to word it correctly, and take mercy on my people. She is an autonomous being and can choose to do that, whatever the Ggdani or the Wandering Cities might think about it."

✕

Fozu's story stuck with Tess for the next several days. She thought about it during mealtimes and while lying awake listening to Jacomo snore. She mulled it over while tying knots for Karus (bungling them horribly) and while taking a turn at the bilge pumps (a large water barrel having mysteriously ruptured down in the hold). And no matter how long she thought about it, the conclusion was always the same: she had to help him see the sabak.

And she didn't see how she could possibly do that.

A week out, near sunset, old Karus got tangled in a line and yanked right off his feet. Tess had been nearby when it happened. He'd muttered, "That's not right," and shuffled over to look at one of the cleats that the lines fastened to. It was wobbling. The moment he touched it, it broke loose, the line whipped around, and Karus went flying up into the air. He dangled from the mainsail spar for ten minutes, screaming, before they managed to cut him down. Once he was down, his daughter Argol (who had been in the captain's cabin, studying, when Karus went up) wouldn't let anyone touch him; she single-handedly carried him below, still screaming, to the ship's surgeon.

Everyone went back to their duties, albeit somewhat subdued.

Then Argol burst back onto the deck, her brown eyes wet and rimmed in red, bellowing for the bosun. Tess's Porphyrian hadn't improved much, but the gist was clear: cleats don't just come loose spontaneously. Either the bosun was keeping a slovenly deck (which even Tess knew was not the case) or someone had set a trap for Argol's father. Either way, it was the bosun she was holding responsible until she knew whom else to blame.

Darvo the bosun shouted back, and others backed him up. Shouting turned into shoving. All over the ship, sailors began coming out of the woodwork, sometimes literally, drawn to a fight like flies to a carcass. Shoving turned into an all-out brawl, Unlucky against Lucky, and then there was a cry of "Man overboard!" followed by "Heave to!" and Captain Claado thundering out onto the deck.

Tess, who'd been watching everything with great round eyes, began to realize that it would never again be the case that everyone was looking seaward, away from the sabak tank, just as darkness was falling.

She sprinted below like her heels were on fire.

Twenty

Fozu didn't want to come at first. "I haven't worked out exactly what to say. I don't do the chirp-speak that well—"

"You can't just touch her and hope for the best?" asked Tess, peeking out of his room, up and down the corridor. It was deserted. Glodus apparently wasn't one to stay belowdecks during a fight, or for *Heave to* and *Man overboard*.

"No, I can't just touch her," griped Fozu, following Tess. "I'm an exile, not a barbarian. I have to do this right."

Tess took the quickest route she knew, up the corridor to a little-used hatch that came out behind the plaion. They crouch-walked to the corner where the tank hulked, and she untied Fozu's hands. He gave her a wide-eyed, almost frightened look.

"Don't make me regret this!" she said, trying to jolly him along.

Fozu, rubbing his wrists, looked like he barely remembered human speech, let alone how to talk to sabak.

"Pathka!" Tess stage-whispered, and the quigutl surfaced. "Can you translate this man's words for the sabak?"

"I could, but mind-to-mind would be easier," said Pathka. He dived again, roused the sabak from her nest, and then floated with her at the surface, hand in hand.

That was all the explanation Pathka was going to give, apparently.

"Speak Ninysh," Tess instructed Fozu, "and Pathka will convey what you're saying." *Somehow.*

Fozu was shaky and sweaty. He swallowed hard, throat knot bobbing, and said—faintly at first, but growing stronger—"Little Light, I am Speaker and Keeper for the seventh generation of the exiled city of Bjoveh, whose people became Jovesh and then Shesh. We accepted our punishment and faithfully carried our own stories against the day when we could return them to the Worldmind. But the Jovesh are gone, and the Shesh are under siege, and I do not know what will happen next or whether I will last. I want to give you our stories, so they will be safe. I know I have no right to ask out of season, but if I die, seven generations die with me."

The sabak glowed brighter. Pathka, in a stilted, trancelike voice, said words the sabak apparently put directly into his mind:

> *O child of Bjoveh, fallen into despair,*
> *Do not carry your nation's burden alone any longer.*
> *The Little Lights accept you on behalf of the One.*
> *We alone decide this, not human laws.*
> *We say it for all to hear, even the watcher in the shadows:*
> *Put your hands in the pool, O Bjoveh. We accept you.*

Fozu stared, stunned. Tess nudged him gently forward. He threaded his hands through the grating and placed them flat upon the surface of the water like two lily pads. The sabak touched his palms with the crown of her head, and Fozu closed his eyes like a man at prayer.

Tess wanted to remember him like this, giving his people's stories to the sabak, grunting with effort, his forehead beaded with sweat. Marga hadn't been wrong about him—the heart of him, that is, the gentleness she believed she'd glimpsed in his riposte, even if she insisted on calling it by the wrong name.

At some point, ever so faintly, his skin began to glow.

Tess sneaked peeks around the end of the plaion, trying to keep track of what was happening. The lost sailor—who turned out to be neither Argol nor the bosun, but some other Lucky unfortunate—was recovered, and then Captain Claado made everyone stand in two parallel lines while he paced up and down between them, loudly conveying his disappointment.

Tess spirited Fozu back to the records room before his guard returned. He flopped onto the sea chests, half weeping, with exhaustion or relief, Tess couldn't tell. She left him to it.

Sailors began descending to the lower decks, grumbling to each other in Porphyrian. Whatever lecture Claado had given them about letting old hatreds drop, it didn't seem to be working—unless, perhaps, they were all now united in their hatred of him.

Tess pressed through the crowd, heading back toward her cabin. She had witnessed a wonder and helped someone—really helped—and she was feeling . . . worthy. Surely what she'd done would qualify. What if they *could* get to Edushuke, somehow, to meet Lord . . . Hami? Fozu would put in a good word for her. It wouldn't have to be the whole expedition, just her and Fozu and Jacomo, if he wanted. Maybe Argol could sail them in the plaion and get some time away from the people who hated her (another worthy deed; Tess would be racking them up).

She opened her cabin door, and there was the one person who hadn't gone above to witness the altercation.

Jacomo leaped to his feet, looking guilty.

Tess quickly took in the scene: He was fully dressed, so *that* wasn't it. His thnik was on its chain around his neck, not in his hand; he hadn't been fending off embarrassing insinuations from his brother. He was standing in front of the open writing desk, trying to block it with his body, and his fingers were smudged with ink. In fact, there was rather a lot of ink dribbling off the corner of the desk and pooling on the floor behind him.

"You knocked over your inkpot," said Tess helpfully.

Jacomo yelped and turned to assess the damage. Whatever he'd been doing was ruined.

Tess brought him the basin of water and sponge, intended for personal ablutions, from the stand in the corner. "More bad poetry?" she said.

"I guess you'll never know," said Jacomo.

As they put the soggy, smudged pages into a bucket—Jacomo's erstwhile vomit bucket, which he'd kept like some kind of talisman—Tess noticed a legible line. She didn't mean to read it, but it's hard to see writing in your own language and not understand instantly.

It said: *Vulkharai, laugh until you cry.*

He'd been writing down the stories he'd heard in Paishesh. Tess shook a finger at him and said, "I heard Mee explicitly tell you not to do this."

Jacomo snatched the page out of her hand. "It's notes, for my own reference. I wasn't going to publish them. But how am I supposed to remember everything otherwise?"

"No judgment from me," said Tess, wringing out the sponge. "But Fozu has seven generations of Shesh and Jovesh history memorized."

"He probably heard it more than once, and wasn't drunk at the time," said Jacomo. He was using one of his shirts to sop ink off the desk, perhaps figuring the black cloth couldn't get any blacker. He was mistaken.

Cleaning up ink is largely a process of transferring the mess from one surface to another. Once the desk and floor were clean, Jacomo rinsed out the shirt and sponge, after which the water was far too dirty to wash the remaining ink off himself.

"It is distressingly tempting to take this as a sign," he grumbled, looking at his blackened hands. "I disobeyed Mee, and now I'll never get clean."

"Poor you," said Tess. "I'll bring you new water."

First she had to dump the ink water. The deck was now deserted, except for the night crew. She went straight to the leeward railing and then took a moment to be pleased that she hadn't had to think about which way the wind was blowing. She'd have a proper weather eye by the end of this voyage. Above her in the sky—also inky—the jeweled stars winked down.

Motion in her peripheral vision caught her attention. She looked toward the sabak tank.

At first she thought the ghostly-pale figure *was* the sabak, escaped through the scupper drain and clinging to the side of the ship. The figure wasn't proportioned like a sabak, however: the head was too small and the limbs too long. There was no tail. How could a human crawl along a vertical wall like a quigutl? And were they . . . naked?

Tess leaned over as far as she dared, keeping a hand on the basin beside her, trying to understand what she was seeing. The figure was crawling toward the sabak tank's scupper drain. They reached their hand inside, presumably feeling for a way to open the drain.

Were they trying to kill the sabak or set her free? Either way, Tess had to do something. She walked quickly toward the sabak tank.

"You there," she called as she brushed past the plaion. "Get away from that scupper!"

The person—a man?—looked up briefly, then seemed to redouble his efforts.

She had nothing else to persuade him with, so she emptied the basin of inky water onto his head. He gave a muffled cry, keeping his grip on the ship with difficulty.

Her shouting had alerted the crew. Darvo the bosun, the senior sailor on deck, quickly took charge, directing the able seafarers around him to fetch nets and hooks to try to apprehend this mysterious saboteur. The man scuttled quickly, but the sailors soon hemmed him in.

"Bosun, report!" barked Captain Claado, coming out of the stateroom with the countess.

Darvo, wrangling the stranger in a net, cried over his shoulder: "Stowaway, Captain. Tried to drain the sabak tank."

The miscreant was hauled up and dumped unceremoniously onto the deck, where he flopped like a herring before springing to his feet. He was a diminutive person, wearing some kind of white bodysuit that clung like a second skin; it took on a silver sheen in the lantern light and covered everything but his pale violet eyes, which blinked against the glare.

Tess suddenly realized he was *literally* wearing a second skin— a sabak skin—and she barely had time to be shocked before he rolled down the flap covering his mouth and nose, revealing the face of Lord Hamish Tacques-Mouton. There were dark circles around his eyes where he'd been spattered with ink.

Absurdly, he gave full courtesy.

"How the devil did you get here?" said Marga, first to find her voice. "I suppose you've come to arrest us for capturing a sabak."

"I probably should," said his lordship. "But my other duty supersedes that now. I was going to content myself with setting her free."

"What duty?" Marga demanded.

His sigh seemed almost heavier than his person. "It's a long story, Countess, but my name is Hami; I'm a Watcher for the Ggdani. I'm here to stop your expedition."

Marga stared a moment, and then she began to laugh.

"The serpent is forbidden to you," said Hami over her laughter. "The pole and her peoples are likewise forbidden to you. If you do not turn back now, this will end badly."

"You're going to stop us how, exactly?" said Marga. "Giles won't draw me a map—is that your nefarious scheme?"

"Fozu knows better than to make a map. I didn't have to tell him that."

"And what did you tell those dragons you were sailing with?" said Marga, sounding irritated now. "You don't seem to have stopped them from sailing on."

"The dragons will fail," said Hami, getting a faraway look. "I've seen to it."

Tess felt a chill. Hami had seemed to be Spira's friend back in Paishesh. Had he been engaged in sabotage all the while? That was cold.

"What was your scheme here?" said Marga, as if she feared his answer.

"I had your sailors at each other's throats just hours ago," said Hami. "Much more effective than fires and leaks. But it's all moot now that you've found me."

"Is it, though?" said Claado. "How do we know you haven't booby-trapped the hull?"

Hami's pale brows shot up. "That's an intelligent question, and I'd be a fool to answer."

"I suspect you'll think twice about answering once you're clapped in irons and stowed in the bilge," said Marga. "Unless you're keen to go down with this ship yourself."

She opened her mouth as if to give some kind of order, but before she could speak, Hami plowed his shoulder into the bosun's chest. Darvo, who'd already been punched by Argol today, seemed stunned; Hami took the opportunity to relieve the man of his cutlass and marlinspike—a foot-long awl used to untie tricky knots and stitch up sails. Most sailors had at least one of these; on a Porphyrian merchanteer they weren't usually used as weapons.

Hami stood en garde, all but daring anyone to try him; the sailors looked to Claado for orders, but he seemed disinclined to order any of his crew to take the Ggdani on.

He didn't need to; his niece was eager to do it. She drew her sword, and everyone backed off, leaving her room to circle Lord Hamish.

Marga tapped his blade with hers in a chiding, almost playful manner. "I've been hoping to face you ever since you claimed to be Master Tacques's relation. I suppose that wasn't even true, though?"

"I was fostered by the family; he taught me," said Hami, parrying her first lunge. He did not riposte. "His brother, Lord Philippe Tacques-Mouton, brought me up from age twelve. With enough gold, you can convince almost any Deadlander nobleman that you're a long-lost cousin."

Marga seemed not to like him besmirching her aristocratic brethren. She launched into a ferocious volley of blows known as the Windmill (Tess watched her often enough to recognize the move). Their blades clashed and rang. Hami parried, dodged, and finally succeeded in a feint that sent Marga's lunge in entirely the wrong direction. Ignoring his opening, he did not counterattack, but rushed toward the prow of the ship. Marga gave chase and caught up on the forecastle, where she pressed hard and nearly pinned him against one of her new cannons. He dodged—her sword struck sparks against the steel barrel—and then he leaped on top of the gun; one more leap to the railing sent him sprinting sure-footedly up the bowsprit.

Marga looked like she was considering going after him, but the sea was choppy and the bowsprit was getting washed with cold spray. "Come down from there," she cried. "Surrender and you won't be harmed."

Hami did not reply, but pulled the flap of sabak skin up to cover his nose and mouth again, tossed the cutlass and marlinspike onto the deck, and did a graceful backspring into the ocean.

"Heave to!" cried Marga, sheathing her blade and whirling about.

"Belay that," her uncle counterordered. "You'll never find him now. We barely found Eludus when it was calm and there was still daylight."

"Don't worry about Hami," called a voice from the leeward rail. "He could swim all the way home in that sabak suit if he wanted to. They really are a wonder."

Everyone turned to look; Tess and the crew had been so focused on the sword fight that no one had observed Fozu creeping onto the weather deck. He grinned and waved. His hands were unbound, and he had his hide coracle strapped to his back like a turtle shell.

Tess froze guiltily. She *had* latched the records-room door, right? She remembered doing that but did not remember retying his hands. Deep down, though, she knew the truth: Fozu could have escaped at any time. What had kept him imprisoned wasn't the door or his bind-ings, but his need to give his stories to the sabak.

He'd finally done it, with Tess's help. His stories were part of the Worldmind, and now he had no reason to stay.

"You can't just abandon the sabak," Tess cried. "What if some-thing happens to *her*?"

"You won't let it," said Fozu. "But don't let that be all you do."

Tess went cold. He hadn't just spoken to the sabak; the sabak had spoken to him.

"Giles—Fozu, don't go," said Marga, extending her hand. "The sea's too rough."

"I've seen worse. And I've got my little boat," said Fozu, tapping his coracle. "Thanks for hanging on to it."

And then he, too, leaped into the sea—inelegantly. Marga, with a cry, rushed to the railing, but he'd already vanished in the darkness. She slammed the railing with her fist. The sea, restless and unsympa-thetic, churned all around the ship.

The crew stood about, looking bewildered, until the bosun crossly whistled them back to their posts. Only then did Tess realize that she still had a basin in her hand, and that she'd left Jacomo waiting for a very long time indeed.

Twenty-One

Mind of the World, sometimes we feel like strangers in our own skin. What used to give comfort now pinches and chafes. The music drifts flat; the very colors have changed.

A cicada cracks its shell, and however much it wants to, it cannot stay inside.

Once upon a time (*time being a prism for understanding*), a countess had spent a week trying to persuade her former navigator to draw her a map, but he'd parried every argument. His ripostes had been stinging. She thought she'd come away unscathed, but there are cuts you don't feel until you see your own blood on the ground.

After Giles's escape, Marga shut herself up in her stateroom for almost a week—the rest of the way to St. Remy—to lick her wounds.

Upon the sixth morning, Father Jacomo was sitting in what had become his usual armchair, cup of tea in hand. He had kindly but firmly taken over tea duty in the mornings as a way of checking in on her, she suspected; Marga had bristled at first, but she was secretly glad. Mentoring her protégé would have been one thing too many right now, wholly occupied as she was by pacing, scowling, and arguing with Giles in her head.

Father Jacomo took everything with equanimity. She supposed that was his job, as a priest.

"How are you feeling today?" he said, leaning back in his chair.

It was not an easily answered question. Her fiancé was dead, Giles had spoiled everything, and today she would be seeing Lady Aemelia Borgo—a dear friend, but not a comforting or entirely unstressful sort of person.

And she'd just gotten irritating news from her napou.

"I've been better," said Marga, forcing herself to stop pacing and sit down. "Uncle Claado will be coming ashore after all—for moral support. *Mortifying support,* more like."

Jacomo raised his woolly brows, looking uncertain about whether that had been funny.

"He always picks fights with Aemelia," Marga explained. "But I can't have him insulting her this time; we need her help repairing the submersible. She gets mercurial when she's upset, and she'll already be upset about William."

"I could tell her about Lord Morney's passing, if that would help," said Jacomo. "Sometimes people take bad news better from a priest."

"I don't suppose you could persuade Napou to stay on the ship?" said Marga, disliking the pout in her own voice. "Usually, he sails circles around the island while I'm visiting."

Jacomo took a sip of tea. "Why does your uncle dislike Lady Borgo? He doesn't seem the sort to insult someone for no reason."

Ah, she'd been hoping he wouldn't ask.

Darienne approached with Marga's best hair (the copper waves, newly promoted); Marga sat up straighter so her maid could pin it on, trying to think of the most diplomatic way to explain Aemelia. "Your father is a duke, Jacomo. You know how powerful people can have powerfully eccentric opinions. Aemelia has no qualms about letting you know what she thinks—and sometimes, I admit, she's uncharitable."

"Uncharitable as in . . . stingy? Or unkind?" said Jacomo.

It was both, of course. Marga flashed a closed-lip smile. "My napou, alas, can't disagree discreetly; he has to challenge her on every point. Loudly."

"He's a man of principle."

"He's intolerant," said Marga with an impatient shake of her head; Darienne dropped half a dozen hairpins. "Maybe all Porphyrians are raised that way. My mother was the same, albeit less prone to tirades. She was stealthy. For example, my father would tell Samsamese jokes—you know the sort of thing: How many Samsamese does it take to sail upriver?"

"One to raise the sail and two more to fill it with farts, if memory serves," said Jacomo dryly. "My mother is Samsamese; I've heard them all. I must've authored half a dozen myself."

"Well, *my* mother hated them. She'd never let my father tell one without attacking him. She'd widen her eyes and say in this little innocent voice, 'I don't get it, Poul.'"

"I don't think I get it," said Jacomo, gazing upward, head slightly tilted. "How is that an attack?"

"She would force him to explain the joke." Marga put on a gruff, embarrassed voice, in imitation of the old count: "It's funny because . . . erm . . . *you* know. The Samsamese eat a lot of cabbage, and . . . erm . . . they're sort of stupid."

Jacomo blinked (he had unexpectedly long lashes), and then he chuckled. "That's actually rather clever. The joke just sounds mean, spelled out like that."

He was missing the point. "She always did it in front of company, and it was mortifying. I don't see why she couldn't keep quiet and pretend not to notice, like everyone else."

"Is that what you want us to do at Lady Borgo's?" Jacomo asked. "Keep quiet and pretend not to notice?"

It just sounded cowardly, spelled out like that.

"Aemelia is my friend; she was William's mentor," said Marga sternly. She took the hand mirror from Darienne and examined her hair. "She's taught me so much; I owe her a debt of gratitude. Whatever her faults, she's one of our leading scientific minds. She's published dozens of anthropological monographs and amassed the largest collection of Pelaguese artifacts anywhere. Her family have been good stewards in St. Remy, ruling with judicious evenhandedness—none of the purges and unrest you find in St. Claresse or St. Fionnani."

"Ruling who? Which nation?" asked Jacomo, all but batting his lashes.

Marga blinked back at him. She'd only ever heard them called St. Remy Pelaguese—

"Pelaguese!" cried Giles his very first day aboard. "You understand that you're killing us, I hope."

"I'm not killing anyone," Marga insisted. "I'm a scientist, not a governor-general. Not a settler or a legionnaire."

"No, it's you," he said. "The simplest way to obliterate us is to deny us our names"—

The bosun's whistle, shrilling from the weather deck, startled her back into the present. St. Remy had come into view. Marga got to her feet, waved off the earrings Darienne was holding, and departed for the waist of the ship. Jacomo tailed after her.

St. Remy harbor lay just half a mile off, gleaming like her fondest hope.

She would breathe easier ashore; she could leave her Giles-of-the-mind behind.

The bucolic countryside, achingly green, transported her back to the Southlands, away from the lichenous rocks and salt-twisted trees that dominated most pelagic landscapes. St. Remy town nestled cozily among low hills, like a hatchling chick. The slate rooftops and limestone facades bloomed golden in the early light, warm and welcoming. The tidy harbor was clean and bright, its warehouses uncluttered. She'd always marveled at how the nets and traps here looked new, like they had only just been invented, and civilization along with them.

It looked like a dream of home, with all the rough surfaces planed away. Ninys had never looked this Ninysh.

Of course, the people looked anything but. Marga watched for "St. Remy Pelaguese" dockhands and stevedores on the bustling pier as the *Avodendron* tied up. Their hair hung straight and sleek in every shade of brown; any reds and golds among them were probably Ninysh settlers. Both men and women wore narrow, calf-length skirts with a vertical seam in back concealing a ream of pleats. Their long, woolly socks were knit directly onto wooden soles. Their wide sleeves were salted with pearlescent buttons that caught the sunlight.

Aemelia lets them wear their own clothes, she told imaginary Giles. *That's not nothing.*

It's pretty damn close.

Usually, Aemelia would have had a carriage waiting, but she wasn't expecting them. Uncle Claado (ashore, as threatened) dispatched a runner to Palasho Borgo, while Marga found a place to sit, low crates under an awning that provided no shade whatsoever. The sun was still too low. Tess sat beside her; Jacomo paced.

Two little girls approached, hesitantly at first, bearing trays of items for sale—poppets, pine candy, lily-of-the-valley bouquets—things nobody needed. It was just a more genteel form of begging, if you thought about it. Marga looked away from the girls, shading her eyes with one hand and pretending to watch ships come in, so as not to encourage them.

Jacomo, on the other hand, set about bargaining with the smaller girl. She was five or six, impossibly apple-cheeked, emitting cascades of giggles. Jacomo loomed over her like a kindly, stout tree. He handed her a coin and received a fistful of pine candy.

The giggles had drawn Marga's gaze; the sweetness of the scene held it.

"I'm Jacomo," he was saying. "What is your name, my queen?"

"Agnes. But"—the girl switched to a breathless whisper—"that's not really my name!"

The taller girl, her sister most likely, swatted Agnes with a button-spangled sleeve. "Hush. He's going to think you're a pagan." She flashed a baleful eye at Jacomo, took the littler girl's hand, and began marching her away.

"I don't mind if you are," Jacomo said hastily. "But what are your people called?"

Agnes looked back, wide-eyed, but her sister hurried her along. Jacomo gazed after, popping a piece of candy into his mouth.

"Nice try," said Tess. Jacomo gave a little bow.

Uncle Claado stepped up, a silhouette against the early sun. "They're called Nutufi," he said. "Circumnavigate the island enough times, you pick a few things up."

So you could have asked your uncle. At any time, Marga's inner Giles needled her.

Claado *would* know; he had always been ostentatiously virtuous. "You're making me look bad, Napou," Marga quipped. She regretted it instantly.

"It's not me doing that," said Claado.

The glare of the low sun on the water irritated her eyes.

A carriage with the Borgo crest arrived, and soon they were rolling away through St. Remy town. Marga leaned her chin on her hand, watching out the window. Ships, shops, people about their morning tasks—she was seeing more Ninysh reds and golds among the populace than she remembered from previous visits.

Claado was animatedly explaining something to Tess and Jacomo.

". . . as if the size of my cranium would reveal the mysteries of Porphyry," he said, waggling his fingers like someone telling ghost stories. "What makes us philosophize? How is it that we were engineering aqueducts back when the Ninysh were still living in sties with their pigs?"

"Living with pigs has not gone entirely out of fashion," interjected Tess.

"But how does the size of your skull pertain to any of that?" asked Jacomo.

Claado was going to fill these two with contempt before they even arrived at the house; it was time to put an end to it. "It doesn't, necessarily," said Marga snappishly. Too snappishly; she didn't like herself like this. "Aemelia has a hypothesis, and she's gathering information. But that's the whole point of science: you don't know the answer beforehand. And she'll never know the answer if you won't let her near you."

"Just watch," said Claado, tapping his head. "Her ladyship follows me everywhere with calipers." Tess and Jacomo laughed.

Marga gritted her teeth and turned toward the window again.

The estate was several miles into the countryside, a limestone manor house surrounded by gracefully manicured parkland. The carriage pulled into a circular gravel drive, and footmen began helping everyone down.

Marga grabbed her uncle's sleeve before he could climb out, and whispered, "Promise me you're not going to pick a fight."

"I will be on my best behavior," said Claado archly, pulling out of her grasp. "But it does expire after a certain point."

That was not reassuring. Marga looked at her companions, standing together on the gravel drive, and anxiously appraised their appearances. Jacomo was rumpled but dressed all in black; a priest could get away with that. Claado had wrapped a garishly embroidered sash over his slops and hadn't even put on shoes, presumably in hopes of giving Lady Borgo an aneurysm. Tess was still dressed in a threadbare doublet like a clod.

"You couldn't have put on something a little nicer?" cried Marga, like steam popping the lid off a stewpot. Ah, cack, she had not been going to say anything about that.

Tess shuffled her scuffed boots. "I don't actually own anything nicer."

Of course she didn't; she'd worn this same outfit to the funeral.

Mercifully, Marga's thoughts of self-reproach were interrupted by Lady Borgo's steward, Tomasino. He was a diminutive man with deep-set eyes and slicked-back hair, graying at the temples; his dapper figure was softened in the middle by a paunch. He'd been directing the luggage removal, but now he saw Claado and cried, "Uncle Captain! It's been a long time."

"Too long," said Claado, giving the man a boisterous, back-slapping embrace.

"Her ladyship is gardening," said Tomasino, extricating himself. He gave Marga a significant look.

This meant Aemelia would be here in moments. This was a game she played—*Oh, la, you caught me in the middle of something!*—when in fact she'd been preparing since the carriage went out.

And sure enough, her ladyship came sailing around the end of the house, gardening hat attractively askew, a bundle of freshly cut jonquils in her arms. She was tall, in her fifties, her golden hair shot through with silver. A few strands had come loose from her bun so beautifully that it was hard to believe she hadn't intended them to tumble down just so. Even the plant stains on her apron seemed to have been thoughtfully placed for maximum aesthetic effect.

Aemelia was always the same: impeccable. For the first time in twelve years of friendship, Marga felt her patience with it beginning to wane.

"Marga, darling!" cried Aemelia, handing the flowers to Tomasino, who passed them off to a footman. "I didn't expect you at all this season. You should be much farther south by now, if you mean to find the Polar Serpent this year."

Lady Borgo took Marga's hands and kissed her cheeks effusively—real kisses, not air kisses. Marga tried to smile back, but her heart was suddenly full.

"We've had some setbacks, Aemelia," said Marga. "I fear we need your help."

"Don't fear—you shall have it, of course." Her ladyship cast a shrewd eye over Marga's companions, noting the absence at once. "Where's my dear Lord Morney? Not ill, I hope."

Marga winced. If Aemelia noticed, she didn't let it stop her guessing: "Was he detained in St. Claresse? I told him not to get sucked into the local troubles. Do you need me to put a word in with Governor Boqueton? That man bungles everything."

"No, alas," said Marga, "it's much worse than that."

Her ladyship seemed momentarily at a loss. She pulled off her gardening gloves; a maid materialized at her elbow to accept them. "Speak plainly, dear girl. What happened?"

Marga reached back for her uncle's buttressing arm and found it. If he'd really come to give moral support, now was his chance. It was Jacomo, however, who cleared his throat and said, "Lady Borgo, I am grieved to inform you that William, Lord Morney, has ascended the Golden Stair on St. Eustace's arm, may Heaven's light enfold them."

Lady Borgo whimpered and then fainted dead away.

Tomasino was miraculously positioned to catch her; a housemaid hurried out with smelling salts. Tess and Jacomo looked impressed by the servants' prescience, and Marga supposed it was impressive, until you realized Aemelia fainted rather a lot, and that a flogging awaited anyone unfortunate enough to let her fall.

Marga had witnessed a flogging—one had been plenty—and since then she had taken great care that one should never happen on her watch again.

"Let's go indoors," said Marga when Aemelia seemed recovered enough to walk. There was a good chance she would flop again when she learned how William had died. Marga would get her to a couch first. If she was sitting, no one needed to catch her.

So you circumvent horrors? said her Giles-of-the-mind. *You don't have the guts to tell Lady Borgo to stop being cruel; you just rob her of an opportunity. You do realize that she can always find another?*

Ah, perfect, that voice again. Giles had lodged himself in her conscience and was going to turn everything sour for her. He had a special gift.

They entered the house, directly into one of the Pelaguese galleries. No couches here. Marga tried to hurry everyone along, but Tess was gawping at floor-to-ceiling glass cases filled with pottery shards, spearheads, painted wooden boxes, carved tusk-seal ivory, obsidian beads. There was a strange hanging made from slats of decorated whale baleen—like some sort of unusable rope ladder—and a display of garishly embroidered boots. In the center of the room, as it always had, loomed a pyramid of skulls.

Marga cringed, expecting her inner Giles to speak up, but he didn't need to say anything. The pile was grotesque; she had always thought it was grotesque, and yet she had done exactly what she'd advised Jacomo to do: kept quiet and pretended not to notice.

Each skull had been a person once. From this very island, most of them. They would have been . . . ah, it was on the tip of her tongue . . . Nutufi? Just like every maid and footman who came in here to dust them. Just like Tomasino, who was standing near them now, hands folded behind his back, his face scrupulously blank.

"So tell me," Aemelia's voice cut through her thoughts. "How did he die?"

With all that death in front of her, it took Marga a moment to understand whom she meant.

William, of course. Marga's voice caught in her throat.

This time, her uncle did come to her rescue. He solemnly intoned in a voice as deep as the sea, "He fell overboard and was eaten by sabanewts, milady."

"Sabak," said someone faintly. Possibly Tess.

Tomasino was beside her ladyship at once, but this time Aemelia didn't so much as sway on her feet. "Sabanewts! Well, he died in a rather exotic way, didn't he? I'd expect nothing less; I'm almost sorry I didn't see it."

"Madam," said Captain Claado with a little bow. "You are a ghoul."

Marga shot him a warning look, but he'd turned his face away. His braids were not intimidated by her glare.

"Oh, fie, how do your people survive without a sense of humor?" cried Lady Borgo, swatting at him. "I shall have my answer once you let me measure that cranium of yours."

Claado did meet Marga's eye this time; it was she who looked away.

"I meant I should like to see a sabanewt someday," Aemelia said, looking down her aquiline nose. "One hears such tales about their uncanny mental powers, and how the oil pressed from their dead flesh is a panacea, worth its weight in gold."

Her ladyship tapped a finger to her chin, considering. "Our St. Remy Pelaguese never kept them, did you, Tomasino?" Before he could respond, Aemelia answered her own question: "You couldn't. The water's too warm here."

"It wasn't allowed, milady," said Tomasino.

"They wouldn't survive," said Aemelia in a correcting tone. "That's just biological fact."

"They *weren't* allowed, though." That was Tess, coming around from behind a display of scrimshaw tigers. "Only five polar nations may keep them. King Moy acknowledged it in a treaty. The 'St. Remy Pelaguese'—who I believe you should call Nutufi—aren't on that list."

Her ladyship stared at Tess, unblinking as a falcon.

"We captured a sabanewt, Aemelia," Marga quickly interjected, with cheerfulness strained nearly to breaking. "A bit unlawfully, ha ha, but I'd love to show it to you—"

"Who is this insolent person?" said Lady Borgo. Her gimlet eyes still hadn't blinked. "Is she supposed to look like a man, or a monkey?"

Tess flushed crimson.

Marga laughed, not because it was funny, but because maybe it *could* be funny, and funny was better than angry. "Forgive me, Aemelia.

I am remiss in not introducing my protégé, Tess Dombegh, as well as our priest, Father Jacomo, who is the youngest son of the Duke of Ducana."

Jacomo, thank Allsaints, was a man of impressive lineage. Her ladyship took his arm and peppered him with questions all the way down the corridor. Jacomo answered everything good-naturedly—his parents, siblings, cousins, second cousins (Queen Glisselda was but once removed), and third cousins made up vast swaths of Goreddi and Samsamese nobility. Marga took a moment to collect herself, and by the time they reached the dining room, she felt ready to handle whatever came next.

What came next was the dining room itself. She'd recalled it as a place of elegant repasts and sparkling conversation; she'd forgotten that the walls were hung with snowshoes, fishing harpoons, and dozens of human bones, embellished just like the scapula Aemelia had given her.

They had never bothered her before. Why did they bother her now?

"Why doesn't any of this bother you?" Giles had asked more than once. "You sail on your merry way, having tea with this murdering governor over here, eating little cucumber sandwiches with that iron-fisted baronetta over there, like none of their abuses matter."

"Just because I'm not fomenting revolution doesn't mean I'm not bothered," Marga flung back. "But my father taught me that you catch more flies with honey than with vinegar."

"No one ever caught a fly with honey. Flies are drawn to corpses"—

Marga shook her head to clear it. Breakfast was being laid out on the dark, polished table; servants uncovered platters of kippers, cheese, and toast, poured tea, and set out pots of jam. A footman had pulled out a chair for her.

"What an efficient house crew," said Marga loudly, trying to wrest her feelings into some semblance of normal. "They could give my Darienne some pointers."

"She's a serf from your estate, I presume?" asked Aemelia, who was being seated. "Well, there's your problem. It's all predicted by skull measurements." She gave Claado a cool look; he glowered back. "Goreddi serfs are unambitious and unimaginative; Samsamese serfs are stoic and resigned. The serfs on Ninysh estates, however, have unexpectedly shapely skulls and may be almost as ambitious and intelligent as our aristocrats."

"Or else your aristocrats are embarrassingly serflike. But please, interpret it to suit yourself," said Claado, helping himself to kippers. His best behavior—which had already encompassed calling Aemelia a ghoul—seemed to have expired.

Aemelia ignored him, which was just good manners. "What you need, Marga, is one of our St. Remy Pelaguese."

"Nutufi." Even after being called a monkey, Tess kept correcting her. It was Claado's bad influence, surely. Or Giles's. It had been a mistake to let them spend so much time together.

"They're short, and they smell of fish," Aemelia continued, undeterred, "and they can be some trouble to train, but once you temper their perversions and make them understand the natural order of things, there are no servants more responsive."

Around the perimeter of the room, half a dozen footmen stood perfectly still. Marga tried to imitate their demeanor as she cringed on the inside.

"I have a couple young females just broken in, if you'd like to try them out—"

"That's it," said Claado in a voice like thunder, slamming down his fish fork. His braids trembled and his beard bristled. "I can't sit and listen to this. I'm going back to the ship."

"Are we quarreling so soon?" Lady Borgo flashed a brittle smile.

"Napou, please," said Marga, reaching out to stop him going. He pushed her hand away.

"She's talking about a pair of women as if they were a pair of shoes," he said. "They're not *things*, whatever her cranial divination might tell her. Someday she's going to realize that phrenology is all nonsense, and she'll devise some other scientific excuse for keeping them down. The shape of the eyes, maybe, or the color of the skin."

"Don't be ridiculous," said Marga, reflexively taking her hands off the white tablecloth.

"Forgive me, Marga," he said. "I tried to play nice, for your sake. I really did try."

He stalked off. His footsteps rattled the bones on the walls.

Aemelia's head bobbed like a heavy tulip on a slender stalk; a servant with smelling salts hovered at her elbow. She waved the man away and gave a shuddering sigh.

"You all saw: I did not pick that fight with him," said Lady Borgo, clutching at her heart. "I've been nothing but generous to your uncle, Marga, and you see how he treats me. He is not welcome back in this house, though it pains me to say so."

"I understand," said Marga, keeping her face so still it hurt.

She hardly tasted her breakfast or heard the conversation around the table, so preoccupied was she. Afterward, she was surprised to find Tess leading them all back down the corridor, through the galleries. Something had caught the girl's eye, apparently.

"I am happy to answer any questions about my collection," Lady Borgo was saying graciously, "or about our St. Remy Pelaguese."

"The Nutufi?" said Jacomo.

"Oh, you shouldn't say 'Noo-too-*fee*' as if it were some sort of name," said Lady Borgo. "It merely means 'people' in the local dialect."

"Here," said Tess, turning a corner into a round atrium. A stone staircase hugged the perimeter of the room, leaving an open center, where a wondrous sculpture stood. It was a flat panel of what looked like wood, fully eight feet tall, that had been carved into a bas-relief of an enormous serpent, looping and coiling. It echoed the graceful curve of the staircase.

Its fearsome majesty gave Marga chills every time. That, at least, hadn't changed.

"Ah," said Aemelia happily. "You have a keen eye. This is the finest piece in my collection. You'll never guess what it's really made of—don't touch!"

"It's got . . . little hairs on it?" cried Tess, folding her hands behind her back again.

"It's the dried tail of a sea beaver," Aemelia announced. "I have many such carvings, all of them ancient, but none as large as this. I shudder to think of the beast it was once attached to."

"And this is the work of the Nutufi?" Jacomo asked.

Lady Borgo frowned at the name. "It's a bit of a mystery who made these fine carvings, or the massive stoneworks all over the island. I've theorized that they're the work of an earlier people, who moved on or went extinct. Our Pelaguese are simple and childlike. They lack the sophistication and artistic sensibility to create something like this."

Every word seemed to be reaching Marga through Fozu's ears, and he was ferociously insulted. *Are you listening, Marga? Do you not hear how patronizing she is? She won't even believe the Nutufi made their own art.*

He wasn't wrong, was the thing. It would have been so much simpler if he were wrong.

Marga focused on the bas-relief, drinking in its calming beauty, trying to shut out Fozu. This had been William's favorite carving. He had come a long way to see it, back when he was one of the few people willing to believe the World Serpents might exist. Marga would never have met him, but for this work of art (*Nutufi art,* interjected Fozu). She gazed at it, heart aching, remembering.

". . . my protégé, Lord Morney, used to theorize that our Pelaguese considered it a deity and prayed to it. After all, he'd say, when you consider their perverse proclivities, what god is more apropos than an enormous snake coming out of the bush!"

There was a long pause, during which Marga's heart seemed to stop. It was a filthy, disrespectful joke, and there was Tomasino standing in the doorway, keeping his face so still it looked like it, too, had been carved.

"I don't get it," said Jacomo.

Oh, Heavens, no. He wouldn't dare.

"Snake? Bush? I know you're a priest, but don't tell me you're entirely unaware of the mechanics of copulation?" said Lady Borgo with a smirk.

Jacomo had turned the color of a beet, but he persisted, bull-headedly, pushing back the way Marga herself had unwittingly taught him: "But why is it *funny*?"

"It's funny because our Pelaguese are a bunch of—"

"Oh, dear me!" cried Marga in desperation, not even sure what she'd say next. "You know, Aemelia, we have been on a ship for two weeks straight, and we are stenchy!" She spread her arms and started trying to herd Jacomo and Tess toward the stairs. "It would be best for these two to locate their rooms and get a bath—has their baggage been taken up?"

Lady Aemelia Borgo, looking mildly affronted at the suggestion of negligence, turned to her steward for confirmation. It was not clear whether she understood or appreciated the embarrassment Marga had just reflexively saved her from.

Would she have been embarrassed, if Marga had let her continue? That wasn't obvious, even to someone who had known her a long time. If Marga hadn't spared her friend's feelings, what the devil had she done?

Spared your own, said her Fozu-infused conscience. *Peace for yourself at our expense.*

Damn it.

"Up the stairs with you. Go," said Marga, shooing Tess along. As Jacomo passed, Marga grabbed his arm and whispered, "I told you about my mother in confidence. I'm disappointed."

"With respect," he said, "I thought you were handing me a tool and meant me to push back on your behalf. I know you feel constrained by friendship, and by whatever you think you owe her. But her abuses matter. I have to believe, at some level, they bother you, too."

Marga, in her astonishment, let go of his arm; he followed Tess up the stairs.

Saints in Heaven, he'd sounded just like Fozu.

And when had she started thinking of Giles as Fozu?

"Here's my offer," Marga said. *"You draw me a map, and I will call you Fozu."*

"So, I should betray the polar peoples and the One in exchange for basically nothing," he replied. *"That is pretty tempting."*

"It's not nothing! You just told me being deprived of your name was a kind of death."

"It is. But not killing me seems like the most minimal courtesy you could extend, not some great gift magnanimously bestowed. Oh, huzzah, she's treating me like any other human being, I guess I'll hand over everything"—

"Marga, darling?" Aemelia had finished consulting with Tomasino. "Did they go up already? Oh, my dear, are you well? Your cheeks are wet."

Marga pulled a handkerchief from her bodice and pressed it to her face. "This sculpture reminds me of William," she said. Surely that was a reasonable excuse for crying.

"Me too," said Aemelia. She gently tucked her arm through Marga's, her crystalline blue eyes alight. "I'm sorry I can't seem to make it work with your uncle. Truly I am. And I was a bit abrasive with your protégé, I suspect—"

"It's fine," said Marga. "I know you mean well."

"I could be nicer. I forget how to make small talk, how to smile and nod congenially, rattling around in this enormous house by myself," said Aemelia. "I still have salons twice a week—intellectuals, artists, and people of quality up from town—but other than that I am quite alone with my work most of the time."

"And your Pelaguese," said Marga. "But perhaps they're too . . . too simple and childlike."

She held her breath, willing Aemelia to say something, anything, kind or contradictory or complicating.

"That's it exactly," said Aemelia, brightening. "You've hit the nail on the head. They don't have the intellectual capacity to keep up, let alone ask meaningful questions or carry on any kind of conversation, really. A sweet-natured race, if you will, but dim."

"Probably not all of them," said Marga. Ye Saints, she pushed back feebly.

Maybe it was a muscle and she'd let it atrophy. Maybe it grew stronger with use.

Lady Borgo laughed. "Come to my study. You must read the draft of my latest article and give me commentary," she said, tugging Marga's arm. "You'll like this: I'm disputing Russo's theory of devolution, which all those bastards of the Academy subscribe to. I'm positing that people get more *innocent* the farther you go from civilization. . . ."

Reluctantly, Marga allowed herself to be led deeper into the house.

Twenty-Two

Tess didn't come down for lunch, pleading headache. Breakfast had been uncomfortable enough. She wasn't sure what was harder to take: Lady Borgo, or Marga desperately trying not to offend Lady Borgo.

Tess lay on her bed, contemplating the carven beaver tail above her mantelpiece and wondering whether to call Seraphina on the thnimi. It had been a long time since she'd reported in, she now realized. Not that there'd been much to report—just . . . Will dying. Their dramatic departure from St. Claresse (Paishesh). And Fozu, Hami, and the sabak.

All right, that was actually quite a lot.

It was embarrassing to call now, after such a long time. Better to start small and work up to it. She should surreptitiously record Lady Borgo saying noxious things and send *that*—maybe the royal cousins could send the fleet just to seize her ladyship's skull collection. That seemed like good international diplomacy.

She shoved her hands into her pockets; one was alarmingly full of lint. Tess extracted the wad of fluff and was about to flick it off the edge of the bed when she suddenly remembered what it had to be. Fozu's eyu. It didn't look as stretched and frayed as she remembered.

It twitched in her hand and she dropped it, alarmed. She rolled onto her stomach and observed it closely: it was moving. She hadn't imagined it. The fibers were like little tentacles, reaching across the gaps, pulling loose sections together.

It was fixing itself. Saints in Heaven, what a strange piece of work this was.

Tess had no idea how long she spent staring at the fluffy device, enthralled, but eventually there was a loud knock at the door. A maid had arrived with an armful of gowns. Behind her was a bucket brigade, ready to fill the bronze tub in the corner of her room.

The maid was a tidy, slender woman called Anna. Captain Claado had said all the servants here were Nutufi—if that really was the right name. Tess did not trust anything Lady Borgo said about them, but a seed of doubt had been planted.

"A bath before dinner?" said Anna, keeping her hands balled into fists while she curtsied. "And I'm supposed to find a gown that fits you."

Tess looked at the steaming buckets regretfully. She really did want a bath, and clean clothes would be nice, but that committed her to dinner. With a sigh, she let the servants in.

They filled the tub with hot water hauled up from the kitchens. The last bucket, carried by a small boy, was full of rose petals; the scent wafted up as he dropped them in.

Anna closed the door behind the bucketeers. "I can have your doublet and breeches laundered for you."

"That would be nice, thank you," said Tess, already stripping down to try on gowns. Might as well get it over with before her bathwater cooled.

The gowns were too long, being Lady Borgo's castoffs; all but one had more slashes and poufs than Tess could stomach. The remaining gown was blue with a reticulated lace collar, which she rather hated but wouldn't feel too silly in. Anna assured her that she'd have it hemmed by the time Tess was out of the bath.

"Unless you'd like me to stay and scrub your back?" said Anna.

"No, thank you," said Tess, casting a longing gaze at the tub.

Anna curtsied; her straight brown hair was parted with geometrical precision. She held out her hands for the gown and laundry, and only then, when she'd uncurled her fists, did Tess notice a fine tracery of raised lines on her palms, crisscrossing in diamond shapes, like the pattern on a beaver's tail.

They looked like deliberate burn scars.

Anna curled her hands shut again.

"Forgive me," said the chambermaid. "That was done when I was a girl, before I knew better. There's no way to undo it."

"What is it? Some . . . Nutufi thing?" asked Tess.

Anna looked so mortified that Tess was immediately sorry she'd asked.

"It's a sin," said Anna, with a pained smile. "The devil's mark. I am branded forever a pagan, even though I've repented. At least I knew better than to inflict it upon my own children."

Tess's first instinct was to comfort; she, too, had been made to feel inadequate by Saints. "First," she said, "the Saints contradict each other. What's a sin to one isn't always a sin to all. But secondly, I know some living Saints. St. Seraphina is my half sister. She's a strange bird herself, and she wouldn't find your scars remotely alarming, let alone a sin—"

"Thank you for your concern," said Anna, kissing her knuckle toward Heaven. "But we were ignorant and uncivilized, and now we're not. Now we're Ninysh."

"All right," said Tess, shaken by Anna's conviction and by a contradictory conviction of her own, that Lady Borgo did not consider her servants to be Ninysh. "I'm sorry."

The chambermaid left, and Tess stepped into the tub, preoccupied now, and unable to surrender to the enjoyment of it.

Jacomo, that ne'er-do-well, pleaded headache to get out of dinner. Tess, who'd pulled that trick at lunch and would have liked to do it again, felt justified in judging him for it.

Marga met her on the stairs, smiling at Tess's new gown, although her approval seemed to snag on the thnimi brooch. "We should find you something less obviously glass," she fussed, reaching out to straighten it.

Tess covered the brooch before Marga could examine it any closer. "It was my sister's."

Marga's mouth turned down. "You and Jacomo were terribly unmannerly this morning. I have never felt so embarrassed. Promise me you will keep your opinions to yourself tonight."

"Maybe you could expound upon a few more of yours," said Tess. The second half of that sentence bounced off Marga's fleeing back. Sighing, Tess followed to the dining room.

There were other people at dinner, to her surprise. Other Southlander guests, that is; servants never counted, even in Ninys and Goredd.

Tess had never really thought about it that way, even when she'd served her own sister. She'd only ever thought to finish her service and be back where she belonged, seated at the table and being waited upon in turn.

She was so preoccupied with this insight that the other guests made little impression. There was a dashing silver-haired explorer, retired, full of stories; a couple of naturalists; an *anthropologist,* which seemed to mean he studied people like the naturalists studied Voorka seals; some philosophers and poets, snubbed on the continent, out to make a name in greener pastures.

Second sons of minor lords? Plausibly. Tess quite lost track of them all.

They'd left an empty place setting, in remembrance of Will. Tess could picture him here, flaunting his credentials as scholar, explorer, *and* lordling. He would have outshone everyone.

Well, everyone but Lady Borgo, who'd donned a bountiful green silk gown, laced and slashed to reveal a pale pink undergown. Tastefully applied crystal droplets gave a dewy effect, making her look like a peony bud about to bloom. Her hair was a cascade of silver, reminiscent of Marga's at the funeral.

Marga herself looked surprisingly dull in comparison.

After dinner, everyone convened in one of Lady Borgo's tasteful salons. Her ladyship stood by the hearth while a servant passed out wine. Everyone knew not to sit on the satin sofas just yet; there was to be a toast, and Tess could guess whose memory they'd be drinking to.

"Dear friends, thank you for attending tonight," said Lady Borgo. "I need your support in this trying time, as does our dear Marga. It's so shocking that Lord Morney is dead. Can a noble soul ever truly be gone? If there's any justice in the world, some part of him should linger."

Tess shuddered. She knew, better than most, that Will lingered. He'd haunted her even before he'd died.

"Let us raise a glass and promise never to forget him," her ladyship continued. "Let us live his noble example by conquering doubt, vanquishing impossibility, and reaching for immortality even if it eludes us."

Everyone drank but Tess.

"He has one legacy still," said Marga, sounding put out. "His submersible."

"Which we shall repair—of course! I just wish there was more I could do," cried Lady Borgo, and then she and Marga were hugging and crying.

Some more toasts and memories of Will were proffered. Tess drifted to a pale gold couch in the corner, away from the eulogizing. She noticed a stocky young man in a sea-green doublet peering around the edge of the doorframe. He wore a starched ruff and a serious expression, and he carried a six-stringed viol. His shiny, dark hair ran loose into the runnels of his ruff.

He waited for Lady Borgo to notice him.

"Sit down, everyone," her ladyship ordered at last. "I almost forgot. My music master, Martin, has prepared an entertainment. The boys' choir from St. Remy Mission will sing one of his hymns, and then he will dazzle us on viola da gamba."

A line of boys filed in, all eight or nine years old, dressed in slate-gray robes like little monks of St. Remy. The young music master set his viol in the corner of the room and joined his charges at the front, smiling at them and leaning down to whisper encouragement. When Lady Borgo cleared her throat, he straightened a bit guiltily, bowed, and raised his arms to direct his choir.

Tess switched on her thnimi. A concert probably wasn't relevant to Queen Glisselda's interests, but it would be relevant to Seraphina's.

The boys' voices rose like skylarks on an updraft of ethereal harmonies. Tess had never heard the like, hopeful and heartbreaking, seven lines weaving in and out and around each other, a cord made of chords, so bright she could almost see a shimmer in the air. She didn't know much about music, but she knew she was in the presence of something remarkable. Seraphina was going to be amazed.

Applause was inadequate to convey how Heavenly it was.

"I do prefer songs in Ninysh, Martin," called Lady Borgo over the clapping.

"Yes, milady," said the music master. "I beg your pardon."

"That won't do," said Lady Borgo. The applause trickled awkwardly to a halt. "This is not the first time I've told you, yet you persist in being insolent before my guests."

Tess glanced over at Marga, who was looking predictably stone-faced.

Martin stared at the ground and muttered something.

"What was that?" said Lady Borgo. "Speak up, child."

The music master took a deep breath. "We can't sing this song in Ninysh because Ninysh doesn't have the right words."

Lady Borgo looked repulsed. "What words could you need that aren't in scripture?"

"Also," said Martin, "Ninysh is not a nice language for singing."

Gasps went up all over.

"Nutufi is softer. Smoother," he said. "It could not be a sin to use it in music, surely, just for the feel of the syllables? You don't ask my viol to play in Ninysh, only to have a beautiful sound. We sing a lot in the . . . the *forest*, and the boys—"

"The boys are meant to be learning Ninysh. You'll impede their education."

"With respect, your ladyship, the most revered Ninysh scholars speak three or four languages. Knowing Nutufi as well shouldn't—"

"Scholars study *complex* languages, not your degenerate forest patois."

Across the room, Marga was squirming as if she'd sat on a shard of glass. It was nice that she found Lady Borgo's opinions troublesome, but it would be nicer if she said something. Lady Borgo might actually listen to a countess.

A monk from the mission, who'd been loitering in the corridor, led the boys out; they stared and giggled and pushed each other in the manner of small children everywhere. Martin busied himself with tuning his viol.

The divot between Lady Borgo's brows was deepening.

"I don't know why our music master is in such an ungrateful mood this evening," she grumbled for all to hear. "If his parents hadn't dumped him at the mission as a child, he'd never have discovered his musical gifts. But is he thankful for the chance to compose motets and concerti grossi? He acts like he'd rather bang two rocks together out in the forest."

"Saints' bones, what happened to his hands?" cried one of the poets.

Martin, who'd been tightening his bow, put his hands behind his back. Lady Borgo called, "Show them properly, Martin. Hold out your hands."

He kept his face expressionless as he spread his fingers; he had the same crisscrossing scars as Anna.

"What kind of monsters would apply hot iron to the palms of their hands?" said the anthropologist. "How do they not cause him pain every day?"

Tess suspected that Lady Borgo made sure they *did* cause him pain every day, in fact.

"Three generations of Borgos have never wheedled it out of them," said Lady Borgo. "I published a paper on the subject once, hypothesizing that it's due to chronic self-abuse." She eyed Martin suspiciously; he gave no sign that he had heard. "Do you object to my theory?" No response. "If so, then please explain what your people do and why they do it."

Martin withdrew his hands from consideration and resumed tightening his bow. The learned men of Lady Borgo's salon, who'd presumably engaged in such activities without scarring their own hands, laughed at his discomfiture.

This was unbearable. Tess stared flames at Marga, willing her to say something, but she only looked at her own hands and frowned.

The viola da gamba concert proceeded apace, as beautiful as the singing had been, although Tess didn't have much heart for listening. Neither, it seemed, did Lady Borgo, who stood up in the middle of the second movement, declaring that she had a headache and the concert was over. On her way out, she knocked over Martin's music stand with her farthingale and berated him for his ill placement of it.

"Eat your dinner and go," said Lady Borgo, pinching the bridge of her nose as she swept out. Martin bowed into the space she'd vacated and then fled the room.

Tess was all but boiling in her gown, she felt so helpless and upset.

If the music master was having his dinner now, he'd likely be down in the kitchens. Tess returned to her room first, to fetch something out of her baggage, and then she walked up the corridor, looking for the doors she wasn't supposed to notice. Manor houses were all alike, made to keep their functioning seamless and invisible. Glitter drew the eye; she turned away from the glitter, found an unobtrusive door, and was soon descending an unadorned staircase, following the clatter of dishes and the sound of warm laughter.

Martin sat at one of the kitchen tables, eating and reading while scullions buzzed about, giggling and gossiping in a language Tess didn't recognize. The music master had removed his ruff and set it in the middle of the table. Anna sat across from him, taking a cup of tea; she leaped to her feet upon seeing Tess. Tess had lived a dual life at court—half lady-in-waiting, half Jeanne's personal servant—so she'd been in servants' spaces before and had practice navigating them. Lady Borgo's cast-off gown made it harder, but she gave Anna quarter courtesy and kept her eyes averted until Anna, still wary, sat down again.

Tess sat beside Martin. He didn't look up.

"I saw your performance," Tess began.

"Yes, I know," said Martin. "It was quite a small room."

"My name is Tess," said Tess, flustered at not finding him easier to talk to.

He turned a page of his book. It was *The Life of St. Remy*.

This would be less awkward, surely, without Anna staring with naked suspicion in her eyes. "Could we go somewhere quieter?" said Tess.

"Regrettably, miss, I'm a Daanite," said Martin, still not looking up.

Tess went red. Saints' bones, they'd really got off on the wrong foot if he thought she was propositioning him. "I'm not here for that," she said.

He finally met her eye. "Ah, I see. There are only two kinds of foreign ladies who come looking for me after a concert. You must be the other kind."

He led Tess to a little storeroom, where the silver was kept. Occasionally someone would carry in a cleaned and polished candelabrum, but it was still more private than the open kitchen.

Martin folded his arms across his barrel chest. "Anna will report to her ladyship that you came here offering to take me away from all this."

Tess was stunned. "Y-you *have* heard this before."

"I told you. Two kinds. But explain how you're different. Get it over with."

She'd intended to ask him to come away on the *Avodendron*, but clearly he'd had that kind of offer before. (Why hadn't he fled, then? It made no sense.) Tess had conceived of a backup plan, however, in case she couldn't manage to stow him away or Marga insisted on returning him. From the bodice of her gown, she fetched Fozu's pale, fuzzy, self-repaired eyu.

Martin's brown eyes widened in surprise.

"This," said Tess, "can be used to contact a man who—"

"I know the sort of person it calls," said Martin, lowering his voice to an urgent whisper. "And I know someone like you could not have come by it honestly."

A servant came in with an ornate gravy boat. Tess, bristling at Martin's accusation, palmed the device until the other man had shelved the dish and left the room.

"Take it," said Tess, holding out the eyu.

"What good will it do me?" said Martin, making no move to take it. "You think a Ggdani would deign to whisk me away? How would he—and why should he?"

"His name is Hami," Tess persisted. "He's a Watcher . . . a good person. A principled person." She was stretching what she knew of him, almost to the breaking point. But someone capable of judging her worthiness was surely a paragon of worthiness himself? He must chafe at injustice. "If he knew how Lady Borgo was treating you—"

Martin actually laughed at this, although he shut his mouth quickly when two more servants brought in an enormous platter. His amusement was still manifest in the hand he'd clapped to his mouth: two fingers tapped a rapid beat upon his lips.

"I don't know how you concluded that," he whispered when they were alone again, "but Ggdani care for nothing but sabak and their laws. Not me. Not you."

Tess felt suddenly like she was looking down from a high, windy ledge; the depth of all the things she didn't know was far more considerable than she'd realized.

Martin's expression softened. "I see that you want to help," he said. "I'm willing to give you the benefit of the doubt that it's because you have a kind heart. But what looks simple to you is not simple at all. If I go, what happens to the boys in my choir? What happens to my village and my people and my forest? You can't take all of us, and we wouldn't go. This is where we were born, where our ancestors sing, where we *live*."

His eyes glittered. "If you really want to help, don't take me. Take Lady Borgo."

Tess's heart sank. "What? *How?* She's—"

"The rightful ruler of this island?" said Martin.

"I wasn't going to say that. I only mean taking her won't solve anything," said Tess. "What about all the Ninysh settlers, soldiers, merchants, sheep . . . ?"

"Please take the sheep," said Martin. He was short enough that he always looked like he was rolling his eyes at her. "But you see how quickly you grasp the complexity of removing her? We Nutufi are every bit as complicated. We're not *children*."

Tess's ears burned; she felt scolded.

Behind Tess, someone cleared her throat, and then Anna's voice said, "You shouldn't be speaking so long unsupervised—'for your very nature, pagan, leads you into sin.'"

"Of course it does. But 'civilized' ladies may do as they like," said Martin, giving Tess one last, reproachful look as he followed Anna out.

Tess was left to find her own way back upstairs. Only when she'd reached her bedroom door did she realize that she'd left her thnimi on the entire time. Seraphina was going to see everything that had just happened; Tess burned with embarrassment.

"You heard him play," she said directly into the device. "I couldn't not try. I didn't know he'd be insulted. I wouldn't have been, but then again, I walked away from my whole family. Maybe I just don't mind being rootless."

In that moment, though, she wasn't so sure. Long after she'd turned off her thnimi, she still clutched it tightly, as if it were Seraphina's hand.

Tess's mind was too unquiet for sleep. She paced her room, turning the same argument over in her mind: *I had to try. I didn't know he'd be insulted. What was I supposed to do?* After an hour of this, reaching no conclusion, she decided to see if Jacomo was awake. Maybe he was feeling better (assuming he'd really been ill). Maybe she could bring him something if not.

Light shone under his door, and the floorboards squeaked at regular intervals as if he, too, were pacing. Tess knocked, and the footfalls abruptly stopped.

"Yes, that's it, go very quiet and maybe I'll forget I heard you," said Tess.

Jacomo answered the door wearing his traveling cloak, leather knapsack, and boots.

Tess sized him up. "You appear to be going somewhere."

"I'd just made up my mind to come tell you," he said, closing his door silently behind him. "There's a, ah, festival that happens on this island. A storytelling festival, called Maftumaiu—which means 'spring festival,' I'm given to understand. Mee is going to be there—"

The Katakutia had said she'd see him soon.

"You said you'd voted to come to St. Remy *on my behalf*," said Tess, swatting his arm. "What a devious villain you are. I know better than to ask whether I can come with you."

"You absolutely can't," said Jacomo.

"Hence the not-actually-asking. But where will you be, and when will you be back?"

"It's held at a place called the Navel of the World—I don't know where that is. I've got to get going, though," said Jacomo. He set off down the corridor.

Tess dogged his steps. "How are you getting to this place you don't know?"

"Mee told me to meet 'the Walker' at the harbor," he said. "The Navel of the World can't be far if we're walking. It might be a tavern—that would be a good tavern name. I would appreciate it if you could prevent the countess and Lady Borgo from noticing I'm gone."

"How am I supposed to do that? I suppose I could claim you're praying." Marga was never going to fall for that. "You'll be back in time to sail, though, right?"

They'd just reached the bottom of the curving stair. The great serpent sculpture loomed in the darkness like a piece of frozen night. Jacomo whispered, "I hope so. The festival seems to last roughly a week? Until the moon is a quarter gone. The countess will want to sail as soon as the submersible is repaired, but she couldn't tell me how long that will take. I suppose if the expedition left without me, I could try to catch up—"

"No," said Tess. "No! You can't leave it that uncertain. Marga won't want to sail without you. You're practically her spiritual adviser now."

"That's overstating it," said Jacomo, growing flustered. "And I think I made her angry this morning."

"You have to come back," said Tess. "Don't make me listen to her cry about Will; I'll never forgive you. And what if this is all a ruse? A duke's son would fetch a sweet ransom—even a ne'er-do-well like you." He laughed, but she insisted: "In all seriousness, I'll never forgive *myself* if I'm letting you naively walk into danger. How would I tell your family?"

He unclasped his thnik necklace and handed it to her. "Here's how."

"More literal than I meant, but thank you," said Tess, pocketing it.

"As for danger . . . it's occurred to me that this might be a trick. Come with me to the harbor and meet this Walker person. Gauge whether he seems trustworthy. Maybe he can give you more detail, because other than 'this island,' I swear I wasn't told where we're going. And this is a big island."

It was not a short walk back to St. Remy town. The palasho was deeper in the countryside than it had seemed from inside a carriage. The full moon rose over the rolling hills as they walked. The higher it rose, the more anxious Jacomo became, and the more he picked up the pace. They reached town at a trot and jogged the last half mile to the harbor.

"Sorry," said Jacomo. "But I was told he'd arrive when the moon is at its zenith."

"And how . . . are you supposed . . . to recognize this person?" asked Tess, irritated that she was out of breath and he was not.

"Mee didn't say," he said, looking up and down the deserted docks. Ships, dotted with roosting gulls, bobbed lightly on the waves.

And then they saw the Walker and realized that there had been no need for Mee to describe him because there could be no mistaking him. He was wading through the ocean toward them, the water up to his waist and then his knees, moonlight gleaming off his silvery scales.

It was St. Pandowdy.

Tess's family had hidden in the tunnels under Lavondaville during St. Jannoula's War, so she hadn't seen the gigantic Saint rise from the swamp or carry off St. Jannoula in his hand. She'd heard Seraphina describe him, though, and she'd seen St. Fredricka's mural of him coming to Seraphina's rescue. Tess had often grumbled about her sister being considered such a hero when this giant had saved her skin.

He was impressively large, however.

Jacomo was having some kind of moment, and when Tess looked at him now, she saw what kind it was. He looked like Frai Moldi gazing upon Anathuthia.

"Oh, Tess," he half whispered, reaching for her hand. "It's a sign."

She squeezed back.

He untangled his hand from hers, looking a little embarrassed.

"You have my thnik, in case this goes bad, but I can't help feeling that everything has come in some kind of circle and is exactly as it should be. Tess, I feel called to this."

Emotion had risen in Tess's chest, and she couldn't speak, but she nodded. She hung back while he walked to the end of the dock. The giant Saint waded toward him, making waves that wobbled every ship at the pier. Without a word, St. Pandowdy scooped Jacomo up and carried him away.

The Navel of the World might be farther away than either of them had guessed. Who knew how far St. Pandowdy could walk in a night?

Tess watched them turn south at the harbor mouth, and then took the long road back to the manor house, alone.

Twenty-Three

Mind of the World, you open ceaselessly.

The world needs every mind it can get. Some are ancient, and some are very young, and some—the ones that never stop questioning—contrive to be both.

Once upon a time (*or was it more than once? Time sometimes goes in circles*), a giant lifted Jacomo and carried him into a new life. Cradled in that enormous, scaly hand, Jacomo rocked with every step the great Saint took. The long island slept, stretched tenderly under a quilt of moonlight. Pandowdy waded parallel to shore, pressing his massive body carefully through the water as if trying not to make too many waves. It felt slow, and yet they moved fast enough for the wind to make Jacomo's eyes water.

Sure, it was the wind. He tried to laugh at himself, but it came out as a sob.

⚔

When Jacomo was very small, his mother had read scripture to him and his older brothers every evening. Not that she tucked them into bed or anything—that was Nurse's job—but she'd come into the kitchen and read while they had their bedtime snack, a roll and a cup of warm milk. Jacomo, at four years old, would climb onto one of the kitchen counters and read along over his mother's shoulder (he'd taught himself to read before either of his brothers had learned to sit still). He liked to see the text for himself, because he'd noticed his mother sometimes misread things. At that age, he innocently assumed this was an accident.

"Remember, brethren, the fruits of the soul," she intoned one evening, reading from the analects of St. Munn. "Faith, hope, and obedience."

"Charity, Mumma," he piped up helpfully. "That word is 'charity.'"

"Sit by the hearth with your brothers, you unnatural child," she snapped at him.

"You fatty fat pig," his brother Heinrigh added.

Jacomo didn't want to sit with his brothers, and besides, the scripture had him bursting with questions. "Do the fruits of the soul have pips, Mumma? Where can you plant them? Is that how you grow a soul?"

"What the devil kind of impertinence is that?" Her breath had that smell, the one they weren't supposed to notice. She closed the book and slammed it onto the counter beside him, hard enough to make him jump. "I won't be corrected by a weird, unsettling child like you."

She stormed out.

"Ooh, how do I grow my soul?" said his brother Richard in a high, mocking voice. "Maybe it needs some manure."

"Pigs like manure—oink, oink, oink," added Heinrigh, who had never been and would never be any subtler than that.

"Stop it—please?" Jacomo cried. He was already taller than both his brothers, but they were older and still somehow bigger in his mind.

"Stop it, stop it, stop it—pleeeeease?" they hooted back at him, cavorting across the red tile floor. Heinrigh stole one of Jacomo's socks right off his foot.

Jacomo pulled up his feet before Richard could snatch the other one. He felt like a treed cat, hounds baying below. He struggled until he had a cramp in his face and then, humiliatingly, began to cry.

Suddenly real hounds came into the kitchen, sticking their noses into everything, and Griss the gamekeeper right behind them (his name was Fritz, but two-year-old Jacomo had called him Griss and the name had stuck). The old man took one look at the boys—one up, two down—and guessed what was happening. "You, Richard, for shame! You at least should know better. Heinrigh, you feral beast, I despair of you ever learning. Both of you, to bed, or I'll see that your father hears of this."

The older boys scarpered. Jacomo, still sniveling on the counter, cringed at the gamekeeper's stern words. Griss didn't have to scold him for him to feel scolded.

Griss glared after Richard and Heinrigh until they were gone, then turned to Jacomo and said in a quieter voice, "Your mother's in a fine state. What was it this time, lad? You didn't find another brandy stash, did you? I told you to stop looking behind things."

Jacomo shook his head, his chest shuddering as he inhaled. "I only—I only asked how do you grow a . . . a soul." He burst into tears again.

Griss was silent a moment. Jacomo ventured a glance at his face, expecting to see scorn there. The old man tugged his beard, his expression almost wistful.

"That's a good question," said Griss at last. "A very good question. I'll warrant not even the wisest priests entirely know the answer." He grabbed Jacomo under the armpits, gently lifted him down, and then bent to the boy's eye level. "Save these questions for them that deserve it. Your mother has troubles of her own; your brothers . . . maybe they'll grow into a bit more wisdom someday. Maybe."

"Poppa?" asked Jacomo.

"No," said Griss. "How about this: save them up for me. You may come out to my cottage anytime and ask."

"But will you know the answers?" asked Jacomo. He was worried about insulting the gamekeeper, but he needed to know.

"Perhaps not," said Griss, never one to lie to a child. "But I expect that if you have someone to ask, that might help you toward answering it yourself. I promise to listen to every question and say 'Good question!' afterward."

This made Jacomo laugh, and for the moment, unexpectedly, that was enough.

✕

The older Jacomo got, the fewer unanswerable questions he asked. He learned to suppress tears and find other ways of dealing with his brothers.

He cultivated an air of devastating cynicism that could wither Richard with a look or cut him with a remark; this earned the grudging respect of his eldest brother. Heinrigh, impervious to both looks and remarks, required a more physical approach. With trickery, Richard's help, and a good deal of luck, Jacomo contrived to ambush Heinrigh and not merely thrash him but break his arm.

Contrary to all sense and reason, Heinrigh was his great friend and devotee after that.

Jacomo was so disgusted with himself that he couldn't meet his own gaze in the mirror.

At thirteen, he was enrolled at St. Gobnait's Seminary. It was his duty, as the third son of the Duke of Ducana, to become Bishop of Trowebridge; the bishopric held lands adjacent to his father's, and he would thereby, sort of, join their estates. It was a fine plan, except that whatever naive faith he'd once possessed had been so shingled over with self-loathing that he couldn't even locate it anymore.

It had surely withered and died without the sun.

As soon as he arrived in Lavondaville, he realized that he was going to wither, too, in the dark and dismal city. At least at home, even if his family was awful, he could climb to the top of Cragmarog and see the whole sky.

He told himself he'd give it six months. Surely he could endure half a year of early mornings, bad food, cold latrines, long prayers, and insufferable classmates?

Four months in, St. Jannoula's War started. Classes were moved to the cathedral crypt in case of dragon attack. The food became exponentially worse, and he never saw the sun. Jacomo decided he could not endure this for half a year after all.

He ran away during meditation, when everyone had their eyes closed.

It was not the cleverest idea he'd ever had. There was a war on, after all. He burst out of the cathedral to see dragons screaming and grappling overhead, crashing into spires and rooftops. The sky was so clogged with dust and smoke that daylight barely shone through; the sun looked like a rotting orange.

Jacomo pulled up his novice's hood against the rain of ash, put his head down like a bull, and ran through the twilit streets. He dodged falling timbers and bricks; a pane of glass just missed him, and he recognized belatedly that it could have killed him. In times of dire stress and fear, people sometimes discover that they have a secret well of faith after all, but not Jacomo. He did not call upon Heaven in his hour of need, nor yet the Saints.

Not even the literal, living Saints who were fighting this war with their minds.

Other people have described it as *mind fire* or *soul light* or even *Heaven's holy glow*. Jacomo was wholly occupied with trying to get out of the crumbling city; if he noticed the Saints' light at all, he took it for lightning or dragon fire.

The city gates were barred against the Samsamese, who'd joined the war against Goredd. They were camped on the plain to the south, so Jacomo headed north. Armies couldn't maneuver easily in the forest and swampland; that direction was probably clear. Indeed, he encountered almost no guards as he climbed to the top of the northern battlements.

How was he to descend the other side of the wall, though? It was a sheer drop, thirty feet onto rock. Jacomo didn't have a rope; he didn't even have a change of clothes. He'd bolted with no real plan and had made it this far on sheer nerve, but at this final insurmountable obstacle, he crumbled. He couldn't go forward and he couldn't go back.

The wall shook; Jacomo clung to a merlon for dear life, certain that this was the end. Before his eyes, a mound was rising in the middle of the swamp. It swelled and grew as something enormous pushed up from below, mud and decay streaming off it in rivulets. Deer and birds fled for their lives. Ancient trees were uprooted and shed like straw. A gargantuan being stood upright and shook itself off, revealing skin covered in tarnished silver scales.

A giant had risen from the swamp: St. Pandowdy.

Jacomo fell to his knees in wonderment and wept, overcome with terror and inexplicable joy. He wept as if he might never stop.

Weeping washed the debris from his heart—an epoch's worth of accumulated sediment, the festering peat of shame. It destroyed, for the moment, the safe, obscure bog where he had buried his innocence and brought his childish faith back into the light.

He had forgotten how painful and beautiful it was.

He had a vision then, of bringing comfort to the indigent, of helping people grow their souls—he would become a good priest, for all the right reasons, not merely because he was a third son and had no choice. He saw the map of his life spread out before him, a worthy life where he was not his brothers' fool or his father's pawn.

The vision faded, but Jacomo promised himself that he would never forget it.

Jacomo leaned back in St. Pandowdy's hand and watched the stars sway overhead.

He *had* forgotten, alas. If anything, he'd grown more bitter after seeing St. Pandowdy because no one had understood, not even his teachers at seminary, who were supposed to understand these things, if anyone was. The shallow tedium of his classes disillusioned him again, and then the dream was gone.

"I ran away from seminary," he said aloud to the night air. "And I found something to believe in, little by little, as I followed Tess and deduced that she was changing. I admired her—from afar—but I envied her, too. She got to see the Continental Serpent; the creature was dead before I reached it."

The giant Saint didn't answer. It wasn't clear whether Jacomo's words had reached him.

It didn't matter—St. Pandowdy had come for him. That was more than enough. Some vast wheel had come full circle, and Jacomo would become what he was always meant to be. A True Priest, Mee had called him. His vision—his purpose—would be fulfilled.

Jacomo reached into his pocket for the one religious token he still carried, a St. Polypous medallion. He pressed it to his lips, then closed his eyes and let destiny carry him away.

Twenty-Four

"Don't tell me Jacomo is ill again!" cried Marga when Tess came down to breakfast. Jacomo was, of course, nowhere to be seen; Tess had planned not to draw attention to his absence, on the principle that she couldn't be caught in a lie if she never said anything, but apparently Marga had already been thinking about him.

"Poor fellow," the countess told Lady Borgo. "He's spent half the voyage over a bucket."

"I could ask my personal physician—"

"No need," Tess interjected. Fortunately, she'd already considered what to say. "He sends his regrets, but it's his Saint's day, and he wants to spend it fasting and meditating."

Both women stared at her from across the table, and Tess got a sinking feeling that she'd said something bizarre without realizing it.

"It's St. Yane's Day," said Marga.

Of course it was. Tess's mother had had an altar to St. Yane; she'd explained him to young Tess as "the patron of married people." The baby-making Saint, in other words. A completely ridiculous patron for Jacomo to be fasting and meditating for.

"Heaven chooses your patron. I expect he's a bit self-conscious about it," Tess said, digging into the breakfast kippers that had appeared in front of her as if by magic.

"So, I've spoken to the glaziers," said Lady Borgo, changing the subject. "We have enough glass and caming to fix Lord Morney's submersible, but they worry whether their technique for greenhouses and church windows will withstand the pressures of the sea. They're also worried about the work space. If the submersible were in pieces, they could easily work from both sides, but to have someone in that enclosed space with an open flame—"

"There isn't time to disassemble the whole thing," said Marga.

"Let Pathka help," suggested Tess. "His flaming tongue would do the trick, and he's not averse to tight spaces."

Marga brightened. "Perfect. Although . . . I haven't seen him since St. Claresse?"

"He's been loafing in the sabak tank," said Tess.

"The sabanewt!" cried Lady Borgo. "I meant to tell you, Marga—you must leave it here with me. You'll never keep it alive on a ship, whereas I already keep a gaggle of penguins and a sea beaver. If I added a sabanewt to my menagerie, I think the masters could trouble themselves to come look at it. After it passes, its dissection would be a momentous scientific occasion—by invitation only. I'll gather every drop of precious oil, sell it to the highest bidder as an elixir of immortality, and finally fund an academy of my very own, even more prestigious than the Segoshi original, with my anthropological museum forming a foundation for . . ."

Lady Borgo went on and on; Tess stayed focused on Marga, who looked perfectly untroubled by the suggestion that she leave the sabak here to be prodded, dissected, and drained of fluids. How was she not repulsed by the very idea? This was a sentient creature, as intelligent as a quigutl. They should release the sabak back into the wild; the creature had only been taken aboard for Fozu, and he was gone.

Of course, Marga had refused to release Fozu, who was indisputably a sentient creature as well. Tess was getting an inkling of yet another worthy act to undertake.

Before noon, they went down to the harbor to look at Lord

Morney's contraption, which had already been hauled out of the belly of the ship and put up on scaffolding at the dry dock. Several guests from the salon the night before showed up to see it as well. At Lady Borgo's request, Marga began explaining how the submersible worked.

Tess skipped the lecture and went aboard the *Avodendron* to fetch Pathka. She borrowed the padlock key, which was hung up in the navigation room, and sauntered over to the tank, whistling. The grating had rusted a little and complained when she opened it. Pathka popped up at once, looking hale and frisky. Tess would not have guessed that seawater would be good for his scales, but he was gleaming.

"They need a flaming tongue over at the submersible," she said. "Can you manage without a translator, though? I have some business with . . ." She nodded toward the sabak.

"Oh, yes, she wants to talk to you again," said Pathka, climbing over the edge of the box. "Don't worry about me. I could fix the thubmerthible by myself, if they have all the materials."

Pathka hurried off, leaving a trail of foot-and-tail drips across the boards. Tess turned her attention to the pale creature in the water; she was looking at her. Tess stared back, her heart contracting. She didn't want to talk to the sabak again. Just thinking about the last time made her squirm. She'd felt a . . . a moment of sympathy for Will, for the haunted confusion he'd lived in the last day of his life. For a moment he had seemed human, breakable, and very, very small—which made her the monstrous one, didn't it, for not forgiving him? That was backward, it was wrong, and she wasn't revisiting those thoughts if she could help it.

The sailors had made opening the sluice look easy, but it was not. Tess finally wrenched the lever enough, and water began gushing out the scupper. It was loud. She looked around, but most of the crew were ashore. She spotted Glodus, up the mainmast, but he seemed to be asleep.

"I'm setting you free," Tess told the sabak. "You'll never swim in the sea again if Lady Borgo finds you here."

Tess wasn't worried about the creature understanding her. Fozu had been so anxious to speak the sabak's own language, but the creature had taught Pathka chirp-speak with a touch. She surely had all of Ninysh and Goreddi absorbed into her mind already from Will. Or from Tess herself—what language had the sabak been speaking in Tess's head?

The water was nearly gone before Tess noticed something she'd forgotten: the grating to stop the sabak escaping while her water was being changed. It was at the far end of the scupper, bolted to the outside of the ship.

There was no way Tess could reach it on her own, let alone remove it. The sabak couldn't get out this way; she'd emptied the tank for nothing.

The creature wouldn't survive long out of water, surely; she lay forlornly at the bottom of the empty tank, a torpid white blob. Tess was going to have to refill the water as quickly as she could. The sailors had made *that* look hard.

Suddenly the sabak hurled herself upward, flowing over the edge of the tank and spilling out onto the deck with a splat. Tess clapped a hand to her mouth to keep from shrieking and backed away from the sabak. She couldn't exactly walk on land, but she dragged herself wetly along, digging her claws into the deck. At first Tess thought she was after her, angry that she didn't want her in her mind again, but the sabak was only looking for another scupper—there was drainage all along the deck, to clear the inevitable seawater. She wriggled, squeezed, and slithered through a hole that looked much too small for her, and splashed down in the harbor below.

Tess gaped stupidly at where the sabak had gone, and then called "You're welcome!" after her. She returned the key and went ashore. A glance toward the submersible told her that Pathka was there; the gathered observers seemed enthralled by whatever he was doing. Good. It would be a while before anyone noticed the empty tank. Tess had time to get herself far from the scene.

It wasn't that she thought no one would figure it out; Marga would, almost certainly. But Tess preferred to be scolded later, in private, after the countess had had time to think it over and realize Tess was right.

She returned to Palasho Borgo—a pleasant walk on a mild spring day—and took lunch in the kitchens. In her room, afterward, she spotted Jacomo's pendant thnik on the table by the bed, glinting accusingly. She had promised to keep in touch with Jeanne, and her single attempt so far had only reached Richard. Now, while she waited for Marga to return and yell at her, Tess had a golden opportunity to talk to her sister.

Except, surely she shouldn't call without knowing where Jacomo had gone? What if Richard wanted to talk to him? He'd never believe his brother was meditating. She needed to figure out where the Navel of the World might be, so she could put everyone's minds at ease—her own included. She set the thnik aside and went in search of Lady Borgo's library.

(She knew it was an excuse, and a flimsy one, to put off calling Jeanne, but . . .)

The library had maps of St. Remy—astonishingly detailed maps, showing individual farms. There were some non-Ninysh names. When Tomasino brought Tess a cup of tea, she noticed for the first time that he, too, had branded hands. "Forgive me," she said, "but do you speak Nutufi?"

He glanced around and then said, "Nutufi?"

Ugh, she hadn't said it quite right. Martin had been correct about Ninysh vowels. Embarrassed, she pressed on: "Do any of these place names mean anything specific?"

It took him some effort to work backward from the awkward Ninysh transliterations, but he found Thoughtful Branch, Hill of Clouds, Never Forget Mazu, the Quiet After Rain. None seemed to mean Navel of the World.

"This is an old map," said Tomasino wistfully. "Most of those places don't exist anymore. The forest has shrunk by half." He traced a line across the narrowest part of the island, two-thirds of the way down. "The center is all sheep now."

Tess asked, not very hopefully, "Have you heard of the Navel of the World?"

"No," said Tomasino carefully.

"Maftumaiu?" He shrugged; she was surely mangling the pronunciation. "Where is the spring festival held?"

He shrugged. "It isn't held anywhere. We're not pagans anymore."

Tess thanked him for his time and the tea, which she took back to her room.

Either he wasn't aware that the festival still happened, or he feared her reporting back to Lady Borgo. Tess couldn't blame him, but it left her stuck. If worse came to worst and it looked like they were in danger of leaving without him, she hoped that she might fetch Jacomo on foot, if need be, but he could be anywhere.

Just thinking about searching the whole island was exhausting, apparently, because she fell asleep before she had a chance to call Jeanne.

Marga all but kicked her door down. Tess sat bolt upright in bed.

"What were you thinking?" the countess cried, marching into the room. "That you'd just set the sabanewt free, without asking me?"

"She was . . . sick?" said Tess, whose half-asleep brain did not have a firm grasp on what lie she'd meant to tell. "Her gills were green—Fozu said that was bad—so I had to act fast?"

Marga sat down heavily on the bed beside her, blinking as if fighting tears. "Glodus tried to convince us that Argol had set the creature free. Of course Napou and I knew that that was nonsense, but Aemelia was irate. She demanded that Argol be flogged."

"Oh, cack," said Tess. In her wildest imaginings, she could not have foreseen that.

"We talked her out of it," said Marga. "Napou had his doubts, but if you wait until Aemelia calms down, she will listen to reason." She got a faraway look, then shook it off. "*You,* though. Why didn't you fetch me before letting the sabanewt go? You didn't trust me."

"Trust you?"

"To do the right thing." Marga's voice grew strained. "To have mercy on a suffering creature and let it go. What did you think, that I wanted to watch it die?"

"Lady Borgo, just this morning, was fantasizing about holding an invitation-only dissection of the corpse," cried Tess, "and you said nothing."

The countess waved off this objection. "Being confrontational doesn't help; politeness is more effective and costs nothing. I wish my uncle understood that."

Politeness might be more effective for a countess, but it just made some people easier to ignore. Now was not the time to confront Marga with this, however. Tess opted for the consoling lie: "It wasn't a matter of trusting you or not. I had to act quickly."

Marga inhaled shakily. "All right. I seem to be a bit touchy on that score. Aemelia told me something about William that really upset me."

Oh, please no.

"Apparently his inheritance was a pittance, and his title in dispute," Marga continued, looking at her hands folded in her lap. "I thought he'd spent most of it on the submersible, but now I learn Aemelia funded that. The submersible was to have made his fortune, so that when he grew rich and famous enough, he might rule his own island like she does."

Tess had heard about the disputed title from Jacomo, but the importance of it hadn't sunk in. "So . . . you feel like William deceived you?" she asked cautiously.

"I feel like he didn't trust me!" cried Marga, bursting into tears. "Did he really think me so petty and shallow that I cared whether he had a title, or a penny to his name? Why didn't he tell me? I wouldn't have begrudged him anything. . . ."

On she went. And on and on. Tess pasted on a smile, turned off her ears, and did her best, but if it hadn't been urgent before, she felt it keenly now: she needed Jacomo back. Tess could not be Marga's shoulder to cry on about Will.

The Navel of the World still eluded Tess, though. Martin might have known where it was; he'd been blunt and forthcoming, but Tess felt too ashamed to approach him again. Anna had seemed mortified just talking about her hands, but surely Tess could find a way to ask about Maftumaiu without causing her distress.

Tess tried the next evening during her bath. Anna had offered again to scrub her back; Tess hunched her shoulders and submitted to the brush. Anna scrubbed with enthusiasm.

"Did you grow up in the forest, Anna?" Tess finally got up the courage to ask.

Almost at once the scrubbing ceased. "That was a long time ago," said Anna. "I don't think about those days."

"I know you're devoted to the Saints now and have renounced paganism," said Tess, trying to be respectful. "I just wondered what it was like."

Anna grunted noncommittally and resumed scrubbing.

What it was like was too vague. Tess tried another angle. "Did you tell stories? I heard the tale of Vulkharai from a Shesh storyteller in Paishesh and really enjoyed it."

Anna grunted again, sharply this time. There was an opinion behind it.

"I liked how Vulkharai is both comic and tragic, all at once," Tess persisted.

Anna couldn't hold back any longer. "If that's how the Shesh tell it, then they're a shallow people, skating over the surface of things. There's nothing *tragic* about Vulkharai."

"No?" said Tess, surprised. "But he accidentally kills the one he loves!"

"He loves wrongly," said Anna. "It's not a literal ice tiger, anyway; it's a metaphor."

"Tell me how," said Tess. They were getting somewhere, even if she wasn't sure where.

"Vulkharai stands for all people. The ice tiger is the violence we are regrettably prone to," said Anna. She began ladling warm water over Tess's shoulders. "Violence may be alluring, but it always destroys you. Vulkharai innocently performs an unselfish act—making boots—and his loving generosity defeats the monster. Only when it's dead, and the infatuation broken, does he see what danger he was in."

"Love conquers violence," said Tess, a bit awed. "That's wonderful."

"It's pagan nonsense," said Anna, a sudden bitterness in her voice. "'But even those who dwell in darkness may see glimmers of the light,' saith St. Remy. We did our best, in our ignorant state, until we learned better."

"You give yourself too little cred—"

"I told you, I don't think about those days," said Anna, bitterness blooming into hostility. She stood and brushed off her knees. "Shame on you for asking me." She was almost in tears now. "Don't speak of such things again, or I shall tell her ladyship."

"All right, I won't," said Tess, cowed.

Tess was left to finish washing herself and to think about what Anna's version of Vulkharai must say about the Nutufi.

Submersible repairs proceeded relentlessly, faster than the moon diminished. Upon the fourth day, Countess Margarethe entered the hollow metal gourd herself and took it on its maiden voyage across the harbor. Tess, without realizing she was doing it, held her breath in sympathy until she almost passed out on the pier. When the submersible finally surfaced again, and Marga emerged, breathless and triumphant, Tess had to admit to herself that she had witnessed something historic and extraordinary.

And that she was out of time to locate the Navel of the World. The repairs were finished. The *Avodendron* would sail the next morning, and unless Jacomo miraculously showed up by then, he wouldn't be aboard.

Tess had expected the meditation excuse to last a day or two at most, and that she'd need a new story after that, but Marga hadn't asked after Jacomo once. It was a little disconcerting.

Dinner was a fine spring lamb, so young and tender the meat seemed to melt. Tess was too preoccupied to enjoy it. The two noble ladies recounted the glorious submersible test, seemingly oblivious to Tess's fretfulness, until Lady Borgo said, "Marga, your protégé seems downcast. Worried, I would say."

"To my dismay, I have to admit you're right," said Marga, keeping her eyes on her food.

"Of course I am," said Lady Borgo, slicing another succulent, bloody tranche of lamb off the bone. She put a slice in her mouth and chewed slowly, never taking her eyes off Tess.

"Tess, let me tell you a story," said her ladyship at last. "When my great-grandfather, the first Lord Borgo, discovered this island, he found it brimming over with pagans. Our St. Remy Pelaguese worshiped a great black stone, different from any other on the island. Perhaps it had fallen as a meteor. The pagans, in their simplicity, believed that it marked the spot where the earth had once been attached to the sun, its mother, by some cosmic umbilicus. The Navel of the World, if you will."

Tess felt the hairs on the back of her neck stand up. She'd thought she'd been so careful in her inquiries, but her ladyship had gotten wind of it somehow.

"The Navel was the site of their notorious spring festival, an unholy orgy of howling, dancing, human sacrifice, and rites too unseemly to discuss at the dinner table," Lady Borgo continued. "It was meant to revive the earth's fertility after the long barrenness of winter."

"Like our peasant revels on St. Yane's Day?" asked Tess, pushing back the only way she could think to. Marga, still, was pointedly not meeting her eye.

"A thousand times worse," said Lady Borgo, her lips pinching together in distaste. "Dark rituals. Witchcraft. Other Pelaguese would sail hundreds of miles to participate in the debauchery and to add their deviltry to the mix.

"My great-grandfather was utterly confounded. He found the Noo-too-fee docile, friendly, and eager to serve, on the whole, but he couldn't convince them that their devotion to this omphalos—that's the technical term—was incompatible with the faith of Allsaints. They would eagerly attend Mass and then pay their devil-stone a visit on the sly, and they would not give up their spring festival. When he posted guards around the stone, the pagans howled like hounds kept out of the kitchen.

"Finally his lordship hit upon an ingenious solution: he built this palasho right on top of the damned thing, and that was the end of his troubles. It's in a locked vault because it still draws Pelaguese like flies if it's out in the open. I can show you after dinner. It's in the cellar."

"The Navel of the World . . . is in your cellar," said Tess, unable to fit the thought into her mind. Jacomo had been carried off by a giant; he wasn't in the cellar. What little she'd thought she knew about where he'd gone was now snatched away, leaving her no place to stand.

"As for the spring festival, that practice has been outlawed," said Lady Borgo. "Alas, it pops up now and again in the forest, like the devil from his hole, and we have to beat it back down."

"Enough," Marga snapped. "Tess, how did Jacomo hear of these rites, and when did he leave?"

Tess met the countess's shrewd gaze and then wished she hadn't. "I'm not sure . . . what?"

"He hasn't been in his room for at least three days. Maybe four. Aemelia asked the servants not to disturb him on St. Yane's Day."

"We did believe you initially," said Lady Borgo into her wineglass. "But he's the son of the Duke of Ducana, and I could not, in good conscience, fail to see to his needs. At first I thought maybe he had sneaked off to dally with *you*." She winked at Tess. "You're not entirely unattractive, however uncouth. But no, Anna affirms that you've been sleeping quite alone."

Tess vainly willed her cheeks not to catch fire.

"And she says you've been asking impertinent questions of her and Tomasino."

All the fire in Tess's body turned to ice.

"I glean from this that they have revived the spring festival yet again," said Lady Borgo, smirking. "It will be out in the forest, where they think we can't find it. Young Jacomo—a sweet-natured naïf, from what Marga tells me—has been lured there, seduced by the primitive."

"He is a priest," said Marga. "I doubt he's prone to debauchery or seduction."

"Are you saying that he couldn't resist the opportunity to convert a whole mass of heathens at once?" said her ladyship, putting on her pious face.

Tess met Marga's gaze; clearly they both knew the answer to that one.

"Priests are not immune to temptation," said Lady Borgo, stating it like a scientific principle. "His intentions may have been pure, but he couldn't know the depth of iniquity he'd face. They possess a thousand foul persuasions. We should fear for his immortal soul.

"I shall send in the militia first thing tomorrow. This has gone on too long. I left a bit of forest at the south end of the island; the trees are so beautiful, it seemed a shame to do away with it entirely. If they're just going to muck it up with their pagan rites, then they've forced my hand. This ends now, even if we have to burn the forest to the ground."

"Jacomo can take care of himself," said Tess. "Give me a horse and I'll fetch him back, no harm done to anyone."

Lady Borgo was brimming with exaggerated sorrow. "I have decades of experience with these people. I can't allow you to risk it. If the son of a duke, armed with scriptures and Saintly virtues, succumbed to their wiles, imagine how they'd trample your maidenly modesty to dust."

"I don't know, I'm pretty uncouth," said Tess.

"This is a job for armed men," said her ladyship. "Soldiers can't hear the siren song of temptation over the ringing of their swords."

"There are temptations *only* soldiers can hear, Aemelia," said Marga.

Tess was too upset to eat after that; the ladies soon finished as well. As they were leaving the table, Marga grabbed Tess's wrist and whispered, "I hope you aren't plotting to steal a horse. That would be madness. Ask Argol to take you in the plaion."

Tess raised her eyes to the countess's face in surprise.

Marga's mouth flattened grimly. "I can talk Aemelia out of this. I know I can. She's a good person, Tess, she's just . . . she'll see reason."

There was no time to argue. Tess rushed to her room, changed into breeches and boots, and ran out of the palasho into the fallen night.

Twenty-Five

The *Avodendron* lay at wharf, her gangplank lowered. Tess clambered aboard, startling the sailor who'd ostensibly been standing guard but may actually have been dozing.

"Where's Argol?" cried Tess.

"Ashore, with the captain," he said, pointing toward a public house on the quayside called the Bletted Medlar. Light and music came out of the open doorway.

"Lower the plaion!" called Tess to the entire night watch. "Countess's order. I'll be back with Argol as soon as I may."

In the tavern, Tess spotted Argol across the crowded room playing backgammon with Captain Claado. Tess must have looked distraught, because they were on their feet almost at once, abandoning their game and threading their way through the drinkers toward her.

"What's happened?" said the captain in a low voice, as if he'd been expecting something.

"Jacomo's gone . . . to the forest," said Tess, her heart racing so fast she could barely speak. "Lady Borgo is sending . . . the militia. Marga wants . . . to dissuade her—"

"Good luck with that," muttered Claado.

"I need to warn the Nutufi and . . . fetch Jacomo back. Argol, would you . . . sail me?"

"Of course," said Argol.

Claado added, "She'll sail us both. I know the southern end of this island, the places to start looking. That's where I go to avoid the Borgo salon. And gods bless Marga for trying, but if I know her ladyship, she's been looking for an excuse to do this. The forest people need to know what's coming. I would be honored to help you warn them."

The crew of the *Avodendron*, to Tess's astonishment, had done her bidding; the plaion was in the water, ready to board. Argol worked quickly, raising the sail and coaxing the wind, and soon they'd cleared the harbor. They followed the coast southeastward.

Tess sat up late into the night. St. Remy was quite a long island, with nothing but blank, moonlit farmland for miles. Still, she kept her vigil. It felt important.

She must have drifted off at some point, because Claado shook her awake near dawn to point out something in the distance. It looked like a low black fog rolling across the island's face, but as the sun rose, and it didn't dissipate, Tess realized it was a dark line of trees, the vanguard of the forest. A dense, ancient wall of spruce and cedar. The trees stretched impossibly tall, as if to touch the reddening sky.

This was what the island had looked like before the Borgos moved in on it with sheep and wheat and settlers. Pasture extended right to the edge of the forest, where lambs nibbled new seedlings down to nubs. The sheep were winning this war.

Past this line of demarcation, St. Remy was a different island, with trees trailing moss, rocky cliffs, crashing surf, gulls and seals and otters. Sometimes massive timber structures, dome-shaped, abutted the water. Tess thought these might be human constructions, until she saw creatures, as large as cows, swimming with saplings clutched between their massive yellow teeth. Their tails spread behind them, black and pancake-flat. Sea beavers.

Soon they encountered a cluster of sea beaver lodges; between them, barely visible, flowed a narrow channel. Tess might've sailed past without seeing it, but Claado knew this coastline. He directed Argol into the channel, which was just wide enough for a boat to pass.

The hidden cove behind the lodges was larger than Tess would have guessed; at one end, narrow fishing boats were clustered, some pulled out of the water and suspended from ropes to make room for other boats beneath them. These were of many shapes and designs—flat or round, with lateen sails demurely furled or wide sails like splayed hands. Boats small enough for a single person; a longboat that might have held thirty. Some painted garishly, some drab as dead leaves. Tess could barely take in all their variety.

Other peoples used to sail hundreds of miles to attend Maftumaiu, Lady Borgo had claimed. Maybe some still did.

Argol maneuvered the plaion up to the landing, and Tess and Claado climbed ashore.

Steep steps were carved into the bank, curving away into the trees. In the upper branches, the low, brittle chatter of wind chimes sounded a bit like distant human voices. Tess looked up and saw they were made of bones.

They were inscribed with intricate carvings, like the scapula in Marga's collection and the bones on Lady Borgo's dining room wall. This was a Nutufi place.

Sunlight filtered through the foliage, making dappled patterns on the mossy path. Captain Claado took the steps two at a time, and Tess scrambled after him. At the top of the ridge he paused for her to catch up. She followed his gaze, but all she saw was a clearing, the forest floor beaten smooth by generations of feet.

"Where's the village?" she whispered, fearing to break the silence.

"Right in front of you," said the captain, stepping toward the clearing.

Tess saw nothing but trees. Well, no, there were small hillocks between the trees, mossy mounds set in a horseshoe pattern open toward the cove. Only when she stood among them did she see that each one had a door. They weren't hillocks, but houses, and the doors were delicately carved sea beaver tails like the ones in Lady Borgo's collection.

There seemed to be no one around.

"Is it usually this quiet?" whispered Tess again.

"I've only stopped here once; I don't know what's usual," Claado whispered back. "Maybe they heard the news already and evacuated."

"Or they're all at the Maftumaiu, wherever it's being held."

A woman emerged from one of the houses, yawning as she ducked out of the low doorway. She was tall, wiry, and well muscled, and her skin was an unexpected gray-green color. Short white hair stood straight up on her head. She was unfolding a piece of complicated basketry, which kept her from noticing Tess and Claado right away.

When she did notice them, she seemed unconcerned. She finished opening her basket—which seemed to be a stiff, woven garment, or maybe armor—and then she refolded it around her naked gray-green torso and over her gray-green shoulders and arms.

"Do you speak Ninysh?" Claado said unnecessarily loudly, enunciating with excruciating care. "Ne camprete Porphyrii? I need to speak to your chief. It's urgent."

The woman stared impassively, as if she didn't acknowledge the noises coming out of his mouth-hole as speech. Claado tried Porphyrian nautical hand signs. The woman gestured back. Claado frowned in concentration and tried a few more; they weren't quite communicating.

The woman's palms were unscarred, which settled it for Tess: she wasn't Nutufi, but she might be someone who'd come from afar to attend the Maftumaiu.

Tess heard soft voices and turned to see two men coming out of another house, holding hands. With their round faces and brown hair, they might have been Martin's uncles.

The gray-green woman saw them, too. She called out haltingly, perhaps speaking their language and not her own, and then she grinned and waggled both her hands beside her head as if to say, *These foreigners are your problem now. Good luck!*

With that, she stalked off into the forest.

Claado addressed the men: "Do either of you speak Ninysh?"

"I do," said the taller of the two, bowing slightly. "In St. Remy town I am called Samuel." His partner said nothing but narrowed his eyes.

"What are you called here?" said Tess, not sure this was an appropriate question. Why wouldn't he have given her his real name? Maybe she wasn't supposed to know.

He broke into a smile. "Solnu. But Samuel is easier for you to say and remember."

"I can remember Solnu," said Tess, although—to gauge by how many times he gently corrected her—she couldn't quite say it. There was some kind of half whistle between the *l* and the *n,* and then the *u* swooped like a swallow in a way she couldn't duplicate.

"Why have you come? It is our holy time, and I fear we cannot give you the attention you deserve," said Solnu at last, giving up on her vowels.

"We're here to warn you," said Claado. "Lady Borgo is sending her militia. You must prepare to fight or flee. Where is your chief? We need to tell them."

Solnu paled. "That can't be right. We have a treaty with Lady Borgo."

"She thinks you stole one of our people and wants to punish you for it," said Tess. "Is . . . is Jacomo here? A big fellow."

"Oh yes," said Solnu. "But we didn't steal him. The Walker brought him."

"I know," said Tess. "But the militia is coming nonetheless. You need to be ready."

Solnu spoke low and briefly to his partner. The other man, who Tess gleaned was named Tafo, seemed angry and had many rapid words to say. Solnu, gentler and more diplomatic, would occasionally raise his chin or jut his lip, expressions that seemed to carry a meaning Tess couldn't discern. Finally he pressed his thumb between Tafo's eyebrows (a surprising gesture that struck Tess as deeply tender), and Tafo stopped arguing.

"Our *king*," said Solnu, emphasizing that this was the word to use, "the one you wish to warn, is at the Maftumaiu."

"Take us to him," said Claado.

Solnu jutted his lip. "You don't understand. You can't disrupt the stories, even for this. If one of you told a story, you might perhaps mention the militia at the end of it."

Tess and Claado exchanged a look.

"I couldn't give the news as if it were a story?" asked Claado. "Once upon a time, that murderous Lady Borgo sent armed men to drive you from your—"

"That would be impiety," said Solnu. "If you prefer, you can wait for Maftumaiu to be over, in two more days."

"The militia will surely be here by then," said Tess.

"Then you'd better start thinking of a story to tell us," said Solnu.

He and Tafo linked arms with Tess and Claado and led them beyond the perimeter of the village, deeper into the forest, around boulders and mossy trees. They descended into a ravine on a trail that was barely a trail, and Tess wondered whether the militia would even be able to find this place. The village, sure, they'd probably destroyed a hundred such villages already; they'd know what to look for, or they'd listen for the wind chimes. Wherever Solnu was leading them was in very deep forest and harder to find.

They reached another clearing and Tess gasped. Before her rose a structure like a rondel barn, only ten times larger. The thatch was foot-long pine needles, not straw; the walls might've been fieldstone, but they were concealed behind leathery panels, intricately carved.

More sea beaver tails. It occurred to Tess that Lady Borgo's collection may not have been as "ancient" as advertised. The carvings might have been made by—and been plundered from—people within living memory.

Her ladyship would have coveted these. The panels were carved with sea scenes, fish and sea beavers and people in boats. Everything was textured with swirling whorls, as if Tess were viewing the scenes through moving water. The great double doors of the building were made of two tails, each six feet high, cut into geometrical lace. Light shone out through the holes.

Inside was a large amphitheater; four terraced levels, wide enough for people to recline on, descended to a central floor, where four thick pillars supported the round roof. Between each of the pillars a cheery fire burned, except in the south, where a storyteller stood upon a great tortoise shell. No one occupied the southern quarter of the room, behind him. That space was dotted with the flames of many tiny oil lanterns; if you squinted, it looked like the night sky.

The rest of the amphitheater was full of people. Tess saw Jacomo and Mee sitting to the right of the stage (was it a stage? Tess didn't know what else to call it). Mee was whispering in Jacomo's ear, presumably translating. Jacomo was behaving himself, not taking notes; he fidgeted with his Saint medallion, which twinkled in the firelight.

Kikiu clung to one of the columns near them; Tess spotted her when her tail twitched.

Solnu squeezed between Tess and Claado. "Which of you will tell the story?"

"Tess should tell it," muttered Claado. "All my stories end with someone drowning."

Tess didn't mind him volunteering her; she knew plenty of stories. The hardest part would be deciding which one to tell.

Solnu nodded, content with this. "Sit with us, and we'll raise you."

"Thank you," said Tess, unclear what the end of that sentence meant, quite.

Solnu and Tafo led them to the western quarter of the third terrace. The floor was of packed earth, covered in layers of furs and textiles. The gray-green woman sat nearby, one level down. At floor level were a group of young people, perhaps thirteen years old, sitting cross-legged with their hands on their knees, palms up. Their hands glistened in the lamplight; they'd been spread with some silver-blue substance.

"Why are their hands shiny?" Tess whispered to Solnu.

"It's a salve, to heal them," Solnu whispered back. "Keep quiet now."

Maybe they'd had their hands branded with that crisscrossing pattern, like Anna and Martin. It sounded painful to Tess, but none of the youngsters seemed unhappy about it. Adults sat near them, feeding them tidbits as if they were royalty.

Some Southlander customs surely looked just as incomprehensible from outside. The Keys to Ascension, for example, were patently ridiculous—if you thought about it—and yet Marga would not leave Will's funeral before placing them on the Golden House. It was just what one *did*; explaining it couldn't quite capture what it meant.

The storyteller on the tortoise shell had finished speaking; he turned and walked up the steps behind him, between the oil lamps— that was evidently what one did as well. Maybe he was supposed to look like he was rising through the sky. The twinkling lights made that part of the theater look like a staircase of stars.

A star-case, Tess decided, pleased with the pun.

As he rose, a humming also arose, undifferentiated notes that quickly resolved into a chord. Seraphina would have been able to identify it, certainly. To Tess it sounded . . . approving?

The gray-green woman was on her feet, making her way toward the top of the star-case.

On the other side of Tafo, Claado grimaced at Tess. She got the message: he did not want to wait through ten more stories before they could give their news.

"May I speak after this woman?" Tess whispered to Solnu. He raised his chin.

The gray-green woman, tall and regal, descended to the stage.

She eschewed the tortoise shell and made a circuit of the stage with one arm raised, her head bobbing back and forth. While she did this, there was more movement, someone else coming around to the top of the star-case.

The second descending star was Mee. She did not come all the way down but stood one tier up, among the twinkling lights.

Mee spoke in her airy voice, understandable to all: "Our storyteller has a name."

"Kluit," the woman announced.

"And she has a nation," said Mee.

"Tshu!" cried the storyteller, raising her hands with her fingers curled like claws.

The hum rose again; Tess was beginning to understand it as applause. She hummed along, trying to blend into the chord.

"Honor upon your words and deeds, O diplomats," said Kluit, per Mee's translation. Tess noted that Kluit had said "Nutufi," not "diplomats"; that was how Mee rendered the proper name.

"Every year we Tshu"—"my nation," per Mee—"send our most skilled storyteller as thanks for your help, long ago, in brokering our peace with the Aftisheshe" ("the dog herders"). "This is my seventeenth year; you all know me. I am the strongest salmon, navigating swift streams of story."

Appreciative laughter rose up. Kluit's grin gleamed in the firelight. She paused with her long arms spread like an albatross's wings, threw her head back, and cried plaintively:

Awake, O tigers, awake!
Your queen is dead—the traitor
Vulkharai has killed her.

I will tell you how it was done,
How he tricked and deceived her in the name of love,
And how we will have our vengeance.

Vengeance on his blood and breath,
Vengeance on his eyes and thought,
Vengeance on his people unto the tenth generation.

The story continued in this vein, a bloodcurdling account of Vulkharai's boot-based crime, followed by a long narration of the ensuing vendetta. Tess quickly lost track of who killed whom. This was nothing like the tragicomic song she'd heard in Paishesh.

The hum-applause was halfhearted after Kluit's tale, truth be told. Solnu whispered to Tess, "The Tshu have violent hearts, but we try to be good hosts and not insult them."

"You think they tell 'Vulkharai' wrong," said Tess, recalling Anna's interpretation.

"Different isn't the same as wrong," said Solnu, looking a little shocked. "But are you ready for me to raise you?"

Tess's stomach dropped. She still hadn't thought of a story.

Solnu rose and gave an unexpectedly long preamble. Mee, still onstage, didn't bother to translate it; she was staring at Tess through the fire, her gaze hostile. The Katakutia had warned Jacomo not to speak of this festival in front of "the Dead"; Tess suddenly worried that he was going to be in trouble with his mentor.

Solnu was nudging her arm. "Go on. I've raised you."

Raised seemed to mean he'd put her forth as a storyteller. Tess circled to the top of the star-case, as Kluit had done, and then descended to the illuminated stage, thinking quickly. A Dozerius tale might do. Not one of the seduction stories, which she couldn't stand anymore, but maybe one with monstrous beasts. Everyone loved battles with monstrous beasts, surely.

Mee gave her a serious look as she passed. Tess was starting to get nervous.

"Our storyteller has a name," Mee announced as Tess took her place on the shell.

"Tess," said Tess.

She expected to have to name her nation next; she would say *Goredd* but would tell the story in Ninysh. Mee, however, didn't give the prompt she'd given Kluit. Instead she said, "This girl comes from the Land of the Dead. Hear her Deadlander story, O People."

Tess told the first tale that popped into her head.

Twenty-Six

Mind of the World, where stories are born, tell us a story.
      Here is what Tess said with her voice, which was one Voice of the World:

Once upon a time, Dozerius ("the trickster," per Mee's translation) defeated Portobaldus ("the dread giant") and took the luxuries of his house—bolts of silk, gold and furs and nutmegs. He particularly wanted the giant's magical heatproof gloves, which Portobaldus had used to dig into a volcano and grab out molten rock to throw. Of course, the gloves were far too big, so Dozerius had his tailor refashion one into a fine suit of clothes.

In a dusty corner of the giant's house, Dozerius found a treasure map, which showed where Portobaldus had buried the magic rubies of Argopoppus ("the irrelevant king"). They were quite nearby, along the seashore, and Dozerius thought he and his valorous crew could certainly spare some time to retrieve them.

Upon sailing to the place indicated by the map, a stretch of white, sandy beach, they were dismayed to see an enormous sand castle standing where the treasure was supposedly buried. Ordinarily this would have been no obstacle—they were pirates; they'd kicked over sand castles before—but this particular castle was swarming with very large crabs.

Dozerius sent forth his seven most fearsome fighters to deal with the crabs. They approached the sand castle and cried, "We have come for the rubies of King Argopoppus! Hand them over, and no one gets hurt."

The crabs scoffed at this, and so the seven pirates attacked the castle. Three were killed, and the rest were beaten and injured. These were exceptionally ferocious crabs. Their carapaces were as wide as dinner plates and as hard as steel; their claws were strong enough to snap a grown man's wrist or put a crimp in his sword.

"Well, this is humiliating," said Dozerius's first mate, Marsupius ("the sidekick"). "We're not going to be driven off by mere crustaceans, I hope."

"Of course not," said Dozerius. "They're tough, I'll grant, but the tougher the foe, the softer his underbelly. Follow my lead; I'll show you how to defeat them."

This time Dozerius himself went ashore, with Marsupius and some other men. He did not approach the crabs' stronghold but began setting up camp a ways down the beach. He had his men bring all the softest cushions and most luxuriant furnishings from the ship, as if this were the campsite of a king. The crabs watched suspiciously, then sent an emissary to parlay.

"What are you doing to our beach?" said the crab crabbily, examining Dozerius's wafting silk tents, gilt tables, and the copper cauldron upon the fire.

"We greatly admire your fine city," said Dozerius merrily, "but noticed you lack a few of the refinements of civilization. We thought we'd found a city of our own, over here, so that we could trade our luxury goods and teach you how to be gentlemen."

The crabs thought this was a splendid idea, so Dozerius traded them seven bolts of silk for a pile of seashells and a sack of sand fleas. His crewmen thought he'd gone mad, but whenever they tried to ask Dozerius what he was doing, he tapped the side of his nose and said, "Patience. All will become clear."

The crabs tried making themselves silk robes, but they fit very awkwardly. "Well, of course they do," said Dozerius when the crabs complained. "Nobody wears silk robes over armor. In fact, nobody wears armor at all in a civilized city. It gives the wrong impression, as if you were frightened and insecure, not the lords of your own destiny."

The crabs removed their heavy carapaces, stacking them behind their sand castle, and found that the silk robes now draped properly and looked much better. However, there was still the problem of the silk getting caught on their claws; it snagged and tore most grievously.

"Well, of course it does," said Dozerius, when they complained. "You don't see my companions and me trying to get dressed with weapons in our hands, do you? Refined people know when to set their weapons aside. In a safe, civilized society, you don't need to go around armed all the time."

The crabs could not set their claws aside, alas, but Dozerius suggested binding them shut with colorful silk thread. It was practical and fashionable. The crabs loved it and stood in line for their claws to be bound.

"You've improved yourselves," said Dozerius warmly. "I would like to have a great feast in your honor, but first I must purify myself before the gods." He stoked the fire under his great copper cauldron until the water was swiftly boiling, and then he leaped in with his clothes on—that is to say, wearing the suit made from the giant's heatproof glove.

The crabs gasped at the steam rising up. "Can you not bathe in the ocean?" they asked.

Dozerius feigned surprise. "You're worried for my safety? How kind. But our gods are very powerful and would never allow their devoted servants to come to harm."

"How do they know you're devoted?" said the king of the crabs greedily, already thinking what he could do with that kind of divine protection.

"We prove it by bathing in a boiling cauldron and demonstrating absolute trust," said Dozerius. "You are welcome to perform these same ablutions with all your people, but first let me come out and dry myself."

Dozerius climbed out, and fresh water was put into the pot. All the crabs eagerly climbed in. At first they were quite content, for the water was only pleasantly warm.

"It's boiling ferociously," said Dozerius. "Do you not feel it?"

The crabs could not feel it, for of course it wasn't true. Dozerius stoked the fire higher.

Some of the crabs began to feel it, but none of them dared admit that the gods had not granted their protection. The water grew hotter, and still the crabs stoically pretended that it wasn't hurting them. Only when bubbles began to rise in earnest from the bottom of the pot did they understand that they had been deceived. Panicked, they squirmed and writhed and screamed for mercy, but their claws had been bound, so they couldn't pull themselves out, and their carapaces had been removed, so they couldn't bear the weight of other crabs upon their backs.

Dozerius enjoyed his promised feast, a great pot of boiled crabs. His crew, finally understanding his purpose, shared it with him.

When they knocked down the sand castle and dug into the strand, however, the magic rubies were nowhere to be found. And thus, Dozerius never considered this exploit a real victory, for he had traded the lives of three men and seven bolts of silk for nothing but a crab dinner and a day at the beach.

Twenty-Seven

Before the audience could hum, Tess had one more thing to say: "Lady Borgo is sending soldiers. I don't know how long until they arrive. My countryman Jacomo is her excuse—she thinks you've kidnapped him. Countess Margarethe is trying to dissuade Lady Borgo, but I'm not confident she'll succeed. You should prepare to fight or flee."

The silence lengthened.

A white-haired, fragile man in the front row rose to his feet with the help of a younger companion. He was wrapped in a cobwebby shawl with scallop shells and chips of obsidian sewn onto it. He turned his back on Tess and called a name: "Solnu!"

Solnu stood up, and although it was hard to see him across the fire, Tess could discern that he kept his eyes downcast and his hands folded in front of his stomach.

The old man proceeded to berate Solnu. Tess couldn't tell what he was saying, but his tone was clear: he was furious. Her heart sank further with every passing moment.

She turned to Mee, who was watching impassively. "What's happening?" Tess whispered. "Why is he scolding Solnu?"

Mee raised one eyebrow and gave Tess a sad, if slightly sarcastic, look. "That man *raised* you. He's your parent now. Here, one never shouts at a child—or a guest. Your misbehavior is considered his fault."

"I told a story before giving the bad news, just like he told me to," cried Tess.

"I feel certain the king is about to explain himself," Mee answered.

The old man, leaning on the arm of his young companion—possibly a granddaughter—was working his way around the perimeter of the columns. He didn't descend the starry stairs, but squeezed past the edge of one of the fire pits onto the center stage. The girl released his arm, and he approached Tess on unsteady feet.

Mee covered her face with both hands and then held them forth, as if offering the old man a mask she'd been wearing. Tess assumed she was to follow suit and did so, not daring to ask what the gesture meant. It was meant as respect, that much seemed clear.

"O King, I present this unworthy incomer," said Mee.

The aged king raised his chin. "Incomer, you have angered me," he said (per Mee's translation). "We cannot leave this place. It is the Navel of the World, and we are the ones who tend and renew it. We do not take up arms against other peoples. Your suggestions—that we fight or flee—are unhelpful, unwelcome, and insulting to our ears."

"Please forgive me. I didn't intend any insult," said Tess.

"However, you may also have given us a gift," said the king, wagging a bony finger. "That story was a parable of your people's deepest desires."

Tess opened her mouth and closed it again. It was a children's story, frivolous nonsense, chosen for no deeper reason than that she'd hoped it would amuse everyone.

Clearly, it hadn't.

"Answer me this," said the king. "If the crabs had given up their treasure at once, would your people still have destroyed them?"

"They're not my . . . that is, Dozerius is Porphyrian. I'm actually Goreddi, not Ninysh, and I'm not here to take anyone's treasure," said Tess.

Mee didn't translate. "Answer him," said the old priest, jabbing Tess with a finger.

The answer, since it was a Dozerius story, was almost certainly yes: the crabs were doomed whether they gave up their treasure or not. Slaying monstrous animals was what Dozerius did. Tess couldn't imagine a scenario where he saw giant crabs and opted to leave them alone. Dozerius was one fictional man, however, whereas this king was asking about a whole nation of people, all with their own ideas and intentions, good and bad. She saw no way to answer his question, and yet she desperately wanted to reassure him.

"I don't know," she said at last. "It might depend on what the treasure is?"

"I know what it is," the king said. "Lady Borgo has told me again and again what your people want."

"They want everything!" cried a voice in the audience, and then Kluit of the Tshu was on her feet (Mee still translating). "Don't be fooled, King Molsu. This story does not contain the secret to placating the Dead. They believe we're monstrous creatures—greedy, grotesque, and foolish. They have no compunction about slaughtering mere animals and taking all they have."

Tess felt unbearably hot. "I didn't mean it that way," she whispered to Mee.

"Did you not?" said the old woman, avoiding her eye.

"I've said this all along, and maybe now you will believe me," the tall gray woman continued. "You call them incomers, but they are invaders. They mean to destroy not just your nation, but all the island and polar peoples. They look at us and see the monsters they brought with them in their heads. What's a monster to do but show them what *monstrous* truly means?"

Nervous laughter went up at this. The king shook his grizzled head.

"We're not the fighters you Tshu are, sister. We're not even hunters. We accept what gifts the sea brings, and it has brought these incomers, full of fearful stories though they are. Every day it brings more.

"How do you stop a tidal wave? You don't. You rush to high ground and hold on."

"Waves recede and let you go home eventually," called Kluit. "What will you do when this wave does not?"

"We will live," he answered. "Differently than we do now, but we will live. When your ice tigers threatened the Aftisheshe, they started living at the tops of cliffs. When the sleeping mountains awoke, the Murkh found new strongholds. We adapt and we survive."

"My Tshu will stop them," said Kluit. "Along with the Murkh, the Aftisheshe, and the Ggdani. We will fight even you, O King, if we must, though these words taste rotten in my mouth. We won't forget how you let the invaders swarm past you, into our territories."

"Think of them as our gift, O Tshu. Imagine how many songs of battle glory you will be able to compose," said the king. "As for my people, I say again: we do not fight. A tree bends with the wind."

All around the amphitheater, people hummed approvingly at his words.

"To this end, we shall do what we must. This story has persuaded me." He raised both hands, thumbs and index fingers touching lightly, and pronounced: "In exchange for this place, the Navel of the World, for the rest of our island, and for peace, we will give the incomers what we once thought it right to deny them—*sabaggatg.*"

Mee did not translate that last word because she was shouting, "You can't!" Kluit leaped up again, crying out in anger. She wasn't the only guest from elsewhere, Tess saw as more outraged people rose. There was a man with dense curls, like Hami's, and a person of indistinct gender (to Tess's foreign eye) who wore a beaded mask, and others rendered in silhouette by the firelight. Even King Molsu's Nutufi subjects shifted in their seats uneasily. Everyone understood what the king had said without translation; this was a word they all shared in common.

"What is he giving over?" Tess half whispered to Mee.

Mee's eyes flashed furiously. "Sabak oil," she snapped. "And it's your fault."

The Katakutia gripped Tess's arm like a crab and marched her out of the Navel of the World, through the wood, and toward the village. Jacomo and Claado followed them out, hurrying to catch up.

"You told her where you were going!" Mee shouted over her shoulder at Jacomo. "And she told the Dead lady, and now the militia is coming."

"I didn't know where to find the Navel," said Jacomo. "You didn't tell me. Remember?"

"Lady Borgo deduced that Maftumaiu had been revived in the forest, but she doesn't know where," said Tess.

Of course, Lady Borgo had proposed burning the whole forest.

"You should have stayed away," cried Mee. Tears streaked her wrinkled cheeks. "Better for the militia to wipe them out than for their coward king to conclude that he could buy his way out with sabak oil. Why did you tell him that would work?" She shook Tess's arm painfully.

"I didn't!" cried Tess, frightened by Mee's tears. "I didn't even know he had sabak oil."

"He gets it in tribute, for settling wars and disputes. You told him that if he gave up his treasure, the invaders would leave his people alone."

"I wouldn't have said that," said Tess, trying to remember her exact words. Dozerius would have killed the crabs just for being crabs; Kluit had understood that better than the king had.

"You are a liar," said Mee, "and I am going to kill you."

She let go of Tess and pulled an obsidian knife out of the folds of her clothing.

Tess was too stunned to move. Captain Claado shoved her behind him, and Jacomo cried, "Mee, wait, please. She never said that. King Molsu heard what he wanted to hear."

With shaking hands, Jacomo pulled his St. Polypous medallion out of his pocket. "I—I can prove it. Listen." He flipped a switch along its edge, revealing it to be a quigutl device. A few strange sounds came out, and then Tess's voice: ". . . hotter, and still the crabs stoically pretended that it wasn't hurting them."

"Oops, too far," said Jacomo.

After one more false start, he found what he was looking for. Tess's tinny recorded voice said, "I don't know. It might depend on what the treasure is?"

King Molsu responded in Nutufi, but the device hadn't recorded Mee's translation. Or rather, there was a sound like wind through cedars that must have been Mee's voice—understood by everyone, heard live, and apparently by no one, heard through this device.

Jacomo switched off the recorder. He couldn't meet Mee's eye.

"I asked you not to write the stories down, because it kills them," said the Katakutia. "So instead, you do something worse. You turn living voices into shadows and vapors."

"But this proves that Tess didn't say what you thought. You heard that, right?"

He was throwing everything away to save her; Tess felt more horrible than grateful.

"I heard the rattling of bones," said Mee. "I understand the language of every living creature who stands before me, but I can't understand these dead words. I only understand it was you who killed them."

Mee held out her free hand and Jacomo gave over the device. The old woman attempted to crush it beneath her heel, but between the pine needles of the forest floor and the soft soles of her boots, the result was toothless. She stabbed at it with her obsidian knife, then cried, "Fire friend!" Kikiu came rustling out of the underbrush.

The old woman tossed the medallion into the air and Kikiu caught it on the fly, iron jaws snapping ominously. Jacomo cringed at the sound.

"You are not the priest you claimed to be," said Mee, looking like she could spit fire herself. She passed the knife from one hand to another. Claado was backing up, herding Tess behind him, but Jacomo stood still, chest out, ready to get whatever he deserved.

"No, Wind Kin, don't do this," said Kikiu. The hatchling scuttled into the gap between Jacomo and the old priest and began to sing:

> O sister, I know these hatchlings.
> I've followed their story-threads a long time.
>
> When my mother was dying,
> In desperate need of someone to bite,
> Teth offered herself. My mother's teeth
> Sank deep into her flesh. Teth didn't flinch,
> Although she might have died.
> That's who she is, and that is what I trust.
>
> She is that person still, whatever errors she makes.
> This I swear, upon my mother's life.
>
> As for the other, look at him.
> It was you, not he, who called him a True Priest,
> And put that burden on his shoulders.
> He did not ask, he did not beg.
>
> It was you who were mistaken.
> Don't make him pay the price for that.

Mee's mouth fell open. She slowly put her knife away.

Tess, too, boggled at Kikiu's song; the hatchling hadn't sung in Quootla, but in the same strange, windy-sounding speech as the Katakutia. How had she learned that language? How did she know how to sing this priest out of a murderous rage? The hatchling seemed to have lived an extra lifetime in the weeks since Tess had last seen her.

"Go back to your people—all of you," cried Mee. "I have a great deal of damage to assuage here, and I don't know whether it can be done. You"—she pointed an arthritic finger at Tess—"I'm sure you meant well, but what does that matter when you set the world ablaze behind you? You may have started a war with your pestilent ignorance."

She turned on her heel, the tassels of her leather tunic whipping around her like flails, and stomped—silently—back toward the Navel of the World. Kikiu took one lingering look at Tess and Jacomo and then followed Mee into the forest.

Twenty-Eight

*M*ind of the World, open your eyes!

Once upon a time, there was a quigutl whose name meant "death." She had always tried not to take it to heart, but that's the sort of name that follows you around and makes you pessimistic about your purpose.

Kikiu had sensed a change before she ever met the old woman, from the first day she set foot on the ship. It had hit her like a new wavelength of light or a sound she should not have been able to hear. It was as if the earth had tilted, and suddenly all roads led downhill toward the Katakutia. Kikiu might have crawled away, with effort, but why would she? For the first time in her life everything felt right side up.

She couldn't understand why Mee didn't feel it, too, but Kikiu knew how to be patient. She'd spent her whole life waiting for Pathka to be nest to her; this was trivial in comparison. The world was bent in this direction. Mee would roll toward her eventually.

It was possible she needed a nudge, though.

Kikiu had tried to be subtle; her cavorting had amused the old woman as they strode the sabak-road between sea and sky. They'd sung to the stars together, danced with fish and whales, contemplated the mournful Voorka on the rocky shores. And Kikiu had listened patiently while Mee detailed her hopes for this tall, fat, sweet-natured human boy-priest she believed she had discovered.

"The Greater Lights told me I would find a True Priest from the north," the old woman often gushed. "I will instruct him in the ways of True Priests so that he can return to the Land of the Dead and change their hearts."

"That's a big task," said Kikiu. "You might be putting more burden on him than he can bear. He's a human, after all."

Mee—who was also a human—only laughed and waved Kikiu's concern away.

That was before Jacomo broke the old priest's heart.

Afterward . . . well, there had been a lot of talking among the Nutufi. Mee hadn't translated it. The Tshu woman had stepped in and maybe resolved things; Kikiu had been less concerned with that than with Mee, who looked like she'd been stabbed through the chest with her own obsidian knife. She was pale and shaky; she hid behind her fringed hood and would not speak.

At nightfall, without a word to anyone, Mee slipped away from the Navel of the World, down to a stretch of rocky seashore where she'd stowed her stilts and wings. She might have left without Kikiu if Kikiu hadn't been resolved to cling to her like a barnacle.

"Don't feel obligated to follow me, little one," Mee said, strapping on her stilts. "I . . . I have nothing to teach you."

"You taught me the wind-speech," said Kikiu.

"I didn't. I don't know how you learned it," said Mee. "And I don't know how I could have been so wrong about the boy. Maybe I didn't understand what the Greater Lights were telling me. I didn't think that was possible."

"Do you understand everything everyone says?" said Kikiu, positioning herself between the Katakutia and the waves so the old woman couldn't walk away.

"Always. It's my gift—and my curse," said Mee. "I understand what people really mean, beyond mere words."

"What if the person speaking doesn't know what they mean?" said Kikiu. "How can you understand them if they don't understand themselves?"

"It's not that hard," said Mee, sounding irritated. "I am wise and have insight."

"So you use your best judgment," said Kikiu. An argument was right in front of her—she could see it, like a glimmer of fish scales in deep water—but she had to creep up slowly or her pounce would miss. "You decide what they must have meant."

"I do not." Mee sounded frosty now. "The meaning is there already. I don't put it there."

"What if they say something you can't understand?" Kikiu pressed, making sure to speak Quootla and not the wind-speech. "Or what if you understand-*utl*?"

The old woman reared back, affronted. "How can I . . . What does that . . . ," she stammered.

"You didn't understand!" cried Kikiu, excited that her gambit had worked. "At least, you're not sure whether you did. But that's how my people talk all the time—in paradoxes! Maybe you've never had to make a contradiction hold still in your mind before. You didn't think it could be done, but it can, and you did-*utl* for a moment. It felt strange."

"I couldn't retain the meaning," said Mee, visibly shaken. "It slithered like a snake."

"That was your mind, your reaction—*you*. You are present in every translation you do," said Kikiu. "It's unavoidable."

Spontaneously, the hatchling began to sing:

> *You see through meatball eyes;*
> *Your tender, gray-and-pink,*
> *Soft, meaty rack of brain*
> *Is what you use to think.*
> *Knowledge is a pot roast,*
> *And feeling, a strong drink!*

Mee blinked at Kikiu, openmouthed, and then she began to laugh, sharp and bitter, like stinging sleet on a winter gale.

"It was you all along, wasn't it?" said Mee. "You were the True Priest I was sent to find."

Kikiu inclined her head. "It was reasonable to expect a human. You did your best."

"My best may have caused unnecessary pain and suffering," said the Katakutia. "I'm supposed to be better than that. I'm supposed to be wise."

"You are wise," said Kikiu firmly, taking the old woman's cheeks between her padded fingers. "There's always more to learn, and one mind can only hold so much. You had never met a quigutl before me. How could you know I might be a priest? Even I didn't know.

"But now that we both know," the hatchling continued, "do not turn away. Please. Do not refuse to teach me just because you still have things to learn."

"We can teach each other, perhaps," said the old woman.

"Two minds are better than one," said Kikiu.

Mee got to her feet, wings spread wide, and stepped into the surf, feeling around for the diaphanous sabak-road. Her sabak companions swarmed around her, emitting strings of sticky spittle, which they wove over and under the road, reinforcing its webbing ahead of her stilts. Kikiu splashed into the ocean alongside them, the moon gleaming encouragingly overhead.

From far away, the Wider Mind heard them singing:

Under the stars we go,
Into the world, oho!
To ask, to learn,
To feel, to know.
Into the world, oho!

Twenty-Nine

The plaion sailed back to St. Remy across a choppy gray afternoon. Tess's mind would not sit still or accept what had happened: Jacomo ejected from Mee's good graces; the king of the Nutufi about to take desperate action and alienate the other island nations; Lady Borgo's militia, unless Marga had performed a miracle, still relentlessly approaching the Navel of the World.

"I only wanted to warn them!" Tess burst into the silence. "And get Jacomo back."

"Well, you got me back," said Jacomo with a pained smile.

She couldn't bear how sad he looked, or how disapproving Claado's expression was.

Claado had some gall, judging her. If it had been him warning everyone about the militia, they would have taken it no better. And he had no right to be annoyed about her choice of story when he'd refused to tell one.

"How could they think I'd given them insight into Ninysh intentions?" Tess cried. "I'm not Ninysh, and more to the point, that was a Porphyrian story."

"Don't bring us into this," said Captain Claado.

Tess leveled her glare at him. "It was from a book I had as a child, *The Adventures of the Porphyrian Pirate Dozerius and His Valorous Crew*."

"I've heard of those books," said Claado, returning her glare with compound interest. "They aren't Porphyrian."

"What?" said Tess.

"They were written for gullible Southlanders by someone who thought a dark, foreign protagonist sounded interesting and exotic."

"I don't want to know that," said Tess.

"Porphyry is home to the great tragedians. Do you really think we'd read such trash?"

Tess felt suddenly shaky and short of breath.

"The name Dozerius should have been your first clue," Claado persisted. "Maybe it sounds Porphyrian to foreign ears, but it sounds ridiculous to us. Imagine if I'd only ever met you two and concluded that I knew all about Goreddi names. I might decide it seemed perfectly sensible to call my characters Mess and Tacojo."

"I named my baby Dozerius," said Tess. Her voice seemed to come from across a chasm.

"Oh," said Claado. "Oh dear."

Poor baby, child of a fool mother. It wasn't his fault. She was Mess after all; she embodied it. She felt stripped, exposed to the buffeting winds, her stupidity plain for all to see.

Maybe she wasn't alone in that, though. Jacomo, at the prow, sat with his head in his arms, his shoulders shaking to a different rhythm than the rise and fall of the sea.

Marga and Aemelia were taking tea in the parlor when Tess and Jacomo arrived (Argol and Claado had gone back to the ship; "Tell Marga it's time to go"). Marga leaped to her feet, several emotions vying for ascendancy. She went straight for Jacomo and wrapped her arms around him.

"How was I going to explain to your parents if you were killed or gone for good?" she cried, pulling back and patting his cheeks as if he were a recalcitrant five-year-old, wandered off at the fair.

Jacomo's chin trembled, but he did not speak. He looked full of emotions, too, like a bladder about to burst.

Tess turned on Lady Borgo. "We found him. Call off your soldiers."

Lady Borgo smirked. "Settle down. Marga has persuaded me not to burn the forest."

"Or kill anyone?" asked Tess. "Nobody sends the militia out against trees."

"Tess," said Marga, her brows lowering.

"You can't think I sent them against the Noo-too-fee?" Lady Borgo pressed a hand to her heart. "That would be dishonorable and cruel. They don't fight back; they don't know how.

"I admit, I was angry, but then Marga reminded me how William valued untouched wilderness. I have decided to preserve these last precious acres as Lord Morney's Park, a place of pristine beauty—once we've removed the shanties, or whatever the Pelaguese are squatting in, and restored the forest to its original state. Nobody wants to commune with nature only to stumble across someone's laundry drying."

Tess closed her mouth, which had fallen open. "But they live there."

"Yes, well, they *can't* live there," said Lady Borgo. "They spoil the landscape."

Marga put a firm hand on Tess's elbow and began drawing her away from Lady Borgo's couch. "It's a beautiful idea. A park for all the people to enjoy."

"All the people?" cried Tess, pulling her arm free.

"And a fitting memorial to Lord Morney," Marga continued. "Thank you, Aemelia—so very, very much—for this tribute, and for helping us repair William's submersible." Marga raised her arms and began herding Tess toward the door without touching her. "Since my uncle is returned, I'm afraid we must catch the tide."

"You won't stay one more night?" asked Lady Borgo, pouting a little.

Marga, lips together, tried to give courtesy while edging her companions out of the room.

Tess would not have another chance to confront Lady Borgo with her own monstrosity; it was now or never. This was for Martin—and Anna. And Solnu. And everyone who'd ever lived in that forest.

"You should leave, too," Tess called over Marga's shoulder. "Go back to Ninys. Leave the Nutufi to their forest."

Marga grabbed Tess's shoulders and turned her around.

"What a perfectly unworkable suggestion," said her ladyship as Tess was marched out of the room. "I've never even been to Ninys. I'm as much a native St. Remyan as anyone."

⚜

The Borgo carriage conveyed them back to the harbor, and they reached the *Avodendron* just as the sun was setting. Jacomo climbed down first; Tess caught Marga's sleeve before she could follow him.

"How could you?" Tess hissed. "She's displacing the Nutufi, and you *thanked* her."

"Since I'm the one who persuaded her not to kill everyone and burn down the forest, yes, I did thank her," the countess hissed back. "And I'd do it again."

As soon as they were aboard, Captain Claado called for the gangplank to be taken up and the lines to be cast off; he was more than ready to go. Jacomo disappeared belowdecks. Tess would have followed him, had not Marga grabbed her arm and steered her toward the great cabin.

"We need to talk," said the countess the moment the door closed behind her. "I tolerate your youthful exuberance as much as I can— maybe you don't realize how much forbearance that requires on my part. I let you correct me about the Pelaguese names for things. I did not chastise you for letting 'Fozu' see the 'sabak' the day Eludus was pushed overboard—yes, I noticed. I say nothing about how you choose to dress like a vagrant."

"You said something once," Tess couldn't help saying.

Marga scowled. "At some point, it is my duty as your mentor to step in and tell you that there is such a thing as going too far. My family did not survive Count Pesavolta's purges by belligerently alienating everyone—especially not potential allies."

"Potential allies who threaten to kill thousands of people?" cried Tess. "Is that who you think I shouldn't have alienated?"

Marga looked taken aback. "You were extremely rude to Aemelia, yes, but I don't mean her. I mean *me*. Even after I talked to you about letting the sabanewt go, you still won't trust me. Do you think I'm your enemy?"

Tess plunked herself down on an upholstered chair. She didn't fully trust Marga, in fact, but had no intention of explaining all her reasons.

"If you had only told me where Jacomo was going and why," Marga persisted, pacing before the windows, silhouetted by the sunset sky, "we might have kept it from Aemelia. She might still have cleared the Nutufi out of the forest eventually, but it didn't have to happen now. Similarly, if I had known you wanted to ask Martin to come with us"—here she gave Tess a sharp look—"I could have arranged for him to be quietly brought aboard."

Against his will? That worked so well with Fozu, Tess wanted to say. Instead she asked, dreading the answer, "How did you learn about that?"

"Kitchen staff overheard you talking. I believed Martin, that you offered to take him away and he refused. Aemelia was inclined to believe the others—ambitious backstabbers all—who claimed he'd cornered you in the silver storage and tried to ravage you among the tureens." Marga clenched and unclenched her hands. "Aemelia had him punished."

"Ye Saints," said Tess. She had harmed him by trying to help. She felt sick.

"You can't just hare off after whatever world-saving project strikes your fancy," said Marga. "It's harder to navigate a moral course in this part of the world; there are uncharted shoals, hazards we can't anticipate. We need to stick together and not work at cross-purposes. Next time you want to help somebody, talk to me. I might already be considering it from a different angle. At the very least, I might have a clearer view of where the pitfalls are, or what the unintended consequences are likely to be."

"I'll . . . I'll try to remember," mumbled Tess, picking at the arm of the chair.

Marga's mouth flattened. "Is it that you're overawed by my rank? Is that the—"

A knock at the door cut off her query, to Tess's relief. Argol entered, a folded letter in her hand. "I was asked to give this to you, Your Grace," she said, handing it to the countess.

Marga unfolded it—it was unsealed—and read quickly. Her face seemed to harden into stone as she read. "Did you know about this?" she cried, thrusting the paper at Tess.

Tess read:

To the Countesse Margarethe:

My family has serfed yours since the day of my grategrandfather, and it has been my joye to carry on this work like my parents before me. I hope I have done so with honor. I have stayed behind in St. Remye. I did not know, until I seen it for myself, that in the Pelagos a serfant may yet be master. I shall have my own farm, or a shop in town, and I who once serfed shall now be serfed in turn.

You told Tess that you two were equals in science, but you never said such things to me. Am I not your equal under the eye of Heaven? Heaven is greater than science or all priests are liars. But I shall be your equal now in truth,

a lady in this new land. It is the Pelaguese who are fit to be
serfants, not your own kind.

> *Sincerely,*
> *Darienne of St. Remye*

"I try to be kind," fumed the countess, "I teach her to write, and she repays me like this. Now who's going to do my hair?"

"It'll last awhile; she left the ends tucked," said Argol. "When it starts to come down, I can teach you to put it up again."

"Maybe," said Marga. "If I ever stop being furious that you let her go. You couldn't have given me this before we sailed out of the harbor?"

"I was heaving the lines, Your Grace."

Tess, for her part, was racking her brains to remember what Darienne looked like, how old she'd been, how tall. She'd been a hovering presence, tying on the countess's sleeves, making hats appear on the countess's head. Tess could not recall ever hearing her voice.

"Well, I'm glad for her," said Tess determinedly, handing the letter back.

"Glad for her?" said Marga. "You're so angry about the displacement of the Nutufi—do you have any idea who is displacing them?"

"Lady Borgo," said Tess.

"If Aemelia were the only person on the island, the Nutufi could gad about as they pleased; there'd be room for everyone. It's people like Darienne—nobodies who decide they could be somebodies after all—who come in and demand a share of the territory."

Tess boggled at her. What must it be like to be so elevated that you could declare some people "nobodies"?

A countess didn't have to care. That right there was half of why Tess didn't trust her.

Marga could stay neutral (for science) while Paishesh burned, and brush off Lady Borgo's threat to kill thousands (what was a little genocide between friends, after all?). She could betroth herself to a handsome young lord and make no inquiries whatsoever into his past (because surely he would never have dared do to a countess what he'd done to Tess).

It wasn't that Marga was cruel or unkind. She cared about Fozu, in her own way; Tess was even willing to believe she cared about Martin. Anytime a countess cared, it was a gift—generous, magnanimous, a delightful surprise—because she never had to. There was no consequence to her for not caring, and so sometimes, if it was going to inconvenience her, she simply didn't.

Somebody had to do a countess's hair, after all, and iron her petticoats, and see to all the trivialities so that she had time to read books and play at swords. The world was full of Dariennes; if they were fleeing to the Archipelagos, it was because nobody cared about them.

Tess herself could not even recall Darienne's face.

"And let's remember, things could be far worse in St. Remy," Marga was saying; she'd apparently kept talking. "Displaced is not dead. By that measure, the Nutufi are *lucky*."

That word again; it struck Tess differently now. She glanced over to see if Argol had reacted to it, but Argol had wisely departed already.

"I'm very tired," said Tess, trying to close the conversation. "May I go?"

The countess reluctantly assented. Instead of going to her cabin, though, Tess paced awhile in the waist of the ship, trying to soothe her agitation. She'd seen the limits of the countess's beneficence—and that her own weren't so dramatically different. Had she ever spoken to Darienne, even once?

As the brisk sea air calmed her, she recalled something Captain Claado had said in the carriage on the way to Lady Borgo's: *Even Porphyry, a nation of enlightened, humane philosophers, rationalized our social striations like anybody else. People suffered for it. People are still suffering.*

But the Porphyrians were trying to make things better, weren't they? Claado was. Surely it was possible, with diligence and effort.

Don't let that be all you do.

What had made the Lucky so lucky, anyway?

Tess walked the length of the deck to the other end of the ship, to a door beneath the forecastle, a place she'd never been. Captain Claado answered her knock, wearing spectacles, a book in his hand. Behind him, a lamp flickered.

"Why are the Lucky called that?" Tess asked without preamble. "Were they living in Porphyry before it was colonized? Were they killed or enslaved?"

"A Southlander always jumps straight to slavery and genocide," said Claado dryly. "Your imagination is a blunt instrument. I assure you, humans commit other crimes against each other. But let's not talk about my foster daughter as if she weren't here."

He opened the door wider and ushered Tess inside. Argol was at Claado's desk, bent over some sort of ledger book, carefully filling in columns of numbers. She glanced up at Tess, something simultaneously shy and defiant in her gaze.

"I'm teaching her the most tedious part of being captain," Claado explained. "Keeping accounts. Depending where she lands, she might have someone to do that for her, but she might not." Captain Claado gestured Tess toward a stool; he took one of the sea lockers. "Argolele, Tess is wondering what makes you so *Lucky*."

"Since you said none of us may use that word harshly on your ship," said Argol, dipping her pen, "I can only say I am lucky to have a captain who believes in me."

Claado looked flummoxed by this response. "I only meant . . . I don't want those louts wielding the word as a weapon. It's past time to put all that behind us. Nobody has been Lucky, officially, in almost a hundred years."

"Unofficially, it was illegal for my father to go to sea thirty years ago," said Argol.

Captain Claado shifted uncomfortably on his locker and turned to Tess. "I don't know how much history you've been taught, but you knew Porphyry was a colony."

"It was the southernmost outpost of the . . . Ephaanos Empire, now defunct?" said Tess, digging deeply to remember even that much. "Was no one there when the Ephaani arrived?"

"It was almost empty," said Claado.

"Officially," said Argol, giving him a sidelong look.

"I said 'almost.' There were a few people," said Claado. "Vegr, they were called. The Great Houses traded with them. I was taught in school that they'd simply disappeared."

"In fact, the Lucky married them, and they became Lucky, too, poor souls." She paused to clean her pen, then said, "The Agogoi seldom want to remember the entire story."

"You've been my teacher, when I set out to be yours," said Claado quietly. "Porphyry was founded by twelve wealthy families—the Great Houses, or Agogoi. House Abraxas, my family, was one. Poorer Ephaani could afford to come to Porphyry only if they were sponsored by Agogoi. They were supposed to work off their debt in the new land within a few years."

"But they couldn't," said Argol, blotting her page delicately. "It was a trick."

"It was a trick," Claado acknowledged. *"Debt has kittens* is a Porphyrian saying, and we Agogoi always made sure it was true. The Lucky couldn't work off the debt. If they came close, we changed the rules. We kept them ignorant so they couldn't check our numbers; we lied and enticed them to take on more debts.

"Over time, we convinced ourselves that nature had done this, not us. Of course they were poor—they were foolish, lazy, and impulsive. Of course they shouldn't own businesses or participate in government—they couldn't grasp such sophisticated concepts."

"We shouldn't go to sea," said Argol. "We might run off without paying."

"In that instance, we told ourselves you brought bad luck," said Captain Claado.

"So *Lucky* was meant ironically?" asked Tess.

Argol gave a pained smile. "No. We were called Lucky because whenever we complained, the Agogoi would remind us that they'd ferried our greedy, grasping ancestors to this shore and that we were lucky to live in Porphyry at all."

Claado looked at the floor, rubbing his mouth. "Eighty-nine years ago," he finally said, "House Perdixis—who've never chaired the Assembly again since—declared an amnesty. All debts were forgiven."

"*Most* debts," said Argol, a sharpness in her voice for the first time, as if she'd reached the limit of historical ignorance she could tolerate in one evening.

"Recent debts couldn't be forgiven, or else no one would have been paid for work they'd done that week," Claado said a little snappishly in return. "But you see, that was decades ago, and yet it's still not over. The present vibrates with the past. You've seen how my men react to having Lucky on this ship. Most captains won't hire them."

"You went out of your way to find us," said Argol, more gently now.

"I did what every Agogox with a conscience should do," said Claado. "I went to the Museum of Outrageous Debt, where the old contracts are filed, and found the ones my house first held. Not easily—we used to swap contracts without warning so that we could fine the Lucky for paying the wrong creditors. The people we originally sponsored have many descendants; I chose the ones I thought I could best help.

"Particularly this lass," he said, clapping Argol's shoulder, "who deserves to be the first Lucky captain. I'll see it happen, if I have to debate the Assembly myself."

Argol lowered her gaze and resumed writing columns of numbers.

"Now, if you'll excuse me, I have to review the night crew," said Captain Claado. He turned to leave, pausing at the door for one last point: "The way you begin is the way you end up, Tess. Even Porphyry, for all our fine philosophy, fell into that trap. You Ninysh are going to make a misery of the Archipelagos if you don't figure that out quickly."

He closed the door. Argol set down her pen and rubbed her eyes.

"Are you all right?" asked Tess, not sure what she would do if Argol wasn't. It was like watching a mountain struggling not to cry.

Argol sniffed and then sighed; the whites of her eyes glittered in the lamplight. "He is a second father to me, and I do not say that lightly," she said, her voice, as ever, incongruously soft. "But the tools at his disposal, the answers he knows, are all Agogou."

"At least he cares. He doesn't have to," said Tess, her thoughts circling back to Marga.

"He cares," Argol agreed. "And it will never be enough until he realizes we can't do this the proper way. He can debate the Assembly until his flesh falls off his bones. They'll never grant me a captaincy." She leaned back in her chair; her eyes were still glittering, but defiantly now. "What I need is my own ship. I'll captain it illegally and evade capture. If the Assembly can't stop me and they can't tax me, they may finally bestow my rank in absentia, as if it were their own idea."

"You'll . . . be a pirate. Essentially," said Tess, her secret heart thrilling at the thought.

Argol took up her pen again. "A pirate with very tidy account ledgers."

Tess left Argol to it and went out to the weather deck, a hand upon her thnimi. The evening's conversations had her thinking about her mission from the Queen more deeply than she'd considered it in weeks.

"Goredd is prepared to intervene, if we must," Queen Glisselda had said.

What did that mean, exactly? War? That was one tool that only a queen had at her disposal, and the most straightforward way to drive the Ninysh off. But even if the Ninysh deserved to be sent packing (and Tess didn't doubt that they did), they would not go quietly. They had cannons. Tess could envision such a war dragging on and on, with the islands and islanders paying the price.

And what would a queen, with all those particular tools in her toolbox, do if Goredd won? Pack up and leave? Or, with every good intention, stick around to "fix" things in Goreddi ways not appropriate to this place or its people?

Tess flipped the thnimi on, then flipped it off again. She did not want Goredd sending troops to the Archipelagos—that much she was sure of—but everything she had to report was just going to convince the Queen and the prince consort, in their philosophical wisdom, that intervention was necessary.

She wished she had somebody to talk to who could advise her, or point her toward an answer. In some idealistic dreamworld, a priest might do that; Tess had never found they did much besides make her feel guilty. Still, her brother-in-law was a good listener, occasionally. If he'd turned out not to be a True Priest, that was only a further recommendation in Tess's eyes.

Jacomo's snoring greeted her even before she'd opened the cabin door, alas. He was curled up on the sea lockers, having politely left her the bunk. Tess tried to be polite in return, taking off her boots and doublet without opening the lantern, but she kicked over a jar in the dark and spilled liquid all over the floor. She smelled it at once: okush. Where the devil had he gotten that? She leaned over him, and there it was on his breath as well. Hm.

Well, she could wait. She lay down and was asleep before he'd emitted ten more snores.

Thirty

Jacomo did not get up the next day, although not because he'd kept drinking; Tess had spilled his only jar of okush. He did not get up the day after that, nor the third day, either, and Tess began to wonder whether he meant to sleep all the way to the pole. Upon the fourth day, the countess asked the ship's physician to have a look at him. The physician was a fastidious little man, dark brown and bald, who apparently lived in the sick bay, because Tess could not recall ever seeing him before. He took Jacomo's pulse, listened to his lungs, asked a flotilla of questions (translated by Argol), and scrutinized the color of his urine (Tess absented herself for this). After nearly an hour, Argol translated his diagnosis: "He has a Tragic Disposition."

"Like melancholy?" said Tess, looking down at her brother-in-law, huddled under a quilt with his back to them. "Are you supposed to drain his bile with leeches or something?"

The physician answered in patronizing tones. "Vigorous exercise. Philosophy. And leafy green vegetables, as often as we can get them."

"No, thank you," muttered Jacomo.

"Tell me when he changes his mind," said the physician. "Or if he gets worse."

Tess did not ask what worse looked like. She'd been there. She was worried now.

Pathka, too, was worrying her. She hadn't thought about how clearheaded he'd been while the sabak was here; now that she was gone, the difference was stark. He frequently woke Tess, muttering to himself. Where he used to hunt rats around the ship, he now staggered around the weather deck, looking confused; Tess had tried to lure him back to the cabin, but he hadn't seemed to recognize her.

She wished Kikiu were there to advise her, but she suspected the hatchling would say, *Get ko to the serpent as quickly as you can.* Which was easier said than done when you were setting off mapless into the unknown.

How much time did Pathka have?

One morning, Tess pulled open the long drawer under her bunk, looking for her spare shirt, and was startled to find Pathka stretched out upon a nest of her clothing, asleep. Tess nudged him, trying to get at her shirt. His skin felt slimy. Quigutl were moderately revolting in a variety of ways, but sliminess was not one of them. Tess stifled a cry, so as not to bother Jacomo, braved the awful texture, and shook Pathka awake.

"You're oozing," Tess whispered. "Come topside, we'll wash you off—"

"Teth, it's all right. It's supposed to happen." Pathka sounded weak but lucid. "It's my thuthmeptha. It's time."

"Time to change back to female?" asked Tess. "Now? Why?"

"Two reasons. One, Kikiu isn't here, so my pheromones won't spark the change in ko against ko's will." He paused, apparently to catch his breath. "Two, I didn't want to admit ko was right, but I'm not myself. I don't know why. I'm hardier as a female. I hope it might help."

"You hope it might," said Tess.

Pathka closed his eyes. "I expect it will. If nothing else, I get to rest for thirty-nine days."

"What do you need from me?" asked Tess, petting his slimy head.

"Stop touching me, first," said Pathka, opening one eye. "The mucus has to harden into a cocoon. If my nostrils crust over, rinse them with water. Once a day should be enough. Also . . ."

"Yes?" said Tess, leaning closer.

"Today, tomorrow, the frozen moon."

"All right, then," said Tess. She gingerly closed the drawer and rinsed her hand at the basin; Pathka kept muttering to himself until he finally stopped.

The expedition carried determinedly, doggedly on. In the absence of a map, Marga and Claado conferred together often. Their strategy, as best Tess could discern, seemed to be to follow any deep strait that led either south toward the pole or east, away from the Sea of Holes. So far, the waterways had all been open; Tess wasn't sure what would happen once the sea started icing up.

Things got harder well before they reached ice, however.

First there was the webbing, the silvery sabak-spittle roads that the Katakutia followed from island to island. The strands grew more abundant the farther south they went. The cobwebby material looked delicate, but it was strong enough to withstand Mee's stabbing stilts.

It was not strong enough to withstand the hull of a deep-keeled ship, although the *Avodendron* felt the impact. Every time it hit one, the ship jolted and shuddered until the strand finally snapped.

The expedition was destroying things just by traveling from one place to another, Tess observed grimly to herself. *Of course we are.*

A single strand was one thing—a channel with multiple strands was quite another. The ship broke through three, each tougher than the last, until it had lost too much momentum to breach another. They were at a dead stop in a strait full of semitransparent, sticky strands. Claado cursed roundly. They had to lower the plaion and tow themselves backward, which took half an afternoon.

Then there were days of fog. The crew spilled the wind from their sails (not that there was much to spill; if there had been, it would have blown the fog away), and the ship crept along at a dismal pace for fear of running aground. A watchman, posted on the mainmast, jutted out of the top of the fog enough that he could see the trees on nearby islands. He signaled to the steersman with bells, maintaining course as far from any islands as possible. The crew, always singing while they worked, sang louder than usual.

Tess found the slowdown excruciating. Midsummer was fast approaching, and if they didn't reach the polar circle soon, there was surely no way they'd make it to the pole this year. The waterways would freeze solid. What would happen to Pathka? Tess didn't know how to plan for that contingency. All she could do was stand helplessly at the forecastle, gripping the railing, white-knuckled, and try not to let despair get the best of her.

Sometimes the fog cleared enough that she glimpsed eerie objects in it. Micro-islands, too low for the watch to notice, that they were lucky not to have hit. A collective of bobbing fishing skiffs; the fur-clad fisherfolk laughed and waved at the *Avodendron.* Once Tess smelled smoke through the fog and an hour later glimpsed an island where everything had burned to the ground. Silhouettes of houses and blackened tree trunks drifted past, silent as ghosts. The crew stopped singing and stared. Tess couldn't tell who had lived there—Ninysh settlers? Native islanders?—or why it had burned, but it felt like a portent.

When the fog finally thinned, the dragon expedition reappeared off the starboard bow. Tess found this unexpectedly reassuring; if her expedition was on the wrong track, well, at least they weren't alone. Marga, apparently enlivened by a bit of competition, called for more speed, and a game of hide-and-seek began. The *Sweet Jessia* was now ahead, now behind, now at anchor in a little bay while the *Avodendron* glided past.

They were everywhere, those rascally dragons. The *Avodendron* turned southeast and then east-southeast to evade them, but the *Sweet Jessia* always managed to find a faster way around and pull ahead again. Marga urged her uncle to make all available speed; the *Avodendron* unfurled sails Tess didn't even know she had, sails on top of sails, catching every lick of wind. They passed the *Sweet Jessia,* cheering wildly, and then they rounded the horn of a large island and saw two more *Sweet Jessia*s blocking the strait ahead.

The *Avodendron* had no choice but to heave to.

Two more *Sweet Jessia*s emerged from some hidden cove behind them, and then they were surrounded.

None of these ships was the dragon expedition. This was something else entirely.

"Someone has gone to a great deal of trouble just to deceive us," said Marga, watching through a spyglass as one of the ships lowered a dinghy.

"Pirates?" asked Tess, whose imagination ran that direction, ever and forever.

"Worse," said Marga, closing her telescope with an irritated snap. "It's Robinôt."

Tess could see him now at the prow of the dinghy, waving as if to long-lost friends. The *Avodendron* threw down a rope ladder and he climbed aboard.

"To what do we owe the pleasure, Lieutenant?" said Marga, her tone making clear that anything owed would not be paid.

"The pleasure is all mine," said Robinôt, which was indisputably true. "We're here to escort you to St. Fionnani."

"We're not going to St. Fionnani. It's in the wrong direction."

Tess knew she should recognize the name, but these Saint islands all sounded alike.

The lieutenant gave Marga a frank, disappointed look. "We can do this pleasantly, Your Grace, or we can do this unpleasantly. Why, look there."

He pointed toward the nearest decoy ship. Square panels in her side had opened up, like the mechanical shutters of a cuckoo clock, and out of these holes protruded cannons. There were twelve, each twice the size of the chasers at the *Avodendron*'s prow.

Tess shuddered.

Marga, steel-spined, did not even look alarmed. "If you suspect I'm harboring a fugitive, search my ship and satisfy yourself upon that point. But I'm *not* going to St. Fionn—"

"Count Pesavolta's own hand says otherwise," said the lieutenant, extracting a sealed letter from his jacket.

Marga unfolded it, looking skeptical; her face went ashen as she read. "This is dated three years ago. He can't issue warrants preemptively."

"He can for something like this," said Robinôt. "You retain your land and title at His Sublime Excellence's discretion. If you get too rowdy and disobedient, that can easily and quickly change. The writ is meant to remind you of that incontrovertible fact."

"As if I could ever forget," the countess grumbled.

"Then it's agreed," said Robinôt, holding out his hand for the letter. Marga reluctantly returned it. "We're off to St. Fionnani."

As the lieutenant was rowed back to his ship, Tess half whispered to the countess, "What was the warrant for, if not the fugitive Giles Foudria?"

"In the event of my defiance of or insubordination to the lawful commands of Count Pesavolta or his representatives," said Marga, "I may be stripped of my land and title, and—depending on the offense—hanged for treason. Technically, having evaded capture by a member of Sixth Division and drawn my weapon on him, I'm already guilty. He's letting me know that he may or may not choose to report it, contingent upon my cooperation now."

She met Tess's gaze, her dark eyes glittering. "Even I, a countess, am sometimes powerless at the end of the day. Napou, let's get under way."

St. Fionnani, the southernmost Ninysh settlement, was the wrong direction, in fact—a half day's sail northward. Tess had never seen an island with so many cliffs. Its harbor was a long, narrow inlet winding more than a mile toward the interior. The north bank was a wooded slope too steep and rocky to build on; the south bank had just enough space between the sea and the cliffs to cram in a narrow band of docks, shipyards, and lumberyards and a rough town consisting primarily of taverns. At the top of the cliffs hulked a fortress, dug in with earthworks and embankments, guarding the narrow harbor mouth.

A hundred ships at least, the greatest part of the Ninysh fleet, were here. The *Avodendron* was towed past half a dozen ships to an empty berth, where they waited for Lieutenant Robinôt to come aboard. His soldiers swarmed the ship like ants. Marga set her jaw but did not try to argue or stop them.

"Saints bless your search" was all she said, putting a little acid into every word.

If they did a thorough search, they were going to discover a strange-looking, crusty cocoon in a drawer. Pathka's chrysalis, if that was the word for it, had hardened into something like flaky pastry; Tess worried they'd break it to see what was inside. The crew were supposed to wait above, out of the soldiers' way, but she slipped below to her cabin. Soldiers had gotten there first. She peeked in apprehensively, only to find that Jacomo had moved from the sea lockers onto her bunk. He'd let the blanket drape down in front of Pathka's drawer.

"So sorry to disturb your lordship," a soldier was saying. "Feel better soon."

"Close the door when you leave," muttered Jacomo. "There's a draft."

They left, chalking an *X* on the door to indicate the room had been searched. Apparently, if you were the son of the Duke of Ducana, nobody was going to look under you.

"Thank you!" she whispered. Jacomo, one arm thrown over his eyes, nodded minutely.

The soldiers weren't as delicate about the rest of their search, finding it necessary to empty the countess's trunks onto the floor and to dig into the flour barrels. No trace of Giles Foudria was found. Indeed, the only trace left, as far as Tess knew, was the eyu in her pocket.

"We're done here," said Robinôt as his men filed off the ship. He leaned against the rail, not looking particularly done, fiddling with the bandage over the injury Marga had given him.

Tess planted herself beside Marga and folded her arms, adding the weight of her glare to the countess's, as if that would help hurry him along. Maybe it would.

"Will told me a thing or two about this World Serpent you're after," drawled Robinôt. "Are you sure two guns are enough? We're retrofitting our fleet here—"

"We don't have time for that," said Marga.

"You misunderstand me," said Robinôt. "I don't mean more bombards for the *Avodendron,* but rather that we might send a prime ship of the line to accompany you."

"No, thank you. Tow us back to open water and we'll be on our way."

Robinôt looked at his boots, which had not a scuff on them. "I realize you're in a hurry, but I also know—having explicitly looked for it as evidence—that you never got a map from Foudria. No wonder you were floundering about."

Tess began to scoff, but Marga was looking suddenly abashed. *Had* they been floundering? "It was the fog, surely," offered Tess.

"It wasn't just the fog," Marga muttered.

"Foudria's not the only person who's ever crossed the polar circle," said Robinôt. "Trappers and traders often stop here on their way back to civilization. There are some at the Citadel now—not trained cartographers, but can beggars be choosers? Come ashore. I'll introduce you."

"Crackpots and madmen who eat their own boots?" interjected Tess witheringly.

Marga, chewing her lip, looked less scornful.

"Your Grace, I feel responsible," said Robinôt. He laid a hand upon his heart to illustrate how much feeling he was doing. "I accused you wrongly in St. Claresse, all but chased you out of town, brought you here against your wishes—"

"Threatened me with Count Pesavolta's displeasure," said Marga.

"And for what?" He mugged mournfully. "Let me make it up to you. Please."

Marga frowned, but Tess could see the wheels of cogitation turning. "Mr. Darvo," said the countess at last, hailing the bosun, "inform my uncle that Tess and I are gone up to the Citadel for an hour or two. Send ashore for any supplies we need, and see if you can't pry Lord Jacomo out of bed. He can help the cook carry leafy vegetables, if there are any to be had."

Robinôt was blocking the gangway. He pointed at Marga's sword. "I'd feel better if you left that behind."

For a moment Tess thought he'd crossed a line, but then Marga unbuckled her sword belt, handed it to the bosun, who had not yet departed, and inclined her head sarcastically at Robinôt.

Saints above, they must have been far more lost than Tess had understood.

"Are you sure we can trust him?" Tess muttered, following Marga down the gangway.

"We absolutely cannot," Marga muttered back. "But our forward progress has been . . . labored. I don't know whether these trappers can help, but even a scribbled diagram would be welcome at this point."

They weren't even going to reach the polar circle this season. Tess felt an eddy of protopanic but pushed it down as hard as she could. For Pathka's sake, she couldn't give up.

The cliffs were so high that Tess wondered whether the town ever got any direct sunlight. The place smelled like fish and vomit, with an undertone of gunpowder. Robinôt's soldiers accompanied Tess and Marga up the switchback road to the fortress. The road wound through a tunnel bored into the cliffs and lit with torches.

"Half our fortifications are underground," said Robinôt, gesturing toward a side passage. His voice echoed. "This whole cliff was riddled with tunnels before Ninys even arrived."

They emerged into jarring sunlight, upon a plateau at the top of the cliffs. The fortress was to their right, sunken and sullen, surrounded by dry moats and earthworks. Robinôt pointed out the different kinds—bastions, ravelins, tenailles—and Marga nodded as if she understood.

Tess looked left across the high plain, vibrant green with young wheat. The fields stretched half a mile until they hit the dark wall of forest. In the middle of the wheat stood a settlement: a church tower and half a dozen thatched roofs just visible above encircling walls. The wooden palisade was being replaced with stone; Tess could hear the stonemasons hammering. The settlement had a dry moat, too, which seemed like a lot of defenses for a small hamlet. Whom did they expect to come out of that forest?

Robinôt followed Tess's gaze. "That's the mission church and farming collective. Our foothold here has been hard-won, three steps forward and two steps back. These wheat fields? All new. This is the first year the Pelaguese have left us alone long enough for anything to grow. They may finally be giving up."

"What are the people called here?" asked Tess.

"We call them Dog People," said Robinôt, smirking. "One look at their women will tell you why. Welcome to Little Bitch Island, my friends."

That name she knew. Fozu had called it that. This was Edushuke.

Fozu had planned to meet Hami here, not realizing Hami was aboard the *Avodendron*.

Some instinct made her look toward the harbor. The inlet was so long that she couldn't see all the ships, but the five decoy *Sweet Jessia*s had not yet been towed out of sight.

She counted six *Sweet Jessia*s.

The real one was here, already at anchor. They'd caught up with the dragon expedition.

Marga's voice broke Tess's reverie: "Twenty cannons? Surely that's overkill." She was pointing at the bastions, or maybe the ravelins.

"You don't know what our people have suffered here," said Robinôt. "Twenty-five years of fighting, and this tiny corner is all we have to show for it. These guns may turn the tide."

"What kinds of devils are these Dog People?" said Marga.

"Fighters, and there are endless hordes of them. More arrive all the time," he said. "They have some homeland, far from here, resupplying them. Great Bitch Island, probably."

With that, he turned and led them into the Citadel.

Tess spotted Spira almost the moment they stepped into the heptagonal courtyard. The trestle tables of the soldiers' mess were set up outdoors, since the weather was fine; Spira and two saar compatriots sat with a leather-faced man, hunched over bowls of stew, speaking urgently. If he was an explorer, the dragons had gotten to him first.

Robinôt led Tess and Marga across the courtyard and indoors, to the low-ceilinged hall where the officers ate. In contrast to the soup line outdoors, this was a formal affair with linens and silver, servants and fortified wine. Twenty men in dress uniform sat around a long table—generals, lieutenants, the governor-general of the island, and the admiral of the fleet. The soup course had already started.

The officers watched Robinôt, that Sixth Division interloper, as warily as if he were a wasp. Some began reluctantly shuffling their chairs to make room at the table.

"Don't trouble yourselves," called Robinôt. He turned to one of the servants. "Prepare three plates. We'll take them outside."

The servant bowed and scrambled off to do his bidding. Around the table, the officers closed ranks and resumed eating without another glance at the visitors in the doorway.

Marga was staring daggers at Robinôt; Tess could guess why. A countess outranked everyone here, even the white-haired governor-general, and Robinôt hadn't introduced her.

It was a barefaced insult. No wonder he'd told Marga to leave her dueling sword behind.

Robinôt led Tess and Marga back outside; servants followed with their food. Spira's group had gone, but Robinôt located a couple of other men, grizzled veterans with wild hair and three-day stubble, and planted himself beside them. Marga and Tess took seats opposite.

The old-timers, Cucuron and Slabireaux, were well into their grog. It took little prompting from Robinôt to get them telling stories. They'd seen ice tigers pacing on icebergs; the cats would leap into the water and swim after your boat frighteningly fast. They'd seen peculiar islands, called Old Floats, that shifted in the night to block your way. They'd seen mermaids (Tess suspected sabak) and gray-green people (these she knew were real). There were cities in the far south—underground cities of pearlescent glass; cities embedded in cliff faces, populated by people who could fly; cities that walked upon the face of the water.

Tess could have listened all night. These were even better than the adventure stories she'd been raised on.

"Take it with a grain of salt," muttered Robinôt. "The midnight sun addles a man's wits."

Marga cocked an eyebrow, the sharpest weapon at her disposal. "Old Floats and Wandering Cities are real. We encountered those on my expedition through the Sea of Holes."

"But have either of you withered coots encountered the great serpent?" asked Robinôt.

Slabireaux seemed suddenly interested in his pease porridge spoon; Cucuron's rheumy eyes drifted toward the sky. Robinôt repeated the question more loudly, and Slabireaux said, "Why d'you think I'm goin' home? Because I onderstand something I dedn't before."

Tess held her breath. That sounded like something someone who'd seen it might say.

"Understand . . . because you saw the serpent?" Marga pressed.

"Because we saw the Ggdani. You en't going to find it unless the Ggdani let you find it," said Slabireaux, tapping his spoon on the bridge of his nose.

"There's a whole mob of Ggdani in the farthest south," said

Cucuron, drumming on the edge of the table. "They pull the strings, make the decisions. You can't go against them if they take against you. They killed our mate Jubenali. Gave him frostbite in his eyes."

"They can't give you frostbite," said Robinôt.

"Believe what you like," said Slabireaux, "but we seen it. Where they touch, it spreads. If they decide you en't gettin' through, you en't gettin' through."

"You got through, though," Tess observed. "They found you worthy."

The old explorers exchanged a glance she couldn't interpret.

"They did *not*," said Cucuron.

"Could you take us as far as these Ggdani, though, or draw us a map?" asked Marga.

"No," said Slabireaux.

"We swore we'd ne'er go back," said Cucuron, his cataract-pale eyes rolling like a spooked horse's. "Anyroad, we can't draw no map. The way changes. The Old Floats shift, the earth shakes. What were passable last season will be blocked now—or worse, full up with whirlpools and geysers and storms."

"Don't tell me they also control the weather!" scoffed Robinôt.

"Clearly, I can't tell you nothin'," said the old man.

"Look, we're going to find our way there eventually, whether you help us or not," said Marga. "We have a good ship, a resourceful crew, and supplies to last a yea—"

Slabireaux reached across and grabbed her hand. Marga's eyes widened.

"It's galling to be told what you can't do," he rasped. "I was like you. If a thing were forbidden, I cried, 'We'll see about that, comrade!' and rushed headfirst into it. But do you accept that you can't go to Palasho Pesavolta and plop yourseln upon the count's fat lap?"

Marga tried to pull her hand back but couldn't. "Of course I do!"

"Then accept that neither can you see the One without the Ggdani's say-so."

Tess interjected, "They sometimes find people worthy, don't they? It's not impossible?"

But Marga was speaking over her: "I don't accept your analogy. A World Serpent is nothing like Pesavolta's lap. It's part of nature and belongs to everyone."

Robinôt drew his knife and pressed it into the folds of Slabireaux's throat. "How dare you manhandle a countess's person, or compare Count Pesavolta to a mob of savages. You will take every word back."

"I'll not," said Slabireaux with utter calm, releasing Marga's hand. "There are things you en't allowed to do in this world—such as stab an old fool in the throat for no reason."

Robinôt, scowling, withdrew his knife. The old men took the opportunity to scarper.

"Well, that was useless," the lieutenant said, hailing a servant to take the empty plates. "I didn't realize those two would be so unhelpful."

Marga sniffed. "If I gave up every time some old man told me to, I'd never get anything done. Anyway, it wasn't entirely useless. Now I know what the final hurdle will be."

"And who you'll need to bribe or kill," said Robinôt, smirking.

Marga did not look shocked by this suggestion. "We should be getting back to the ship."

"It will be dark soon," said Robinôt. "It's highly inadvisable for two ladies to traverse St. Fionnani town alone after dark."

It wasn't dark, in fact, although it was late. Tess flashed an anxious glance at Marga, but the countess was staring hard at Robinôt.

"Give me a sword," said Marga, keeping her voice light. "And you can judge tomorrow whether the town or the ladies got the worst of it."

"Quite impossible, I'm afraid," said Robinôt.

"Send men to accompany us."

"There are none I can spare," said Robinôt. "But we can quarter you here until morning."

Tess couldn't fathom how Robinôt withstood Marga's glare; his ears should have melted, and then his eyes. Alas, the immovable object remained unmoved. Marga finally flagged and gave a gesture of grudging assent.

Tess was put into a small, square room with a narrow bed—reminiscent of a monastery cell she'd been briefly imprisoned in. This window had a shutter, though, and no one had bothered to whitewash the walls. She flopped onto the cot with her clothes on and had nearly drifted off when there was a knock at the door.

It was Marga, her arms full of blankets and pillows from her apparently much nicer room.

"I hope you won't mind," she said, "but since we're roughing it anyway, without even a change of clothes, I would feel better sleeping on your floor. Does your door lock?"

It did, but not to Marga's satisfaction; it could still be opened from outside with a key. The countess insisted on moving the bed in front of the door—not an easy maneuver in such tight quarters. Once they'd got it moved, she made a nest of blankets in front of the window.

"You don't think Robinôt would really try to harm you?" said Tess, wrestling the mattress back into shape. It had fallen off the bed frame, and the straw was all down at one end.

"I think he wants to humiliate me," said Marga. "It's been obvious since we came up. He didn't introduce me to the officers. He found us the worst explorers and then threatened one, just to show what a hothead he is—as if I weren't clear on that point. Now he's forcing us to stay the night. He's desperate to put me in my place, after the sting I gave him on St. Claresse. He surely isn't finished yet, but he'll get no opportunities while I'm asleep."

Tess looked at Marga's nest guiltily. "Would you rather have the bed? I don't mind."

"Hm? No, no," said Marga, wrapping herself up like a cocooning quigutl. "You've had your doubts about me, and I mean to show you that we are in this together. I accept the floor in solidarity. Besides, this gown should wrinkle spectacularly against the planking. I can whine about it tomorrow, and perhaps that will satisfy him that I've suffered enough."

They both lay quietly for a while.

"I find it disheartening," said Marga at last, her voice small in the darkness, "to think that he was one of William's dearest friends. If there's a silver lining to my darling's death, it's that I won't have to pretend to enjoy Robinôt's company on feast days for the rest of my life."

Tess found this oddly poignant and was awake thinking about it long after Marga had begun to snore.

Thirty-One

*O*pen *your eyes, and notice that your hands are the Hands of the World.
What can the world do, without your hands? How would it put
itself to rights?*

Once upon a time, while Tess and the countess were sleeping,
a diminutive woman darted across the new wheat fields toward the
farming collective. She slipped through the gap between the palisade
and the new stone wall when the watchman's back was turned, as she'd
done many times before. In her hands she carried a basket, and in the
basket were sachets of dried herbs and a single stoppered bottle.

She was a node, a knot, a place where the threads of many different stories crossed. Her name, these days, was Berekka.

She crossed the colonnaded plaza toward the mission school dormitory, smelling all the mission smells: garlic, wool, and woodsmoke.
Her dark clothes and complexion helped her blend into the shadows;
her bluebird-blue hair, visible a mile away in daytime, was not a liability with no moon to illuminate it. The dormitories were locked at
night, except once a month the little service door at the back was left
open by the youngest of the nuns—Sister Marie, a small, scared pi-
geon of a girl—whom Berekka had managed to persuade to her cause.

One of Berekka's foster mothers had been a nun, back in Segosh
(the other was a whore). Berekka knew how to talk to them.

It was usually Sister Marie who met the herb delivery at the door, but tonight it was three of the girls, out of bed after hours. It was dangerous (Sister Marie could not protect them; she would have to plead ignorance), but they risked it because they had to know.

There had been four girls waiting for her last month. Berekka suspected she knew where the missing girl was tonight, and it made her feel sick.

They didn't talk much, lest they wake the older nuns. Berekka didn't have to explain about the tea or how to brew it; she'd been delivering her abortifacient herbs here for half a year. She silently passed the sachets to Zivekhi—the youngest, and the only one shorter than Berekka. The girl gathered them in the skirt of her nightdress.

"Did you bring it?" the tallest girl, Ebushai, whispered, unable to contain herself.

She spoke in Ninysh. Berekka's heart broke a little, but she didn't pretend not to understand. She lifted the stoppered bottle for them to see. The girls looked awed.

"Please, auntie, can I give it to him?" asked the last girl, Rimeshe, chin trembling. She was Father Erique's great favorite and had the most burning need for vengeance.

"No," Berekka whispered firmly in Aftishekka, putting the bottle away. "I told you: you have enough to endure. Murder sounds like a welcome release, but it stains the soul. I've been through it before; I know what I'm in for. I willingly take this on for you."

From deep within the dormitory darkness, an elderly voice called, "Who's there?"

The girls quickly closed the door and latched it. They knew how to scamper, hide, and sneak back to their beds; they might not get caught. Berekka still worried for them.

She didn't worry for herself. She'd been observing this priest all month, ever since the girls had solicited her help, and she knew his habits. He would just be returning from the library, where he liked to take the girls. He would drink cognac before bed.

The priest had his own room because he'd come with a bit of an endowment; a Ninysh count had once had enough faith in Erique's piety to leave him some money. Berekka hoped that old count didn't have a moment's peace up in Ninysh Heaven, that he spent his days screaming in horror when he looked down and saw he'd funded a terrible priest—kicked out of his last parish for abusing his serving girl and banished to a mission church in the Archipelagos, where he carried on with even greater impunity.

It was just as likely that a Ninysh count would look down and see nothing wrong, alas.

Berekka knocked on Father Erique's door and waited. A strong waft of woodsmoke caught her attention; these northerners were so delicate, keeping their fires stoked high even with midsummer only three weeks away.

The priest finally answered, already in his night robes. He could not have been much over thirty—about Berekka's age—for all that his fine pale hair was already thinning. He was much taller than she was, and she wondered whether she looked like a child to him.

"Hello, little bluebird," he said merrily. For a moment she thought he'd already had his cognac—but no, there it was on the table across the room, the glass still clean and empty. "I've seen you flitting about the compound. What good fortune brings you to my door?"

Berekka smiled prettily. "I'm here to poison you."

Berekka had poisoned only one other man. Fozu had unwittingly helped her.

She'd met Fozu at the Academy, where she would sometimes attend lectures by apothecaries and herbalists with her foster mother Sister Monica. She'd been afraid to go at first, for fear of running into Master Russo, who'd captured her in the wild (as he put it, as if she were a tiger), but he was now too grand and important to spend time among the humble botanists. Still, she wore a novice's veil to lectures so no one could see her face.

Fozu somehow knew her for an island girl anyway. He tried getting her attention in a variety of ways—waving, winking, speaking words to Sister Monica that were really meant for her. "I think that young man likes you, Rebecca," Sister Monica said encouragingly.

Rebecca (that was Berekka's name in those days) had no interest in this skinny, redheaded boy. One day he passed her a note; she opened it scornfully. There were no words on the page, just a drawing of boots.

Not hard, plain, ugly Ninysh boots—soft, embroidered, beautiful Aftisheshe boots.

She confronted him after the lecture, flapping the note in his face. "What is this?"

"Vulkharai's boots," he whispered, glancing around to make sure no one was eavesdropping. Sister Monica was closest, but she was determinedly not paying attention. "I don't know who your people are, exactly—I'm guessing Murkh?"

"Aftisheshe," said Rebecca, deflating a little. She'd felt seen, but he hadn't really known.

"But I knew you'd know those boots," he persisted. "Every nation tells that story."

"It's not a story," she hissed. "It's how our war with the Tshu began."

He looked taken aback, but only for a moment. "I'm an islander, too. I've been trying to tell you."

Her veil probably dulled the sharp skepticism of her expression as she looked him up and down. His hair. His pale complexion, complete with freckles. He looked Ninysh to her.

"But your name is Giles," she said, feeling foolish.

"It's not. I'm Fozu," he whispered. "Don't tell anyone."

They were friends after that, although not in quite the way Sister Monica would have liked (she seemed anxious that Rebecca marry a nice boy and not take up either of her mothers' professions). Fozu was sweet, but a weight on Rebecca's heart wouldn't let her feel the right things for him.

Sweet Colette, Rebecca's other foster mother, laughed at her lover's concern. "Don't mind Monica," she'd say. "When you're sixteen, old enough to be on your own, I expect you to run back to your home island. And I hope we will have taught you enough medicine and midwifery that you will always find work, wherever you go."

In fact, Rebecca had learned it all early and well. By fifteen, she could treat any women's ailment, deliver a breech baby with a double nuchal cord, and brew up abortifacients for the red ladies. Still, there was one particular tincture she wanted to learn to concoct. Sister Monica refused to teach her (and may very well not have known). Sweet Colette looked a bit askance when Rebecca asked, and said, "We do not poison our patrons—even the very awful ones—but I do know something that works quite well on rats."

Rebecca learned to make it, and then she returned to the old neighborhood where she'd lived when she first arrived in Ninys. The apartment had been above a bookseller's, but the whole street was full of booksellers. It took several days of haunting to find the right steps, but when she knocked on her old door—she remembered the graffito of a mermaid beside it—a woman with hollow eyes and six children answered. Master Russo didn't live there anymore.

Her mothers didn't ask where she'd gone; she was too old for them to keep track of her every minute.

Fozu was mostly a geographer, but he sometimes attended Master Russo's lectures. Rebecca started asking Fozu for stories. The anthropologist had become quite famous; he'd won the Academy Prize for his theory of devolution—that the races of humankind became corrupted and degenerate the farther they wandered from civilization. He'd become a moral crusader against the red ladies (he must've worked out that Sweet Colette had spirited Rebecca away). He'd gone abroad for a season and returned with a new Pelaguese pet, a little Nutufi boy named Loso (called Louis) who sat onstage during lectures, drinking tea from a saucer and saying "please" and "thank you."

"The devolved degenerate can be partially rehabilitated, and taught manners just like regular people!" Fozu sneered after telling this story, imitating Russo. "I'd like to skewer him."

"Do you know where Master Russo lives?" Rebecca asked. "We could go to his house and confront him. Rebuke his vicious lies to his face."

"Wouldn't you be afraid he'd recognize you?" asked Fozu, who talked big but would not have skewered a mouse, even if it bit him.

"I want him to recognize me now. It will be all right," Rebecca assured him. "I'll bring him a gift, to show there are no hard feelings."

Fozu took her to Master Russo's house a week later. The decorated academic had moved up in the world, to a half-timbered town house; he accepted Rebecca's bottle of wine as her apology for running away, and he poured them each a glass to celebrate their reunion. She ensured that Fozu spilled all of his, and surreptitiously watered a plant with her own.

It was a quick poison, very quick. First it burned a hole in Russo's throat. He collapsed on the carpet and lay gasping like a fish while it burned out his stomach. Rebecca knelt beside him and said a few words, a prayer to Edushuke, the first of many she would utter to cleanse the miasma from her soul.

Fozu threw up everywhere and ran away crying. She regretted that; he'd been a kind friend and would surely never forgive her.

She hurried to the river, stole a little boat under cover of darkness, and tried to remember how to sail it. Only then, smelling the wind on the water and feeling the tug of the lines in her hands, did she finally begin to cry—for her mothers, whom she could never face again, and for all the things Russo had taken from her that even his death could not return.

Berekka was sitting at Father Erique's little table, her stoppered bottle in front of her. He sat opposite, smirking, having brazenly invited her in despite her threat. She was too short to be taken seriously, apparently.

There was no fire in his grate, but she could still smell smoke— just a *bere* smell, blurred and indistinct. It had been stronger outside.

"I've been wanting to speak with you," said Father Erique. "You see, there's been a bit of a mystery here at the mission for several months. Previously, many of our girls would find themselves with child—an unfortunate circumstance brought about by their lascivious natures, but one that we forgive, since they can't help themselves. Their children are brought up properly in the faith of Allsaints and will live the pious lives their mothers were too heathen to manage.

"About six months ago, we saw four miscarriages and a stillbirth. Since then, not one of our girls has conceived."

"I've been giving them an abortifacient tea of Queen Rhademunde's balm. I'm glad to hear they've been using it," said Berekka, unwilling to play the game of pretending not to know how any of this had happened.

Father Erique looked discomfited, the way he should have looked (but hadn't) when she told him she meant to poison him. "That's a mainland herb," he said.

"It blooms in all our meadows now. A couple years ago, I returned to Ninys, even though I'd sworn never to set foot there again." Berekka swirled the green liquid in her bottle. "I brought it back, along with harshmallow and dragonsbane. I knew what you would resort to if you couldn't quickly eradicate us with war."

Father Erique sneered. "I'll give you a choice, little witch, which is more than you deserve. You may drink your own poison, every last drop, or I will march you up to the Citadel, to be hanged for witchery."

"Hanging sounds unpleasant," said Berekka. "But I suppose I deserve it, as a witch and murderess."

"A murderess only of yourself if you take the wiser course," said the priest. He uncorked his cognac. "Here, let us drink together. I shall salute your passing and say a prayer over you."

"Very well," said Berekka. He passed her an empty glass, and she poured her concoction into it; the liquid was thick and green, and its putrid smell quickly filled the room.

"How on earth did you expect to induce me to drink that?" said Father Erique, half laughing, half gagging. "It even smells like death."

Berekka, who knew what death smelled like, did not bother to correct him.

He lifted his glass of amber liquid in a small, sarcastic toast. She saluted him back, and then they downed their drinks.

He felt it immediately; she could see it in his eyes. He was telling himself it was the alcohol, that it burned because he'd drunk too quickly, that he was imagining things.

"You're not imagining things," said Berekka calmly. "I doctored your cognac this morning. If there are any curses you wish to utter, utter them while you still can."

"But . . . but . . ." His eyes bulged and flecks of pink foam dotted his lips. He gestured wildly toward her glass.

"Oh, this?" she said, examining the green residue. "Something I've been experimenting with for the hounds. It does nothing for worms, alas, but it should give me a shiny coat."

He flopped out of his chair, clawing at his throat. She ignored him and started looking for something to write with—a quill, charcoal, anything. Simply killing him was not enough. The other priests needed to understand: *This is what happens to rapists.* The lesson was wasted if no one could learn from it.

Her eyes began to sting and then water, which surprised her. For a moment she wondered whether she was weeping, whether she felt pity or remorse—she was certain she did not—or perhaps sorrow for her poor, stained soul. Only when she coughed did she realize that there was a perplexing amount of smoke in the room. Something was very wrong.

The mission bells began to peal out an alarm. Berekka cursed. She was going to have to haul Father Erique outside. If this place burned down around him, the other priests would assume he'd died in the fire and none of them would learn anything.

He wasn't dead yet. He'd contrived to make himself vomit, annoyingly.

Berekka was short but sturdy, and he was as thin and wiry as a hunting hound (though not nearly as elegant). She hefted him over her shoulders and carried him out to the courtyard, still moaning and gurgling.

Priests were hauling buckets of water out of the well, while the sisters herded panicking children toward an escape tunnel leading out to the wheat fields. Berekka skirted the chaos, hoping they were all too busy to notice her.

There was fire in all directions, which was confusing. Fire usually started in one place and spread, leaving an obvious direction to run, but every way Berekka turned, she saw another blaze.

And then she looked up to the roof of the church and saw why.

He had a beard now, and he looked like the sea had recently puked him up, but she knew that slender frame and those eyes, even if they'd once been gentler.

"Fozu," she whispered, and then someone tackled her from behind.

Thirty-Two

Alarm bells woke Tess in the middle of the night. She smelled smoke and for a panicked moment thought the Citadel was on fire. Stepping over the countess, she threw open the shutter and saw the mission burning across the plain. Massive bright flames leaped toward the sky; she could hear them roaring on the wind. Soldiers rushed out from the fortress to help.

"Thatch goes up quickly," said Marga, who'd risen and was standing behind her, "but those huge palisade logs would require an accelerant to really get going."

"What are you suggesting?" said Tess, who suspected she knew.

"That we know someone who came here carrying pyria," said Marga. The conflagration cast an orange glow upon her face.

"They wouldn't waste it on this, surely. Spira said they brought exactly enough to kill the serpent with," said Tess.

The whites of Marga's eyes glittered in the firelight. "After all we went through with Giles and Lord Hamish, you believe the *dragons* were being truthful? Maybe they brought more than they said, or they've decided they can't make it to the pole. Maybe they sold it; maybe someone stole it. Either way, Robinôt heard Spira mention it. He's bound to make the connection, as I did, except he'll tell the governor-general straightaway."

With that, she closed the shutter. Tess shuffled back to bed.

She was awakened early by Marga shaking her shoulder. "We should go, while everything's still in confusion. Robinôt surely isn't focused on humiliating me now."

The courtyard was swarming with people—refugees from the mission, soldiers who'd been up all night, and civilians up from the harbor town to pass out food and blankets. Tess followed Marga around the perimeter of the heptagon toward the front gate, trying to avoid the dense crowd. About halfway along, a figure stepped out of a recessed doorway into their path.

It was Spira. Ko's eyes were ringed in shadow, as if ko hadn't slept.

"Out of our way, dragon," said Marga.

"Did Lord Hamish arrive with you?" asked Spira. When Marga tried to push past instead of answer, ko added, "I know he stowed away on your ship."

"We discovered him and he fled. I don't know where he went," said Marga. "I'm going to do you a favor, Scholar, out of the goodness of my heart. You should know that Lieutenant Robinôt was not shipped back to the mainland. He's here."

"I glimpsed him yesterday," said Spira haughtily. "He doesn't concern me."

"He should." Marga lowered her voice. "Your pyria was undoubtedly used to set the mission fire. Who did you sell it to?"

The edges of Spira's mouth quivered; ko blinked twice. Tess felt she'd had a fleeting glimpse of something beneath the hauteur. Not fear, as she might have expected, but sorrow.

Hami had set the dragons up to fail. He'd said exactly that aboard the *Avodendron*.

"The Dog People?" Marga pressed. "I won't be telling Robinôt, if you're afrai—"

"I tried to sell it," Spira blurted out, glancing around. "I want it off my ship. But Hami's contact couldn't pay. She laughed at us. I had samples in my room, but they've been stolen."

"You mean someone sneaked into an impenetrable fortress—"
Marga began.

"It's hardly impenetrable," said Spira.

Before ko could say more, the gates opened. The crowd of refugees and townsfolk split in two, clearing a path for five riders on horseback, a pack of enormous war mastiffs, and two soldiers on foot leading a woman between them. She was short but not scrawny, and as brown as a Porphyrian. Her long hair was an impossible iridescent blue. Her hands were bound.

The soldiers each held a guideline to keep her moving; they began jerking the lines to make the blue-haired woman stumble. The crowd jeered. There was not a lot of spare foodstuff to throw, nor rocks, so they threw dirt and pebbles. The woman plastered on a grim, brittle smile and dodged what she could.

"That's . . . that's my contact," said Spira, turning pale. "Berekka."

"You should leave, before she decides to take you down with her," said Tess.

"Leave how?" said Spira. "They've closed the harbor. Nobody is allowed in or out until they catch whoever set the fire."

"What?" cried the countess, her indignation echoing even over the jeers of the crowd. "But they've caught her, clearly. Why else would she be bound?"

As if in answer to her question, two more soldiers rushed through the gates, carrying a stretcher with a dark-robed priest on it. His throat was bandaged, his face slack. A gaggle of sooty, worried-looking monks jogged along behind the stretcher. This group veered toward Tess and her companions, who were apparently standing right in the path to the infirmary.

Tess glanced at the injured priest's face as he was carried past.

Holy cack. She knew him. She would have known him anywhere.

"Erique!" shrieked the countess, clapping her hands to her mouth. "Sweet Heavenly home, what have they done to you?"

"What has *she* done, you mean," cried one of the monks in a voice rough with smoke and sorrow. He pointed toward the blue-haired woman. "It was Berekka the witch. She tried to poison him. We caught her in the act."

The last time Tess had seen Father Erique, the rapist priest of Anshouie, he'd been tied naked to a chair. She herself had tied him there. His long-suffering servant, Angelica, had given him a well-deserved, accurately placed kick and then taken off.

At least Angelica wasn't the one tied up and accused of poisoning him. She deserved a better fate than that. Tess hoped she was happily cooking somewhere.

The people of Anshouie were supposed to have brought Father Erique to justice, though, not released him back into the wild to carry on as before. Tess had left them a note, detailing his crimes. Had they even read it?

Was she supposed to have killed him herself? She shuddered to think.

She glanced over to where Spira had stood, but Spira had taken the opportunity to disappear.

"Let's go," said Marga, grabbing Tess's elbow. "We'll see about this harbor closure."

The countess hustled Tess down to the lower city, where they found that Spira had reported correctly: a great chain had been raised across the mouth of the harbor, keeping all ships in. It had lain on the bottom long enough to acquire barnacles and a wispy seaweed fringe.

There was nothing for it but to wait, so of course Marga went back to the Citadel directly, to speak with the governor-general.

Tess, for her part, was being followed by a vague, pervasive guilt. She tried to quell it by keeping busy. She checked in on Pathka and Jacomo, but that took all of five minutes; they were still cocooning. She walked up to the shipyards and did some recording with her thnimi. She'd abandoned the idea that Goredd could intervene in the Archipelagos without making a bigger mess, but the Queen still needed to know how many ships were being retrofitted with cannon.

Those weapons could be used against Goredd as easily as the Archipelagos.

The next morning, Tess awoke to a rapping at her cabin door. She found the countess outside, buckling on her sword belt.

"How's Jacomo?" Marga asked.

Tess glanced over; he was curled on the bunk, his back to the door. "About the same."

"Damn," said Marga. "I really could use some moral and spiritual support."

If she'd hoped those words would goad Jacomo out of bed, she was sorely disappointed. He began to snore aggressively.

"I can help you," said Tess, grabbing her boots.

"Are you sure?" said Marga as Tess pulled the door shut. "Jacomo says you're not comfortable with pain and grieving. Not that I think any less of you for it."

That was apparently the reason he'd given as to why Marga shouldn't talk to Tess about Will. Tess gave what she hoped was a wry smile and said, "I expect I can handle a bit."

Marga nodded cordially and set off for the weather deck.

Tess followed. "But what sort of pain and grief are you anticipating?"

"I'm going up to the Citadel to see Father Erique," said Marga. "They told me last evening that he should be stable enough to receive visitors today."

"Oh," said Tess, her feet slowing.

Marga doubled back, took her arm, and led her down the gangway.

"Are you *sure* you'll be all right?" asked Marga. "His injury is quite gruesome, I'm told. That vicious herbalist—I refuse to call her a witch—made a great bloody hole in his throat."

It wasn't his injury Tess dreaded. It was her own creeping guilt.

The question from yesterday returned: *Should* she have killed him? She could imagine the sabak accusing her of taking the easy way out, and yet it hadn't been easy. She'd wanted to hurt Father Erique. She'd had to pull herself away.

Who would she be now if she'd killed him? Surely it would have broken her. How do you kill—even someone who deserves it—without wanting to do yourself in next?

Tess pondered this all through the narrow town and up the winding cliff road. She hardly registered that Marga had kept talking until these words cut through her self-absorption: "Poor Erique. I've known him forever; we practically grew up together. He's the son of my father's loyal old steward. He officiated at my wedding and at Albaro's funeral. He didn't deserve this."

Tess's first instinct was to clamp her mouth shut, let the countess have her illusions. But then she heard the sabak again, plain as day: *Don't let that be all you do.*

She couldn't change the past, but there was always another choice to be made, right now.

If Father Erique survived his injuries and was allowed to carry on as before . . . she couldn't let that happen. She had to reveal what he had done.

Marga was the logical one to tell, but maybe also the hardest.

"What if he *did* deserve it, though?" said Tess. Her heart felt like a trembling bird. "That herbalist must've had a reason to do what she did."

Marga boggled at her. "Not a good reason. You should've seen him as a child, how pious and unearthly he was. He had the scriptures of St. Munn memorized by age four. My father sent him to study with the Bishop of Modera, and by fifteen, our Erique had become the youngest priest of that order in a century. Papa always said he'd be bishop someday."

The temptation to keep silent almost overpowered Tess; again she forced herself to speak. "If he was so wonderful," she said as they entered the Citadel, "why was he banished to a run-down country church and then to the Archipelagos?"

Marga puffed up with indignation. "He wasn't *banished*. He always preferred to walk among the common people. Devoting himself to missionary work is entirely in character."

Cack. "Run-down country church" was supposed to have made Marga wonder how Tess knew all that, which would be Tess's invitation to go into detail. It was awfully hard to just blurt out his crimes without preamble.

But she would if she had to.

Across the courtyard of the Citadel, Robinôt came out of the infirmary and headed toward the officers' wing. He spotted Marga, waved, and changed course to intercept her. "Are you come to see our mangled priest?" he called. "I just left him. He's awake and in good spirits now that I've told him the little witch is to be hanged."

Oh Heavens, no. The priest free and the herbalist dead?

"Doesn't she get a trial?" asked Tess.

Marga frowned. "She was caught in the act, Tess."

"And she's a Dog. You don't try Dogs," said Robinôt. "She was already on the governor-general's wanted list as a witch, spy, and abortionist. I'm told the mission priests have been complaining about her for ages. She'd've hanged already, except I asked to interrogate her."

He smirked at Marga. "You'll never guess who she spotted at the scene of the crime, Countess. Your man Giles Foudria. The little witch knows him, apparently."

Marga hunched her shoulders as if against a cold headwind. "Did the little *herbalist* explain why she tried to kill Father Erique? She must have had a reason, however misguided."

So Marga hadn't simply dismissed her argument? That was an encouraging surprise.

The lieutenant shrugged. "She said he's molesting girls at the mission. It's all lies."

Tess couldn't stop herself: "What if it's not lies?"

"You're really going to impugn men of the cloth?"

"An abortionist is there so often they've complained. Who's she offering her herbs to? Father Didn't-Do-It?"

Robinôt's face went hard as glass. "You're not funny," he said.

"Enough," cried the countess. Her brow was deeply furrowed now, the corners of her mouth creased. "I am trying to go see an old friend, Tess, not start a fight. Lieutenant, good day." Marga turned her back on them both and set off for the infirmary again.

"I have things I'll want to discuss with you later," Robinôt called after her.

Marga didn't look back, didn't wait. She let the infirmary door fall shut in Tess's face.

Tess could read the signs: the countess no longer required moral support. Not from Tess, anyway. As much as she wanted to, Tess couldn't turn back now. She let herself in.

The infirmary was a long, cool room, its rows of cots empty but for Father Erique's at the far end. He was propped up by pillows, his wrecked throat pristinely wrapped in white. He was looking up, eyes alight, at Marga, who'd bent over to smooth his thinning hair from his forehead. Behind them, a military nurse rolling bandages called over his shoulder, "He can't speak, Your Grace, but I could find him something to write with, perhaps."

"I would appreciate that," said Marga, pulling up a stool.

Tess drew closer, on tiptoe. She intended not to interrupt Marga's reunion, but to wait and talk afterward. She would stand to one side, unobtrusively—

As if he could feel her eyes on him, Father Erique looked up and saw Tess. His face crumpled. He opened his mouth to scream, but only a horrible gurgling sound came out.

It was Marga who screamed. Two nurses rushed in from the back room.

Of course he'd recognized Tess—her face had surely been seared into his memory.

More nurses materialized, along with a physician and several monks. They descended like a flock of gulls, forcing Marga from her seat, calling out loud speculations: "Is he in pain?" "Does he need more tincture?" "Is the bandage too tight, Alphonse?" "Is infection setting in?"

Father Erique, still gurgling, began flailing as well. The nurses tried to hold him down, perhaps thinking he was having a seizure, but Erique worked an arm free and used it to point—urgently, unambiguously—at Tess.

"What have you done to him?" cried the physician. "Get out of my sickroom!"

Tess considered refusing—it wasn't altogether unsatisfying to realize her presence was a thorn in Erique's side—but then the first nurse returned with paper and ink. Erique might not be able to speak, but he could still lie. Tess knew who would be believed. She beat a hasty retreat.

To her surprise, Marga followed. In the courtyard, Marga grabbed Tess's shoulder and spun her around.

"What the devil was that?" cried the countess.

Tess took a deep breath; her heart was racing. "He recognized me."

"I noticed," said Marga.

There was an edge to her voice, which made Tess's insides contract, but there was no turning back now.

"I met him in Anshouie when I was traveling south." She forced herself to hold Marga's gaze. "He had been abusing his serving girl, Angelica. I saw what was going on. I helped her escape and exposed him to his village."

She'd tied him to a chair, naked, holding a sign explaining his crimes. How had that not been enough?

"You saw what, exactly?" said Marga. "Do you mean to say you watched him do terrible things with your own eyes, never lifting a finger to help?"

"No!"

"And yet you're certain there's no scope for error or misunderstanding? You couldn't possibly have seen or heard something out of context and jumped to conclusions?"

"I know what I saw," said Tess. Her head felt hot; she could hear her pulse in her ears.

"And I *know* Erique from childhood. I know what he's made of," the countess insisted. "'Show me the steel and I will show you the sword,' Master Tacques used to say. Erique could never do something like that. It's against his nature."

Tess gulped air, trying to keep herself under control. Every feeling she'd suppressed was rising in her throat like bile. Her mouth soured; she fought it down.

"Whatever you saw was upsetting, clearly," said Marga. "At least consider that perhaps you were misled, caught up in the hysteria of a troubled young girl."

"I was a troubled young girl once," said Tess. "And I know what I saw in her eyes, because it was like looking in a mirror. *I know* because the same thing happened to me."

Her voice had shrilled; it echoed. There weren't many people in the courtyard at that hour—just a unit of pikes returning from drills—but they were all staring.

"Tess," said Marga, raising her hands like someone approaching a spooked horse, "lower your voice, please. I realize—"

"You realize *nothing*," cried Tess. "I am sick to death of your pithy sayings about seeing people's souls in their swordplay, or being neutral, or some cack. You see what you want to see and disregard the rest. You may as well walk around with your eyes shut."

"Be fair, Tess! A child may exaggerate."

She should not have said *child*.

"I bore a child when I was only a child," said Tess. She needed to stop talking right now. Every word was tearing a fresh wound, and yet it was too late to hold them in. They were poison. They seemed to tear a hole in her throat and let themselves out: "And you know who did that to me? Your precious Lord Morney. I was fourteen. He nearly destroyed my life."

Marga looked like she'd been slapped.

"Every time you tell me how wonderful Will was," said Tess, swaying on her feet, "or how Erique was a pious little angel, all I hear is you bragging that you get to sashay through life ignoring the ugly parts and pretending they don't exist—"

"How dare you?" cried Marga. "I loved that man, and he is *dead*!"

He couldn't die, though. There was always another to take his place. The whole world was Wills, all the way down.

Tess turned tail and fled.

Thirty-Three

As Tess's feet rushed her down to the harbor, she knew it was over—all of it: the expedition, her friendship with Marga, any hope of finding the Polar Serpent. The countess would hate her now; this would stand between them forever.

Tess trotted up the gangway of the *Avodendron*, smiling and waving at the sailors, pretending nothing was wrong, but inside she was terrified. She had to leave, there was no way around it, but she did not know how to go forward from here. She had to get Pathka ashore, do whatever it took to get ko where ko needed to be. Maybe she could steal a dinghy—and magically figure out how to sail. Maybe one of the old explorers would take them.

Ugh, there was baggage to haul as well, unless she wanted to freeze on the ice. She wasn't going to get far without help.

In principle, help was waiting in her cabin, if only she could pry him out of bed.

She braced herself and opened the door. Lord Morney's cabin, which had once seemed so spacious, seemed small and dingy now; the windows were clouded, the corners embroidered with cobwebs. There was a smell, probably unwashed Jacomo, that Tess had begun thinking of as despair. He lay with his back to the door. She'd let him keep the bunk since landing in St. Fionnani; she wasn't sure he'd ever left it.

"Jacomo," she half whispered. He didn't stir. She gently shook his shoulder.

"No," he said into the pillow.

Tears filled her eyes. "I told the countess about Will—in the worst possible way. I was unnecessarily horrible about it, and she hates me now. I can't stay. I have to get Pathka ashore, and I can't do it without your help."

He put his head under the pillow.

"Please." Tess shook him a little harder. "Come with us? I'm embarrassed to ask, because I don't see a way forward yet, but I hoped . . . You're my friend, Jacomo. I've missed you, holed up in here. But this is a fresh start. You'll feel better, out and about in the clean air."

"Go on without me," he muttered under the pillow. "I ruin everything."

"Is that what you think?" she said, angry with him now. "You fail at one thing, and now you're going to lie here feeling sorry for yourself until the end of time?"

He didn't even grunt in answer.

Tess regretted the outburst, even as she itched to say something worse, to rage at him, push him out of bed, and kick him back into the world. That would have been cruel, though.

She'd already been cruel today.

She set about getting Pathka out of the drawer. It was hard—ko weighed more than a human of corresponding size. Tess grunted and strained, halfheartedly hoping that the sound of her struggle would awaken sympathy or curiosity in Jacomo and rouse him from bed.

It didn't.

A shadow loomed across the open doorway and Tess quailed, expecting that Marga had come to shout at her some more. A gentle voice put her fears to rest: "You seem to be having difficulty. Can I do something?"

Tess looked up at Argol and burst into tears.

A square stone tower housed the mechanism for raising the chain across the harbor mouth. Beyond it, on the seaward side, the coastline was rocky and wild. Waves beat against the base of the cliff; gulls flocked there, fighting over refuse that was regularly dropped from the Citadel high above.

There was a ledge on the seaward side of the tower, and it was here that Tess asked Argol to set Pathka down. Argol had carried Pathka single-handedly, following Tess through the low town; now that they were here, and this seemed to be the end of the road, Argol asked only, "Are you sure?"

"Yes," said Tess firmly, trying to sound more certain than she felt. She tried to shake Argol's hand; Argol turned it into a hug, and then she went back to the ship.

Tess looked around her. Maybe this wouldn't be so bad. She didn't mind camping out, and it was only until she could find a way off the island.

Her options were few, however. Any explorer she might have traveled with was stuck here until the harbor reopened. A rowboat might have squeezed underneath the harbor chain; she didn't really know how to use one, though, and she would surely have been seen and stopped by one of the three Ninysh warships anchored in the open channel outside the harbor mouth. They must have arrived after the harbor closed.

Tess had done her share of stupid things, but trying to outrun three ships of the line in a rowboat would have topped everything.

The only other option Tess could see was to pick her way along the bottom of the cliffs until she reached the other half of the island, and then look for a settlement. The Dog People . . . no, that wasn't right. Had she heard their proper name? Somewhere deep in her memory she found *Aftisheshe*. Anyway, if they had boats—all island peoples surely did—maybe she could persuade them to take her away from here.

The tide was low, so Tess jumped down from the ledge onto the wet sand. The promontory came to a point near the chain tower; she couldn't see around it until she skirted the garbage pile. As cautiously as she moved, she still flustered the gulls. They erupted upward in a screaming cloud.

Around the end of the promontory, the island was sheer cliffs for miles. Tess picked her way along the rocky strand, looking for a way up the cliffs. A quarter mile along loomed a huge chunk of fallen rock, big as a barn, and she told herself she'd turn around as soon as she reached it. When she got there, however, she saw that beyond it a channel had been cut through the beach. She waded in a little ways, just far enough to see what had been concealed: a man-made cove dug into the cliff face, where four little dinghies bobbed beside a stone pier. Above this was the entrance to a tunnel, covered with an iron grating.

It looked like it might lead back to the Citadel.

The boats, though, apparently unguarded, were exactly what she needed. All she had to do was learn to sail on the fly.

Pressure against the backs of her boots made her realize the tide was coming in. She didn't know how high or how fast it would rise, and though it pained her to do so, she forced herself to turn around and run back to Pathka. This would all be for nothing if ko was washed away. She would come back when the tide went out again—come back with a plan.

At twilight, soldiers lit the oversized oil lamp at the top of the chain tower. Tess flattened herself on the ledge beside Pathka and attempted to settle in for a cold, hungry sleep. It was quite late, but the sky was still light; her eyes kept popping open. Her thnimi brooch jabbed her if she lay on her side; if she rolled onto her back, it seemed to compress her heart.

When was the last time she'd contacted Seraphina? She couldn't remember. She was the worst informant ever. She fumbled with the device and flipped a switch. No one would be awake to answer a call, but no matter; she'd record a message. She'd speak into the void and pretend she'd done her due diligence.

"Tess?" said Seraphina.

Oh. Right. There was a baby in the house; why wouldn't they all be up?

"I'm quitting," said Tess. "I was just calling to let you know. I've already left the expedition. The countess and I quarreled, and I'm at the point where I can't watch. I can't stop what's happening, and I can't be a part of this anymore."

There was a long caesura, during which her sister, no doubt, was cogitating.

"You saw what a hash I made of trying to help Martin," cried Tess. "I was patronizing."

"I did, and you were," said Seraphina. "But I also heard you say you couldn't *not* try. Your intentions were kind, even if the execution was clumsy."

"My good intentions earned him a beating," said Tess. "They were worthless."

"If you could control every outcome of your actions," said Seraphina, "then I would judge you exclusively by those outcomes. Since you can't, I believe your intentions still matter—not to absolve you, but to goad you into doing better next time."

How did Seraphina always turn everything into a philosophical discussion? "I'm going to try to get Pathka to the pole on my own," said Tess, turning the subject.

"If Marga's angry with you, I could talk to Marga."

"I don't need you interceding like some *Saint.*"

"Ouch," said Seraphina. "Do you need a ship? We could divert a ship of the Goreddi fleet south. The *Marigold* is probably closest, but she would be weeks away."

"I don't want your ship!" cried Tess. "And don't you dare send the

Goreddi fleet down here. The last thing these islands need is Goredd stumbling in and making a bigger mess."

There was a pause, and then Seraphina said tersely, "You're lucky I answered, and not your Queen or prince consort. Everything you've sent us has further convinced them that Goredd has a moral duty to intervene in the Archipelagos."

"With a newly expanded fleet?" But of course: a queen had a queen's tools at hand. "Please remind them of my clumsy efforts with Martin, and advise them to hold off. I'm down here making mistakes so they don't have to."

Seraphina snorted at this, a half laugh, and the tension broke. "It's true," she mused. "The urge to swoop in and save people is strong. As is our wont to believe the Ninysh are monsters."

"The Ninysh *are* monsters—and so are we," said Tess, the weight of that truth almost bowling her over. One of St. Polypous's legs was the devil; it had been his all along. "If Goredd wants to intervene, they can intervene with Count Pesavolta. That might actually do some good."

"You do realize . . . I take *monster* rather personally," said Seraphina.

"I know," said Tess. "Me too."

Seraphina laughed in earnest then. "Safe travels, little sister, to you and Pathka both. But quitting doesn't mean you get to stop calling. Let me hear how you are, or I shall worry and send the fleet after all."

Tess switched off the thnimi, smiling at this, and lay down on the cold, hard stone beside Pathka. The crusty cocoon emitted a little warmth, she found, so she put her arm around it and was more comfortable, even knowing she wouldn't sleep.

Tess must have slept a little, because she was awakened by a scrabbling sound. It was finally dark, and Tess could just discern, in the yellow watch-lamp light, a figure crabbing sideways along the cliff face. It eased onto the top of the wall and crouched there, staring into the lower city.

Whoever it was didn't seem to have noticed Tess, so she was about to close her eyes again when something in the person's posture struck her as familiar. She sat up.

"Fozu?" she whispered.

He turned sharply toward the sound, drew a knife, and scrutinized the shadows.

She crawled forward into the lamplight.

"Tess! What are you doing here?" he said. He put the knife away.

"I've left the expedition," said Tess. "Marga and I had a fight, and . . . I couldn't keep sailing with her."

"I know the feeling," he said, rubbing his beard. The sides and mustache had started to fill in again. "You know, I never did thank you for helping me with the sabak. Knowing the Generation Songs are safe is a weight off my shoulders. I feel like I could do anything, now."

"I didn't do much," said Tess, feeling her face warm.

He hesitated. "The sabak isn't still on the ship, I hope?"

"No, no. I set her free," said Tess.

"Thank the Lights. I felt guilty leaving her behind," he said. His teeth gleamed in the lamplight as he smiled. "Is that why you quarreled with Marga?"

"One of several reasons," said Tess, not liking to go into more detail. "But what are you doing here? Something nefarious? Should I be trying to stop you?"

Fozu laughed. "I'm here to steal the *Sweet Jessia*. Is that nefarious enough for you?"

It was terribly nefarious, and yet it gave Tess hope. Fozu knew the way south, knew his way around a boat. "Would you take me with you?" she asked. "And Pathka?"

His eyes widened, as if she'd overwhelmed him with her eagerness. "I'd be glad to. I could use your help with the harbor chain, in fact. The mechanism for lowering it is inside this tower, but it's quite loud and will wake the town. You must wait until I've brought the *Sweet Jessia* around, otherwise they'll have time to cast off and come after us."

"Of course," said Tess. "How do I get inside the tower?"

"Follow me," said Fozu. He circled the tower toward the town side, Tess at his heels, balancing on the narrow ledge. The door was below them, but he wasn't going for the door. He climbed up two more tiers to a window with a padlocked iron shutter. He picked the lock and held the heavy shutter open while Tess crawled inside. It was very dark.

"The mechanism is in the room below," he said. "But like I said, don't start it until the *Sweet Jessia*'s prow is almost abutting the chain."

"How will you move the ship by yourself?" Tess asked, suddenly realizing this could take a while. "And what about the dragons and crew?"

"They're all ashore except for a watchman, but I'm not worried about him," said Fozu. An emotion crossed his face like a cloud. "Is Marga ashore?"

"She's been sleeping on the ship, with everyone else," said Tess.

"I'm sorry," he said, his voice suddenly tight. He closed the shutter and climbed down.

There was a horizontal slit in the shutter, which allowed Tess a view of the harbor. Fozu crept along the docks, keeping to the shadows; she saw him only when he scurried through a pool of light. The eighth ship along was the *Sweet Jessia*—the real one. The *Avodendron* was farther down, number fifteen; several men-of-war lay between them.

No one in this crowded harbor would be able to move out quickly in pursuit; even the three ships anchored outside the harbor probably didn't have full crews aboard. The *Sweet Jessia* should be able to get a lead on any pursuers.

How did he intend to get Tess aboard, though? And what about Pathka? Tess tried not to fret about it—Fozu was clever, he'd think of something—but her palms began to sweat.

Fozu had reached the ship at last; she could see him moving around on deck. He'd managed to cast off the mooring lines, it seemed, because the *Jessia* was drifting toward one of the Ninysh warships. That was no good. How would he move into open water? Maybe he'd lower the dinghy and tow it himself? He was fussing around on deck, busy with something, but she couldn't see what.

Then she saw. He'd made himself a torch, dripping with pitch, which he lit at one of the lanterns. That was going to draw attention.

"What are you doing?" Tess muttered. As much as sailors dreaded an open flame, it was surely the height of idiocy to carry a big flaming torch belowdecks on a ship—

Full of pyria.

Saints' bones.

The *Sweet Jessia* exploded, shooting a column of fire almost as high as the cliffs. The boom reached Tess a second later, like thunder after lightning.

The ships in the crowded harbor bucked and rocked, straining at their lines like frightened horses. The warships to either side of the *Jessia* had massive holes blown in their hulls; they listed and quickly sank. Three harborside buildings collapsed into heaps of rubble as flaming debris rained over everything. Tess watched in horror as fires sprang up on rooftops, net lofts, sails, and decks. Warehouses went up quickly.

People swarmed the docks, some fleeing burning buildings, some rushing out with heavy mats to start beating the smaller fires, others working the pump in the center of the wharf, eight to a side. It sucked up seawater and sprayed it a long way, but there seemed to be only one pump.

Then a second ship, laden with black powder, exploded into thousands of vicious splints, blasting through the docks and mowing the water pumpers down.

The debris flew so fast and far that some of it smashed against the iron shutter of the chain tower. Tess reflexively ducked, but nothing came through the gap. Fozu must have put her in this tower on purpose, she suddenly realized. To keep her safe.

She was too appalled to be grateful.

"I'm sorry," he'd said upon hearing that Marga was aboard the *Avodendron*. Tess should have realized right then what he was up to. She could have run and warned them; the whole crew could have been halfway up the road to the Citadel by the time the *Jessia* blew up.

The pyria had formed a flaming slick upon the surface of the water and was creeping ever farther down the inlet, finding new ships to consume.

Some ships had had holes blown in their sides by the two explosions; these sank before their powder could ignite, their masts jutting out of the pyria slick like a forest of burning trees. Others, not yet stocked with supplies for their new cannons, went straight up in flames.

She couldn't see the *Avodendron* through the smoke, but the slick must be close. The ship had a hundred souls aboard, and black powder. . . . How much did it take to blow a hole in the side?

It was madness to leave the tower, but she couldn't stay. She rushed down a spiral stair, past the chain mechanism, to the iron door. It was easy enough to unlock once she found the right lever in the dark. She was about to rush outside when there was another massive blast; she slammed the door, threw herself against it, and waited for the hail of debris to subside.

Some of the thumps sounded softer. When she finally emerged, she saw a foot and a forearm. There was no time to feel the horror; she wrapped her arms around her head and ran.

Everything was on fire and everyone was screaming; it looked like the aftermath of a dragon attack. Tess could not make fast progress along the pier, between people moving the dead, people trying to get the pump working again, and soldiers arriving from the Citadel to help. Tess climbed a pile of bricks, the collapsed facade of a warehouse, which elevated her enough to see that the *Avodendron*'s sails had caught fire.

Water erupted in a geyser as one of her sides blew out.

The *Avodendron* sank, or tried to. She was moored in a shallow section and didn't have far to go before she reached the bottom. She listed to port as she sank, masts ablaze, setting the ship beside her on fire.

Tess fell to her knees in shock and disbelief. Maybe they'd all gotten off in time. Surely everyone had fled the moment they heard the *Sweet Jessia* go up.

But no: there were still people aboard, scrambling frantically across the tilted weather deck. Several jumped overboard and swam to a skiff that was still clear of the pyria. They paddled it back toward the ship, where others were lowering someone down the side in the bosun's swing. The sailors in the skiff reached up to help him down.

Tess could tell even from this distance that it was Jacomo and that he was injured—his left thigh was one long red gash. There was such cacophony around her—flames crackling, the pump shrieking, boards shattering, soldiers clanging and shouting—that she could not possibly have discerned Jacomo's screaming, and yet she was certain she did.

The last few sailors leaped from the *Avodendron*, and then came Marga and Claado, holding hands and jumping together.

Tess was trying to get to her feet again, trying to go to them, when someone nearby roared, "Duck!" She threw herself down the leeward side of the brick heap and covered her head with her arms as another warship exploded.

Thirty-Four

Mind of the World, sometimes it is unbearable to be so small.

The Ggdani call you the One, and the quigutl call you the Most Alone, perhaps imagining you peerless and singular. It's the many who are truly alone, though. You hear the voices of all; we hear only ourselves and have to trust that others are out there. It takes faith to reach across the gap, and sometimes that faith is more than we can muster.

Once upon a time (*just the once*), a dragon (*most alone*) stood on the windy cliff at the top of the Citadel road as the sun rose, watching the harbor explode and calculating how long they had to live.

Spira had two weeks' worth of medicines, plus that pot of salve, in their satchel. It could probably be stretched to four if they started on half doses now and resigned themself to a certain amount of joint pain—the salve might help but would have to be rationed, too. Then there would be a month or two spent in ever-increasing agony before their heart deigned to give out.

Unless, of course, the governor-general learned that Spira had brought a hundred barrels of pyria into the crowded harbor and decided to hang them for it. They might welcome a good hanging, once their symptoms got bad enough.

Or sooner. This broken heart, on top of everything else, not easily borne.

Screams rose from the harborside. Half the town was on fire. Soldiers shoved past Spira, rushing down from the Citadel to help; mobs of civilians, sooty and wailing, battled their way up to the Citadel, fleeing the town. The only road between the two passed through a tunnel in the cliffs, and a nightmarish bottleneck was forming in both directions.

Spira moved away from the frantic traffic, toward the wheat fields, keeping one eye on the inlet below, trying to see how far the pyria slick had spread. Smoke smudged their view.

How much of this had Hami intended to happen, and how much had been an accident? Had he known most of Spira's medicine might go up in flames? Had he cared?

That question hurt like a physical blow.

Spira expected another blow imminently: the mutiny William's horrible girlfriend had alluded to. Dragon graduate students wouldn't just slink off, though, not like some people. Dragons always felt compelled to give a long explanation first.

Hami had given only one hint about his plan—and it was a hint only if Spira read a lot into it, with every ounce of hindsight at their disposal. It had been that last evening in St. Claresse, when they'd walked down the pier arm in arm (the memory ached, even with destultia; it was going to burn like pyria after four weeks at half dose). Hami had explained everything to Spira by then—that he was a Watcher, charged with keeping the One safe, and he had an obligation to sneak aboard the *Avodendron* and stop the countess's expedition.

A smarter dragon—a normal dragon, not addled by feeling for this little man—would have gleaned that a Watcher was obliged to stop all expeditions, not only the human ones.

Hami had tugged at an earring fretfully and said, "I wish I had an extra eyu to give you. But listen, in case of emergency, I have a contact on the Fiornani, a Sergeant Luy—"

"...hat a wide web of spies you have," Spira had said, charmed by H...secret life.

"Not a very useful web," he'd replied. "Luy was my eyes in Sixth Division, but he got transferred. Now he gives the same report every week: eternal stalemate in Edushuke."

Spira should have interrogated the word *emergency* more closely. *What do you imagine might happen, Hami? What have you set me up for?*

"Scholar Spira." A voice broke their reverie. Spira turned to see all four of their graduate students emerging from the crowd at the tunnel mouth, shedding articles of clothing as they walked. Behind them, the tumult paused as people stared after them, confused.

Spira's foolhardy students were about to get themselves killed.

"I have contacted Professor the dragon Ondir," said the lead student, a tall male called Fekra. "You are relieved of leadership, Scholar Spira. You will return home at once."

Around Spira, the other dragons began transforming; wings unfurled like sails, necks stretched like spyglasses, fangs and horns and spines sprouted all over. Townspeople, emerging from the tunnel to the sight of full-sized dragons, started screaming; Spira had no attention to spare for them.

Spira would not make it all the way home with only the medicines they had left, but they could still try to talk these ridiculous youngsters out of throwing their lives away. (Had Hami realized they would die? Did any of this weigh on his conscience?)

"You should all return home," said Spira as Fekra's wingspan expanded to blot out half the sky above them. "Do not fly south from here. The ring of volcanoes—"

"You've mentioned the poisonous clouds at least twenty-three times," screamed Fekra in Mootya now. "We'll fly below such clouds."

"Where the Murkh can shoot you down," said Spira. "Very clever. I must have only mentioned the Murkh twenty-two times, if that danger made no impression on you."

"You entangled us in human politics, and now our ship is blown to smithereens," roared Fekra. "You don't know everything, Scholar Spira. You were born empty, out of ard."

The others began to roar—and why not? They couldn't fly for several minutes after transforming; there was nothing to do but berate their former leader.

Spira, empty, hobbled off toward the Citadel.

The courtyard was full of casualties—burns, breaks, lacerations—lying on blankets or on the grass. Spira kept to the perimeter and tried not to make eye contact with anyone. Nobody would look at them twice if they kept their head down. All Spira wanted right now was a seat in the shade, someplace they could rest and think about next steps.

Or wait for death. That had a certain appeal.

And suddenly there was William's horrible girlfriend—Tess?—the last person they wanted to see, standing in their way. Smudged face, hair full of brick dust, eyes wild. "Have you seen anyone from the *Avodendron*?" she was asking. "Countess Margarethe? Jacomo?"

"No," said Spira, turning to walk away.

Tess followed. "I lost sight of them. I thought they might've come up here."

Spira picked up the pace; Tess did, too, as if glued to their elbow.

"Hey, did all your herbs get . . ." She gestured toward the harbor, grimacing. Spira didn't answer; that didn't deter her. "Will you be all right? Do you have enough?"

That cringing solicitousness. That faux sympathy. This girl had been hounding them at every opportunity, desperate to have her apology accepted. Spira was done with this.

"Enough for *what*, exactly?" they snapped. "To get home? To go forward? Of course I don't. Why are you asking me? As if you were concerned—as if you could help!"

Tess looked stricken, but then she looked . . . amazed?

"Saints' bones, maybe I can, though," she said. She paused as soldiers trotted past with a stretcher, then said in a low voice, "I need to get Pathka to the Polar Serpent. You need medicine. There's an herbalist down in the dungeon who might be able to help us both if we can help her." When Spira didn't respond, she added, "Berekka. Your buyer who wasn't. She's an herbalist skilled enough to poison a priest. She might know of substitutes for the things you lost."

Spira gripped their cane tightly, and was gripped in turn by multiple emotions. The girl had had a good idea. They hated to admit it, and they hated the prospect of spending more time with her, but the possibility of living—longer than the few weeks they'd calculated, minus the agony they'd anticipated—filled them with such longing they were almost overcome with dizziness.

And with such doubt that they wanted to cry. They were overdue for destultia, clearly, but they didn't dare take any yet.

"Spira, please," Tess was saying, plainly having emotions of her own. She both smelled and looked afraid. "This is my last idea, and it's not much. I don't actually know whether she can save you, or get Pathka to the pole—I don't even know how to get her out of the dungeon—"

"I . . . *might* know," said Spira, surprising themself.

If ever there had been an emergency requiring Sergeant Luy, this was it.

Spira had scoped out the man's office, in addition to all the fortress's tunnels, just in case; it was always prudent to have another way out. They led Tess through a gate, down a winding stair, into the deepest tunnels under the star-fort.

Sergeant Luy, a requisitions officer, sat at his desk behind a tidy fortress of paperwork. His graying hair was trimmed short, and he wore tiny reading spectacles. "If you're after splints and blankets," he said, hardly glancing at Spira and Tess, "everything has been sent up already."

Well, either this would work or it wouldn't: Spira uttered the Ggdanu word for *Watcher*. It had more different flavors of *g* than Spira was capable of producing without gagging.

Sergeant Luy looked up, his expression suggesting that he thought Spira was coughing up a hair ball. For a frozen moment Spira feared that this, too, had been a setup. Then the sergeant stepped around his desk and closed the door. "Thank all Saints and Lights," he said in a half whisper. "I haven't been able to reach Watcher Hami on the eyu in weeks. What's going on?"

Spira stared, openmouthed, trying to think of anything to say besides *He abandoned me.*

"The Watcher has had his hands full," interjected Tess. "The Nutufi threatened to let the Ninysh have sabak oil, and two expeditions are searching for the One."

What a brazen liar she was—and what harm she'd done with her deceit, even if she was using it to help now. Spira glared at her, resenting the tool and its wielder.

"He has a mission for us," Tess was saying. "We need to free Berekka."

The sergeant looked like a hare, frozen in the light of a hunter's lamp. "Not possible."

"It will never be easier than it is right now, while the harbor's on fire."

"I can't just walk in there and—"

Tess put her hands on her hips. "Are you Shesh, by chance? Because it was a Shesh anarchist—a fellow called Fozu—who burned the mission and blew up the harbor."

Sergeant Luy's expression shifted. "Fozu? I knew his father. Is he . . . dead?" He seemed to glean the answer from Tess's face. His throat bobbed as he swallowed.

"Fozu gave the Generation Songs to a sabak before he died," said Tess. Spira had no idea what this meant, but it seemed to reassure the sergeant. "But your superiors may suspect that you, his fellow Shesh, were in on the plot. Your life is about to get very complicated. Help us free Berekka, and then come with us. We'll get you free in turn."

That was an awful lot of supposition. Spira could barely breathe, waiting.

Luy finally nodded, his brows drawn. "If Fozu had the courage to defy our exile, surely I can find the courage to do what's needed now."

He opened the office door again, looked both ways, and set off up the corridor. As Spira turned to follow, Tess touched their sleeve and whispered, "This was a good plan. What a good team we make!"

Her determined friendliness was too grating to endure any longer. "You can stop fawning so hard. We're not friends, and we're not going to be."

The blood rose to her face. "A-all right. I didn't mean to—"

Spira walked away before she could finish.

Luy led them to the cell block, where the last three guards played dice on the flagstone floor. The sergeant seemed to grow taller as he approached them. "We need strong arms for carrying stretchers," he called. The men looked up guiltily. "Up, all of you. I'm requisitioning your muscles. There's a severe shortage of help at the dockside. Up. Out. Now."

"B-but who will guard the Dog cages?" asked one guard. They were all bigger than Luy, but he'd spoken with such authority that they were cringing.

"I will," said Sergeant Luy. He held out his hand for the keys; he didn't even have to ask. The guards filed out, and then Luy collapsed back against a wall, rapidly deflating.

"I can't believe that worked," he said, his voice rising an octave as anxiety caught up with him. "It helped to know I'll never have to face them again. But come, there's a dozen Aftisheshe down here. We might as well free them all."

He unlocked each cell, telling prisoners, "Wait at the end of the passage. I know the tunnels; I'll lead you out." Before the final door, he handed Spira the keys. "I'll leave the Watcher's task to you. There's a cove, with a dock, down the stair at the end of the passage—"

"I've seen the place you mean," said Tess, who was always butting in.

"We'll leave you a boat," said Luy, clasping Spira's hand and then Tess's. "Give Watcher Hami my thanks for this opportunity. I'm sorry I hesitated."

"You have nothing to be sorry for," said Tess, that blatant bootlicker. "Shesh Paishesh."

Spira, on the verge of snorting scornfully, noticed Luy's lips quivering.

"I am from Paji-Jovesh," said the sergeant, his voice brimming over. "One of the last. But that was kind, and I appreciate the sentiment." He clasped her hands gratefully, then turned down the corridor to where the freed Aftisheshe were waiting for him.

She's not as kind as you think she is, Spira wanted to shout after him. *It's all a lie.*

Even the Watcher was a lie—and they should have known better.

Only one key on the ring was large enough for the cell doors. Spira unlocked the last one.

The creaking hinges woke Berekka; she pushed her blue hair out of her face and sat up. "My pyria seller," she said, recognizing Spira. "I told Robinôt I didn't buy any—I hope you confirmed that. I'd hate to be hanged for arson, on top of everything else."

"We're here to rescue you," said Spira, trying to head off Tess's inevitable interruption.

Berekka stood and brushed straw off her kirtle. "You don't look like much, but when Edushuke offers just one hare, you chase it. Lead on."

Tess, ever in motion, grabbed a torch and led them in Luy's footsteps, up a twisting tunnel and down a long spiral stair. They emerged onto the dock of a hidden cove, carved out of the cliff face. The glare of sky and sea made their eyes water after the long darkness.

Luy, as promised, had left one boat. Spira didn't particularly know boats, but this was like no boat they'd ever seen. The bow and stern looked alike, both coming to a pointed tip that curled back inward toward the benches. Each curl was intricately carved into a stylized animal, a dog with bared teeth, its eyes brightened with mother-of-pearl disks.

Berekka smiled at one of the carven dogs and laid a hand fondly on its head. "How thoughtful," she said. "Luy left us *my* boat."

The three of them piled into the craft. Tess, with more bravado than competence, cast off the mooring line. She handed Spira a pair of oars (also carved with canine motifs) and shoved off. The waves shoved the boat back. Tess shoved again, harder, and set to rowing with a will.

The tide pressed them into the sandstone wall of the cove.

Berekka observed all this with one eyebrow cocked. "You understand that you're rowing against the whole ocean, right? The ocean is bigger than you, and it's going to win."

"Suggestions?" asked Tess crossly.

Under Berekka's guidance, Tess and Spira began laboriously poling the craft along the shallow channel that led to the open sea, pressing oars into the sand at the bottom. Once out of the cove, Spira—like any sensible individual—attempted to row away from town, fortress, and the three Ninysh warships anchored in open water outside the closed harbor. They made no progress and soon realized it was because Tess was trying to row in the opposite direction.

"Don't row that way," the girl cried. "We have to go back to the harbor tower."

"Are you stupid, in fact?" Spira shouted back.

"That's where Pathka is," snarled Tess. "We're not going without Pathka. You're getting herbs, I'm going to the pole, that was the deal."

It was a stupid place to have stowed her quigutl, in full view of literally everyone. Spira plied their oars harder but only succeeded in turning the boat in a circle.

"Excuse me," called Berekka over their quarreling, "but since neither of you have apparently ever used a boat before, would you mind if I took it from here?"

"Be our guest," said Spira, tossing their oars into the bottom of the boat. Tess, that cheater, took the opportunity to row as hard as she could toward the harbor.

"Where were you planning to steal me away to?" asked Berekka as she tipped the mast.

"Nowhere specific," said Spira.

"I need to fetch my quigutl," Tess piped up, "and then I need to get to the pole."

Berekka laughed as she tied off the shroud lines. "We're not going to the pole in this boat," she said. "But I should be able to dart in and grab your lizard before those warships can get up a chase. After that, if it's all the same to you, we should get as far from here as possible. I'd suggest Aftisheshe Home, where I know the people and the herbs."

"Good. Fine," said Tess. "We'll find our own way south from there."

Berekka soon had them running parallel to the cliffs. Near the harbor mouth, a column of seagulls pointed at the tower like a great finger out of the sky. Spira had not quite understood that this *Pathka* was undergoing quigutl grotesquerie; that explained why it hadn't been with the girl the whole time. It had cocooned, and the aggressive birds were picking at it. With no warning but an anguished cry, Tess leaped overboard and began swimming for the tower.

"She's a woman of action, anyway," said Berekka, staring after her.

"She's impulsive and reckless," said Spira.

The diminutive woman eyed them. "How did you two end up together?"

"Not by my own choosing," said Spira, and then Tess was shouting for the boat to be brought nearer, and there was no more chance to talk.

Somehow herbalist and dragon together managed to maneuver the craft closer to the tower, cast out a fishing net, and haul Tess and the cumbersome cocoon in without being dashed upon the rocks. If Berekka was half as good at herbs as she was at boats, maybe there was hope after all.

A glint in their peripheral vision made Spira turn to look. The crews of all three warships had spyglasses raised, observing Pathka's rescue and Berekka's brilliant blue hair.

A capstan was clanking as one of the ships raised anchor.

"The *Indomitable* is setting sails," said Tess.

"I see that," said Berekka. "And I'm sure they see me. I chose a bad time to color my hair."

Berekka caught a breeze and they were off again, scudding along the shallows parallel to the cliffs, trying to take a route the tall ships couldn't.

A second one was unfurling its sails. And the third.

"They'd send three ships of the line after a fishing boat?" Spira asked.

"It's called a kuro, and it's got Berekka the witch in it," said Berekka, tacking east in search of better wind.

She found it and darted off southward, but not before losing ground to the warships. They were closing, inexorably. Berekka tried to lose them among a cluster of micro-islands; they found a way to flank her. She managed to trick one into following her between two islands, where sabak secretions slowed and tangled the deep-keeled ship. The others were too smart to follow her into that trap and circled to intercept. She eked out just ahead of them.

Suddenly Berekka gave a triumphant yelp and pointed at the horizon, where a bank of greenish, sickly-looking fog had appeared. It was unnatural, undoubtedly—even a dragon born empty could tell that. Berekka held course as if she intended to lose the Ninysh in the mist.

"We're not going in there, surely?" cried Spira.

"That would be folly," said Berekka with a wicked grin. "We'll lure them out to us."

Spira did not find this reassuring.

Berekka subtly spilled wind from the sail, letting the kuro slow without appearing to. As the Ninysh ships closed the gap, she began singing at the top of her voice:

Upon the moonlit path
A hound,
Upon the moonlit air
The snow.
Let's walk among crisp
Pine needles
And wind our love into
A skein.

The song was beautiful, incongruous, and unexpectedly terrifying as the warships bore down on them. If they weren't going into the fog, Spira saw no other escape route.

"Beat the sides of the boat," Berekka ordered. "They must be sleeping at their posts."

Spira, like one in a dream, slapped the kuro in time as she sang; Tess joined in.

A swift galley ship, sleek and bristling with oars, sprang out of the fog toward them like a spider from its burrow. Tess screamed; Spira ducked behind the gunwale.

Whatever prey the galley had expected to find—a fishing boat full of singing drunkards?—it found itself face to face with two large Ninysh men-of-war.

The galley's steersman blew three sharp blasts on a horn, and six more galleys plunged out of the fog, charging the Ninysh ships and ramming them with their pointed prows. The ships did not have full complements of gunners or marines; the sailors fired crossbows at the galleys.

Berekka, meanwhile, trimmed her sails and darted away as fast as the kuro would go.

Spira kept an eye aftward, watching for pursuit. "We're safe," said Berekka, noticing. "Those warships will keep them busy. We're minnows compared with those treasures."

One ship was sinking; the other had tried to turn back and was being surrounded. The galleys were narrow as needles and traveled shockingly fast.

"Was that a . . . a Wandering City in the fog?" asked Tess, sounding awed.

"The Wandering Cities are actual cities that walk across the water," said Berekka. "It's the Aieat who live in a fog of their own making. They hunt whales and they hate company."

Tess, for no apparent reason, started laughing, and then Berekka was laughing, too.

It had been a long day, and it should have been over long before now, even if the sun couldn't seem to make up its mind to drop beneath the horizon. It lingered, red and petulant, like an exhausted toddler refusing to go to bed.

Spira leaned back into the prow, melting as the tension dissipated. They could barely keep their eyes open, and finally gave up trying. They heard Berekka quietly ask Tess, "I didn't get an answer out of that one. What are you two doing together?"

"I need to get to the pole, and Spira needs—"

"Yes, yes, I get that," said Berekka. "And you each thought I could help you. But how is it that you're working together? You don't even seem to like each other."

For some moments there was only the sound of water against hull. Spira opened one eye a crack and glimpsed Tess staring out to sea (chin on fist, short curls blown back). They closed the eye again and strained to hear what she would say.

"I'm not sure how to tell this story," she said at last, very quietly, as if she didn't quite believe that Spira was asleep. "I feel like I could write five hundred pages, and then five hundred more, and still not get it all. But the short version is: I did something to hurt Spira—on purpose, years ago—and I'd like to make up for it, if I can."

"So you're on a journey of restitution," said Berekka, as if this were a thing people did. Maybe it was, among her people.

"Ko has Tathlann's syndrome and needs a dozen herbs just to manage it," said Tess. "There was this boy I liked—"

"Ah, that old story," said Berekka.

"He was a terrible person, and I was a sad, lost child," Tess continued. "I wanted him to love me. I would have done anything he asked, however cruel. He hated Spira, and so he stole ko's medicines and destroyed them. I helped him. Ko almost died."

Ko, ko, ko, as if they were some revolting quigutl. Every *ko* chafed like sand in Spira's stockings. They couldn't take this anymore. "If he was so terrible, why were you traveling with him on the *Avodendron?*" they asked, not opening their eyes.

"I tried to tell you—it was a misunderstanding," said Tess. "The countess kept referring to some *Lord Morney*, which was not a name I ever knew him by."

Spira's eyes popped open. "The last time I saw you in Lavondaville, just after my illness, you seemed desperate to find him. You were begging people to tell you where he'd—"

"He left me pregnant! I was ruined. It took me years to put myself back together, and to finally admit how he'd used and abused me." Tess seemed to realize she was shouting; she paused and took a deep breath. "Spira, I was wrong. I was grandly, spectacularly wrong, as stupid as I feel admitting it. I was wrong about him, and I was wrong to follow his lead in tormenting you, and I am so, so sorry."

"I can't forgive you," said Spira.

Tess looked as if she'd been expecting this. "It's all right. There are people I can't forgive, either." Her face crumpled, but she recovered quickly. "I've been on both sides of this kind of thing, Spira, and the obligation is all on my side, not yours."

"Restitution," Berekka repeated with a firm nod. "But I've never heard of Tathlann's syndrome. What are you taking for it, Spira?"

Spira grudgingly sat up, opened their leather satchel, and brought out vial after vial of herbs, naming each one. Twelve in all.

Berekka gave a low whistle. "Chiromastic and destultia will be particularly hard to substitute. I'll have to experiment, which could make you sicker in the short term."

Spira shrugged and started packing up the vials. "*Not* experimenting makes me dead in about three months, and leaves me wishing I was dead long before that." Tauntingly, their heart gave a little lurch. It wasn't impending pyrocardia, but the other problem. The thought of surviving a long time, endlessly hurting after Hami.

But broken hearts healed, didn't they? That was something humans would know.

"Are you in pain already?" cried Tess, probably responding to Spira's expression. She flung open the storage box—the one that had held the fishing net—saying, "Is there a blanket or something we could give ko?" Berekka started helping her look.

Spira couldn't take one more *ko*. "Do you have any idea how insulting that is to a dragon?" they groused. "'Ko' is a quigutl word. It implies changeability. The one thing I'm unlikely to do is change."

Tess looked up, eyes wide and cheeks flaming. "I was trying to be respectful, rather, because 'ko' is ungendered—and you . . . I mean . . . I thought . . . aren't you?"

"What would you prefer that we call you?" Berekka interjected.

Spira flopped back in the prow. "I don't *care*. It's not like any of them actually fit."

Except, there had been a word that fit, a word that had made Spira feel . . . expected. And not so alone. Hami had taken it with him when he left, alas. Spira couldn't bear to think it now.

Isn't that proof of concept, though? said imaginary Aganat in a surprisingly gentle tone. *Words applied kindly carry a different weight—it's even better when you choose one yourself. Berekka is giving you a chance to choose.*

Spira blinked at the two women at the other end of the kuro. Aganat had claimed gender was communication, but it was also connection. Hami had shown Spira that. What if . . .

"You could use *she*," said Spira at last. "If you insist."

"We don't insist," said Berekka. "Are you sure?"

"No," said Spira. "But I'd like to try it. Just to prove it doesn't work."

"There is a blanket," said Tess, "but it smells like seaweed. Would you still like it?"

Spira shook *her* head (it felt funny; the pronoun, that is, not her head). "Is there anything in there for a broken heart?" she asked.

Tess and Berekka stared at her a moment, and then Tess said, *"Men!"* and they began to laugh. Spira, understanding it this time, tried laughing just a little, and found that she could.

And for the moment, they were three women in a boat (to say nothing of the quigutl). Three together. Spira pulled that gender over and around herself like an old quilt, ragged but clean, smelling a bit of seaweed. It wouldn't last forever—she was only borrowing it, after all—but for the moment it was real enough to keep her warm.

Thirty-Five

Awaken, Mind of the World!

The recursive beauty of a mind is that it can think about its own thoughts. It can track reason through the forest of emotion and see where it went wrong.

A mind can change its mind. Understanding unfolds like a flower under the analytic eye of the sun.

Once upon a time (*upon a mind?*), a harbor blew up, and many people were injured.

The nave of St. Fionnani's church had been carved into the cliff, and this was where many of the wounded were taken, on principle that a cave church was less likely to burn down or collapse than a freestanding building. Marga and Argol claimed a side chapel for Jacomo and their other casualties. The *Avodendron*'s physician had survived; being Porphyrian, he was unsentimental about repurposing Saints' draperies as bandages.

Once she felt assured that everyone was being looked after, Marga turned to leave. "Don't go back out there!" cried Claado, gripping her like he wasn't prepared to let go.

Marga pried his fingers off her arm as gently as she could. "I'm whole and hale, so I am obligated to help however I can. You taught me that."

She kissed his cheek and strode determinedly through the crowded nave toward the doors, untying the sash of her sailor's slops as she walked. She wet it in the holy-water font beside the door and tied it around her nose and mouth. She took a deep, rose-scented breath and opened the church door.

Outside was an infernum of flames and blowing ash.

Inexplicably, her spirits lifted.

She was well educated enough to recognize the pathetic fallacy in herself—the idea that the world seemed organized to reflect her mood—and yet here was the blasted, devastated town, looking like a mirror of her heart. The collapsing buildings, the screams, the smell of smoke and blood—she'd been here even before the harbor exploded.

At least she could do something about the world. She wasn't so sure about her heart.

Marga joined the first work crew she saw, a bucket brigade, and passed slopping pails of seawater for an hour or two. It was mind-numbing, but not entirely satisfying.

She left the bucketeers when they were called to douse a different warehouse, farther up the wharf, that was more important or more easily saved. Marga drifted, broken glass crunching under her boots, until she spied a squadron of soldiers lugging wet woolen blankets for beating out small fires. This was what she wanted to do. The soldiers didn't object to another set of arms, even if they belonged to a stout, middle-aged woman none of them knew.

The soggy blankets were heavy; Marga beat them against smoldering barrels and beams, relishing every wet, satisfying slap. If she kept this up for long, she was going to hurt tomorrow.

It would hurt even more to stop, though.

The first fires she beat into submission were all Tess. *Slap*. That liar. *Slap*. How dare she malign the memory of a dear, dead man?

The stink of smoky wet wool made Marga's eyes sting.

At some point, the fires changed. Some were William-shaped, inconsiderately dying when she had a hundred pointed questions to ask.

Some became Aemelia; maybe they meant well, but Marga was having a harder and harder time believing it. Some were that villain Robinôt, William's inexplicable, unaccountable best friend. . . .

The trouble was, Robinôt wasn't nearly as inexplicable if Marga was willing to believe Tess's account. But how could she? William was dead. She couldn't know. It was a betrayal of his memory even to consider the possibility.

Surely she wasn't considering it?

Marga beat furiously. She smacked down blazes until her shoulders burned and her forearms felt molten. The soldiers drew straws for who had to tell her to stop, that night was falling, that the only fires left were the ones no one could extinguish, the ones that were going to have to burn themselves out.

Marga had begun to resemble one of those fires.

"Ma'am? Hey there," said the unlucky lad, waving to get her attention. He couldn't tug her sleeve because she wouldn't hold still long enough. "Time for a break, maybe? There's soup at the Little Piglet, I hear. You've earned it, eh?"

Marga stopped, panting, and removed her sash from her face. It was black with all the soot she hadn't inhaled, but her throat still felt raw.

"Thank you," she croaked at the soldier, handing him the charred blanket. She turned and staggered back to the cave church, and they never did learn her name.

Marga slept like the dead on the floor of the chapel, surrounded by the *Avodendron*'s crew, and when she awoke, her arms were so stiff and sore that she could hardly lift them. She didn't eat breakfast, not wanting anyone to see her struggle to raise a spoon, and certainly not wanting anyone to raise a spoon for her when there were more-serious casualties to attend to.

Her uncle had begun sending out teams, as soon as it was safe, to see whether anything could be salvaged. They reported back one by one. All her books and charts: ruined. All her clothes: ruined. All their food supplies: ruined.

The submersible, surprisingly, seemed intact, but it was at the bottom of the harbor and would take some effort to raise.

A lone trunk had popped to the surface like a cork; the *Avodendron*'s crew had seized it ahead of another salvage gang. They brought it to Marga, looking pleased with themselves. When she saw what it contained, her heart sank, but she couldn't bear to bring down morale.

"Good work," she rasped through a throat like a pincushion. "Keep looking."

The trunk was Lord Morney's. It was full of journals that might answer her questions.

She felt sick just thinking about it.

Uncle Claado, perhaps sensing her exhaustion, shooed everyone out of the chapel and left her alone with her thoughts. Well, alone with Jacomo and her thoughts; he had sustained a large burn on his thigh, the worst injury of all the surviving *Avodendron* crew (there were a dozen lost, Heaven hold them). He was in no condition to go on salvage runs.

He didn't seem to be asleep, however; his breathing was irregular.

"Jacomo," said the countess. "Did Tess ever talk to you about Lord Morney?"

He opened his eyes. "I . . . ah . . . What about him?"

"The sort of thing you might choose to keep from his fiancée," said Marga. "The sort of thing that you would know, without having to ask, *must* be what I'm talking about."

Jacomo cleared his throat. "Um. Yes? She did?"

Marga's breath came out like a little sob. "And you found her credible?"

He propped himself on one elbow, grimacing, and wiped the hair out of his eyes. "You didn't, I take it."

"I don't think she's lying, exactly," said the countess, lying. "But there must've been a misunderstanding. Some kind of mistake. Because he wouldn't . . . I knew him, and he *wouldn't.*"

"I didn't know him," said Jacomo, lying back again. "But I know Tess spent years trying to pretend nothing had happened, and it almost killed her. You met her back then—at my brother's wedding."

Marga hadn't forgotten the rude, drunken girl who'd almost spoiled the wedding. *This is why I don't believe her,* she wanted to say. *She's clearly not trustworthy.*

It was an uncharitable, unworthy thought, and the woman who'd just spent an entire day in a fugue state, smothering fires until she could no longer move her arms, was perhaps not the right person to be casting stones.

Still: she was a scientist. Even if she'd wanted to believe Tess (and in her heart of hearts she did *not*), she required proof. It wasn't fair otherwise. People might accuse a dead man of anything, and he couldn't defend himself.

Beside the chapel altar, a chest full of potential proof hulked malignantly, if only she dared look.

Marga took up the lantern, her arms screaming agony, and opened the lid.

After a sleepless night spent reading by lamplight, Marga ventured outside again and blinked disorientedly in the gritty sunshine. The town was less smoky than the last time she'd seen it. Some effort had been made to shift debris and clear rights-of-way; the last of the smoldering warehouses had burned itself out. The dying had died and the wounded had been carried up to the Citadel, leaving an eerie silence behind. Ash danced in eddies at her feet.

She felt like the only person in the world.

For a bitter moment she wished she were. Life would be so simple.

Nothing was simple now. She'd emerged into a new, devastating, postjournal world. She was on the cusp of something; she wasn't quite sure what, but she had only one more puzzle piece to gather, and then she would know. She set her feet toward the Citadel, and Robinôt.

The lieutenant was in a meeting with the generals, the adjutant in the anteroom office told her, blocking her way. Marga stepped around him, then stepped around him again, and got as far as the open doorway of the conference room before he dared to touch her and pull her back. She'd spotted Robinôt within and met his eye, however. Now she would wait.

She didn't expect him to come out of the meeting right then.

"Do you have something to report?" he asked under his breath, pulling her out of the adjutant's earshot, as if she were one of his informants.

She hadn't come here to report, but she had the distinct impression that if she wanted anything from Robinôt, she was going to have to give him something first.

"It was the dragon expedition who tried to sell pyria to Berekka the witch," she said. "I presume the dragons died when their ship went up."

Robinôt's expression informed her this was not news. "They survived," he said. "Four transformed and flew away. A fifth—the pasty one—escaped with Tess and the witch."

There was one question answered without her having to ask, although she would have liked more detail. "You don't know where Tess has gone, I suppose?"

"I had hoped to ask you that," he said. "Three ships of the line couldn't catch her."

"She fled by boat?" cried Marga. "She doesn't even know her knots properly. How could she possibly outmaneuver three—"

"You seem surprised," said Robinôt, eyeing her appraisingly. "So I suppose it will also be a surprise to you to learn that Giles Foudria was, in fact, here and that he's the one who ignited the pyria aboard the *Sweet Jessia?*"

Marga hadn't anticipated a blow from this direction; she struggled not to reel from it.

"I'll take your evident confusion as a yes," said Robinôt.

"You're sure it was him?" she said shakily. "They found his body?"

He shrugged. "His involvement is not in doubt. Some things are so clear in hindsight that one doesn't require proof."

Absurdly, she felt relief. No body surely meant Giles might still be alive?

What an awe-inspiring capacity for denial she had.

"I am struck once again, Countess, by your very convenient ignorance," said Robinôt. "I'm sure there's a logical explanation."

Tess doesn't trust me was part of it. In that moment, Marga couldn't blame her. How do you trust someone who closes her eyes and refuses to see?

Robinôt glanced toward the room where the generals were waiting. "I don't have time to discuss this now. Stay, though—Pauli can make you a cup of tea—and when I'm finished, you must help me make sense of everything."

He spoke reasonably, warmly even. If he had asked this of Marga on any previous day of her life, she would have waited and cooperated. But postjournal Marga knew things she hadn't known before: if she stayed, she was giving up her liberty and with it any hope of doing right.

She'd come here to learn one thing. She had to ask now, or she'd never ask at all.

"Lieutenant," she said, touching his arm. "If you don't trust me completely, I wouldn't blame you. There's an old habit of neutrality in my family; we've always weathered storms by refusing to take sides. Some conflicts are so important, though, that neutrality is tantamount to betrayal. Let me assure you that I am on your side—on *Will's* side."

She hated the nickname but forced herself to use it. It was all or nothing now.

"Will told me what you'd planned together, including the Last Resort." She paused to let that sink in, but Robinôt's face let no trace of recognition show. "I confess I was initially skeptical. Your methods seemed extreme. I thought assimilating the Pelaguese into Ninysh society, like they do in St. Remy, seemed more humane."

"Things have hardly gone seamlessly in St. Remy," said Robinôt.

"I lost confidence in that model during my last visit," said Marga. In this, at least, she was being honest. "But the harbor disaster has opened my eyes. I'm angry now, and willing to concede that maybe . . . maybe the Pelaguese . . ."

"Must be dealt with definitively and soon?" said Robinôt, inadvertently saving her from having to utter the repugnant words aloud. "I'm so pleased to hear you say so, Marga. This is one of the things we're finalizing in this meeting."

"Genocide," said Marga, hoping that a thin smile could veil her despair. Some part of her still wanted to give William the benefit of the doubt, to believe she'd misunderstood.

Robinôt did not recoil from the word; the terrible light in his eyes was her affirmation. Marga forced herself not to look away, for once in her life.

She had almost married his co-conspirator.

"Do you want to sit in on this meeting?" he asked.

"I want that cup of tea," she said. "You can tell me your blood-thirsty plans later."

Robinôt emitted a chuckle, snapping his heels together as he bowed. As soon as he returned to the generals, Marga made for the door.

"Have a seat," said Adjutant Pauli, leaping to his feet. "I'll bring you that tea."

"I have some important papers that Lord Morney left me," said Marga, putting on her most authoritative air. "The lieutenant would find them useful. I shall return directly."

The young adjutant hesitated, but her conversation with Robinôt had ended cordially, and he had not been ordered to detain her. Something was making him stare, however. Maybe it was her sailor's slops (she felt a pang for her gowns, being nibbled by fish at the bottom of the harbor). Or maybe it was something else, something she'd been able to ignore all her life.

"Do you know who I am?" she asked pointedly. "I am Countess Margarethe of Mardou."

The man startled as if he'd been asleep. "Of course," he said. "Forgive me—"

"I don't look Ninysh to you, do I?" she said.

"W-well, you are wearing foreign slops," he said feebly. "And the Dog People are also a bit, ah, you know. Swarthy."

Marga bit her tongue. Getting out of here was more important than putting this rapscallion in his place, and she dared not give Robinôt a reason to come back out. She flashed the young adjutant a smile, which evaporated the moment she turned her back on him.

What a massive mountain of denial she'd lived under. It was a miracle she's been able to stagger around under all that weight.

By the time Marga reached St. Fionnani's church, she'd made up her mind. She took Argol aside and questioned her about the logistics of bringing the submersible to the surface. Argol seemed to think it was feasible and agreed to make it so. In a storage room, Marga found some parchment, upon which she wrote several short messages. These she took to her uncle.

"I need you to send these notes to Lieutenant Robinôt at the Citadel," she said, fanning them out like a hand of cards. "The first immediately, and then another every couple days. They should prevent his understanding that I've eluded his grasp until I'm far enough away."

Claado scanned the messages, a fiction of how she'd discovered that Giles Foudria was still alive, and how she would gain his trust and lure him out, if only Robinôt would give her time and space. The last one, done in a hasty scrawl, suggested that she was in trouble.

"He's going to come looking for you after this one," said Claado.

"Exactly," said Marga. "That will delay his moving forward in other pursuits."

"You're buying time—for what?" asked Claado, narrowing his eyes.

"It's better if you don't know where I'm going," said Marga. "And you should definitely find somewhere else to be before Robinôt decides to come question you. Up the inlet, toward the shipwrights? They'll want to repair the warships first, of course, but it couldn't hurt to get the *Avodendron* into the queue as soon as possible."

Her uncle grumbled. Marga kissed his cheek and whispered, "You might be proud of me by the end of this. That'll be a nice change."

"I have always been proud of you," he protested, even though they both knew it wasn't true. He seemed to think she was feeling fey.

She was not. But let him believe she was courting death; it would lend real sadness to his words if and when Robinôt decided to question him.

Marga had one more person to talk to before she left; she barged into the chapel, where Jacomo was sleeping. "Did Tess give you any hint where she was going?" Before he could respond, she added, "She must be scheming something, to have taken the dragon and the witch."

"What?" said Jacomo. Something in his voice made her look at him more carefully.

He was deathly pale, and the front of his shirt was drenched with sweat. Marga frowned and pressed a hand to his forehead.

"Physician!" she called. The man was asleep in the nave; he leaped at the sound of her voice and hauled himself to the chapel. "He's feverish. Infection must have started in his leg. What can you do for it?"

"Nothing, except amputate if it goes septic," said the physician. "My draconic salves are at the bottom of the inlet."

"Shit," said Marga. She knelt by Jacomo again. "Can you sit up?" she asked, and then helped him rise. His head wobbled on his neck as if it weighed more than usual.

"Help me," she ordered the physician. Together they each took an arm and led Jacomo into the nave. "I've got him," said Marga, readjusting her position under Jacomo's arm. "Pack up a bundle of dressings for me to take."

"He can't travel," said the physician, seeing what she was about.

"Well, he can't stay here," said Marga. "There's an herbalist where we're going, I hope."

It took a long time to reach the waterside; Jacomo couldn't put weight on his leg, and he kept needing her to re-explain where they were going. Marga propped him up, ignoring her still-aching arms, and bullheadedly kept him moving. By the time they reached the docks, Argol had succeeded in raising the submersible with the help of a crane and seven divers. It hovered at surface level, scarred and dented but intact.

"I can't promise it works," said Argol, helping Marga unlatch the hatch.

"It will," said the countess, letting denial have full rein one last time.

Jacomo, whose fever was quite high, was too dizzy to climb in under his own power. Argol fixed up a rope harness and lowered him through the hatch with the crane. Marga got him settled in his seat and then popped her head back up for one last conference with Argol.

"Take care of Napou," said Marga. "See to it that the *Avodendron* gets repaired."

"When will you return?" asked Argol.

"Not until I've stabbed Robinôt in the back," said Marga.

Then she closed the hatch, said a little prayer, and started up the engine.

The harbor was full of scavenging fish, feasting on corpses and spoiled provisions. The cracked, charred ribs of ships loomed in the twilit water, casting ominous shadows. Marga steered around, between, and under them, trying not to contemplate the weight of water above her, or how quickly they would drown if the windows broke again.

Only when she'd found her way out of that harbor of horrors, past the chain and into open ocean, and only when she was quite certain Jacomo was unconscious, did the countess permit herself to weep—for Will, for Giles, for herself.

Perhaps even a little bit for Tess.

"It's going to be all right," Jacomo muttered.

This only made her cry harder.

He reached out with his fever-hot hand and patted hers consolingly. She grabbed his hand and squeezed it; with her other hand she wiped her eyes.

And then, having poured some of the poison out of her heart, she was ready to do what had to be done.

Unsure where Tess and the others had gone, she reasoned out a course of action for herself. She'd travel to the other end of St. Fionnani, to the Dog . . . that is, to Berekka's people (she would learn their proper name at the first opportunity, she resolved). Berekka might have returned to them. If not, they might have some idea where she could've plausibly gone.

Berekka would heal Jacomo, and Marga would help these people drive off their Ninysh oppressors. It seemed the least she could do, after what William had been planning for them.

The coast was all cliffs and fallen rocks. Marga began to despair of finding a suitable place to land. The submersible was meant to be hauled out by crane; it wasn't simple to get in and out of otherwise. After careful consideration, she decided her best option was to wedge her vessel in the shallows between two rocks that would keep it upright and still. She found a cove where the water was relatively calm and rammed the contraption into a tight corner. It shuddered as the waves beat against it, but it held.

Getting Jacomo out was a struggle; he was shivering and light-headed. Once they'd climbed out and down the rocks, they had to wade through hip-deep water toward shore, which only made him shiver the more.

Marga kept him upright. They'd just reached what looked like a carven pathway up the cliffs when she heard the horrible grinding screech of metal against stone. She turned to see the submersible succumbing to the suck of the tide. It teetered precariously and then rolled seaward. She'd closed the hatch but apparently hadn't secured it, because it flopped back open. The water glugged as it filled the interior of the craft.

Will's legacy—as she had once called it—washed out to sea. Marga watched, numbly, and then she began to laugh.

Marga headed inland on foot, struggling to keep Jacomo moving. A pack of curious dogs soon found them, nine motley mutts, who sniffed but didn't bark. Marga was wary at first, thinking them feral, but she soon saw signs of care: each dog wore a braided cord around its neck, from which hung a tiny bell made of shell. The whole pack tinkled faintly as it moved.

"Can you lead us to people?" Marga asked, not expecting an answer. The dogs did seem to be herding her, however, surrounding her like an honor guard. She let them lead, and hoped they weren't leading her over a cliff.

Her honor guard soon encountered a real guard: a half dozen patrolling soldiers, men and women, armed with bows and pole arms, who seemed to come out of nowhere. They wore cured leather cuirasses that left their brown arms bare, checked woolen trousers in unexpectedly riotous colors, and long cloaks in a uniform gray. Tall, slender dogs accompanied them, like greyhounds but with a rougher coat. They were unleashed but strictly disciplined, hunters pressed into service for war. The hounds curled their lips and growled; their teeth were an unsettling green. Marga raised her free hand, hoping that they understood it as a gesture of surrender.

The patrol group looked at Marga's canine honor guard in mild surprise, but no one spoke or raised a weapon. Marga's swords were rusting in the wreck of the *Avodendron,* but even if she'd brought one, she knew she was too plump and middle-aged to look like much of a threat to these warriors.

"Do any of you speak Ninysh?" she asked, self-conscious about using that language, but it was all she had. "I need to find Berekka, the herbalist. This man is very ill and needs her help."

The two who understood whispered a translation to their comrades. There was no debate; they circled Marga and Jacomo and escorted them up the ridge and down into the next valley.

Halfway down they encountered another dog, a mastiff, the first of any breed Marga could recognize. It was in rough shape—a torn ear, one eye nearly swollen shut, a bald patch on its shoulder—but it seemed pleased to see them. It wagged its stub tail and whimpered. The soldiers formed a defensive line. A sharp whistle kept their hounds behind them; the hounds, in turn, snapped at the dogs of Marga's honor guard and stopped them from approaching the strange dog. The scouts struck swiftly; the mastiff was dead before it even had time to yelp.

"Why did you kill it? It wasn't threatening you," cried Marga, appalled.

"It was Ninysh," said one of the soldiers, a woman.

Marga couldn't stop her voice from trembling. "I'm Ninysh."

"Are you full of worms? Will you infest the sacred pack?" said the woman.

"We might be full of spiritual worms," Jacomo muttered.

The woman translated his utterance, everyone laughed, and they got moving again. He was clearly delirious with fever, to be saying such things, but the image still gnawed at Marga and wouldn't let her go.

⚔

Marga had expected some sort of hamlet, hastily thrown together like the mission before it burned, but what she got was a town.

It was called Mivikh and had flagstone roads, over which carts of firewood and vegetables trundled, pulled by yet another kind of dog, sturdy and woolly. The streets were lined with houses and workshops, like no buildings Marga had ever seen. Their tiered, thatched roofs echoed the shape of the surrounding fir trees; their wooden columns reflected the trunks. Where doors had been left open (for the day was warm and fine) Marga spotted little balls of fluff zooming around the interiors, making hiffing sounds; the door thresholds were a foot higher than the ground to keep these tiny dogs contained (they hardly looked like dogs at all, but Marga couldn't imagine what else they could be).

There was no surface the Aftisheshe didn't embellish. Some of the doorways were decorated to look like mouths; the walls were painted with eyes and ears and hands, as if these houses were living beings.

Workshops were everywhere, often indistinguishable from homes. There were forges, bowyers, tanners, dog-harness makers, bootmakers, pikestaff makers.

What fascinated Marga most, however, were the fighters drilling in an open square beneath a tall, spreading fir, trimmed like an umbrella. Each had two hounds and a long staff tipped with a vicious metal spike at each end. At their commands—whistles and gestures—the hounds ran in elaborate figures, leaped obstacles, or tore into woolen dummies. If the warriors crouched, their dogs would bound up their backs, leap into the air, and tear into targets dangling from the branches of the fir tree.

It was an ingenious martial art, practiced by formidable fighters. If they hadn't driven the Ninysh off their island by now, surely it was only because they lacked organization and leadership—things Marga herself could provide. She saw the raw materials of a great army here, the army she would use to stab Robinôt in the back.

First things first, however. She grimaced, adjusting Jacomo's weight against her shoulder, and followed where her guard led.

It seemed to be a council house, with the council consisting of twenty old women with gray braids wrapped around their heads who sat in a circle of carven chairs, some with plump cushions. They were discussing something, sipping from two-handled cups, when Marga and Jacomo were ushered in at spearpoint. The council fell silent, more curious than hostile. Marga didn't know which way to look; she hated turning her back on anyone important (or who might have a weapon). There seemed to be no option but to stand straight, speak clearly, and try to get this over with quickly.

"Thank you for seeing us, esteemed council," she said, unable to give proper courtesy while keeping Jacomo upright. This made her feel unexpectedly naked. "My comrade is dangerously ill. I'm looking for Berekka, the herbalist, in hopes that she can cure him."

One councilor—whom Marga took to be the eldest because she was so shrunken—raised a crooked finger. A Ninysh-speaking guard approached her. He whispered in her ear and she whispered something back. "Berekka has been captured by the enemy and is imprisoned at the fortress," he translated.

Marga's heart sank. Tess and Berekka hadn't stopped here, then. That was a problem.

Jacomo interrupted her thoughts with a loud groan.

"He's in bad shape," said the councilor through her translator. "He won't make it to the fort. We will care for him in the Goddess's house."

Four guards entered the circle and took Jacomo away. Marga couldn't stop them; there were too many, and they were armed while she was not. She registered her disapproval, however: "He has an infection. He needs medicine, not prayers and incense. Berekka was trained in Ninys, at the Academy—"

"Stop shouting," said the eldest councilor.

Marga clamped her mouth shut and watched, fuming, as Jacomo was led away.

"Why are you really here, Ninysh spy?" said the eldest, her eyes glinting like milky opals. "It was clever of them to finally send someone brown, but you don't fool us. You're no different—just as loud and disrespectful."

Marga felt a frisson as she realized what a deep hole she had to dig herself out of already.

"I'm not a spy," she said, clasping her hands behind her back. "I'm here with the joyous news that the Ninysh fleet has been destroyed by fire. The settlement at St. Fionnani is in utter disarray, the Citadel full of dead and wounded."

"If what you say is true," said the eldest, "it gladdens our hearts."

"Gladness is fine, but action is better," said Marga, encouraged. "The time to strike is now, before they can reorganize. I know the layout of the Citadel, her strengths and weaknesses. I know her commanders, and more than that, I know my people. That canine martial art I saw in the square—we could use that—"

"We *have* used that," said the eldest. "For centuries. Since before our hundred-year war with the Tshu."

"Of course," said Marga, "but there's tactics and then there's strategy. You've got the former in spades, clearly, but I suspect you've been lacking the latter."

"Upon what basis do you conclude such a thing?" another councilor piped up.

The air in the room seemed suddenly colder, but Marga persisted, undeterred. She had no qualms about telling difficult truths, even if the council didn't want to hear.

"Why, the fact that they have occupied this island for more than twenty years," Marga patiently explained. "You've held them to one corner, sure, but you haven't driven them off. That sort of thing requires long-range vision. Planning. I'm offering to help with that. I'm a sword master, and strategy is the air we breathe."

"You seem to think it was a small thing to have kept them contained so long," said the eldest, her mouth puckering. "Look around. In twenty years have the Ninysh reached this city?"

Clearly they hadn't; they would have razed it to the ground.

"Holding them off is admirable; I wasn't trying to denigrate your achievements," said Marga. "But the Ninysh are a danger as long as they're here, and now is the time to—"

"The Ninysh are a danger?" cried one of the younger councilors shrilly—in Ninysh, without the translator's help. "Why are we only learning this now?"

Her words were pure, acidic sarcasm. Marga felt like she'd been slapped.

"How dare you come here and insult us?" shouted another. The younger women spoke Ninysh, it seemed. "We fought the Tshu for a hundred years—the Tshu! Do you understand?"

Marga understood only that her face was growing unbearably hot and her ears were buzzing. She didn't deserve to be shouted at; she was trying to help.

"We have a strategy, thank you, and it will come to fruition soon. Tigers are coming, even now, so do not presume to lecture us on our deficiencies. You think you can come in here, knowing *nothing* of our history, *nothing* of what we have already accomplished, and—"

"Councilor Vufekhi, stop talking!" cried the eldest, whose translator had been frantically whispering in her ear, trying to keep up.

"I had to answer her insults," Vufekhi replied.

"I sympathize, but now we can't let her go. You've said too much. She might run back to her people and tell them what's coming."

What was coming? Marga, in her defensiveness, had had a difficult time listening.

The eldest spoke a bit more, words no one bothered to translate. Apparently they were instructions for the guards, who bound Marga's hands and led her off to an isolated cell.

The man who brought Marga meals spoke no Ninysh (or pretended he didn't). Her cell was carved into the side of a hill, so there was no view and little light. She had a pallet of sweet-smelling grasses to lie on, at least, but for five days she had nothing to do but watch the shifting shadows and think.

She found she didn't mind. She needed some time to reckon with herself; it was overdue.

On the sixth morning, her doorway darkened more completely than usual. She assumed a new guard had taken breakfast duty and so didn't look up until a gentle voice said, "Countess?"

She sat up at once. Jacomo, leaning on an intricately carved cane, smiled wanly while her warden unbolted the door for him. He stepped inside, limping; with effort, he lowered himself onto the pallet beside her. The warden left two bowls of the usual stew on the floor and then bolted the door.

"You're all right," said Marga, her heart full. "So they've stuck you in here with me."

"I asked to be here," said Jacomo. "I figured we well-intentioned, desperately clumsy outsiders belong together."

"No!" cried Marga. "You've done nothing wrong. I'm the one who insulted them by—"

"I have indeed done wrong," said Jacomo. "Back on St. Remy. Did Tess not tell you? I put myself in a terrible prison afterward—the one in my own head. This prison is light and airy compared with that one. I don't mind it in the least."

Marga fetched the stew bowls and let him tell her what had really happened on St. Remy: how he'd been so certain he was special, a True Priest; how he'd recorded the stories, intending to preserve them; Mee's anger and his own unrelenting shame.

"You're too hard on yourself," said Marga.

"No. I appreciate your faith in me, but . . . no," said Jacomo. "Unless you're trying to say I didn't need to flagellate myself for quite so long—that, I might agree with. But that's the other reason I'm here. It occurred to me that you might be doing the same thing."

Marga kept her eyes on her stew and said nothing. When Jacomo made no attempt to fill the silence, she sighed and said, "How long are you supposed to self-flagellate, then, when you realize that your neutrality—which you considered a proper, useful position, maybe even a moral position—has been enabling evils all around you? When you finally understand that your friend is trying to develop a scientific basis for oppression and your dead fiancé was designing a genocide? When you realize your painstaking, scrupulous care was more for the retention of your wealth and property than for the people who depend upon you?"

Her head bent over her stew, as if it were so full of guilt she could not hold it up. Jacomo hesitantly put an arm around her shoulders; she leaned against him and wept.

"I know," he said at last. "I know. Oh, Countess, I—"

"Marga," she said sternly through her tears. "Don't ever call me Countess again."

"Marga," he affirmed. "I felt exactly this after I failed Mee and the Nutufi. And the worst part is, I knew better. I'd had an epiphany, earlier, about Tess and the best way to help her, but maybe epiphanies aren't enough. You've got to apply them consistently."

Marga straightened, wiping her eyes. "What happened with Tess?"

"Well, first I stepped in it, of course. She'd told me about her history with Lord Morney."

"Call him Will," said Marga bitterly.

"After dinner that first evening—which none of us realized was his last evening—he followed us out and said threatening things to her. Tess looked so appalled and frightened that I . . . I told him she'd had his baby, to shock him. I vaguely threatened him as well."

Marga laughed mirthlessly. "He deserved as much."

"That's what I thought! But Tess was furious," said Jacomo. "I was mad at her in turn, for being ungrateful when I was only trying to help.

I stayed up all night arguing with myself, though, and by morning I saw she was right.

"St. Seraphina once spoke at my seminary—a history lecture about St. Jannoula's War. She said that most people believed St. Pandowdy had rescued her, since that's how it looked from the outside. Casual observers couldn't see the brave, difficult thing she'd done in her mind, breaking down her mental defenses, making herself vulnerable to St. Jannoula's power, and finally fighting back. Pandowdy, who *could* see the color of her mind, had noticed her doing all that and that she was struggling. So do you know what he did?"

"He rescued her," said Marga, who'd heard the story.

"He offered to help," said Jacomo. "He made himself her sidekick."

"I love Seraphina dearly," said Marga, "but are you sure she wasn't trying to convince you that she was the real hero, and not the giant who carried off St. Jannoula?"

"You can take that up with her," said Jacomo. "I'm trying to explain my epiphany. I suddenly saw, clear as day, that Tess didn't need me to protect her from Will. She resented it, in fact; it made her feel helpless and weak. What she needed was a sidekick."

"You are *not* saying, I hope, that I should be Tess's sidekick," snapped Marga, her hackles suddenly up.

"N-not at all," said Jacomo, eyes widening in apparent alarm. "I meant that both of us might be sidekicks to the *Aftisheshe*, instead of thundering in like knights-errant to save them, whether they need it or not."

Marga exhaled, her ire deflating a bit, although something at her core still quivered indignantly. "You must understand," she said, "*sidekick* carries a different weight for me than for you. The world never told you your life would be better spent in service to a husband and children. Scholars and swordsmen never patronized you; your family never considered you too Porphyrian—or too Ninysh—to amount to much. You were born a protagonist; some of us have had to fight for it."

Jacomo opened his mouth as if to argue but seemed to think better of it. "There are other words," he said at last. "How about *accomplice*? Or . . . what do you call someone in cahoots with you? A cahootier?"

That made her laugh. "Could we use *sidekick* as a verb? That, I might endorse."

"Whatever you like," said Jacomo. "And I know I'm ham-handed, but all I'm trying to say is that we protagonists—whether born or made—are not diminished or lost when we help others become the heroes of their own stories."

Another long silence ensued. Marga finally said, "You make it sound so simple."

"It is absolutely not simple," said Jacomo. "The moment I thought I was special—a True Priest, chosen by the Katakutia!—every selfless notion flew out the window." He gave a self-deprecating laugh. "I offer my self-important foolishness as a bit of sidekicking for you, Marga— consider me an object lesson."

She rested her head upon his broad shoulder again. "You know," she said at last, "you may not be a True Priest, in the specific way Mee meant it—"

"I'm not a priest at all," said Jacomo. "I ran away from seminary before taking orders."

Marga punched him lightly in the arm. "That's chapter fifty-eight of *Everyone Lies to Marga* . . . but fine, have it your way. You're not a priest. But if you ever did become one, you wouldn't be terrible."

Jacomo choked on his stew; Marga slapped him on the back until he quit coughing. "Thank you," he finally gasped. "Tess once told me I'd be a terrible priest. If I've graduated to not entirely terrible, that's quite an advancement."

Marga was only half listening. "I've done my share of terrible. I came here believing myself entitled to lead Aftisheshe armies," she said. "I don't know if they'd be willing to give us a second chance, but I think we need to determine what we can offer that would actually help."

"I may be able to assist you with that," said a vaguely familiar masculine voice from outside the cave. A silhouette, peculiarly stream-lined, as if he were wearing no clothing, darkened the doorway; the man approached the cell door. With the light behind him, his features were hard to see, but Marga could discern enough to affirm that her first impression was correct.

"Hami," she said, nodding as to a respected opponent. "Were you eavesdropping?"

"Eavesdropping was a large part of my job for many years, Your Grace," he said.

"Please don't call me that," said Marga. "But how did you get here?"

"Slowly," he said. "I had to swim, if you recall."

"Giles arrived much sooner."

"Fozu was a resourceful individual," said Hami, "and I presume he told a fine tale to a passing vessel and got a lift. No Ninysh ship is going to pick up a man in a sabak suit."

"Were you following him?" asked the countess.

"I was supposed to have met the dragons' expedition here," said Hami. "Do you know what happened to them? Were they aboard their ship when it blew?"

"They escaped and flew away."

"Then they're as good as dead," said Hami. "But surely they didn't all fly? There was one who couldn't easily do so—Scholar Spira?"

"Spira sailed off with Tess and Berekka," said Jacomo. "No one here has seen them."

"They eluded three warships, I heard," Marga added.

Hami nodded vaguely, in a reverie, then sighed. "But this isn't why I intruded upon your notice. I heard you expressing a desire to do restitution."

Doing restitution seemed an awfully humble and contrite way of putting it, and Marga had more than half a notion to revise the phrase to *making amends,* or even better, *being genuinely useful.* She met Jacomo's eye in the semidarkness, however; he shook his head almost imperceptibly, and she saw what she was doing and why.

She could shed her title, but she was still a countess to her core. That was hard to counter.

"Restitution, yes," she said determinedly.

"Good," said Hami. "Because I am on a similar journey. I've seen you fight, and I know what kind of sway your rank holds among your people. It occurs to me that we might work effectively together."

"What do you have in mind?" asked Marga.

"Nothing set in stone yet. As you say, it will depend on what the Aftisheshe need. If I can persuade them to release you—if I vouch for you, Margarethe—would you be willing to help me?"

"Yes," she said.

He gave solemn half courtesy, turned on his heel, and left.

Thirty-Six

Tess spent a sleepless night in the bottom of the kuro, beside
Pathka's cocoon. She had thought her stomach quite unshak-
able, but the little boat rocked constantly, and eventually it was too
much for her. She threw up once, over the side, and spent the rest of
the night wishing she could do it again. Fortunately, night was only
a few hours long this time of year. Even in the predawn gloaming, as
long as she could see the face of the water, Tess began to feel better.

Mostly better. She felt a few pangs and assumed they were her
conscience.

Spira, most probable source of conscience pangs, was curled into a
ball at the prow, asleep. Ko—*she*, that is. It was going to take practice
to think of Spira as *she*. Even before Tess had (apparently ill-advisedly)
settled on *ko,* Spira's pedantic peevishness had always struck her as
masculine, if anything.

Tess gave a mirthless chuckle. She was chronically wrong, as well
as unforgiven, but she never really got used to it.

Her ruminations were interrupted by splashes off the port side.
Dark shapes under the surface of the sea were creatures with full, fat
bodies, swimming faster than the boat; they would occasionally leap
from the water, revealing black backs and white bellies. Their fins

flapped like ineffectual wings, failing to keep them aloft, but they were so sleek they dived back under with hardly a ripple.

Berekka was up and stirring, making some adjustment to the sails. Tess, trying not to wake Spira, pointed excitedly and stage-whispered, "Flying fish?"

Berekka shook her head. "Birds."

"Birds that can't fly? I thought flying was the definition of a bird."

Spira, who may have been awake all along, muttered, "Chickens can't fly."

"We call them mekhivolhai—'noisy stinkers,'" said Berekka. "They're delicious, in fact."

"Don't say they taste like chicken," said Spira.

"They taste like fish."

The kuro sailed past a dozen islands, some with Aftisheshe settlements. "For historical reasons, we tend to prefer islands with cliffs," Berekka explained. "The Tshu knights use ice tigers in war, and those can't climb sheer rock."

"How do they move tigers from island to island?" asked Tess. "Tiger boats?"

Berekka was frowning at the horizon. Tess turned and saw yellow sails coming into view, a few at first, then a dozen, then more than fifty. An armada of longboats, coming toward them.

"Are these your people?" asked Spira, shifting to look.

"No," said Berekka. "They're Tshu. Tess is about to have her tiger question answered."

Berekka dropped sail; the kuro slowed and bobbed like a cork. "We'll have to wait this out. If the tigers think we're fleeing, they will chase us. They're hard to control at sea."

As the longboats neared, Tess began to see creatures in the water. The sea roiled with swimming tigers, their white noses protruding above the waves, their tails rising like curious sea serpents. "The fleet looks like it's headed for that island," Berekka whispered, pointing out an island to their north, plainly fearful of drawing attention. "Tigers get exhausted if they have to swim too far."

Whispering didn't help; a bevy of curious cats spotted the kuro and began swimming toward it. A clash of gongs from the Tshu ships commanded the tigers to return. Most did, but some had other ideas. Soon, a half dozen tigers were swimming around the kuro. Tess might have reached out and touched them, if she hadn't been overly fond of her hands.

Berekka hefted an oar as if gauging its suitability as a weapon.

"Surely they can't climb into our boat," muttered Spira.

"They don't need to," said Berekka. "They're trained to tip us over or tear the hull."

"Can you swim, Spira?" asked Tess, ready to keep the scholar afloat if necessary.

"It won't help," said Berekka. "It probably hurts less to drown before you're eaten."

"I thought your war was over," cried Spira, struggling to sit up straighter.

"The Tshu won't command them to attack," said Berekka, "but tigers don't always wait for a command. They're not as smart and disciplined as dogs."

One of the longboats had oars in the water and was rowing toward them at full speed. A clear pattern rang on the gong—Tess would be hearing that beat in nightmares for the rest of her life—but the tigers weren't listening. A tiger-knight climbed onto the prow and perched there, spear in hand, looking ready to skewer a tiger if that's what it took. The knight's basket-armor gleamed in the sun.

A pale paw with long, wicked claws groped the edge of the kuro experimentally. Berekka slapped it hard with the oar and it retreated into the water; the kuro rocked.

Suddenly most of the tigers stopped circling and abruptly swam off westward. Tess soon saw what had happened: a pod of noisy stinkers had surfaced, and the tigers had decided they were the easier meal. They tore the fat birds to pieces with much thrashing and screaming.

Berekka scoffed, "So undisciplined. Our war dogs would never break formation to—"

A horrifying crunch interrupted her as powerful teeth punctured the hull of the kuro. One tiger, at least, had managed to stay focused.

The longboat had drawn close enough for the knight to leap onto the tiger's back.

The cat's mood shifted at once: it became immediately obedient and contrite. The knight directed it toward the others and their greasy seabird feast, and swatted all the tigers' noses with a long switch. The battalion began swimming sheepishly back toward the longboat.

This was all well and good, but the kuro was still sinking. The water, bitterly cold, was up to Tess's knees. Spira, who'd been slow to rise, was drenched to her waist and shivering miserably. Pathka's cocoon bobbed; Tess tried to keep a hold on it so it didn't wash away.

The tiger-knight called out to them—in Tshu, apparently. Berekka called back in a different-sounding language, looking supremely irritated. The knight laughed and then hailed the longboat. The crew threw the kuro a line and managed to haul the little boat close before it sank entirely. Everyone was brought aboard the longboat, even Pathka's cocoon, and soon they were huddled at the foot of the mast, wrapped in wool blankets. Spira was still shivering.

The Tshu let the kuro sink, over Berekka's vociferous protests.

The longboat had a yellow sail and more than thirty oars. The rowers wore woven basket-armor and were bristling with blades; their bare arms, straining at the oars, were gray green.

The tiger-wrangling knight climbed back aboard and removed her helmet, exposing a shock of short white hair. Tess was surprised to recognize Kluit, the Tshu storyteller from the Maftumaiu. Kluit spoke to Berekka in not-quite-fluent Aftishekka.

Berekka was frowning afterward. "They won't take us to Aftisheshe

Home. They're headed toward an island called Shevkha. We'll have to find our own way from there."

"What's in Shevkha?" asked Spira. "They're not invading your people again, are they?"

"Quite the contrary. Our peoples are joining forces. We're taking Edushuke back."

The Tshu fleet crept relentlessly, like an oil slick, resting the tigers every couple of hours. They found a pair of small islands for nighttime. Normally the tigers would sleep on an island and the Tshu would sleep in their boats, but this time a few Tshu put ashore on the tiger-free island and set up camp for their guests on solid ground. Tess was glad to get Spira in front of a fire; the scholar had never stopped shivering.

Tess didn't mind being off a boat for a while, either. She'd stopped feeling nauseated, but the pangs had gotten worse. It wasn't conscience after all: her stomach hurt.

Kluit came ashore with them, as one of the better Aftishekka speakers. She seemed the most senior of the shore party, directing her underlings to build a fire and catch some fish. As she set up the griddle, the tiger-knight kept sneaking sly glances at Tess. Kluit definitely recognized her, which made Tess cringe. It wasn't pleasant to be reminded that a stupid story you'd told may have accidentally started a war.

To distract herself from the tiger-knight's gaze (and from her abdominal pain), Tess took out her thnimi. She hadn't dared to look at it since diving into the ocean to save Pathka's cocoon. A test button, supposed to make it chirp, wasn't working. The device seemed to be dead.

How long would it take Seraphina to get worried and send the fleet?

The pain was beginning to radiate into the tops of her thighs. Only one thing hurt quite that way: her monthlies. She had completely lost track of the weeks, and here she was, in a strange place with nothing for it. She'd had anxiety dreams like this.

Then again, she was here with an Aftisheshe herbalist and a Tshu tiger-knight. They surely had this problem sometimes. What did they usually do?

"I'm embarrassed to ask," Tess said to Berekka, "but my monthlies have come, and I left my lunessas, to say nothing of my clothes—"

"Of all the problems you've presented," said Berekka, "this one is most easily solved." She said a few words to Kluit, who immediately handed the fish turner to an underling and bounded back to the boats. She returned with a small cauldron of water, which she placed upon the fire, and a wooden box that she handed to Berekka.

"I didn't bring any bulbs," said Kluit, per Berekka's translation, "but they're better fresh. I'll be back before the fish is done." She grabbed a large knife and took off toward the shore.

Berekka opened the little box, sniffed it, and smiled. "Teta root," she said, adding three big pinches to the water. "This will soothe the pain. In fact, Spira, you should have some, too."

Spira made a sulky noise, and then all of a sudden Kluit was back, grinning and brandishing a bouquet of kelp floats. She thrust these at Tess.

Tess took them, feeling terribly confused. The bulbs had a strong smell.

Kluit stared at her. Tess stared back.

Kluit burst out laughing.

She took one of the bulbs back, trimmed the stem and leaves, and cut it in half to produce a flexible, if stenchy, little cup. Through gestures alone, Kluit was able to communicate exactly where Tess should stick it.

"Does . . . does that work?" Tess asked dubiously, her eyes darting to Berekka.

"It catches everything," said Berekka, stirring the pot. "You do have to change it out for a new one several times a day, so hang on to those other bulbs."

"Throw the old one into the ocean," Kluit advised, "and shout, 'Breakfast for sharks!'"

Apparently the Aftisheshe did this, too; Tess left the two women laughing together while she wandered away from the fire and did her best to insert the damned thing. By the time she figured it out and returned, they were chatting like old friends and Spira was holding the first warm cup of teta-root tea in her hands.

The tea was bitter, but it worked quickly. Tess could feel her gut unclenching.

Kluit snapped her fingers, and one of her underlings brought her a curious tool, like a narrow, elongated spoon made of antler. Talking all the while (Berekka didn't bother to translate), Kluit held out her bare forearm; her skin looked more gray than green in the dwindling twilight. She scraped the tool along her arm in a wiggly wave. To Tess's astonishment, this created a pale line on Kluit's skin. Kluit pulled the gray-green strip out of the bowl of the spoon and handed it to Berekka, who accepted it reverently.

Kluit scraped some more, making elaborate geometrical patterns on her forearm. Tess found it hard to watch. "Why is she peeling off her own skin?" Tess cried. "Doesn't it hurt?"

Berekka translated, which only made Kluit laugh the more. "It's my second skin, not my first," she said, sticking her arm under Tess's nose. "You see? Everything is all right."

"They cultivate a kind of algae on their skin," Berekka explained, tucking the strips away in a leather bag one of Kluit's underlings had given her. "Several polar nations do this; it keeps them warm. They scrape some off in summer to get some sun, or else their bones go soft.

"She claims it has medicinal properties. I still don't know what Spira is going to need, but I don't think I can afford to turn such an offer away."

Tess glanced at Spira to gauge her reaction, but the saar was already asleep.

It took four days to reach Shevkha; Berekka grumbled about this frequently. The kuro could have made the trip in a day, it seemed, but there was a large interisland sea in the way, too far for the tigers to swim across. They had to sail around it, island to island.

Tess didn't entirely mind. She was learning about the Tshu. Their basket-armor was woven from strips of whale baleen, and they considered themselves one of the civilized nations because they were allowed to keep sabak (Berekka rolled her eyes at this). Kluit had three husbands and five grown children on this boat; the rest she'd left at home (the rest of her husbands, Berekka had clarified—that would not have been Tess's guess).

Shevkha finally came in sight, a broad, low-lying island with a generous harbor. It was neutral territory, a good place for the two armies to gather. Some Tshu and Aftisheshe forces had already arrived and were encamped in the middle of the island, using their collective mass to keep the tigers and hounds apart.

Kluit beached the longboat nearer the Aftisheshe side, so Pathka's cocoon wouldn't need to be hauled across the middle of the camp. Of course, then her tigers had to be herded around to the other side; her children took care of that, while Kluit hefted the cocoon over her shoulder and carried it single-handedly up the beach. Berekka gave Spira her arm, and Tess took up the rear.

Someone was shouting: "Teth—Teth!" And then Kikiu came whipping through the tent maze, sprinted across the beach, and just about bowled Tess over in the surf.

"You're here, you're here!" Kikiu yammered excitedly. "And you brought my mother—I knew she'd be in thuthmeptha! Ko is transforming to slow down ko's illness, but it isn't going to work. At least, I think it won't. I'm not very good at interpreting the future yet."

"You're . . . what?" cried Tess, who was having difficulty interpreting the present.

"I understand so much more now. I've delved into the World-mind, and I know where Pathka's mind got lost. I was the True Priest all along. Me!" said Kikiu in the wind-speech, running in a splashy circle.

At the mention of the True Priest, Tess raised her eyes toward the camp, and sure enough, there were half a dozen Katakutia crossing the camp on stilts, fringed hoods obscuring their faces, presumably here to translate for the Aftisheshe and Tshu. Tess's heart sank.

"Don't be afraid," said Kikiu. "She won't try to kill you again. I'll go warn her you're here, though, because she'll want to avoid you."

With that, the hatchling scampered back up the beach. Tess's companions stared at her.

"No one's considerately helping me avoid you," Spira muttered first.

"Did a Wild One try to kill you?" said Berekka. "What on earth did you do?"

"I . . . may have started a war," said Tess.

"You almost did," Kluit interjected (per Berekka), "but King Molsu saw reason in the end. I had traveled there with a Wandering City, which hadn't wandered far, and they were willing to evacuate the Nutufi. I arranged it. I owed the Nutufi that, as a Tshu."

"What about their land?" said Tess. "What about the Navel of the World?"

"The Navel of the World is wherever the Nutufi are, because contemplating the world's navel is their main occupation," said Kluit. "I mean that admiringly."

"That's not a happy ending," said Tess.

"It's not an ending at all," said Kluit, curtly now. "It's a continuation, and the best we can do for the moment.

"I also blamed you at first," she added, more gently. "It was easier: you're a manageable size, and the Ninysh armies aren't. But we only have two arms, and we can only do what we can do. Your story gave me insights, and in the end I am glad to have them."

"Thank you?" said Tess, recalling how cutting those insights had been.

Kluit laughed. "We storytellers get blamed for all kinds of things— corrupting the young, failing to paint a glorious enough picture of our queen, insulting the priests—but our obligation is to dig into our own hearts and expose the truths there. Sometimes our hearts are full of monsters. It takes valor to look them in the eye."

She shifted Pathka in her arms and continued up the strand toward the Aftisheshe side.

After finding Tess and Spira a tent to rest in, Berekka went out for the remainder of the afternoon. She returned in the evening with sup-per, a meaty stew called *upuki*, and she wore the expression of some-one with bad news, trying to make it sound not so bad. "We're going back to Edushuke," she said as soon as Tess's mouth was full. "There are no spare boats to take us to Aftisheshe Home and, ah, they realized who I am. We need every healer in wartime."

The stew was full of tiny bones; Tess was busy trying to chew around one, or she would have had some words. She couldn't go back to Edushuke, away from the Polar Serpent and toward the countess (whom she'd quarreled with) and Jacomo (whom she'd abandoned). How was she supposed to get Pathka to the pole now? Wait until this war was over and beg one of the tiger-knights to take her as far as Tshu territory?

How long did Pathka even have? Kikiu had said ko was getting worse.

"Edushuke would be better for Spira, honestly," Berekka was say-ing. "My hothouses, my herbs, all my equipment, are there. I know you want to go south, Tess, but when the hounds of need are pulling in different directions, you've got to choose."

"Nrrn" was all Tess managed to say, picking a bone out of her mouth.

"You're supposed to eat those," said Berekka.

They slept in one small tent—not quite in a quigutl-pile, but close—and left early with the first wave of kuros. The capacious war kuros carried supplies, fighters, and dogs. Tess, relegated to a kuro full of tents, pined after the hound transports. Berekka tried to dispel her illusions: "War hounds are as dangerous as tigers. You don't want to ride with them. At my house in Mivikh, I have a dozen upuki you can pet."

Tess leaned her cheek on her hand and sighed after their pointy snouts nonetheless.

Edushuke was a two-day sail without tigers. It was well past bedtime but not yet dusk when the fleet of kuros reached it. Tess and her companions were dropped off at a cove carved into the relentless cliffs—a particularly Aftisheshe style of landing place, easily defensible. The rest of the Aftisheshe fleet did not stop, but sailed on toward the western end of the island, to the only place on Edushuke where one could land with tigers. The Tshu would join them there.

Tess was so exhausted that everything became a blur. Somehow she and Berekka got Pathka and Spira up the steep steps. Somehow Berekka acquired a dogcart to carry Spira and Pathka up the coast to Mivikh. Berekka and Tess walked alongside. Tess must have sleepwalked, because the next thing she knew, they'd reached a forest—except not a forest, a cliff-top town full of oddly tree-shaped buildings. People came out to greet them, even though it was the middle of the night (the sun had set at some point). Tess was led to a one-room house, warned to step over the high doorsill, and allowed to fall face-first onto a sleeping couch.

Something started yipping bright and early. Tess startled awake, alarmed that she couldn't remember what had become of Pathka's cocoon. But there it was, across the room, under Spira's bed. Spira had a blanket wadded over her head to block out the yipping, which seemed to be coming from a dozen little balls of pale fluff; some of them were zooming around the floor, some snoring on a folded blanket near the hearth, some up on the bed sniffing at Spira.

These must be the upuki Berekka had mentioned. Berekka was nowhere to be seen.

Then she was stepping over the high threshold, bearing a basket of fresh-cut herbs.

"Oh, good, you're awake," said Berekka. "Clean up outside, then come help."

Tess went outside and got a good look at the town; in the clear, bright sunlight, she could see why she'd taken the tiered rooftops for pine trees. She wondered whether they were meant to be disguised from a distance. There was a washbasin behind Berekka's house, as well as an ocean cliff from which Tess could feed the sharks. Tess took care of necessities and, when she got back, found Berekka sitting on a cushion on the floor, plucking leaves into a mortar. "Nudge the fire and wake it up," she said, gesturing toward the hearth with her chin. "Get the pot boiling, and then under my bed you'll find my basket of joy."

Tess had a moment of déjà vu—she knew the phrase *basket of joy*. Her good love, Josquin, had kept one under his bed. Dear Josquin. It must be a commoner thing than she realized.

"Powdered teta root is in the square box," Berekka called. "Three scoops into the pot."

Tess scooped. The instructions kept coming: "Stir so it doesn't boil over. Take it off the fire as soon as it develops a kind of . . . bere smell. Bah, my Ninysh gets so rusty. Not that Ninysh has good words for smells."

"I've never encountered a human language that can describe smells," said Spira, peeking out from under the blanket. "I assume it's because your noses are terrible."

"Compared with yours," said Berekka, crushing the herb with a pestle. "Aftishekka has ways to talk about smells, though. In Ninysh, everything smells like a thing. My foster mother Sister Monica could discern all kinds of things in a glass of wine—blackberries, leather, smoke—but if I described the smell's timbre to her, its depth or density, she was completely lost."

"Dragons can tell you the number of parts per million," said Spira haughtily, "and graph their velocity and trajectory."

"This is fascinating, but what's a bere smell?" interjected Tess, stirring frantically.

"A blurry smell?" Berekka offered, adding oil to her mixture. "A smell that's only halfway there. If the teta smells full and bright, its medicinal properties are breaking down and you have to start over. It's almost there, in fact."

Tess took the pot off the fire and set it on a trivet to cool.

"So does your name translate to . . . 'blurry speech'?" asked Spira.

"Well done," said Berekka, pouring the contents of her mortar into another pot. "It's kind of a funny story. *Berekka* is our word for a foreign language, because you can tell someone is talking, but not what they mean. When I was nine, I was abducted to Ninys by a master of the Academy. He must have asked me my name. I didn't have a name—we don't get named until we're thirteen—and didn't understand the question anyway. I tried to explain that his speech blurred in my ears, and he mistook the word for my name. He thought I said *Rebecca*. I was called Rebecca for many years.

"When I made my way back here and told them my name, it was almost the same thing in reverse. I said, 'I'm Rebecca,' and they laughed and said, 'Sounds more like Berekka to me.'"

Tess, kneeling beside the fire, seemed to be having a blurry memory. She could not quite put her finger on it.

Spira said plaintively, "Speaking of smells, there is someone pacing in front of your door. I do not wish to speak with him. Would you tell him I'm too ill and tired, and send him away?"

Tess could think of only one person it might be. Berekka set her mixture aside, wiped her hands, and cautiously approached the door. Tess shadowed her.

Watcher Hami looked up as the door opened. His first instinct was apparently to give three-quarters courtesy, despite the fact that he was no longer dressed as a Ninysh lord. He'd been given an embroidered tunic and a pair of Aftisheshe checked trousers, rolled at the cuffs. His white curls were more disheveled than Tess had seen them, but he had not lost his lordly mien.

Berekka stepped over the doorsill toward him; Tess followed, closing the door.

Hami removed his dark spectacles, as if he needed to see without their mediation to believe that Tess was there. "They said strangers had arrived. It sounded like you and Spira."

"Spira is too ill to see anyone, Ggdani," said Berekka. "Can I do something for you?"

The diminutive man pressed his lips together. "I'm sorry to hear that," he said. "Would you convey a message? I came to apologize; Spira will know for what. And to say goodbye, in case . . . I've been given a mission, a bit of trickery to start off the campaign. Things could go wrong. I abandoned teu once without a goodbye. I didn't want to do it again."

Berekka nodded cordially. "I will tell Spira what you said. And if she, ah, feels up to seeing anyone later, how long until you head out on your mission?"

"Tomorrow night, directly after the performance, I set out for the Citadel with Marga."

"So there's still some time," said Berekka.

Tess, however, had just heard the last name she'd expected to hear, and it filled her with wonder and dread. "The countess is here? How?"

Hami's pale-lashed eyes blinked owlishly. "She's helping us. But ask her yourself. She's at the smithy by the training grounds—see the smoke, just there?—and Jacomo with her."

Tess had never run so fast.

If Jacomo had not been so large and sturdy, Tess might have bowled him off his bench and into the smithy's slack tub. He half laughed, half yelped. "Watch the leg!"

"Sorry," said Tess, realizing she'd bumped it. "But what are you doing here?"

"Marga is choosing a weapon from the vast collection of rusty swords they've captured in skirmishes with the Ninysh," he said. "And I'm waiting for her."

"I meant that a bit more globally," Tess said, punching his arm.

"I know what you meant," said her brother-in-law, grinning a rapscalliacious grin.

It felt like eons since she'd seen him smile. Or upright, for that matter.

The smithy was open on all sides—a roof on six legs—its forge geared toward making spearheads, cooking pots, and parts of boats. Marga was standing on the other side, a silhouette before the sunlit training field, speaking to the smith through a Katakutia. It wasn't Mee, although her name, insofar as she had a name, was probably also Mee. About thirty swords were arrayed on the ground.

"The Ggdani looked for two minutes and pointed to the one he wanted," Jacomo was saying. "Marga apparently has to swing each one, set it aside, take it up again, put it in the *perhaps* pile. . . ."

Tess studied him sidelong; he had a fond, silly look on his face.

"Hami said you'd been given some sort of mission?" said Tess.

"Not me! That is, I have a bit part where I stand around looking injured." He stretched out his bandaged leg. "I expect I can manage that rather well. She and Hami are the main event, though. They shall attempt to trick the Ninysh into invading a place called Long Red Valley."

The countess had stepped out from under the roof, into the training field, and was slashing and whirling with one of the blades. Either she hadn't noticed Tess, or she was ignoring her.

Tess sat down next to Jacomo. "Hami seemed to think . . . they might not come back."

"Hami is a dismal pessimist," said Jacomo, "and I say that as someone who couldn't get out of bed for weeks. But he's not wrong, unfortunately. If they fail, they're likely to fail hard."

Tess shifted in her seat, considering. "What happens to the campaign then?"

"It proceeds just as it would have if she and the Ggdani hadn't asked to help—the fight will be harder, but the Aftisheshe and Tshu together are formidable. They believe they'll win."

"That's a great risk to her for a small benefit to the Aftisheshe," said Tess, looking toward Marga again, feeling an unexpected tug at her heart.

"I know you two quarreled," said Jacomo, lowering his voice. "She and I discussed that at length, sitting in Aftisheshe prison."

"Prison?" cried Tess, loudly enough that Marga looked over. Jacomo smiled and waved, and the countess went back to lunging and parrying, her brows raised in a quizzical quirk.

"You think you're the only person who's been having adventures? I nearly died," said Jacomo, his grin growing more infuriating. "But what I want to say is, remember back in Paishesh, when I stupidly told Will about your baby? You gave me a second chance, and I hope I've done well with it."

He paused until Tess looked him in the eye. She knew where this was going, and wasn't entirely pleased, but if he'd ask her directly, rather than hinting and expecting her to—

"Give her one more chance, for my sake," he said. There it was, curse him. "She has a good heart, even if she's only beginning—at age thirty-two—to notice that the world is not as just and reasonable as she always told herself it was."

"We'll see," said Tess, but she knew that her heart had already begun to thaw, even if it wasn't quite finished yet.

Jacomo gave her a one-armed, extremely brotherly hug and said, "Now tell me what you've been up to."

They exchanged stories; Tess never took her eyes off Marga, who was glancing over at them more frequently now. When their gazes met, it was like a clashing of blades.

That might be a good thing. The countess dearly loved her swords.

"Can you have this one sharp by tomorrow?" Marga said at last with the Katakutia's help. The smith assured her he could. He touched his forehead lightly, then tapped his heart. Marga made the gesture back, then turned toward Tess and Jacomo.

"She's renouncing her title," Jacomo whispered as she approached, "so don't use it."

Tess stood as the erstwhile countess drew near. Marga stopped about five feet away; the awkwardness between them was too thick to allow a nearer approach. It felt almost too thick to speak through.

"Tess," said Marga stiffly, like someone trying to stifle pain, "I owe you an apology. I doubted you. You told me about Father Erique and . . . and *Will*, and I didn't want to believe a word of it. That must have hurt you, not to be believed. I don't know how you had the forbearance and grace to even consider traveling with Will—or with me, afterward, going on about him constantly and whining that you didn't trust me.

"I read his journals and learned a number of things I wish I could forget. He was worse than even you might have realized. There were signs, not least the company he kept, but I didn't care to see them. As for Erique, I'm ashamed of the excuses I made for him.

"I feel like such a fool, and I'm sorry I refused to see."

Tears rolled down Marga's cheeks, unnoted, and then Tess could no longer stop her own.

Tess held out her arms. Marga hesitated, then came in for a timid embrace. Jacomo rose and put his arms around both of them, crushing them all together.

"He fooled me, too," said Tess in a muffled voice.

After a moment Tess pulled away, leaving Jacomo with his arms around Marga, his cheek pressed to the top of her head. They stayed that way until Marga, looking flustered, stepped back. Jacomo didn't take his eyes off her. The fond, silly look had returned.

Tess, now that she'd heard his story, saw with new eyes. Marga had saved his life, and it was just possible that he had also saved her. Tess teetered briefly upon the knife edge of jealousy—she'd occasionally felt things for this sweet-natured student-priest, and maybe even (if she was being completely honest) for this dashing, brilliant no-longer-a-countess—but she resolved it quickly in herself. They were beautiful; this was right. She was happy for them.

"When I return—if I return—I shall want to discuss my estate with you two," Marga was saying. "I want to renounce my title, but I still can't countenance the thought of Count Pesavolta getting his grubby, murderous hands on the estate. There might be a way to—"

"Marga," said Jacomo. "You'll come back. We'll be waiting. Tell us then."

Marga nodded tearfully. She took his arm and extended the other one to Tess. "Let's ask what else we can do. There will be a war on soon."

They went together to the council house.

⚔

That day and the next passed slowly and too fast. Tess helped Berekka pack supplies to take to the front, and learned to make rukkefa—the herb pellets that gave the war hounds their poisonous green bite—from some of the older women. Berekka gave her instructions for the care and feeding of the upuki, and even more detailed instructions about what to give Spira when.

"I promised to help her," Berekka fretted, "but I don't even know how long I'll be gone. I've left enough algal tincture for five days. Spira knows the rest of her regimen, if you could fetch things for her so she doesn't have to get up—"

"All will be well," said Tess, trying to sound reassuring. It was easy to sound hopeful when you weren't going to war, though.

Pathka was due to hatch out any day; Tess had a definite knot of anxiety about that, and what came after, whenever she let herself think about it.

The second evening arrived; the tigers had landed, and some of the knights were coming up to Mivikh for the "performance," as Hami had called it. Tess crossed town with Berekka in the long-lingering twilight; all of Mivikh, and some of their dogs, were headed in the same direction.

They reached a kind of amphitheater, a great green bowl perched dramatically atop the cliffs. Behind the stage, the open ocean spread forever, dotted with islands.

"Do you always have an evening of theater before going to war?" Tess asked.

"Not usually," said Berekka. "But the Tshu are here, and one of the conditions of our peace, as set forth by the Nutufi, is that whenever we're together, we must perform 'Vulkharai.'"

Tess was beginning to feel like the tiger-loving bootmaker was following her around.

"I know this story," said Tess, hurrying down the slope after her. "What's the Aftisheshe version like? Comedy? Tragedy?"

"History," said Berekka.

Kluit was waving them over to sit with her. Marga and Jacomo soon joined, and then Hami approached, looking uncertain. "Spira didn't feel well enough to come," said Berekka, anticipating his question. Hami turned as if to go, but Marga leaped up and brought him back, and they all sat together on the mossy ground.

This "Vulkharai" was as elaborately staged as anything Tess had ever seen. There were dancers, singers, well-trained dogs, glittering costumes, and the boots—the boots!—were individually played by well-muscled warriors, leaping about with graceful absurdity. All around her, Tshu and Aftisheshe laughed together. They chimed in at designated intervals with barks and howls, chants and jeers, applause and false tears.

It was a hundred years of war reduced to an interactive farce where both sides ritualistically laughed at each other and themselves, drank okush, and ended up friends. Katakutia—there were three here, plus Kikiu—stood to each side, translating furiously, but everyone had seen this drama many times, and there was no misunderstanding it. As darkness finally fell, Kluit threw her arms around Tess's and Berekka's shoulders, singing along with the final song.

Tess felt swept away, almost in tears, and she wasn't even sure she got it all.

Afterward, everyone rose to say their farewells. Tess, with Berekka's help, had one question for Kluit: "Your 'Vulkharai' at the Maftumaiu was completely different. Did the Nutufi not make your people tell the same story?"

Kluit patted Tess's cheek. "We don't need the same story, little fish. The Aftisheshe take such pride in all their arts—even those damned boots. They have to learn not to take themselves so seriously. We Tshu, on the other hand, need to channel our rage through poetry, not endless vendettas.

"We bring ourselves to stories. Someday you will find a meaning in 'Vulkharai' that only you can see. It will be yours and no one else's, and it will be exactly what you needed."

With that, she gave Tess a back-breaking hug and took off after the other tiger-knights.

Marga and Hami had slipped away toward their perilous task already. Berekka left with the Aftisheshe fighters; Jacomo trundled along with her supplies in a dog-drawn cart. The Katakutia followed the troops.

Tess returned to town with those who were staying behind, the very old and very young. She opened the door of Berekka's house quietly, in case Spira was asleep. It was hard to tell; the fire burned low and none of the lamps were lit. The upuki, who were supposed to sleep under the bed, had found their way up to Spira and nestled in every curve of her body.

Tess filled the upuki's water, emptied their necessity basket, and started getting ready for bed. She became aware of a muffled sound, maybe an upuki whining in its sleep. She tiptoed over to Spira's bed and leaned over it, hoping to remove the creature before it woke Spira up.

Spira's shoulders were shaking. It wasn't an upuki making that sound.

"Is there something I can get you, Spira?" Tess whispered.

Spira rolled onto her back, scattering the upuki, and rubbed her swollen eyelids. "It's this reduced dose of destultia. It makes me so emotional . . . and I'll be completely out in four more days." She wailed and buried her face in the blankets.

"Berekka had something to alleviate that, didn't she?" asked Tess, opening the basket beside the bed and looking through the boxes and vials. "Was it the algal tincture?"

"I hate the algal tincture!" cried Spira. "It tastes like human epidermal cells."

"But does it help enough to make it worth the—"

"It does *not*."

"All right," said Tess. "How about some teta? That would help you sleep, anyway."

Spira nodded assent, and Tess set some water to boil. The upuki resettled themselves.

Spira's voice eked out from under the upuki: "How was 'Vulkharai'?"

"Good," said Tess, surprised by her interest. "Unlike any version I'd heard before."

"Hami told me the story once," said Spira. "He said it's . . . it's about inevitability."

"The inevitability of what?" asked Tess, turning to look at her. This was such a different Spira than she'd known before: mournful, vulnerable. Heartbroken.

It wasn't just the destultia wearing off, Tess suspected. Calling her *she* seemed to have softened and rounded her hard edges—in Tess's eyes, if not in objective fact. What Tess used to call peevish now seemed melancholy; the pedantic had become precise.

"Vulkharai's gift kills the Queen of Tigers. We destroy what we love," said Spira. "We don't mean to, we don't try to, but we can't help ourselves."

"What a dismal interpretation," cried Tess. "I can understand finding it tragic, but . . ."

And that was when it hit her, just like Kluit had said it would: her own understanding. Vulkharai, however well intentioned, had spent a great deal of time and effort making boots for a tiger who couldn't use them.

In no version of the story had he asked the tiger what she actually needed.

"Spira," said Tess, the glamor of understanding upon her, "what do you need?"

"A time machine," said Spira without hesitation, as if she'd been thinking about this.

"What would you do with a time machine?" asked Tess, taken aback.

"I would go back to . . . to before Hami left on his . . . his mission, and I'd say . . ." She was starting to cry again. "I'd say goodbye at least. Not . . . not hold my stupid grudge and refuse to . . . to see him. . . ." She began crying so hard she couldn't speak.

The teta-root tea was getting fragrant; Tess quickly pulled it off the fire. She poured Spira a cup and brought it to her, along with a square of linen from one of Berekka's baskets—possibly a bandage, but it would do for a handkerchief.

Finally, she reached deep into her pocket, where a bit of fuzz had been shoved and forgotten. She held up the eyu in the firelight and then set it beside Spira's pillow. Spira blinked at it for a moment, but then she took it in her hand.

Tess stepped outside and sat on Berekka's colonnaded porch. She could hear Spira's voice but couldn't make out the words. She sat a good long while, watching the stars reel overhead, until Spira had finished talking and fallen back asleep again.

Thirty-Seven

*M*ind of the World, unite with hand and heart, with eye and voice! *Together, there is no stopping you.*

Once upon a time, two very different people found a reason and a way to work together.

Night had faded into the sickly twilight of dawn by the time they reached the edge of the forest. It was still very early, so they found a place to hide—a hollow under the roots of a spruce—and waited until the sun was a bit higher in the sky, sharing some fish jerky between them.

"Who contacted you?" Marga asked at last, quietly. "Was it new instructions?"

"Ah, no," said Hami. "A friend. Just some closure."

It sounded personal; she didn't press. She had her own festering regrets.

"There's something I want to request, fencer to fencer," she whispered. "The success of this plan hinges on an accurate reading of Robinôt, and I . . . I have to admit to myself, at last, that I'm not as good at reading people as I always believed."

"You know him better than I do," said Hami. She noted he hadn't disagreed with her.

"But you're the better swordsman," she offered. "I know that much, having faced you. The council didn't understand that your eye is as good as or better than mine. I want you to take your own judgment into account."

"And if my judgment contradicts yours?" he said.

"Follow your instincts. The foster nephew of the great Master Tacques has the right of way," said Marga.

"No," said Hami. "We have three options: press strength, feign weakness, or remain neutral. If we disagree on which of the first two is best, I'll take the third path."

That sounded like the worst path to Marga, but she didn't have a better idea for taking both their judgments into account. He was right that they should both have a say. Deferring to him seemed polite, but it might also be a way to dodge responsibility if things went wrong.

The sun was well up now. It was time. Hami bound Marga's hands in front of her.

Atop the promontory, the Citadel hulked sulkily. From afar, it looked more like a series of lumpy hillocks than a fortress; the low inner curtain wall was surrounded by a moat, ravelins (where the bombards were housed), and earthworks. It wasn't like an ordinary castle, with a clear facade and way in.

But they didn't need to get inside, just to be seen approaching. That part was easy; the only cover the plain offered was the burned-out shell of the mission.

They walked without speaking, conscious of the image they had to convey: a pale man shoving his captive ahead of him; an injured, exhausted woman with bound hands clasped atop her head. Hami held a sword in his right hand; the other sword, the one Marga had chosen for herself, was slung across his back as if he'd confiscated it from her.

The bombards seemed to follow their progress like cold, expressionless eyes.

The guards who were hunkered down beside the guns didn't speak or raise the alarm, apparently assessing the threat to be minimal. From a distance they would discern the contrasting complexions and take Marga for one of the Dog People and Hami for one of their own. Hami stopped twenty yards from the ravelins, pulling Marga roughly to a halt.

He shouted, "I demand to speak with Lieutenant Robinôt!"

"Who are you to demand any such thing?" one of the guards called back.

"I am Lord Hamish Tacques-Mouton, and I come bearing a message from Giles Foudria. Now fetch the lieutenant before Her Grace the Countess Mardou gets hurt."

They quickly determined who had the unenviable task of summoning the lieutenant. Marga called plaintively to the unfortunate loser as he climbed out of the ravelin, "Please, let my uncle know I'm alive!"

Hami shoved her to her knees; she gave an anguished cry.

The guard leaped down into the dry moat and scurried out of sight.

Robinôt must not have been far away, because within minutes he was clambering onto the grassy top of the ravelin. Marga knew it was his job to suspect that the people around him weren't what they seemed; he would be considering the possibility, even now, that she and Hami might be in cahoots. They didn't dare give him the smallest hook to hang his suspicions on.

Hami pressed his sword against her throat. He had to, but it still made her blood run cold.

Her hands were not particularly tightly bound; she started picking at the knot, confident that Robinôt would notice even these subtle, small movements.

"Ye Saints above, Countess," Lieutenant Robinôt drawled. "I could have told you that pursuing Foudria on your own would not end well. The arrogance of women, thinking they can tame a man with love. I trust you've learned your lesson."

His taunts put her mind at ease—her uncle had delivered her

notes, and Robinôt had read them. Whether he really believed them was another question.

"I confess myself surprised to see which side you've come down upon, Lord Hamish," Robinôt continued. "I knew there was something off about you, an unnatural sympathy for the Pelaguese, but I wouldn't have taken you for a traitor—a man of your illustrious pedigree!"

Sweat trickled into Marga's eye, but she didn't dare wipe it away. Uncle Claado still hadn't arrived; maybe he wasn't coming. Maybe he would come too late. At some point Robinôt would decide to kill or capture them; she wasn't sure how long a yarn Hami could spin before Robinôt lost patience.

She eyed the cannons, recalling what kinds of lethal shot they were likely loaded with. You wouldn't use iron balls here, like you would ship to ship; you'd use grapeshot or explosive shells. She and Hami could be very quickly dead.

"Ah, you fool, how I have fooled you," Hami was proclaiming behind her. "Now I will tell you how Giles Foudria and I have outwitted you every step of the way."

He told a good story—a remarkable story, which made Marga wonder how much of it might possibly be true—about how he'd been a spy in Ninys for more than thirty years, earning the trust of baronets and manipulating the political climate behind the scenes, trying to prevent or at least slow the colonization of the Archipelagos. He gave names and dates. Robinôt's hands opened and closed as if he were itching for a pen to write this down, all these traitors to report, these gullible fools who'd betrayed Count Pesavolta's trust. It soon became clear, though, that Pesavolta himself had been taken in by this pallid little man and his impeccable manners.

And yet Hami's best efforts had not been enough. The Ninysh were here. Even if the united Tshu and Aftisheshe won the day, Marga knew her people would be back again, wave after wave of second sons and Dariennes.

There was nothing for them at home, that was the trouble.

A clanking broke her reverie—the ratcheting crancquin of a cross-bow being wound. More than one crossbow, by the sound of it, in two separate ravelins. They were preparing to fire on Hami from two directions.

If she warned him, she'd give the game away. She hoped to Heaven he knew the sound.

There was a sickening twang, and then another. Hami batted one bolt out of the air with his sword and rolled to avoid the second. Marga couldn't help it: she screamed. Hami recovered his feet, grabbed her roughly, and forced her in front of him as a human shield.

He exhaled something that might have been "Sorry."

Marga wasn't sorry—she'd just finished untying her wrists, and here was Uncle Claado climbing up beside Robinôt. He had heard her scream and seen Hami manhandle her, and was now frantically berating the lieutenant: "How dare you let them fire upon my niece!"

Robinôt scowled deeply without replying. They weren't supposed to have missed.

It was time. "Napou . . ." She managed to make it sound like Hami's arm was choking her.

Her uncle turned to face her, anguish in his eyes.

With her newly freed hands, she made a Porphyrian nautical sign: *Giant squid.*

His eyes widened. That was their sign, their secret uncle-and-niece code for *All is well.*

It was time for Hami to start grandiloquently outlining his demands so that she could sign to her uncle, apparently under her captor's very nose.

"Here are the demands of His Eminence Giles Foudria—long may he lead us!" cried Hami. "First, we require that the governor-general fall upon his sword and all Ninysh forces surrender their arms."

The problem with Porphyrian nautical signs was that they mostly pertained to nautical things. Marga was going to have to approach certain subjects metaphorically and hope that her uncle—or

Robinôt—had enough imagination to understand what she really meant.

It was just one of the many ways this plan could fall through.

She signed: *Convey this message.* Then: *Large school of fish.*

Claado frowned, clearly not understanding, but then the best possible intervention happened: Robinôt noticed her signing. He held a whispered conference with her uncle.

"Thirdly," Hami was announcing behind her, "we require the removal of all buildings, shipyards, and debris from the bottom of the inlet."

Under Robinôt's apparent instruction, Claado signed back: *How many?*

Robinôt, at least, had deduced that she meant the Aftisheshe army.

Seven hundred, she signed. *And dogs.*

"Fifthly," Hami declaimed. He was growing hoarse; his light voice wasn't made for shouting. "Ninys will pay recompense for the slaughter of the Jovesh."

Where? her uncle signed at Robinôt's behest.

East-southeast. Three miles. Long strait. That was as close as she could get to *valley;* she hoped the lieutenant's imagination was up to it.

She coughed, letting Hami know she'd finished. It was time to wrap things up.

"Lastly: the Ninysh will abandon their ill-advised project of colonization and remove themselves from the Archipelagos entirely. These are the demands of General Giles Foudria," shouted Hami. "What answer shall I give him?"

General would hit Robinôt like a poke in the eye; for a fleeting second he was utterly transparent to her, but then he raised his sneer again. "Tell your so-called general that his petition would receive more serious consideration if he were to come in person."

This was it, the moment of truth: Did she think Hami should feign weakness or project strength? Her fencer's eye tried to gauge Robinôt's vanity and the gambles he'd be willing to take. She could almost see him adding up a ledger sheet of possible risks, likely gains, and inevitable losses. This was going to be a close thing.

What was the best way to put a thumb on the scales? What would draw him out from behind the walls with an army?

She whimpered, the prearranged signal to Hami, indicating her best guess for how to proceed: *Project strength.*

"You fool," Hami cried with the last dregs of his voice. "You don't know who you're dealing with. General Foudria—the Island Fox, the chess master—has you boxed into a corner and you can't even see it. You are in no position or condition to make demands."

Hami had agreed with her assessment; Marga almost melted with relief.

"I will return for your answer at this time tomorrow," the Ggdani croaked.

"You and what army?" Robinôt roared back, fully believing he knew.

Hami began an awkward, backward retreat across the plain, keeping Marga in position to shield him from crossbow bolts. Uncle Claado looked like a kicked puppy, but she dared not signal him again, lest she press her case too far. It was not too late to overplay her hand.

Once out of crossbow range, they were finally able to turn their backs on the Citadel, but Marga still had to pretend to be Hami's prisoner all the way to the valley encampment. This was for the benefit of the scouts that Robinôt (please Heaven) was scurrying to send after them even now, to affirm that the Aftisheshe army was just as she'd described it, not too large and in an eminently ambushable position.

She would be tied up very visibly in the center of camp (she understood why, even if she didn't like it). The miraculously alive Giles Foudria, a thorn in Robinôt's side for so long, would be strutting around camp giving orders; he'd be taller and stouter than the original, but his genuinely injured leg would go a long way toward convincing the scouts that this was a man who'd recently and improbably escaped an exploding ship.

The scouts would see exactly what the Aftisheshe wanted them to see: a force that could be beaten once and for all, if the Ninysh were bold enough to venture outside their walls. Who in their right mind would choose to endure a long and painful siege when the war might be ended with a single raid? That was the argument she expected Robinôt to make to the generals.

They didn't know the Tshu proverb, the hard-won wisdom of a hundred years: *Never let the Bootmakers choose the battleground.*

Thirty-Eight

*V*oice of the World, sing to us now.
Help us remember. Show us compassion.
Once upon a time, after the war was over, the poet Kluit taught her grandchildren thus:

Here is how the tide of the incursion turned.

The incomers from the Land of the Dead called themselves Ninysh. Island after island had fallen to their spears, their cannons, and their enormous ships. Some now say that they weren't worthy, that they let their cannons do the fighting for them. This is not true. I faced them, and I vouch that they were brave.

But there were things they didn't understand. In Edushuke, they let the Bootmakers choose the battleground. A Ggdani Watcher and one of their own women tricked them into sending an army to Long Red Valley—yes, that valley, the one our saddest dirges refer to, the one your ancestors watered again and again with their blood.

But we have renounced vengeance.
We gave away that blood, squandered it;
Let no one claim it was stolen from us.

It was nice to have the Aftisheshe and their trickery on our side for once. They will show you what you want to see, embroider you a flowery path to a victory so certain you'd be a fool not to rush after it. It is always an illusion. They know their own islands, and they are using the very landscape against you.

I had considered these Ninysh rather clever, digging in their fortress and clearing the plain in front of it. For a generation, they forced the Aftisheshe to come to them and fight them on their own terms. They did not seem to see that while their fortress protected them, it had also become a cage.

It had certainly never occurred to them that it should be tiger-proof.

While they were throwing good warriors down the gullet of the Long Red, we were approaching their fortress's flank—from a direction they never anticipated—with a blizzard of ice tigers. But here, I've made a song about it:

> *I, Kluit, daughter of the sun and moon,*
> *Daughter of pine pollen and the swollen sea,*
> *Sing you this song on behalf of my tiger-patron, Meketsh.*
>
> *Upon Edushuke's beak stood the Ninysh Citadel,*
> *And before it spread a broad, blasted plain;*
> *All who crossed that plain would be cut down,*
>
> *So we went around. From the tip of the inlet, we wound*
> *Through the empty shipyards and the ruined town.*
> *Our tigers stalked the gray predawn.*
>
> *Broken masts jutted out of the sound,*
> *Charred corpse fingers; the town had been a pyre,*
> *Ravaged by fire. The heart within me cried.*

Alas, this was war. We would all lose more.
The Nutufi say: Do not throw good lives away,
But consider well who needs to die, and why,

For Nutufi's sake, for Paishesh and Pa'-Jovesh,
For all who remain in the Dead's cruel way,
Their incursion ends at last upon this shore.

A winding road burrowed through the cliffs,
Sheltered from their guns and from their sight.
We crept up from below as it grew light.

How did the Deadlanders feel, at first,
To see a hundred tigers burst out of that tunnel?
It was like the glorious birth of the world.

Some laughed, some stood in shock, some raged.
Their guns, thunderously futile, roared dismay
To realize that they could not kill us all.

The ravelins round their guns had stumped
The Aftisheshe hounds for years,
But they were nothing to our tigers.

They leaped! No words can catch their grace.
Meketsh soared through the air like a tern,
And I, astride her, sang bright hymns of war.

In our shadow, gunners wet themselves.
The smart ones fled; the stubborn stayed,
Faced claws and fangs, and soon were dead.

The cannons were ours, caught with ease.
Those belching, roaring cast-iron beasts
Are not so awful once their keepers flee.

We did not pause on the bulwarks, though.
From that height, we could leap the dry moat.
Soon tigers filled the whole star-fort.

The army was off facing death in the vale;
The fortress held townsfolk, the wounded, some sailors.
They fought us awhile, until wisdom prevailed.

I know what you expect from a story,
To hear war is glorious, valorous, right.
It was necessary, but it still weighs on me.

Eighteen, I killed. I will carry them forever,
Their weeping faces, contorted in fear,
Not at all ready to see their "Heaven."

As is necessary, I have done restitution.
I have been cleansed with the priest's ablution.
War, just or unjust, is still a transgression.

Listen well, children of the sea's swelling:
Glory in victory, but do not glory in killing.
Only tigers may kill without mourning.

Thirty-Nine

Tess, while others fought their war, dreamed forward.

She did whatever the old people of Mivikh needed of her—weeding, herding upuki, winding skeins of dog-wool yarn, pressing rukkefa into molds—physical labor that left her plenty of time to plot and plan her way forward. She still had to get Pathka to Kapatlutlo. She did not know the islands and their channels, but she was beginning to realize it was more important to know which nations lived between here and there, and how to approach them.

Kikiu, who knew the wind-speech, might agree to translate. Then she just needed a boat.

First things first, however—she would ask the old-timers in the weaving workshop for their advice. One weaver, a younger woman named Emaisha, was one of the few people left behind who spoke Ninysh. Tess asked if she would translate, and she agreed. Tess sat with the children, winding skeins, but raised her voice to address the elders at their looms. "Respected elders, I could use your advice. I need to travel south from here. Who will I encounter as I go, and how do I approach them so they will let me travel on?"

As Tess had anticipated, the elders were full of opinions. The Tshu would expect a demonstration of bravado—even Tess had had some inkling of that. Tess would not get far with the Wandering Cities unless she had something novel to show them. After much discussion, the elders decided a quigutl might do. When it came to the Murkh, however, there was some vehement disagreement. At first Tess thought maybe the elders didn't know, or that the Aftisheshe weren't friends with the Murkh. The argument was of a different nature, however.

"They want to know one thing," said Emaisha, gesturing with her shuttle. "What is your reason for going south? I warn you: you must be completely honest."

"I'm trying to save the life of my friend," said Tess. Emaisha translated. No one blinked or spoke. "The quigutl," Tess added, hoping that would help.

The eldest elder, a woman named Bayekh, spoke: "Your friendship with those creatures is curious—and admirable. I will vouch for you." She snapped her crooked fingers, and one of the children brought her a spindle whorl—a flat disk with a hole in the center—and a jar of dye. Using a tassel for a brush, the eldest elder dipped the end in dye and began drawing on the disk, so beautifully that you would have thought she was a painter and not a weaver.

She presented Tess with the painted whorl. Tess took it carefully, balancing it on her fingertips so as not to smudge the wet dye.

"They will know that this was made for you by an Aftisheshe elder," said Bayekh, through Emaisha. "And that I would not have done such a thing if I did not believe you."

Tess was particularly anxious to ask about the last nation she would encounter, but she realized the presentation of the disk was, itself, a kind of test. "Thank you," she said. "I appreciate your faith in me."

Bayekh and the others looked pleased. Tess hoped that meant it was safe to ask her next question: "But what about the last nation—the Ggdani?"

That, none of them knew. They'd only ever met one Ggdani, the one who'd helped coax the Ninysh out of the Citadel. He'd apparently struck them as conscientious but inflexible. "You'll have to ask him," said Emaisha at last. "We counsel humility."

At noon, when they broke for naps, Tess returned to Berekka's to feed the upuki and prepare Spira's dosages. While she was honored to have received the eldest elder's spindle whorl (it had dried and was in her pocket now), she wished they could have reassured her about the pole and its people. Fozu had told her she would never reach it without the Ggdani's blessing; the old explorers had backed him up. It would be tremendously frustrating to convince the Tshu, Wandering Cities, and Murkh to let her pass, only to have the Ggdani turn her back.

Tess had tried all along to find ways to make herself worthy, since that was the only other hint Fozu had given her. Not everything had worked; Martin still pricked her conscience, as well as that war she'd almost started and the displacement of the Nutufi. But she'd enabled Fozu to give his history to the sabak, and she'd set the sabak free. She'd confronted Lady Borgo at the last (for all the good that had done). Father Erique . . . she didn't know what had become of him, but he was probably back out in the world despite her best efforts. Tess felt quite certain—Seraphina's insistence upon the value of intentions notwithstanding—that she was going to be judged by results and not attempts.

Fine: she'd helped Spira and Berekka after the harbor blew. She was still helping Spira, and Spira and Hami seemed to mean something to each other.

Even as she thought that, Tess knew in her heart that personal considerations wouldn't sway Hami. Hami would do whatever he perceived his duty to be, every personal consideration in the world be damned.

As Tess climbed the last hill toward Berekka's house, Kikiu bolted out the door. "Help me!" she cried, spotting Tess. "We have to move my mother before ko burns the house down."

Tess ran after Kikiu, leaping the high doorsill and startling Spira. Together, Tess and Kikiu managed to drag Pathka's cocoon out from under the bed. It was beginning to smoke.

"Hurry!" cried Kikiu as they hauled it into the road. "Now leave it. Back off!"

At first the cocoon smoked silently, twitching and rattling at fitful intervals. Then something flexed under the surface—Pathka's head spines trying to rise. There was a sound like a cat coughing up a hair ball, and then the cocoon burst into flames.

Tess gave a cry of alarm and a sympathetic lurch, as if she wanted to run to Pathka and help (as if there were anything she could do). Kikiu planted herself in front of Tess's feet, keeping her a safe distance back.

A plume of flaming fragments—like leaves or paper—whirled on the updraft, most quickly extinguishing themselves. Pathka, now female, crawled out of her crumbling cinder cage. Kikiu rushed up to greet her, but Pathka flattened herself to the ground and hissed.

Kikiu froze. "Mother," she said in ordinary Quootla, "it's me, Kikiu."

Pathka got shakily to her feet and walked in a tight circle like a broken windup toy.

"Are you usually disoriented, coming out of thuthmeptha?" asked Tess.

"I wouldn't know," said Kikiu.

Someone behind Tess cleared her throat. Spira stood on the porch of Berekka's house, frowning pointedly at the quigutl. "Your quigutl is concussed. Did you drop it on its head?"

"No!" cried Tess, trying to recall whether she had. The cocoon had been through a lot.

"I'm telling you," Spira insisted, "I've seen this before. Our headmistress at the orphanage used to throw quigutl against the walls when they displeased her—or when the orphans did. Their little brains can only take a couple hard blows at most."

Kikiu considered, head spines twitching. "Ko might have been concussed when Anathuthia was killed," she said. "But this is something more. It's the strangeness."

"Thuthmeptha was supposed to slow its progression," cried Tess.

"Well, it didn't. Ko is worse, and running out of time."

"How do we get her to Kapatlutlo like this?" said Tess. Pathka was biting at a patch of weeds beside the path. "She doesn't seem to know us."

"All is not lost," said Kikiu with a new gentleness. "While the Katakutia are assisting the armies, they left the harbor full of Mindlets. I think they can help."

"Pathka did seem more clearheaded while the sabak was on board," said Tess.

Kikiu waggled an eye cone at her. "They can't cure this—only the Wider Mind can do that—but they might be a stopgap and a balm."

Tess and Kikiu slowly herded Pathka toward the harbor; they accumulated an entourage of curious onlookers as they crossed town. Pathka snapped at anyone who tried to touch her.

Mivikh harbor, like all Aftisheshe harbors, was a cove carved into the cliffs, accessible only by a narrow stairway. Tess saw no sabak at first. Kikiu raised her chin and whistled eerily, like the wind through trees, and suddenly a constellation glowed under the water, a dozen or more. They raised their noses to the surface and whistled back, a choir of intricate, layered notes that echoed off the stone walls and danced upon the dark face of the water.

Kikiu nudged her mother, then head-butted and nipped at her, until there was nowhere left for Pathka to go but the water. She fell off the dock with a clumsy splash, and then sabak surrounded her, buoying her up in a corona of blue light.

"They want to talk to you, Teth," said Kikiu. "Prepare yourself, and enter the water."

Tess's heart recoiled. "Do I have a choice?" she asked Kikiu.

"You always have a choice," said Kikiu. "But you always choose the same thing."

"No I don't," Tess objected, but at the back of her mind she heard that voice again.

You, too, did what was easiest.

And still, she couldn't bear the thought of getting in the water.

In the center of the swimming sabak, a darker, scaly head popped out of the water and looked around. "Teth?" said Pathka. "I hope I didn't scare you. All will be well."

Tess waved, unable to speak around the lump in her throat.

"Ko may stay here with us," Kikiu announced. "Until such time as the Mindlets have to scatter to the winds with the Wind Kin. Then ko will need to find a way to the Most Alone."

With that, Kikiu dived into the crystalline water and joined the others.

When the war ended, the stories returned to Mivikh before the fighters did.

The Tshu had captured the Citadel with few casualties. The civilians of St. Fionnani town—who'd sheltered in the Citadel and been left behind when the army moved out to Long Red Valley—had not been keen to take up arms against tigers. They had sensibly surrendered once the fort's military resistance crumbled. There was still some question of what to do with these settlers, but this was for the Aftisheshe to answer, not the Tshu. A delegation of elders was dispatched from Mivikh to help settle the matter.

The Battle of the Valley was hard-fought, with many casualties on both sides, but in the end the Aftisheshe had prevailed. Lieutenant Robinôt had been captured alive; he'd grown in symbolic stature as rumors had circulated of the plans he'd made with Lord Morney to cleanse the islands of their peoples as efficiently as possible. The two men had intended to use every terrible tool one could imagine— poison, disease, fire, imprisonment, slaughtering people like animals. It was almost too awful to believe, and yet this Lord Morney had been killed by sabak the moment they'd gleaned the truth of him. That was a judgment, and not to be taken lightly.

A war court was convened upon the field of battle. Aftisheshe and Tshu sentenced Lieutenant Robinôt to be left upon an iceberg of a tiger's choosing. A longboat was dispatched to do the deed at once.

The fighters came home, bearing their dead, who were quickly commended to the care of their gods. After the funerals—or maybe because of them, Tess wasn't sure—an enormous bonfire was lit in the place where "Vulkharai" had been performed. Aftisheshe and Tshu alike gathered there, singing, dancing, drinking the okush the Tshu had thoughtfully brought with them in seven sloshing sealskins. Tess found Jacomo and Marga there, and let herself be smothered in a hug.

"How was the Battle of the Valley?" Tess cried. "Tell me everything."

"I didn't fight," said Jacomo, releasing her. "And nothing I saw made me want to learn."

Marga smiled enigmatically. "I'll go fetch us some okush," she said, and went to do that.

Tess and Jacomo watched her go. "Did *she* fight?" asked Tess.

"She did. I glean it was less amusing than dueling noblemen in town," said Jacomo. "In fact, I would suggest we change the subject altogether."

When Marga returned with the mugs of okush, however, she changed it for them. "My uncle reports that the *Avodendron* is unsalvageable," she said as she distributed mugs, in a tone that suggested this was supposed to be a cheerful turn of conversation. "He's retiring from the sea. He means to stay here and learn to build kuros."

"And the crew?" asked Tess. There were a hundred of them to account for, at least.

"Some will make their way home, some may stay," said Marga. "The people of St. Fionnani town, and all transients who happened to be stuck there when the fighting broke out, have been given a choice: to leave peacefully, or to stay on, accepting Aftisheshe sovereignty and Aftisheshe laws."

Marga took a swig of okush and wiped her mouth on her sleeve. "Argol is staying. Argol will finally be a captain on her own terms."

That was good news, at least. They all clinked their mugs together.

Jacomo made a face as he swallowed his drink. "So how are we getting home?"

"I'm not sure yet. Something will present itself, I hope," said Marga. She drank deeply and then looked up at the stars. "Now listen, you two, there's something I wanted to say before the battle. I've thought of a way to renounce my title while still keeping Pesavolta's grubby hands off my estate. We become priests."

"What, all of us?" asked Jacomo, as if he'd never considered doing such a thing.

"Even Tess. But let me finish—we start our own order, and then I give my estate over to it," said Marga. "Then we can use my fortune for good in the way we see fit, without fear of Pesavolta snatching it if he doesn't approve of every little thing we do. That's how we stop our people—the common people of Ninys, at least—from invading the Archipelagos. Give them purpose and dignity, a reason to stay, and not by swooping in to save them, but by sidekicking."

That last word made Tess think the okush had gone straight to Marga's head, but Jacomo elbowed the erstwhile countess, laughing, and Marga elbowed him right back. There was clearly some joke between them that Tess wasn't party to.

"I would free my serfs," said Marga. "And there would be no hierarchy among us."

"I don't see how that's going to work if you're a religious order," interjected Tess. "The church is hierarchical. The *Saints* are hierarchical."

"We get to choose," said Marga. "And we get to tell the Saints' tales our own way. And we will call this benevolent endeavor . . . the Society for the Prevention of Future Dariennes."

"That doesn't sound as charitable as you seem to think it does," said Jacomo, a spark of fond amusement in his eye.

Marga laughed and leaned her head against the side of his arm.

He hesitated, then put the arm around her shoulders. "My brain is tired," she said. "You come up with a name."

"The Beneficent Order of St. Pandowdy," said Jacomo as if he'd already been thinking this through. "We could call ourselves Walkers."

Tess had not been considering joining them, not even a little bit, but *Walkers* sent a chill down her spine. She could picture herself as a Walker. She'd already been one, kind of—walking from place to place, helping them that needed it. She could travel the Southlands again, spreading purpose and dignity, dropping by Segosh to see Josquin and avoiding the places where she might run into her mother. . . .

The thought of her mother dampened her enthusiasm. Anyway, what was she thinking? She couldn't go. She still had to take Pathka to the pole.

"Is there a cricket down your shirt?" Marga was suddenly asking Jacomo. He swatted at his chest a few times, then got a supremely foolish look on his face. He pulled on the gold chain around his neck, fishing out the square pendant thnik, the source of the chirping. Unlike Tess, he seemed to have managed not to ruin his thnik with seawater.

"Jackie!" crackled his brother Richard's voice. "Where are you? Who's singing?"

"Sorry, these folks have just won a war," said Jacomo, stepping away from bonfire and crowd; Tess and Marga followed. "They're a bit exuberant. I'm a little drunk. What's going on?"

"I'm calling to congratulate you—you're an uncle!"

Jacomo gave a startled laugh and looked at Tess. "So . . . so Tess is an aunt?"

"Yes, you clever scholar," said Richard. "You're drunker than you think."

It was a girl, and they'd named her Verica Sandrine. Tess hardly heard the rest; she was counting frantically in her head, trying to work out what month it was, because it seemed to her that the baby should not have come yet, and if that was true—

She couldn't take it anymore. She burst out: "Did she come early? Is everyone all right?"

"Almost a month early," said Richard. "But our Verica gave a lusty cry, so the midwife says all is well. Your sister is sleeping now, but she would love to talk to you. . . ."

Tess could only nod in response, because a fear she hadn't known she was carrying was finally loosening its talons from her heart. And then Jacomo and Marga were folding her in another hug, because apparently she was crying.

Mind of the World, the circle is closing. Show us the one we were surprised to love.

Spira's eyelids flicked open, once, twice, and there he was, that dear, small Snow Lord, and for a fleeting instant everything was all right. Spira was where teu belonged—was *teu* again, this time maybe for good.

"I told myself . . . to hold on until you got here," said Spira, letting teur eyes fall closed.

Berekka had been horrified by teur sudden turn for the worse, but it hadn't seemed sudden to Spira. The new herbs had been only minimal help all along; the algal tincture had done nothing but make patches of algae spring up behind Spira's knees (admittedly, those were mildly soothing). Spira had lasted this long only by eating Aganat's salve. *That* had been so potent that Spira had been up and about the day the quigutl hatched, but when it wore off, teur joints, which had slowly been turning molten from the inside out, were instantly aflame.

Every joint. Where ribs connected, spine, nose, ears, anything cartilaginous.

Hami laid a hand over Spira's, light as a butterfly, trying not to hurt teu. Spira turned teur hand over underneath it, so teur inflamed fingers could touch Hami's cool palm.

"I've brought you something," said Hami. Spira dragged teur lids open and saw a cup in his hand. "It's sabaggatg. Just a few drops in okush. It will help, although not permanently."

"Don't tell me you held some back from your sacrifice," Spira mumbled, trying to tease him. His face suggested teu was not succeeding.

"I did not," said Hami. "And I'm now in debt to a Tshu. But if you will drink this, my . . . my dear, the Tshu has offered her family's longboat to take us to my people. You should be well enough to travel that far, and then I will take you to the One, who will heal you fully."

It hurt to even hope for that. Spira whispered, "Impossible."

"Possible," said Hami. "It comes with obligations—don't imagine this is simple. The first step is for you to drink this, though."

Spira nodded assent, and then Hami cradled teur head and put the cup to teur lips.

The warmth was instantaneous, although Spira suspected that was the okush. It spread beyond teur esophagus and stomach, though, radiating outward—it was light as much as heat, and it overpowered any pain it encountered, like a hot iron smoothing a wrinkled linen cloth. The sabaggatg untangled knots, planed jagged edges, quenched fires, stilled tempests, paused the very planets in their orbits.

For a moment, Spira saw it all. Teu was *everywhere*—among the stars, upon the waters, in the chambers of teur own beating heart. Teu was made of mind, and the mind was unfathomable.

Understanding was electrifying.

And then teu was back in Berekka's little bed, looking up at a man with tears in his violet eyes and wondering how much time had passed. If time was a thing that happened anymore.

"May I?" said Hami, reaching out. Spira had barely nodded before he'd wrapped teu fiercely in his arms, something that would have been agony before.

And it was delightful, but not as delightful as not hurting. Who knew *normal* could feel so euphorically good?

Spira was still marveling, still wrapped in this warmth, when the door flew open and Tess burst in on them, out of breath and wild-eyed. Spira didn't mind—nothing on this earth hurt right now—but Hami seemed annoyed at having the moment interrupted. He leaped to his feet and tugged at the hem of his doublet.

"I'm told you're leaving for the pole tomorrow," said Tess, her urgency overriding her manners. Spira could see (this was new) that the girl immediately regretted not giving full courtesy before speaking, but it was too late now. "I want to go with you. My friend Pathka—"

"Out of the question," said Hami.

"Everyone says, *Ask the Ggdani, he'll judge if you're worthy, you can't get there unless the Ggdani says so*," cried Tess, throwing up her hands. "And I have been trying to be worthy, in fact, but then I come here to talk to you and you won't even let me finish my story."

"I know your story," said Hami. "The sabak know it, the Katakutia know it, it is everywhere. And I don't know who told you you had to be *worthy* of the One, but that's not how it works.

"Do you imagine I know the One personally? That we Ggdani all eat Voorka pie with her every afternoon? Even we do not lightly visit the One. I've seen her once, when I was consecrated as Watcher. I will be calling upon every bit of favor and influence I possess—and borrowing a lot more—just to get Spira to her. I don't have anything extra to spare for a mere tourist like you!"

The girl was blinking and stammering, as red as if she'd been slapped.

Spira still didn't like her, but Spira also didn't like *that.*

"Hami," Spira murmured, reaching out to tug on his Aftisheshe tunic. In an instant, Hami was on his knees beside the bed, leaning in so Spira only had to whisper to be heard. "Hami, she helped me. Quite a lot. And she didn't have to."

"My love," he whispered back, "be that as it may, I can't—"

"I know. But surely you could take the . . . the quigutl."

Hami went still as a stone; Spira watched him think (recognizing, fleetingly, how it had felt to be Mind). Finally he nodded slightly and stood up again. Spira felt teuself melt more fully into the bed, as if some burden had been taken off.

". . . the quigutl doesn't need our permission," Spira heard him saying as teu drifted in and out. ". . . it can travel the last leg under the ice with the sabak . . . the best I can do . . ."

Sleep was a fuzzy upuki. Spira woke when Hami sat on the edge of the bed.

"She agreed," he said, brushing a wisp of hair off Spira's forehead, "although she hated to give up her right to see it done. I can understand that. Sometimes you get so focused on your task that you grip it too hard and it hurts to let go."

"I'm glad we can do this for her," said Spira muzzily, then wondered at the words. Teur mouth seemed to have spoken teur heart, without any intercession from teur brain.

Except . . . it was all the same thing. That was the secret.

"Don't tell me you've forgiven her?" asked Hami.

"No," said Spira. "I have only so much forgiveness in me, it seems, and I'm going to need every bit of it for someone else." Teu didn't bother staring pointedly; Hami knew who the guilty party was.

Anyway, Spira didn't have to forgive Tess or even like her to suspect that the world was better off with her in it, or to *know* for a fact that helping her was the correct thing to do. It was the principle of the thing, teu decided, nestling up against Hami's leg. And that wasn't just the vision of the Worldmind talking; Spira had begun to understand it for weeks now, to see glimpses of good in her even when teu didn't want to. It wasn't the things she'd done for Spira (these had struck teu as manipulative and pandering, right up to the end), but the way she'd cared for those stinky, revolting quigutl. She *loved* them. Spira didn't see how that was possible.

To love the unlovable, though. That was surely the profoundest miracle.

And there was Hami's hand upon teur cheek, as proof.

Tess—the girl who loved quigutl, the girl who'd gripped her task too hard and made promises she couldn't keep—spent a terrible night alone on the cliffs, racked by grief and rage. She coughed up every hard feeling imaginable, and even though her mind knew better, there was no way not to feel all of it.

She'd failed. Her promises meant nothing. Her entire purpose had been stolen from her, and now she had nothing. She would never see Pathka again. She wasn't strong or capable enough, whatever the Ggdani had tried to tell her. And then those damned sabak, telling her she always took the easy way out . . .

"Does this look easy to you?" she shouted at the sea, her voice echoing.

Every feeling reeled and buffeted her, but she endured them all, and when they'd blown themselves down to a more manageable size, she threw each one over the cliff, crying, "Breakfast for sharks!"

It kind of helped. Mostly it left her feeling empty, which wasn't so terrible.

When the sun came up, drying her cheeks, she saw a tall ship out on the water—not a sort she recognized, but indisputably some Deadlander vessel. She stood up, brushing off her knees. It seemed to be circling the island, but very slowly.

Marga and Jacomo were right, that this wasn't over. Maybe she should join their order. She didn't see many other ways forward at the moment. She stumbled back to town.

The longboat carrying Hami, Spira, and Pathka south was to leave that day from the place the Tshu had landed, a gracefully curving pebble beach with tall sea stacks at either end, half a day's journey from Mivikh. Tess joined a great convoy of people traveling there together; many Tshu were leaving at the same time, now that the funerals were finished. Spira was carried along by dogcart, as was Pathka. Tess walked alongside the quigutl, her hand on Pathka's head, her heart too full to speak. Kikiu was behind, now ahead, now running around them in circles.

When they reached the bay, two ships were already out in the water, rowing away from shore and beating their gongs for the tigers to follow. Once the cats were all in the water, the other ships began loading. Hami, Spira, and Pathka were traveling in Kluit's family longboat, although Kluit was staying behind for now. "I will go another way and see how the Nutufi are getting along, if they've found a place to settle or if they need my help," she explained (Kikiu translating). "I'm never home for long. My family like that about me."

Tess helped Pathka down from the dogcart, pulled off her boots, and waded with the quigutl alongside the beached longboat. Pathka climbed up the side and stopped at the top of the railing to look back at Tess. "Be well, Teth," she said. "Don't feel sad that you can't come the rest of the way. You came farther than you had to already."

"Can I be sad because I'll miss you?" said Tess.

Pathka touched Tess's cheek with her padded fingers. "We're still nest. Only our nest is as big as the world."

Then Pathka dropped down into the belly of the longboat and Tess stepped away. Her whole face hurt from trying not to cry.

Hami and Spira went aboard, and then Kluit's husbands and grown children shoved off and began pulling at the oars. The boat gradually maneuvered itself into deeper water. Tess waded alongside until the water was up to her stomach, then up to her shoulders, not caring how cold it was, not wanting to see the last of Pathka.

Back on dry land, Kikiu began to sing in the wind-speech:

> *Mother, farewell! Go to your rest,*
> *While I, your nest, a new-hatched priest,*
> *Go back. It is my lot, my heart, my work,*
> *To tell our people where you've gone*
> *And help them understand the rest.*

Sunlight glittered on the water all around Tess, dazzling her eyes, and then she noticed a glow under the water as well. A herd of sabak were swimming around her in an elaborate pattern, some clockwise, some widdershins, weaving in and out.

She knew what they wanted, and her instinct was to balk—but no. No, she would not. She would do the more difficult thing, and swallow her fear, and show these arrogant, oversized newts what she was made of.

Tess laid her hand flat upon the face of the sea, daring them to touch her.

And then we were together once more, and we saw all she had accomplished and endured, and what she thought of us. She was hot defiance, and it stung a bit, but we understood.

"None of this was easy," she pushed back at us.

"And yet none of it was as hard as the thing that is hardest," we replied, as soothingly as we could. "You would rather face whirlpools, storms, endless ice, and certain death than go back home and face the things that are yours."

She was stunned. "If you're talking about my mother, that I should make peace and forgive her, you can go right to hell," she said.

"Not your mother," we said, "but near enough to be frightening. Near enough that you may be unable to see what you—and only you—can do."

Words weren't working. We showed her a vision: two young girls in regal finery, a princess and a duchess, Z. and V. Between them on a table was a map of the world.

She was silent, but we felt her understanding dawning.

"Home is hard," we said, "but at home you know the rules and how to break them. You know the pitfalls, and you know what the goals are. We know you are afraid, but you're not returning to the past. You're going

into the future, for the future. These are the mountains that are yours to move."

She didn't answer. She didn't promise. But her understanding had hardened to a diamond.

And then Tess was back in the water, gasping. The tide must have been rising while she communed with the Little Lights, because it was so deep she was treading water now. She paddled back until she could touch bottom, and waded the rest of the way to shore.

Kluit, grinning at her, called Kikiu over to translate. "You look like someone who's been given a holy task by the Lights."

"I might be," said Tess. It came out rather glumly, but she wasn't actually sure how she felt yet.

Kluit laughed uproariously. "You definitely are. None of us are happy to know our purpose at first, little trout. It always seems too big to manage, or too mundane to endure. But I'll tell you a thing I've learned in forty-seven years: there's more than one way a story can end, even with destiny in it. Your life is still yours, whatever they told you."

"I'll try and remember that," said Tess.

The gray-green woman grabbed Tess's head in a ferocious embrace. "Get it done quickly and well, in that case, so that you may come to Tshu and see us again. We'll find you a husband—two husbands! And a tiger."

This made Tess laugh, which mitigated some of the terror she'd been feeling. There were still so many ways this could go—and it was nice to think there would be a tiger waiting for her afterward.

The crowd on the strand, mostly Aftisheshe by this point, broke out in worried murmurs. Tess followed their pointing fingers and saw a tall ship gliding into view, the same one she'd seen before, only now it was flying the Goreddi flag. Tess couldn't read the name, but the figurehead was a lady all covered in golden flowers, and Tess had no doubt that this was the *Marigold*, sent by Seraphina after however many weeks of thnimi silence on Tess's part.

Tess glanced around until she spotted Marga and Jacomo, who had also come down to see the longboats off. They'd noticed the *Marigold* as well and were chatting eagerly together as Tess approached. "Are you sure you're ready?" Jacomo was saying.

Marga, her eyes shining, said, "Let's go sidekick the world."

And Tess couldn't help smiling then—at their eagerness, at all the work before them. She caught their eyes and nodded, to show them she was ready.

It was time to head out, into the next story.

Epilogue

Mind of the World, open your eyes.

He tried. He couldn't. His whole being was an extended groan.

Not those eyes. The eyes of your mind.

He did not understand how to comply, and yet somehow he did it. His mind unfolded like a flower and he perceived a dazzling brightness like sun on the water.

"Where am I?" he cried without sound.

Here, we replied. *We found you after your ship exploded, and we carried you here.*

"Am I dead?" His fear rippled outward, cold against the cheek of dawn.

No, we replied. *Although in the way you probably mean it . . . yes.*

He panicked a little, struggled. It was hard to hold him.

Look around, we said. *We asked you to open your eyes. Try to remember what eyes are for.*

He calmed, and he looked.

Everything he remembered was here, and everything he didn't remember. There were sunsets over icebergs, classrooms full of dusty charts, his heart at war with his mind. There was his father's death, which he hadn't seen before, and the miles and miles of guilt, of which he knew every inch. There was an eerily familiar boy, unloved by his lordly grandfather, breaking his grief upon the back of the world; there was another boy, who'd died as an infant in arms, grown in his mother's imagination and frolicking upon the verdant lawn of her dreams. There were four dead dragons frozen in a starlit sea, and two women he had loved—both brown, one with blue hair and one with a gleaming sword.

For the first time, he saw the vast, extended pattern of the web, and it eased his heart.

"Where am I?" he asked again, less anguished this time.

In memory, we answered. *In story and in history. Before the beginning and after the end.*

This is the place where the threads all cross.

You are the Mind of the World, perceiving itself.

You are the Hand of the World, enacting itself.

You are the Voice of the World, speaking its truth.

Remember, Fozu.

And be at peace.

Acknowledgments

No book is an island. My deepest thanks to those who've helped me keep this one afloat.

Fearless sailors: Jen van Tassel, Arushi Raina, KC, KY, TA, my sisters, my mother, my brilliant students, CL, TE, the QuasiModals, Dori Jaffe, Rosaria Munda

Navigators who kept me off the shoals: Karen New, Fran Wilde, Wayde Compton, Brent Draney, Phoebe North, Leah Bobet, and others (you know who you are, and I hope you know I'm grateful). Any scrapes I've gotten into are my own doing.

The stars in their firmament: N. K. Jemison, Amal El-Mohtar, Cutcha Risling Baldy, Charlie Jane Anders, Robert Sapolsky, Chelsea Vowel, Matthew Salesses, Alexandra Erin, Nafiza Azad

Able shipwrights who made us seaworthy: Jim Thomas, Dan Lazar, Jenna Lettice, Mallory Loehr, the whole crew at Penguin Random House

Musicians on the fo'c'sle: Gesualdo, William Byrd, TF, Porcupine Tree, Thank You Scientist, Adam Neely, VOLA, Iarla Ó Lionáird

And the dear ones I've shared a dinghy with through plague times: S, B, and U

Cast of Characters

On the Good Ship Avodendron

Tess Dombegh—world traveler, aspiring naturalist, trying to do right in the world

Jacomo—youngest son of the Duke of Ducana; Tess's brother-in-law and friend

Pathka—a quigutl, friend of Tess

Kikiu—a quigutl, offspring of Pathka

Margarethe, Countess Mardou—leader of the expedition, a dashing swordswoman

Captain Claado—her uncle, captain of the *Avodendron*

Darienne—her maid, serfing faithfully

Karus—a Lucky sailor, since before it was legal

Argol—his offspring, Lucky in more ways than one

Glodus—a pockmarked sailor of mean disposition

Mr. Darvo—the bosun

Lord Morney—the countess's partner, in more ways than one, whose contraption is in the hold

Giles Foudria—the countess's ex-navigator, a man she thought she knew

On the *Sweet Jessia,* the Dragon Expedition

Spira—a dragon scholar who has a history with Tess
Lord Hamish Tacques-Mouton—the enforcer of southern treaties
Fekra—one of the dragon grad students under Spira's supervision

The Ones We Left Behind

Professor the Dragon Ondir—sent Spira to the ends of the earth
William of Affle—Tess's bad ex-boyfriend, finally behind her
Josquin—Tess's good ex-boyfriend, fondly remembered
Anne-Marie—Tess's mother, still unforgiven
Jeanne—Tess's twin, pregnant and worried
Lord Richard—Jacomo's brother; Jeanne's handsome husband
Their baby—yet to be named
Lord Heinrigh—Jacomo's other brother, the unsubtle one
Lionel Pfanzlig, Duke of Ducana—Jacomo's father
Griss—the Pfanzlig family's gamekeeper, long ago
Seraphina—Tess's half sister, a half-dragon, considered a Saint by some
Queen Glisselda—Queen of Goredd
Queen Lavonda—her grandmother, deceased
Prince Consort Lucian Kiggs—Queen Glisselda's official spouse; her cousin
Princess Zythia—the official baby of the royal cousins
Mother Philomela—a nun of Tess's acquaintance
Frai Moldi—a monk of Tess's acquaintance
Father Erique—a terrible priest of Tess's acquaintance
Angelica—Erique's long-suffering serving girl, now free of him
Master Bartomeo Tacques—the countess's sword master, long ago
Albaro des Fleris—the countess's husband, dead of a rosebush
Count Pesavolta—the ruler of Ninys, possibly a usurper
Anathuthia—the Continental Serpent, now dead

Colonizers of the Archipelagos

Lord Aveli—the lord governor of the penal colony at St. Vittorius

Aganat—the dragon who perfected black powder

Governor Boqueton—the lord governor of St. Claresse

Lord Morney—again, sorry; some people take up more space than they should

Lieutenant Robinôt—a member of Sixth Division; a friend of Lord Morney

Lady Aemelia Borgo—the baronetta of St. Remy, having inherited it from her father

The governor-general of St. Fionnani—who didn't even merit a name, apparently

Master Russo—an anthropologist and kidnapper

Cucuron and **Slabireaux**—explorers, moderately repentant after all they've seen

Father Erique—*this* bastard, again

Denizens of the Island Nations

Fozu—Keeper and Speaker for the Shesh; needs a sabak and fifty barrels of pyria

Martu and **Reta**—a pair of Shesh storytellers

Hami—Watcher for the Ggdani, retired; just wants to go home

Archivist Oggmi—one of Hami's childhood teachers

Mee—a True Priest of the Katakutia; on a mission from the Little Lights

Martin—the Nutufi music master at St. Remy Mission

Anna—a Nutufi seamstress and maid

Tomasino—a Nutufi steward

Solnu and **Tafo**—adopt Tess at the Maftumaiu

King Molsu—the sovereign of the Navel of the World

Kluit—a tiger-knight of the Tshu

Meketsh—her tiger, whom we dare not omit

Berekka—also called Rebecca, an Aftisheshe herbalist and survivor

Zivekhi, Rimeshe, and **Ebushai**—three more survivors

Vufekhi, Emaisha, and **Bayekh**—Aftisheshe women of note

Sergeant Luy—is Jovesh, in fact, thank you for asking

Where Life and Legend Meet

Vulkharai—an unlucky bootmaker, subject of a hundred stories

Dozerius the Pirate—a trickster, nastier than Tess realized as a child

St. Polypous—another trickster, but wise

The Walker—the giant Saint, Pandowdy, in a delightful cameo

The sabak—distant cousins to dragons, not supposed to exist

Kapatlutlo—the Polar Serpent, whom the Ggdani call the One

Glossary

Aftishekka—the Aftisheshe language

Aftisheshe—the inhabitants of a number of islands, including Edushuke (St. Fionnani) and Aftisheshe Home

Agogoi—the members of the founding families and ruling class of Porphyry (singular: Agogox; adjective form: Agogou)

Aieat—a seafaring nation of fog-bound whalers

Allsaints—all the Saints in Heaven. Not a deity, exactly; more like a collective

Archipelagos, the—the islands south of Ninys, extending to the Antarctic

ard—order, correctness (Mootya)

aurochs—large, wild cattlebeast, extinct in our world

Avodendron—Captain Claado's ship; a mythical eggplant tree (Porphyrian)

baganou—eggplant stew (Porphyrian)

Bapa—Dad (Porphyrian)

baranque—a three-masted Porphyrian ship

bere—blurry (Aftishekka)

bikeki—hardtack (Porphyrian)

Bjoveh—formerly one of the Wandering Cities, exiled seven generations ago

bombard—a cannon

bosun—the ship's officer in charge of deck crew and equipment

bowsprit—a long spar extending from a ship's prow

chaser—a small cannon at the prow or stern of a ship

Continental Serpent—Anathuthia, the World Serpent found by Tess

coracle—a light boat made of hides stretched over a wooden frame

Cragmarog Castle—the Duke of Ducana's estate

cranequin—a crossbow crank

Daanite—homosexual; a follower of St. Daan

Deadlander—Southlander, according to the Katakutia

destultia—an herb used for various draconic ailments

Dog People—the Aftisheshe, according to the Ninysh

doublet—a short, fitted man's jacket, often padded

Ducana—a province of Goredd

dzeni—a foreigner (Porphyrian; plural: dzenia)

Edushuke—an island in Aftisheshe territory, named for a goddess; St. Fionnani

Ephaanos Empire—a vast northern empire, of which Porphyry was once the southernmost colony

eyu—a communication device, made from sabak spittle, that links users through the Worldmind

Femefu-syu-la-Nutufi—the home island of the Nutufi; St. Remy

forecastle—the elevated foredeck of a ship

Frai Leporello—a micro-island named for a monk

Frai Piscento—another micro-island named for a monk

fthep—a stinging tail-swat (Quootla)

Ggdani—the nation that dwells closest to the polar region; guardians of the One

Ggdanu—the Ggdani language

glaive—a weapon resembling a cleaver on a long pole

Golden House—a model of Heaven at the center of every Southlander cathedral

Goredd—Tess's homeland, one of the Southlands (adjective form: Goreddi)

Greater Lights—the World Serpents; the Worldmind

grog—rum mixed with water

gunwale—top edge of a ship's hull

Heaven—Southlanders' afterlife, as outlined by the Saints in scripture

heave to—to stop a ship by turning across the wind

ice tiger—fictional Antarctic felines; just tame enough to carry a knight into battle

Indomitable—Ninysh man-of-war

Infernum—Hell, home of the devil; not all Saints believe in it

Jovesh—the original inhabitants of Paji-Jovesh, also called St. Vittorius

Katakutia—wandering priests of the Archipelagos; sometimes considered a nation for treaty purposes

kedge—to move a ship by dropping anchor at a distance and then hauling in the line

Keys to Ascension—ceremonial keys placed upon the Golden House at a funeral in the absence of a body

kikiu—death (Quootla)

ko—ungendered pronoun that quigutl use for each other (Quootla)

kuro—an Aftisheshe boat; comes in several sizes

Land of the Dead—the Southlands, according to the Katakutia

Lavondaville—the capital of Goredd

leeward—the side of a ship away from the wind

Lesser/Little Lights—sabak, according to the Ggdani and Katakutia respectively

Light Mother—Katakutia, according to the Shesh

Little Bitch Island—Edushuke

Long Red Valley—a site of many battles on Edushuke

Lucky—Porphyrian settlers who arrived deeply in debt

Maftumaiu—the spring festival, two weeks of storytelling at the Navel of the World (Nutufi)

Mardou—a Ninysh port city

mekhivolhai—noisy stinkers; penguins (Aftishekka)

merlon—the raised portion of a crenellated wall

Mindlets—sabak, according to the quigutl

Mivikh—an Aftisheshe town on Edushuke

Mootseye—dragon university

Mootya—the language of dragons, rendered in sounds a human mouth can make

Most Alone—a World Serpent, according to the quigutl

Murkh—a nation near the South Pole

Murkhee—the Murkh language

napou—younger emergent-masculine maternal uncle (Porphyrian)

Navel of the World—wherever the Nutufi are; consecrated space for the Maftumaiu; possibly also a meteor rock

Ninys—a country southeast of Goredd (adjective form: Ninysh)

Nutufi—a nation centered around the Navel of the World on Femefu-syu-la-Nutufi (St. Remy)

okush—a beverage of fermented seal milk

Old Floats—moving islands of the far south

Paishesh—the home island of the Shesh; also called St. Claresse

Paji-Jovesh—the home island of the Jovesh; also called St. Vittorius

palasho—a palace (Ninysh)

Pelaguese—what Ninysh colonizers call the peoples of the Archipelagos

plaion—a Porphyrian dinghy

Polar Serpent—Kapatlutlo, the One, Aachi Zedelai; the World Serpent at the south polar region

poop deck—the aftmost raised deck of a ship

Porphyry—a small city-state northwest of the Southlands (adjective form: Porphyrian)

psei—Porphyrian point-neuter pronoun

pyria—an oily, flammable substance originally used by Southlander knights to fight dragons

quarterdeck—the raised deck behind the mainmast, traditionally reserved for officers

queue—a martial pigtail

quigutl—a small, flightless subspecies of dragon with a set of dexterous arms in place of wings and a tube-shaped tongue that can produce a flame

Quootla—the language of the quigutl, mutually intelligible with Mootya

ravelin—detached triangular fortification

red ladies—Segoshi prostitutes

rukkefa—an herbal biscuit that gives dogs a poisonous bite (Aftishekka)

saar—a dragon (Porphyrian)

saarantras—a dragon in human form (Porphyrian; plural: saarantrai)

sabaggatg—sabak oil (Ggdanu)

sabak—an aquatic polar subspecies of dragon, resembling a large white axolotl; sabak spin underwater webs, speak with chirps, and seem to have psychic powers

sabanewt—the Southlander term for sabak

St. Asparagus—possibly apocryphal; St. Polypous's companion in stories

St. Brandoll—patron of hospitality

St. Capiti—patroness of scholars

St. Claresse—St. Clare in Goredd; patroness of the perceptive; another name for Paishesh

St. Eustace—patron of the dead

St. Fionnani—St. Fionnuala in Goredd; lady of waters; another name for Edushuke

St. Ida—patroness of musicians and performers

St. Jannoula—a living Saint; started a war between dragons and the Southlands

St. Jobertus (St. Bert)—patron of natural philosophy and medicine

St. Kathanda—lady of beasts

St. Lars—a living Saint; a Samsamese inventor

St. Looli—St. Loola in Goredd; patroness of children, the sick and indigent

St. Masha—beloved of St. Daan; patron of romantic love

St. Munn—patron of merchants, popular in Ninys

St. Polypous—a trickster Saint, famous for having many legs

St. Remy—patron of mercy and introspection; another name for Femefu-syu-la-Nutufi

St. Vittorius (St. Vitt)—defender of the faith; another name for Paji-Jovesh

St. Wilibaio—St. Willibald in Goredd; patron of marketplaces and news

St. Yane—a trickster Saint, famous for having many children

Samsam—a country southwest of Goredd (adjective form: Samsamese)

scupper—a hole permitting water on deck to drain back into the ocean

sea beaver—a fictional beaver as big as a cow

Sea of Holes—the oceanic region to the west that seems to be full of holes, in fact

Segosh—the capital of Ninys

Shesh—the nation of people descended from the Jovesh and Ninysh settlers; live in Paishesh, also called St. Claresse

Shevkha—an island in Aftisheshe territory

Sixth Division—Count Pesavolta's secret police

Southlands—Goredd, Ninys, and Samsam together

Sweet Jessia—the ship carrying the dragon expedition

Tanamoot—the homeland of dragons

Tathlann's syndrome—a serious medical condition afflicting dragons who received no maternal memories, due to being ripped from the mother's oviduct

teggdi—a third gender (Ggdanu)

teta—an herbal painkiller (Aftishekka)

teu, teur—pronouns pertaining to teggdi (Ggdanu)

thnik—a quigutl device that allows the transmission of voices over long distances

thnimi—a thnik that also transmits images

thuthmephtha—when a quigutl metamorphoses from one sex to another, which happens several times across their lifespans (Quootla)

Tshu—a nation of tiger-knights living far to the south

Tshu-veit—the Tshu language

upuki—small, fluffy animals raised for food

-utl—Quootla suffix indicating contradictory case, wherein a word also means its opposite

Voorka—a tusked seal, eaten widely, named for a Tshu god

Wandering Cities—a mysterious nomadic nation

warp—*see* **kedge**

Watcher—a Ggdani spy, sent to the Southlands to discourage island colonization

Wild One—a Katakutia, according to the Aftisheshe

Wind Kin—a Katakutia, according to the Ggdani

Worldmind—the collective consciousness of sabak and possibly World Serpents

World Serpents—vast creatures out of quigutl mythology, believed to have created the world and to hold it together

Ziziba—a nation north of Porphyry (adjective form: Zibou)

RACHEL HARTMAN is the author of the acclaimed and *New York Times* bestselling YA fantasy novels *Seraphina,* which won the William C. Morris YA Debut Award, *Shadow Scale,* and *Tess of the Road.* Rachel lives with her family in Vancouver, Canada. In her free time, she sings madrigals, walks her whippet in the rain, and is learning to fence.

rachelhartmanbooks.com
@_rachelhartman